D0051745

Also by
EMILY MARCH

A Stardance Summer
Christmas in Eternity Springs
Reunion Pass
Heartsong Cottage
Teardrop Lane
Dreamweaver Trail
Miracle Road
Reflection Point
Nightingale Way
Lover's Leap
Heartache Falls
Hummingbird Lake
Angel's Rest

The First Kiss of Spring

EMILY MARCH

St. Martin's Paperbacks

This is a work of fiction. All of the characters, organizations, and events portrayed in this novel are either products of the author's imagination or are used fictitiously.

THE FIRST KISS OF SPRING

Copyright © 2018 by Geralyn Dawson Williams.

For information address St. Martin's Press, 175 Fifth Avenue, New York, NY 10010.

ISBN: 978-1-250-13170-6

Our books may be purchased in bulk for promotional, educational, or business use. Please contact your local bookseller or the Macmillan Corporate and Premium Sales Department at 1-800-221-7945, ext. 5442, or by e-mail at MacmillanSpecialMarkets@macmillan.com.

Printed in the United States of America

St. Martin's Paperbacks edition / March 2018

St. Martin's Paperbacks are published by St. Martin's Press, 175 Fifth Avenue, New York, NY 10010.

10 9 8 7 6 5 4 3 2 1

To Bill and Mary Litty, dearest of friends
for more years than I want to count.
Your friendship is one of the true blessings in our lives.

Bill, sorry the cover model thing hasn't worked out.
Yet.
I'm still writing . . . .

Acknowledgments

I am beyond blessed to have so many fabulous people helping me bring Eternity Springs to life.

Thank you to Holly Ingraham for your invaluable editorial input. It's been a joy to work with you on this book.

Thank you to Jennifer Enderlin and everyone on the team at St. Martin's Press for the support you've shown this series.

Thank you to my spectacular agents, Meg Ruley and Christina Hogrebe, at Jane Rotrosen Agency, head cheerleaders for Team Eternity Springs.

Thank you to Eric Draper, MD, for your time and expertise in answering my long list of medical-related questions and to Carol Draper for answering my call for help and volunteering your husband! You've earned your Emily's Angels wings!

Thank you to Sarah Phillips, RN, for reading my draft pages for medical mistakes and to Amanda Williams for pestering . . . um . . . inviting . . . Sarah to read my draft pages for medical mistakes.

Thank you to Nicole Burnham, Susan Sizemore, and Christina Dodd for the plot help.

Thank you to the bestest sister in the world, Mary

Acknowledgments

Lou Jarrell, and to the rest of my family for putting up with me. I know it's not easy.

And finally, to my own personal Celeste Blessing, aka the incredible Mary Dickerson. I have no words. You go above and beyond the call of friendship every single time. Love you forever.

Journal Entry

They told me I was an angel.

I sang like one, they claimed, and I was such a pretty child, what with my rosy cheeks and blond curls and big, bright eyes that changed from pale blue to gray depending on the lighting. I had eyelashes the envy of every woman who saw me and a smile that lit up a room.

I was smart, too. Memorized lines easily and delivered them with skill. So gifted. It was in the blood, they said. A family dynasty of talent.

Such a charmed life, I led. Travel, fame, and fortune. The envy of all.

I was five years old the first time he hit me.

Chapter One

Home.

Caitlin Timberlake exited the Telluride Regional Airport terminal and turned in a slow circle as she feasted on the scene. Colorado's Western Slope was a world of jagged, rocky mountain peaks, of icy-cold streams that burbled and frothed and grew silvery fish that tasted like heaven when cooked over a campfire for breakfast. The San Juan Mountains in summertime presented a banquet of color—hills of green and gold; red rocks and alpine meadows blanketed in wildflowers of pink, blue, purple, and yellow, all presenting majestically beneath an azure sky.

Home.

She filled her lungs with clean mountain air, smelling pine and fir and forest, and tension melted from her bones like snowfall in spring.

Home.

For the better part of eight years, she'd lived in New York City, hustling and bustling and busting her butt as a textile designer, trying to build a life for herself. She specialized in fabric design for bedding and while she liked the creative aspects of the job, work fulfillment remained elusive. After all, pretty bedspreads would never change the world, and Caitlin wanted her work to matter. She wanted her life to matter.

Caitlin's discontent had been born in the moment when she'd learned that her brother Chase had gone missing in a war-torn part of the world, and it had grown in the weeks that followed. His safe return home hadn't squelched the emotion. She'd discovered too much about herself and her wishes and desires during that troubling time.

Primarily, she'd recognized that she'd spent too much time living thousands of miles away from those she loved. It had taken her some time to figure out what she wanted to do about it and even more time to make the decision to act. A few significant hurdles remained in her way, but she was closer than ever before to becoming her own fairy godmother and making some of her wishes come true.

She exhaled loudly, grinned, and announced, "Hello, Colorado. I've missed you."

She'd have sworn she heard the wind whisper back, *Welcome home, Caitlin.*

"I'm doing the right thing," she told herself. Now if she could only convince her mother of that fact.

Well, that was a battle for another day, one after she'd cleared her hurdles and had her fairy wand in hand. Today it was time to shift into bridesmaid mode.

Caitlin had flown to Denver yesterday after work and spent the night in an airport hotel. This morning's flight into Telluride had landed right on time, and the hotel shuttle was waiting for her. After wrestling with her purse, her tote, her computer case, and two suitcases stuffed to overflowing with necessities for her role as bridesmaid, she wanted to kiss the friendly van driver who introduced himself as he took the burdens off her hands.

The fact that Will Gustophsen was cute and about her age didn't hurt, either.

A year ago when her college friend, Stephanie Kingston, asked her to be a bridesmaid at her destination wedding, Caitlin hadn't hesitated to say yes. She just wished she'd known sooner about all the stuff Steph needed her to bring with her and she'd have shipped it ahead.

"You here for an extended stay?" Will asked as he lifted a suitcase into the back of the van.

"Because I have so much luggage?" Caitlin smiled ruefully and explained, "I'm here for a wedding."

"Ahh. In that case, you travel light."

With the luggage loaded, she climbed into the shuttle and, as the only passenger, had her pick of seats. She buckled her seat belt, then settled back for what should be a short drive to her hotel.

As the driver turned onto Last Dollar Road and headed down the big hill he asked, "Where are you from?"

"Here. Well, not Telluride. I grew up in Denver. But I went to college in Tennessee and moved to New York City after graduation."

"Should I offer my congratulations or condolences?"

Caitlin laughed. "I'm glad I had the experience. I'm ready to come home, though."

"Back to Denver?"

"No." Her gaze focused on the small town nestled into the valley below. "I've developed a fondness for mountain towns."

Will Gustophsen glanced into the rearview mirror and wagged his brows flirtatiously. "Please tell me you're moving to Telluride."

His obvious interest soothed the spot on her heart still achy from a breakup last Christmas. Doug Wilkerson hadn't broken her heart when he dumped her, but he had bruised it. "I doubt it. This place is a little too pricy for me. Besides, I have family in Eternity Springs."

"That's a nice little town, but then so is this. It's

possible to live here without breaking the bank. You just need to be smart about it." He launched into a Telluride pitch that sounded as if it had been written by the Chamber of Commerce.

Caitlin couldn't argue with him. The scenery was spectacular and the activities he rattled off sounded inviting. As they approached her hotel in Mountain Village, the pedestrian-friendly, European-style planned resort community built above Telluride and connected to the historic mining town by a gondola lift system, she was anxious to get out and explore. She'd been a kid the last time she'd visited this part of Colorado, and she was sure the place had changed. She had a few hours to kill before meeting Stephanie for a drink, so this was her time to play tourist.

"I get off work at six," Gustophsen said. "I'd love to show you around. Buy you dinner."

"Thank you," she responded, meaning it. Having a cute guy hit on her was nice. "But I'm afraid I already have plans this evening. The bride arrives this afternoon and the weekend is jam-packed from there."

He gave an exaggerated sigh. "Always my luck."

The friendly chatter continued until they arrived at the hotel. After he wrestled her luggage from the van and gave her his number in case her plans changed, she gave him a large tip and thanked him for the hospitable welcome.

Caitlin checked into her room and spent some time answering a few of the unending stream of work-related e-mails. She would miss a few things about her job. The mountain of e-mails that required her constant attention wouldn't be one of them.

With her professional fires put out, she shut her laptop with a satisfied thump, grabbed a hat and sunscreen, and left the hotel. She walked around Mountain Village a bit and was suitably impressed with the style and elegance of the resort town. However, she didn't feel quite at home until she took the gondola down into Telluride and wandered up and down the streets, reading historical markers and inspecting the shops, comparing them to those in another small, historic mining town near and dear to her heart.

Eternity Springs might not have a gondola and ski runs, but the bakery, handmade soap shop, and Christmas store could definitely hold their own against these. People came from all over the country to shop at Vista's art gallery and Whimsies glass studio, and her mother's Yellow Kitchen was the best five-star restaurant in Colorado.

She couldn't wait to be there.

She ate lunch at the Thai spot that her driver had recommended, then indulged in a chocolate ice cream cone for dessert. Taking a seat on a park bench near the gondola station, she savored her treat and people-watched.

The town was bustling this August weekend with tourists and locals alike out enjoying the afternoon sunshine. She grinned as a pair of preteen boys whipped past her on mountain bikes, their mud-caked clothing providing as much evidence of a fun-filled, reckless ride down the mountain as did the joy in their smiles.

Too bad her weekend was packed with wedding activities. She wouldn't mind giving that a try herself. She was impressed by the way the ski resorts had found ways to attract vacationers, athletes, and daredevil fourteen-year-old boys during the off season. Such was the way little mountain towns became tourist destinations and supported thriving economies throughout the year.

She knew that such success didn't happen on its own. She'd had a front-row seat during the revitalization of Eternity Springs and saw how people had worked together to make it happen.

Eternity Springs. It's funny how the little town called to her. It wasn't even home. Not the home of her childhood, anyway. She'd never even visited Eternity Springs until her parents lost their minds and separated after she went off to college at Vanderbilt and her mother ran away from home.

The ringing of her cell phone interrupted her thoughts. She dug the phone from her backpack and checked the number and the time. Stephanie. They were due to meet up in Mountain Village in half an hour. "Hello, bride."

"Hey, Cait. You won't believe what happened. Our plane out of Logan was late and we missed our connection. We won't get to Telluride until late tonight."

"Oh no." Potential ramifications of such a delay flittered through Caitlin's mind. "What did you have scheduled for today? What can I do to help?"

"It's all covered. I built extra time into the schedule, thank goodness. I'm just really disappointed that you and I won't have our girl-time this afternoon to catch up, and of course, missing dinner with George and Nathan. Nathan was really looking forward to spending some time with you before we dive into wedding business. Tomorrow will be jam-packed."

Stephanie had been trying to set Caitlin up with her work friend ever since Doug dumped her. However, the guy's Instagram was a total turnoff and Caitlin simply wasn't interested. Unfortunately, Stephanie was a terrier when she set her mind to something, and she'd decided Caitlin and Nathan were made for each other—despite the little issue that she lived in NYC and he in Miami.

This plane delay might be a blessing, Caitlin decided. "Don't worry about it, Steph. You and I will both be at Marsha's wedding in October. We can have a nice long visit then."

"That's true. And maybe you and Nathan can find

time to grab a drink together tomorrow. It might fit after our spa appointments and the guys' round of golf. I don't want you to miss the opportunity to meet him. Telluride is such a romantic place."

Caitlin closed her eyes and worked to keep the sigh out of her voice as she said, "Telluride *is* beautiful, Steph. It's a gorgeous place to have your wedding. And the weather for Saturday is supposed to be spectacular."

They discussed arrangements for meeting the following day. Before ending the call, Stephanie said, "If you happen to meet a tall, dark, and handsome stranger tonight, feel free to invite him to the wedding. I had six last-minute cancellations, and I've already paid for the meals."

"I thought you have your heart set on me and Nathan."

"I do, but it never hurts for a guy to have a little competition."

Thinking about her lack of a love life put a damper on Caitlin's day. Maybe she should have taken the shuttle driver up on his offer, after all. As luck would have it, as soon as she slipped her phone into her backpack, her gaze landed on a couple about her age, holding hands and stealing kisses as they walked along the sidewalk. This time, she couldn't hold back her sigh.

She was alone. Again. Still. How was it that she could live and work in a city of more than eight million people and always feel alone? Even when she *was* dating someone? But she *did* feel alone and she was tired of pretending otherwise. Tired of pretending, period. Hadn't she been partially relieved when after eight months of dating, Doug sat her down and gave her the "just friends" talk?

Thinking about relationships while sitting in a mountain town caused her thoughts to drift back toward her parents. In hindsight Caitlin could see that she shouldn't have been so hard on her mom when Ali ran off to Eternity Springs. If Ali Timberlake's feelings back then had been anything like those Caitlin experienced now, then Cait could better understand her mom's actions. Ali had tried to explain, using terms like "lack of fulfillment," "yearning for more," and "unwillingness to settle." Caitlin hadn't wanted to hear what her mother had been trying to say. For a while, neither had her father.

But Ali hadn't let anyone stop her, had she? She'd left Mac, left Denver, and eventually opened a restaurant in Eternity Springs. She'd made new friends and a place for herself in the community. In proving to herself that she could live without Mac, Ali had realized that was the last thing she wanted to do. Living alone in Denver, Mac had come to a similar conclusion.

"And all was well that ended well," Caitlin murmured, tearing her eyes away from the lovers. Guess her parents hadn't lost their minds when they separated, after all.

Caitlin polished off her ice cream, licked her sticky fingers, and decided she'd had enough sightseeing. She'd go back to the hotel, maybe change into her swimsuit and do a few laps in the indoor pool. Shoot, maybe she'd change her clothes and rent a bike and act like a fourteen-year-old boy.

Making her way to the gondola entrance, she took a place at the end of the line. A group of college-age tourists fell in behind her, laughing, talking loudly, smelling strongly of weed.

Caitlin stepped forward and as the gondola attendant opened the cabin door for her to climb inside, the constant stream of foul language coming from two girls behind her put her off. She stepped aside. "I'll let them go first."

They giggled and stumbled and f-bombed their way

into the cabin. The attendant met Caitlin's eyes and rolled his, then shut the door.

As she watched the next cabin approach, a male voice spoke behind her. "This is one of the pet-friendly cabins. I hope you don't mind sharing with my dog?"

Caitlin glanced over her shoulder and saw a tall man with sun-streaked dark hair and striking high, defined cheekbones. But it was his eyes that demanded a woman's attention. Framed by long, thick lashes, they were the color of a stormy spring sky, and they were mesmerizing. She stared into them just a little bit too long.

What had he said? *His dog.* "I love dogs."

Embarrassed, she finally jerked her gaze away from those fabulous eyes and toward his dog. Because he'd asked if she minded sharing, she expected to see a big, hairy, scary-looking dog. Instead, she saw a pretty miniature long-haired red dachshund with her hind legs propped up by a doggie wheelchair.

The hot blonde went gooey. They always did. It was one of the few perks Josh Tarkington had found of being the owner of a dog with a broken back.

"Oh no." Her moss green eyes softened, her bee-stung mouth rounded. "What's wrong with him?"

"Her," Josh corrected as the cabin arrived and the attendant opened the door for them. "She's a girl. She jumped down from a sofa and hit wrong. She's paralyzed from the middle of her spine down."

"That's so sad," the blonde said, stepping into the cabin and taking a seat.

"She's actually a happy girl." Josh scooped up the dog and wheelchair and set her on the seat opposite the woman. He shrugged out of his backpack, sat beside his dog, and smiled at his gondola companion. "The woman who owned her at the time of the accident said Penny was depressed for about three days, but after that she recovered her usual sunny disposition."

A large group of children and adults asked to wait for the next cabin since they traveled together, so the attendant shut the door with Josh and the blonde as the only passengers.

"Her name is Penny?" she asked.

He nodded, and when the woman extended her hand to let the dachshund sniff her, Josh noticed she wore no ring on her left hand. "Copper Penny. I'm Josh, by the way."

She lifted her gaze from the dog and smiled at Josh brightly. "Nice to meet you, Josh. My name is Caitlin."

"Are you a local, Caitlin, or are you visiting?"

"I'm here for a college friend's wedding. I live in New York. How about you?"

"I'm playing tourist here this weekend. This is my first trip to Telluride."

"It's the first time I've been in years. It's gorgeous here, isn't it?"

"Definitely." Josh said it without looking away from her.

Judging by the flutter of her smile and sudden shift of her gaze, his subtle flirtation did not go unnoticed. Caitlin returned her attention to the dog and asked, "So, how long have you had this precious Copper Penny?"

"Not quite a month. Her owner had to move into an assisted living center that doesn't allow dogs, so she asked our local vet to find Penny a home. I'd gone to the adoption center to get an appropriately manly dog. I'm still not sure how I walked out with a crippled doxie."

"Obviously, you needed a little good luck."

Josh needed a couple of seconds to make the connection. "Ah, as in 'See a penny, pick it up?'"

"And all the day you'll have good luck," Caitlin finished.

"It must be working. I get to share the gondola with a beautiful woman instead of the campers standing behind me in line. They obviously don't have showers at their campsite."

"I'm flattered." After a brief pause, she added, "I think."

The gondola exited the station and started up the hill.

Josh leaned forward and spoke earnestly. "I'm shooting for flattery. I'm not always very good at it, I'm afraid. I have a tendency to put my foot in my mouth whenever I attempt to flirt."

A smile played at her lips. "Is this an attempt at flirtation?"

"I'm bad at it. I know." He gave her his go-to sheepish grin. Her eyes went gooey again. *Damn, I'm good.*

But after only a moment of goo, Caitlin's eyes narrowed. "Actually, I think you're probably very good at it."

Busted.

"In fact . . ." She folded her arms and studied him. "I have two older brothers. I know how these things work. Is the dog even yours?"

Josh sat up straight and added an offended note to his tone. "Are you insinuating that I use Penny's handicap to help me pick up women?"

Her eyes glittered with amusement. "Before they met their wives, my brothers would have done it in a heartbeat. Stephen borrowed a puppy one time to attract a girl's attention."

Josh laughed. "Okay, so maybe it hasn't escaped my notice that Penny is a bit of an icebreaker, but she *is* my dog. A high-maintenance one at that."

Then he rolled out the winner. He had yet to meet a

dog-loving woman who wasn't impressed by the fact that keeping Penny healthy and happy meant he had to manually express her bladder three times a day.

"Okay, I never would have thought of that," Caitlin said. "That's dedication."

Josh decided to save the daily dog-laundry ammo for later. "She's worth it. She really is a sweet dog. So do you have a pet?"

"No. My apartment doesn't allow anything bigger than fish, and besides, I travel too much with my job."

"What do you do?"

"I'm a textile designer." She named the famous fashion design house she worked for and explained a little about her work.

He was impressed. "So, you're an artist. I'm always intrigued by creative people. Do you work on a sketch pad or at a computer?"

"Both. I usually begin with sketches, but most of the designing is done on the computer."

"I think it must be very rewarding to create something out of nothing. Bet it's neat to see your work in a department store."

Caitlin offered him a brilliant smile. "It is. I was so excited the first time it happened. I knew the date the line was due to be released. My mother flew in and we went to Macy's together." She laughed softly and added, "She bought one of everything and then we went and drank champagne. I think she was even more thrilled than I was. But enough about me. How about you? What work do you do?"

"I'm an engine mechanic. I work for myself. Opened my own shop earlier this year."

"Now *that* is awesome. I dream of working for myself."

"Being your own boss is rewarding, but it's also the

hardest work you'll ever—" Josh broke off abruptly when Penny's ears perked and her head came up.

The gondola cabin shuddered, jerked, and stopped its forward movement.

"What happened?" Caitlin asked, alarm in her voice.

Josh looked up and down the line. He saw no sign of trouble, but plenty of evidence of panic. Behind them, children cried. Ahead of them, one of the female partiers screamed.

I am so glad that wasn't a pet friendly cabin.

"We seem to be stable," he said. "I think . . ."

Static emerged from a speaker above them, then a male voice said, "Attention passengers. Please remain calm. There is no cause for alarm. I repeat. There is no cause for alarm. Your safety is not at risk. Due to a mechanical issue, the main line from Telluride to Station St. Sophia has been halted. We are working to get it back up and running as soon as possible. We ask for your continued patience."

In the wake of the announcement, Caitlin shrugged. "It could be worse. We could be in the cabin with the potheads."

"Or the crying kids."

"I'm not on a schedule. Are you?"

He'd planned to drive toward Delores and find a place to camp, but he could adjust. "Not at all. If you are here for a wedding, I'm surprised you don't have every minute booked."

She explained about the bride's plane delay and confessed to relief about it, considering the woman's matchmaking ideas. It provided a natural segue into the question he very much wanted to ask. "So, you're not with anyone back home?"

"No. I'm single." She reached across the aisle, scratched Penny behind her ears, and casually asked, "How about you?"

"I'm single, too. I live alone now, well except for Penny. This time last summer I lived with a whole gaggle of women, but they wouldn't quit feeding me and I was getting fat, so I moved into a house by myself."

At Caitlin's owl-eyed blink of shock, he laughed aloud. "The look on your face is priceless. Before I decided to open the shop, I lived and worked in an RV park. The average age of the ladies was around sixty, and they liked to bake."

"So you're one of those," Caitlin observed with a roll of her eyes.

"Those?"

"You like to tease."

He had the sudden vision of curvaceous Caitlin lying on his bed, naked and shivering as he teased the tip of her breast to a point with his tongue. "Oh yeah."

"Just like my brothers," she said with a sigh.

That comment managed to pour icy water on his fantasies.

Reminded of thirst, he started to reach into his backpack for his water bottle when the speaker sounded again. "Attention, passengers. Stoppage is due to a mechanical malfunction that does not affect your safety. I repeat. Safety is not affected. The line from Station St. Sophia to Mountain Village will be restarted. That from Telluride to Station St. Sophia will be evacuated by our highly trained team. Again, we ask for your patience."

"Evacuated?" Caitlin asked. "We're a hundred feet off the ground! How will they evacuate us?"

Josh peered through the window, looking straight down. "No more than eighty feet. I've suspect they'll use a rope system. They'll buckle you into a harness and lower you to the ground."

"Oh."

She didn't sound the least bit enthusiastic at the prospect. "Are you afraid of heights?"

"No. Not really." She showed him an embarrassed smile. "When I was in college I went climbing with my brother and one of his friends. To call him a daredevil doesn't begin to describe him. Anyway, his friend missed a handhold and slid into me and knocked me off the mountain. I dangled at the end of my safety rope for the longest, loneliest five minutes of my life before my brother managed me pull me up. I can't say I enjoyed the experience."

"I wouldn't think so."

"How long do you suppose it will take them to get us down?"

"Depends on how big their team is and where they begin. We're about halfway in between the town and Station St. Sophia."

"So we probably won't be the first they get to."

"Probably not."

She pursed her lips and thought about it, then nodded. "I'm okay with that. Will Penny be okay?"

Josh tore his gaze away from Caitlin and glanced down at his dog. "She'll be fine. She's had about all the exercise she can handle today."

Though she could probably use the water he'd been about to pour for her a few minutes ago. He reached into his backpack for his water bottle but his fingers found the Corkcicle bottle he'd filled that morning instead.

"Since it looks like we're going to be here for a while," he said, wrapping his fingers around the bottle's neck and pulling it from the pack. "Care to join me? I have blood orange kombucha."

"I'd love some. Thank you."

He reached back into his pack for the water and

collapsible dog bowl, filled it halfway, then set it down for Penny. Next he pulled out the nesting wine glass and the collapsible water cup he carried.

He handed her the wine glass and she assembled it.

"Don't tell me. You were a Boy Scout."

"Always prepared," he quipped. That much was true. Sometimes in certain company, it was easier to drink his own "wine" than explain why he wasn't drinking.

As he filled her glass, she observed, "You're the first guy I've met who drinks kombucha. Are you into the natural health scene?"

He eyed her speculatively. "See, I don't know you well enough yet to know how to answer that."

"I don't understand."

"I've lived in California and Oklahoma. If I told you I eat tofu and bean sprouts and you're a California girl, chances are you'd be impressed. However, an Oklahoma girl possibly would dismiss me as a weak little weirdo."

Caitlin gave him a fast once-over. Dryly, she said, "You're obviously not weak or little. *I* don't know *you* well enough to judge the weirdo part. Personally, I won't go near tofu, but I don't hold tofu against someone. Do you eat red meat?"

Solemnly, he nodded. "Every chance I get. Do you eat junk food?"

"I order Cheetos by the caseload."

"That's it, then. We're meant to be. Will you have my baby?"

She almost choked on her kombucha. "Weirdo."

He laughed aloud and they shared a grin, then the conversation settled into more first-date type of questions. She asked where was his favorite place in the world. He asked her who influenced her most in life. She asked him what made him laugh. As always, Josh deflected questions about his childhood and steered the conversation away from family. They talked quite a bit about dogs.

More than an hour passed before they saw any sign of rescue. Josh didn't mind the delay. He hadn't flirted with a woman in a long time and he enjoyed himself. She was witty and intelligent and so very fine on the eyes. Caitlin didn't appear to mind the delay, either. She flirted right back.

He decided to ask her to dinner. He'd take her to one of the fancy restaurants in Mountain Village. He actually had a suit in the trailer because he'd attended a funeral for the elderly mother of the mayor of Eternity Springs the morning before he headed out on this trip.

While he waited for the right moment to pose that question, he continued the small talk by asking, "So, did you always want to be a textile designer and live in New York?"

She hesitated, a shadow crossing her face. "Not exactly. I've been living my mother's dream."

"That's an intriguing statement."

"She was a stay-at-home mom who wanted to be a career woman. She—whoa!" The gondola cabin swayed as a loud thump sounded above them. "What's that?"

"I think we're being rescued."

"Oh."

She sounded almost as bummed about it as he felt.

A moment later, the cabin door opened and a man loaded down with equipment swung inside. "Everybody okay in here?"

"We're good," Josh responded.

"So we have two adults and a dog to go down? Is the dog paralyzed?"

"Yes."

"I've seen those wheelchairs on Animal Planet. Cool contraption. I have a pet harness. Any reason she shouldn't go down that way?"

"Not that I know of. She's a calm dog. She should be fine. It is better to send her down alone than with me holding her?"

"Yes sir. It's safer for her to go alone. She'll be completely secured."

"If that's best, then let's do it."

"Good. We'll send her down first."

While the rescuer deployed the rope system, Josh devoted his attention to Penny. He wasn't worried about sending her down by herself. She'd already proved herself to be a scrapper. So far, he hadn't found anything that phased her. He dug a dog treat out of his backpack and fed it to her while the rescuer strapped her into the pet harness.

Following a short discussion with Josh, the rescue worker attached the three-pound wheelchair to the rope, too.

Caitlin scratched the dachshund behind her ears and made kissy noises. Josh told Penny to behave, sneaked her one more treat, then watched her ride the rope down. The rescue team on the ground greeted the dog enthusiastically.

"Nothing pulls the heartstrings like a crippled dog," Josh observed, turning toward Caitlin with a grin that quickly faded. The woman had gone green around the gills. "Caitlin? Are you okay?"

"I shouldn't have watched that," she said. "I'm not a cowardly person. I ski black diamond trails. I've ridden Class V rapids. But I really, really don't want to leave this cabin by rope."

The rescuer frowned at her. "Ma'am, you don't exactly have a choice."

"I know. I'll handle it." She smiled weakly and added, "I'm sorry. I have this . . . thing."

"You'll be perfectly safe. Even if the worst case happened and something failed, there's a backup safety system."

Josh eyed the harness and asked, "Do you have a tandem harness?"

"We have one we use for children, but adults——"

"She doesn't weigh a hundred pounds. We can go down together."

"One-oh-five," Caitlin corrected, turning a hopeful gaze toward the rescuer.

Josh didn't know how any red-blooded man could resist that look, so he wasn't surprised when the rescuer reached for his radio and spoke to his partners on the ground. A few minutes later after the deploying the rope system, a different harness arrived from the team on the ground. The rescuer secured Josh first, then assisted Caitlin. Her cheeks turned bright red when he told her to wrap her arms and legs around Josh and hold on tight.

"Don't worry. I'll be a perfect gentleman."

"Says the stranger with his hands on my ass," she murmured.

He was laughing when he gave the rescuer a thumbs up and they swung out into the air.

Although they descended the eighty feet slowly, it went by much too quickly for Josh. Caitlin kept her eyes closed and her head buried his against his chest, but her mouth ran the entire time.

"I wish I'd had a glass of wine instead of kombucha. Two glasses of wine. One wouldn't be enough. It's humiliating to be so afraid. I'm gonna kill my brother——it's all his fault. I'm shaking like a baby."

And I'm hard as the granite on Mt. Wilson.

She was soft and warm and she used coconut-scented

shampoo. Josh didn't care for the taste of coconut, but he loved the scent. To distract them both, he said, "So you're a Denver girl. Someone told me that Mt. Wilson is the mountain depicted on the Coors beer logo. Is that true?"

"What? Oh. The logo. Yes, I think that's true. The logo depicts the Wilson Group. Mt. Wilson, Wilson Peak, Gladstone, and El Diente."

"The tooth," Josh translated. "It does look like a tooth, don't you think?"

Caitlin lifted her head and looked toward the mountains. "How beautiful," she said, her head swiveling. "Oh wow. What a view this is."

When the smile slowly spread across her face, a captivated Josh couldn't help himself.

He kissed her.

Journal Entry

I learned early that not all kisses were the same.
There were air kisses that Mama and Father exchanged with guests when they arrived at the parties. Head kisses that women pressed against my hair when I was beneath their notice. Cheek kisses that sometimes lingered when I was older.

I vividly recall the first time I was kissed on the mouth.

It was right after the divorce. I was at a party at my mother's current boyfriend's house. Mama never sent me to bed. She mostly ignored me. I craved her attention, but looking back I see that I fared much better when she forgot I existed.

Because then, she didn't take me to parties.

Parties where she disappeared and predators entertained themselves by giving me drinks. Giving me drugs.

Giving me kisses on the mouth.

That first kiss—I was eight years old.

Chapter Two

She invited him to the wedding.

Caitlin couldn't believe she'd actually invited him to the wedding, but it had seemed like the right thing to do. He'd also been a gentleman at the end of the evening. He'd walked her to hotel room door and kissed her good night. His intense eyes had held her spellbound as he waited silently during the pregnant moment afterward to see if she'd invite him in.

She'd been tempted. Seriously tempted. But Caitlin had never slept with a guy on a first date, never been somebody's one-night stand, and she didn't intend to break that streak now.

When she told him good night, he smiled and kissed her lightly and turned to leave.

He'd been halfway to the elevator when she stepped out into the corridor. "Josh, wait. Would you be my plus one for the wedding tomorrow?"

He'd hesitated only a moment. "I can do that. I'd like that, Caitlin. Where and when?"

As she resisted the urge to dance a happy jig, she'd considered the question. "The wedding is at five, here at the hotel. I'm tied up with bridesmaid duties all day tomorrow, but maybe you could meet me just before it starts?" She gave him the details of exactly where on the hotel grounds the ceremony would take place and added, "If you'll be there at . . . say . . . four thirty . . . I'll come out and say hello before the ceremony begins."

"Sounds like a plan. See you tomorrow at four thirty." He'd taken three more steps toward the elevator, pushed the down button, then pivoted.

Caitlin's eyes had widened as he strode back toward her, his gaze locked on hers. Upon reaching her, he'd pulled her into his arms and kissed her long and thoroughly.

She'd melted into a boneless puddle. When the elevator dinged and he'd finally released her, remaining on her feet had been touch-and-go for a minute. He hadn't spoken again, but his steamy gaze held hers until the elevator doors closed between them.

She'd slumped against the wall for support and once she'd caught her breath, floated back to her room.

That night, she'd dreamt that a hundred and one Dalmatians attended Stephanie's wedding—only the dogs were miniature dachshunds and they all were in wheelchairs.

Saturday morning at nine, Caitlin exhaled a relieved breath when she arrived at the resort's café for the bridesmaid's brunch and spied the bride. "You made it," she said to Stephanie as she gave her old friend a hug.

"Finally. It was after midnight before we made it to the resort. Can you believe we got a flat tire driving down into town?"

"You're kidding."

"No! We're on the side of a mountain in a rental car stuffed to the gills with packages and bags and the wheel starts going *whop whop whop whop*. Even my mother muttered a curse word."

"She *never* curses."

"She did last night. She had visions of a bear lumbering out of the forest and running off with my veil."

Caitlin laughed. "I take it you avoided the wildlife?"

Stephanie nodded. "We did. Even my grumpy-Gus groom after midnight, though that took some doing."

Caitlin took her seat as Stephanie moved to greet more guests. The next time she had the opportunity to speak privately with the bride was later that morning during the spa appointment portion of the day when they sat side by side in pedicure chairs. Stephanie slipped her feet into bubbling, lavender-scented water, sipped from a champagne glass, and confessed, "I'm nervous. I didn't think I'd be nervous, but I am. Not about marrying George. I'm totally sure of him. It's the ceremony. What if it rains? What if I forget my vows? What if a bear really does gallop in and run off with my veil?"

Caitlin ran her tongue around the inside of her mouth. "I don't think bears gallop."

"If they're riding horses they do." Stephanie wrinkled her nose. "Distract me, Caitlin. Tell me something to take my mind off galloping bears."

Caitlin sipped her champagne, then nodded. "Okay, I took your suggestion and I invited a tall dark handsome stranger to your wedding."

"What?" Stephanie's hand jerked, sloshing her champagne.

Caitlin's lips fluttered with a smile. "Actually, I don't know that it's totally accurate to call him dark since his hair has these lovely sun-streaks. But he's very tan and his eyes are storm cloud gray. The tall and handsome labels fit him to a tee."

"You met a guy? Here? Last night?"

"Yesterday afternoon. We got stuck together in a gondola."

"Just the two of you?"

"Three of us. He had a dog with him." Caitlin paused theatrically before delivering the denouement. "His dog is in a wheelchair."

Stephanie patted her chest and said, "Awwww . . ."

While they finished their pedicures, Caitlin successfully distracted the bride by sharing details of her meeting with Josh Tarkington. Stephanie wasn't the least bit disappointed that Caitlin had found a way to avoid the set-up with Stephanie's friend from work; she simply wanted her dear friend to be as happy as she was.

Caitlin enjoyed the day, but she found herself watching the clock, anxious for four thirty to roll around. She loved the dress she'd be wearing tonight. Stephanie had asked her attendants to wear dusky blue in whatever style suited them. Caitlin's dress was a fitted, sleeveless, shimmering silk Dupioni with a sweetheart neckline. She planned to wear her grandmother's pearls and three-inch nude-colored heels.

At four fifteen in the bridal party's dressing room, she finally put on her dress. She touched up her lipstick, checked her hair, and climbed into her heels. "I'll be right back," she said to the bride. "I told Josh I'd meet him when he arrived."

"Okay." Stephanie's teeth chewed at her lower lip. She was getting nervous. "You won't be long, will you? We will be lining up soon."

"Five minutes. No more."

Steph's gaze flew to the clock on the wall. "Ten is okay. Maybe you could peek into the garden and see if anyone has come? I dreamt last night that nobody showed up."

"Now you're worrying about stupid things. Can I get you anything before I go? How about a bottle of water?"

"That would be great. Thank you."

After tending to the bride, Caitlin slipped outside of the dressing room and made her way to the garden.

Stephanie couldn't have asked for better weather for an outdoor wedding. A day filled with sunshine had warmed the summer breeze carrying the perfume of roses from the garden, and the wispy clouds dotting the western sky promised a spectacular sunset without a threat of rain. Caitlin followed the sound of music played by a stringed trio toward the spot where the ceremony would take place.

She stopped for just a moment to greet another friend from college, and after promising to spend some time catching up at the reception, she continued on her way.

She spied Josh leaning casually against a wooden support post. He wore a dark gray suit that matched his steel-colored eyes. Seeing her, he straightened away from the wall. "Wow. You look fabulous. Aren't you worried about outshining the bride?"

Both pleased and embarrassed, Caitlin sensed the sting of a blush in her cheeks. "Stephanie is positively gorgeous and beyond happy. I doubt the sun could outshine her today."

"She's not nervous?"

"A little. She'll be fine once she starts down the aisle. When she had to give presentations in college, she'd be a wreck until the moment she stood up in front of the room. She's the type who feeds on the energy of crowds. I always thought she should go into acting."

Josh grimaced. "Don't wish that on a friend."

"You have something against actors?"

For a second, he went still, then he lifted his shoulders. "Not against actors. Acting is a craft—I respect that. It's celebrities that turn me off. Just because someone can act or play sports or sing doesn't mean they are any more knowledgeable or important than the guy who works in an insurance agency and brings me his car to fix. My heroes are those who put their lives on the line for their fellow man. Those who dedicate their lives to the service of others. Those who—"

He broke off abruptly, winced, and apologized. "Sorry, that pushed a button. I'm opinionated on the subject."

"I noticed," Caitlin replied. "I'm also right there with you. Though I will admit if I had the opportunity to meet the Queen of England and browse through her jewelry box, I wouldn't turn my nose up at the chance."

"Like jewelry, do you?"

"Love it. Not that I own any super-expensive pieces, mind you—except for the pearls I inherited from my grandmother—but I'm a sucker for jewel exhibits at museums. The more sparkle, the better. . . . Which reminds me of the tiara Stephanie is wearing today and the fact I'd better get back to the bridal party. We'll be taking a few pictures immediately after the ceremony. If you'd like to wait for me that's fine or I can meet you at the reception."

"I'll wait here."

"Great." She beamed a smile at him. "See you shortly."

Caitlin floated back to the bride's dressing room where she discovered that her visit with Josh had been spied upon by three of the other bridesmaids.

"He's so hot!" said the bride's sister.

"Those eyes!" said the bride's cousin.

Caitlin and Stephanie's suite-mate in college waved her hand in front of her face. "That's it. The minute the reception is over, I'm going to start riding the gondola."

The teasing continued until the wedding planner announced, "Okay, ladies. It's time."

Caitlin marched up the aisle to Vivaldi's "Spring" and took her place in line in front of the rose-covered arbor. Her gaze immediately sought Josh and she found him easily because he stood a head taller than most of the other guests. His gray eyes stared intently into her own, capturing her attention so completely that she almost missed the moment Stephanie stepped into view.

As usual, Caitlin got a little teary-eyed during the ceremony. Stephanie looked like a princess, and the love in George's eyes when he spoke his vows to his bride made Caitlin's heart fill with yearning. She wanted this—the white dress, the adoring groom, the happy-ever-after. The whole fairy tale. Her brothers had found love. She wanted to believe that someday she'd find it too.

Her gaze stole toward the next-to-last row where her date sat. This time Josh wasn't watching her, but rather the bride's four-year-old niece and flower girl. The grin on his face as he watched the little girl twirl her dusky blue hair ribbon around her finger made Caitlin's heart melt. A drop-dead gorgeous single man who obviously likes children?

He must be hiding some fatal flaw. Nobody can be this perfect.

Caitlin dragged her gaze back to the bride and groom as Stephanie began to repeat her vows. Her voice shook with nervousness at first, but she settled down at George's encouraging smile and finished strong. They exchanged rings, and soon the recessional music swelled and Caitlin was gliding back up the aisle.

Josh gave her a wink and blew her a kiss as she passed. As a result, her smiles during the picture-taking that followed held extra sparkle. Caitlin happily introduced Josh to her friends. He was outgoing and friendly, a fabulous dancer, and he displayed an amazing memory for names. Over dinner he told stories about Penny chasing birds that had the whole table laughing.

"I'm jealous," she observed when he performed introductions between a group of eight, all of whom he'd met within the past half hour. "I'm terrible when it comes to remembering names."

"Memorization has always come easily to me. I do have two tips that can help when it comes to names. First is to meet and repeat. Speak the person's name during the introduction. The second trick is to associate the name with someone or something else. For instance, one of the first people I met here tonight was Barrett Holden. I'm in bear country. He has a habit of pulling his beard. Holding it."

"Bear holding. Barrett Holden. I get it." Grinning, she tilting her head and studied him. "So what did you associate with my name in order to remember it?"

He hesitated before speaking in a casual manner.

"Wood. Water."

"As in wood for timber and water for lake?"

"Sure."

He said it so quickly that Caitlin narrowed her eyes, suspecting there was something more to this. But before she could challenge him on it, the band played the first notes of "Unchained Melody" and Josh invited her back onto the dance floor.

He held her close and moved like a dream. Being vertically challenged—to use her brothers' teasing term for short—Caitlin usually felt awkward when dancing with someone as tall as Josh. But he made her feel like she belonged in his arms. "You're an excellent dancer, Josh."

"My mother taught me. She considered dancing to be an essential skill. You're good too."

"Six years of ballet. Three of modern dance. Then four dedicated years of dance hall Saturday nights. I went to college at Vanderbilt."

"Nashville." Josh nodded, then heedless of the rhythm of the music, twirled her into a two-step. She followed him with only a slight misstep, laughing.

His dark eyes twinkled wickedly as he asked, "So tell me, Caitlin, do you swing?"

Startled, she tripped over his foot and lost her balance. His hands swooped in to catch her, clamping around her hips and preventing a fall. For a long moment and with apparent ease, he held her suspended, her feet dangling above the dance floor. He continued to move gracefully to the music and amusement lightened his tone as he clarified, "*Dance. Swing dance.* Western swing dance."

"I knew that," Caitlin said with her chin lifted and a defensive note in her tone. If her mind had gone to sexual swinging first, well, who could blame her? Not that she was into that sort of thing, but still. The longer she remained in his arms, the less she thought about dancing and the more she thought about sex. Her voice squeaked a little as she said, "You can set me down."

"I will. Eventually. I like holding you, Caitlin. Put your arms around my neck."

She did as he asked and he supported her weight until "Unchained Melody" segued into "Summer Wind." The faint scent of his aftershave wafted over her—woodsy and exotic—and made her want to burrow her nose against his neck. Made her want, period. Josh's gaze locked on her mouth, and a shiver of excitement skidded up her spine. Would he kiss her again right here on the dance floor?

Instinctively, she licked her lips. He leaned in and traced the path her tongue had taken with his, then murmured, "Mmm . . ."

Caitlin spent the rest of the song lost in a sensual fog that ended only when the last note faded and the band's lead singer announced the time had come for the bride to throw her bouquet. Caitlin didn't try to hold back her groan.

She despised this particular wedding ritual and she usually made excuses to avoid it. Not because she never caught the bouquet, but because she almost always did.

She had to be up over a dozen by now, and she'd never once come close to a marriage proposal. Shoot, Melanie Harris had thrown the first bouquet Caitlin had caught and Melanie now had three children! And yet, as the single ladies congregated around the bride, Caitlin joined them. She was a bridesmaid, after all. It wouldn't be right to duck it. Besides, tonight she was feeling lucky.

Josh first sensed danger when Caitlin turned those sparkling green eyes toward him and spoke about jewels. The picture flashed into his mind of her lying naked against red satin sheets with the Sokolov emeralds nestled between her breasts. He had yet to banish it completely.

His sense of peril escalated when he danced with her. Graceful as a ballerina, poised as a princess, she fit into his arms as if she'd been born to be there.

He didn't want to let her go.

Danger. Danger. Danger.

Josh should have started running away the minute the gondola rescuers lowered him to the ground. In hindsight, he'd been primed to do something foolish. He'd lived at Stardance Ranch RV Resort until he'd moved into his new place a month ago, so he'd had a front-row seat as lovebirds Brick Callahan and Liliana Howe planned their wedding and future together. Their happiness had made him yearn a little for things he'd never have. Made him restless. Borderline reckless.

She caught the damn bouquet.

Thank God she lives in New York.

He would remember Caitlin Timberlake for a very long time. Timber. Wood. As in, he got wood the moment saw her. Lake. Water. And he absolutely would love to get her naked in water. The hot springs up at Brick's isolated river camp came to mind.

They could get there in two hours going up the back way. One, if he unhooked the trailer.

He could get her up to his room in three minutes flat. *Danger. Danger. Danger.*

He should leave the wedding right now, go up to the room he'd rented for the night and throw his stuff back into his duffle, pick up Penny from the boarders, and high-tail it out of town. Before . . . .

Caitlin returned holding a bouquet of coral-colored roses and wearing an impish grin. "Look what I have."

Too late. Josh held up his hands palms out. "Whoa there, missy."

She giggled. "Don't worry. I've caught plenty of bouquets in my day, but I've yet to land a husband. I think you're probably safe."

"Probably?"

She shrugged, her eyes sparkling like champagne. "Like they say, there's a first time for everything."

"Not for me, there's not," he warned, making sure to meet her gaze. "Not when it comes to bridal bouquets."

A teasing note lingered in her voice when she said, "You sound serious."

"I am very serious."

"I sense a story there. I guess it's your good luck that I don't have a reason to move to Oklahoma." She slipped her arm through his and said, "These heels are starting to talk to me. Shall we sit down for a bit?"

Relieved by the change in subject, he escorted her back to their table. "Would you like another glass of wine?"

"Yes, I do think I would. Thank you."

"Be right back."

While Caitlin surreptitiously kicked off her shoes and massaged her instep, Josh made his way to the bar station and ordered champagne for her and a club soda with lime for himself.

On the return trip to the table, the sight of Caitlin's bare leg revealed to the thigh by the side slit in her dress distracted him. He only vaguely noticed the stir in the crowd of wedding guests, the hoots, the catcalls, the wolf whistles.

So Josh was totally unprepared when a black satin garter came sailing over the heads of the crowd—and landed in his lowball glass.

Soda splashed. The crowd gasped.

Still seated at their table, Caitlin's laughter rang out over the room like wedding bells.

Danger. Danger. Danger.

Disaster.

His stomach sank. His hopes evaporated. *There goes my plan to seduce her into bed tonight.*

Hooking up with Caitlin Timberlake in the wake of this double wedding—tradition whammy would be begging for a visit by bad karma.

Josh admitted to being superstitious. He was the king of snakebit, as they called in it Oklahoma. Extremely unlucky. Maybe even cursed. He'd been born with a target tattooed on his back. How else could you explain taking a tornado hit four times?

His cursed luck was one of the reasons that the bride's garter currently swimming in his club soda gave him the heebie-jeebies.

Once years ago, he'd planned to get married. Never again. He'd intended to be a father. Never, ever again. How did that old saying go? Fool me once, shame on you. Fool me twice, shame on me? He'd challenged fate once and it had bitten him in the ass. Not only did he have genetics working against him, but destiny appeared to be his own personal bitch.

Pasting a good-sport smile upon his face, he fished the garter out of his drink and held it up like the prize it was meant to be, not the omen he considered it. The photographer snapped his picture. The groom threw his arm around Josh and camera shutters clicked.

The bride and Caitlin arrived laughing at how the groom overshot his groomsmen. The photographer took a series of photos with the bride and groom, Caitlin and Josh, and the bouquet and garter.

"I can't believe this," his date said to him. "You weren't even trying to catch it. What are the chances that we'd both end up with the prize?"

"What are the chances?" Josh repeated, a wave of unease rippling through him.

"After all the dancing and standing and leaping, I really need to change my shoes. I forgot to bring my flats to the bridal suite, so I'm going to run up to my room. I'll just be a few minutes."

"I'll walk with you."

"Are you sure? They're about to cut the cake. I've noticed how you've been eyeing the chocolate groom's cake."

"I do have a sweet tooth that doesn't stop," Josh admitted, setting his soda and the garter on their table. "But I can wait until after you change your shoes. It's a big cake."

Caitlin laughed, set the bouquet down next to the garter, and looped her arm through his. They walked out of the ballroom and into the hallway. There, she surprised Josh by pulling on his arm to stop him. "This has been fun. I'm so glad you're here. Getting trapped in that gondola was the best thing that's happened to me in a long time. Thank you."

Then she went up on her toes and kissed him.

Josh kissed her right back. The touch of her lips

torched his bad-karma spidey-sense to ashes and left in its place the need to get her into bed as soon as possible.

Why she finally broke the kiss, he croaked out, "Thank *you.*"

She grinned up into his eyes, then turned toward the elevators. That's when the hairs at the back of Josh's neck rose. He glanced around until a pair of glaring eyes froze him in his tracks.

If looks could kill.

In his mid-fifties, the man had silver at his temples, piercing blue-gray eyes, and a distinguished manner of carrying himself that suited a former federal judge and Eternity Springs' only resident attorney. His wife owned the Yellow Kitchen, Eternity Springs' best restaurant. She was classy, poised, and had a smile that lit up the room. She was looking the opposite way.

Their last name was Timberlake.

The same as the woman at his side whose lips were still swollen from his kiss.

No. No. It couldn't be. She's from New York!

She *lives* in New York. She never said she was *from* New York. Josh slowly released his hold on Caitlin's arm.

Oh holy hell.

He knew that Mac and Ali Timberlake had a son. Chase lived in Eternity Springs and was a good friend of Josh's foster brother, Brick Callahan. Chase was married to Lori, the town's pretty veterinarian whom Josh had come to know quite well since he'd decided to adopt Penny.

Josh hadn't known that Chase had a sister.

Yippee.

He tried to tell himself that he was jumping to conclusions. "Timberlake" might not be as common as "Smith" or "Jones," but this *could be* a coincidence.

Maybe Mac Timberlake wasn't shooting daggers at him because he'd just caught Josh with his tongue down his daughter's throat. Maybe that look was nothing more than a bad case of indigestion. Or hemorrhoids.

Even as the seed of hope sprouted, reality smiled and finger-waved. Reality in the guise of Celeste Blessing and her impishly twinkling blue eyes.

Josh swallowed a groan.

Celeste's presence put whole new spin on the moment. Since the day he moved to Eternity Springs, Josh had heard tales of Celeste's "coincidences." People said she was wise beyond measure and that if she happened to give you a bit of advice, you'd be darned smart to listen to her. Celeste claimed that the valley that was home to Eternity Springs had a special healing magic to it, and Josh would be lying if he said the idea hadn't played a role in his decision to move there permanently. He fought the battle to stay healthy every darn day.

Well, he wasn't in the valley now, was he? He'd left the safety of Eternity Springs to play tourist, and now the bridal bouquet and garter were hanging over his head. It appeared that he might be about to get the boutonnière beat out of him—and he hadn't even gotten laid!

Am I lucky or what?

Journal Entry

Funny how certain memories from childhood stick with you. I think I was eight or maybe nine . . . it was after the divorce . . . and we were working in Austin. A crew member's wife taught fourth grade and she invited us to speak at their career day.

I remember it was sometime in the fall and it was hot. I didn't want to go. It was a day off, and I wanted to stay at the hotel and swim, but my mother insisted we go. I'll never forget walking into the building. It smelled like someone had opened a thousand crayon tins at once. Man, I loved that smell. Still do.

My mother and people in the office started talking and quit paying attention to me. I wandered away. Walked down a hall. My sneakers squeaked.

I remember looking into a classroom. They were kids my age. Twenty of them. Maybe thirty. Some of them had their hands raised, waving them around. It was a history class. The teacher asked a question and I knew the answer. I stood there in the hall and raised my hand. I wanted to answer the question. I so badly wanted to answer the question.

Then my mother called me and we went to the classroom and she did our presentation. Afterward, the kids asked me questions. I told them this was the first time I'd ever been to an actual school. I could tell that most of the kids thought that was the greatest thing ever. One of them said, "You're the luckiest kid in the world."

But there was this one little girl . . . I'll never forget her. She had blonde hair and freckles and she said, "I'd be lonely."

My eyes watered up. I remember I was so afraid I'd start bawling right there.

After that whenever I needed to cry and couldn't, I mentally put myself back in that classroom. Worked like a charm.

Chapter Three

My parents?

My parents are here?

Caitlin stared at Mac and Ali in shock. What in the world were her parents doing here?

They hadn't come for the wedding. They hadn't been invited. They had never even met Stephanie.

They hadn't come to Telluride to see Caitlin, either, because she hadn't told them she was coming to Colorado. This was an in-and-out trip because her boss had denied her request for an extra day's vacation. She didn't have time to drive to visit Eternity Springs, and she hadn't asked them to drive to see her because she hadn't known how much free time she'd have for them.

But here they were.

She couldn't believe it. They were here and they'd seen her. Even now, they moved up the hallway toward her.

My parents are here and there goes my hope to se-duce Josh Tarkington tonight.

"Sunshine!" Mackenzie Timberlake threw his arms around Caitlin and pulled her close for a hug. "What a great surprise. I had no clue we were coming here to visit you. Whose idea was it, yours or your mom's? You sure had me fooled. I didn't suspect a thing."

Yes, well, neither had she.

Her father had some suspicions now, though, didn't he? His words might be friendly and mild, but his eyes shot daggers at Josh.

"It's a surprise to me too, Mac," Ali Timberlake said. "Caitlin, don't you look gorgeous. I think I've figured this out. You look like you're dressed for a wedding, and didn't you have a college friend getting married this month? A destination wedding? I didn't know it was in Telluride."

"I never told you," Caitlin admitted.

Ali gave her daughter a hug. "Because you wanted to surprise us and you arranged for Celeste to get us here."

Celeste? Caitlin looked beyond her parents and spied their family friend. Celeste Blessing was dressed for up-scale restaurant dining in a flowing teal skirt and match-ing jacket. She smiled and finger-waved hello.

Well, good, Caitlin thought. *I won't be alone with them.* Dad wouldn't give her the guilt full-court press in front of someone else.

She returned Celeste's wave and confessed, "Yes, it's my friend Stephanie's wedding. She got married here to-night. But I'm afraid I didn't arrange anything. Running into you is as big a surprise for me as it is for you."

Mac's brow dipped in a frown as he shifted his gaze from her to Josh. "Did your car break down?"

He totally lost her on that one. "My car? What car? Daddy, I flew in from New York."

"Then why were you giving Celeste's mechanic a thank-you kiss?"

Caitlin gaped at her father. *A thank-you kiss? Dad. Se-riously?* That had been a take-me-upstairs-and-have-your-way-with-me kiss. Was he blind?

No, not at all. Hence the arrow eyes.

With that, Caitlin grew annoyed. What was with the overprotective-father act? He had no business acting that way.

"Josh isn't just *my* mechanic, Mac," Celeste said, stepping forward. "He's the newest member of the Eternity Springs Chamber of Commerce and a mechanical magician. I'd had two other mechanics tell me my Gold Wing needed to be sent to the motorcycle graveyard, but after Josh had it a week, it purrs like an angel."

"I didn't know angels purred," Josh mumbled.

Caitlin shifted her gaze from her father to Celeste, and finally, to her date. "Wait a minute. You live in Eternity Springs?"

"Yes."

"But you're from Oklahoma. You said you'd lived in Oklahoma and California. You never mentioned Colorado."

"I've lived a lot of places, but I consider Oklahoma my home. You didn't mention Eternity Springs, either."

It's true. She hadn't. All she'd told him was that she lived in New York.

"So you're a guest at the wedding too, Tarkington?" Mac asked.

"Yes."

Caitlin didn't like the note of challenge in her father's voice and she'd had enough. Annoyance sharpened to anger. She didn't lose her temper often, but when she did, she made it count.

It didn't help any that her feet were killing her. Thus fueled by fury and foot pain, she slipped her arm through Josh's, lifted her chin, and said, "I invited him, Daddy. I picked him up in a gondola cabin yesterday, and we've been having wild monkey sex ever since."

"Oh geez, Caitlin." Josh grimaced, dropped his chin to his chest, and murmured, "I might as well have put the garage up for sale now. Mr. Timberlake, that's not what happened."

Caitlin gave her hair a toss and showed a pugnacious chin. "Josh, it's none of his business. This is ridiculous. I'm almost thirty years old. He's acting like he just caught us naked and going at it like rabbits in the middle of—"

"Sweetheart." Ali Timberlake raised her voice, interrupting her daughter before turning a friendly smile toward Josh. "Hello, Josh. We met last summer at one of the Callahan parties, I believe."

"Yes, Mrs. Timberlake, we did."

"Call me Ali, please. Mac and I did so much traveling this past year that we're a bit out of touch with events in Eternity Springs. The automotive center that opened recently is yours?"

"Yes ma'am."

"Well, you did a fabulous job renovating your place. It's so great to see the old buildings in town come alive again."

"Thank you."

Caitlin stood silently fuming while her mother made small talk with Josh, using good manners to smooth the choppy emotional waters. Ali was a pro at that sort of thing. Traditionally, she'd played the peacemaker in the Timberlake family.

But at the moment, Caitlin didn't want peace. She was embarrassed and angry and, well, sexually frustrated. She wanted to tell her father to climb down off his high horse, but the longer her mother talked, the less likely Caitlin was to do it.

Finally, Ali's exchange with Josh ended. Caitlin narrowed her gaze toward her father and framed the perfect subtle-but-effective jab, but even as she opened her mouth to let it fly, her mother smiled at her and continued, "Caitlin, your father, Celeste, and I have been meeting with the management here at the hotel, and I've been on my feet all afternoon. These heels are killing me. We were just going upstairs to change. Would you and Josh like to meet us for a drink in half an hour?"

Caitlin briefly closed her eyes and admitted defeat. "The wedding won't be over until midnight, Mom. In fact, I'd better be getting back there. I am a bridesmaid, after all."

"Oh. Yes, of course. You need to get back to the wedding. Why don't we meet for breakfast? Say, eight o'clock in the main restaurant?"

"We can wait until midnight," Mac protested.

"No, we can't," Ali crossed to the elevator and pushed the button. "Good night, sweetheart. See you in the morning. Good night, Josh."

The elevator doors opened and Ali dragged Mac inside.

Celeste gave Caitlin a quick hug, looked up at Josh and smiled. "I can't wait to hear all about how you two met. I've always heard that Telluride was a great place for romance."

Mac held the elevator doors for Celeste until she darted into the car.

Once the doors finally shut, Caitlin closed her eyes. "Are you going to tell me I had one too many glasses of champagne and I'm really passed out and dreaming?"

"No," Josh said, his tone flat. "I'm afraid this was all too real."

Caitlin buried her face in her hands. Her shoulders started to shake. Finally, she couldn't hold back her hysteria-tinged laughter. "I can't believe this. I seriously cannot believe this."

"I can. That's the way my luck always runs." Josh gestured toward the elevator. "Still want to go change your shoes?"

"More than just about anything, but I don't dare. The way my luck is running, my parents are liable to be in the room across the hall from mine. No way I'm gonna risk running into them again tonight." *Especially not with you in tow,* she added silently. "I'll just go barefoot. Won't be the first time I've danced barefoot at a wedding. Let's go back into the ballroom."

He visibly hesitated and Caitlin got the impression that he was about to beg off. If that happened she just might cry. She had plans for Josh Tarkington. She wasn't going to let her parents or his current place of residence ruin them.

Caitlin caught his hand and pulled him toward the ballroom. "We'd better hurry or the cake will be gone. Your sweet tooth will never forgive you."

She wasn't certain he wouldn't decamp until the hostess handed him a piece of cake. Despite the fact that he didn't seem the type to eat and run, she nevertheless kept watch on his progress with the dessert and coaxed him back onto the dance floor as soon as he finished.

"I thought your feet hurt," he protested as she reached up and linked her hands behind his neck.

"They do." She put some smolder into her eyes and licked her lips as she smiled up at him. "I'm hoping you'll do that lift-me-off-the-ground thing again."

He sighed audibly. His gaze fastened on her mouth.

"You are dangerous, Caitlin Timberlake."

His hands gripped her hips and he lifted her, twirling her in a slow circle once . . . twice . . . three times. On the third rotation he lifted her a little higher and his lips brushed hers, a soft, swift kiss, but one that made her lips tingle.

"You must be a fabulous mechanic," she murmured when her feet touched the ground.

"Hmmm?" His hand skimmed up and down her spine. "Why's that?"

A little embarrassed by the corny truth of what she was about to say, she peered up at him from beneath her eyelashes and confessed, "You have my engine humming."

He chuckled softly then moved his thumb to the pulse point on her wrist. "Might be skipping a little. Professional pride makes me want to hear it purr."

"In that case, maybe you should take me out for spin."

"Maybe I should," he murmured. "Maybe I will."

Caitlin thought her pulse really did skip a beat then. But instead of whisking her off the dance floor and to the elevator and up to his room, Josh tightened his hold and led her into a spin worthy of Fred Astaire. When the song ended he led her back to their table and said he was going for seconds on wedding cake and did she want a piece?

"Yes, please."

But cake wasn't really what she had in mind. They stayed at the reception until the bride and groom's departure. Caitlin was almost able to put her parents' presence at the hotel out of her mind. Almost. If it was a niggling thorn of reality in the sweet, sensual haze of desire running through her . . . well . . . she could ignore it. She would ignore it.

She wondered if Josh would invite her up to his room for a drink. Or would he expect her to issue the invitation to come to her room? She didn't know the details about how something like this was done. For a woman of her age and experience, she was woefully naive when it came to . . . well . . . hook-ups? First-date sex? She didn't quite know how to define this.

It wasn't a hook-up. It might technically be a first date, but she didn't view it that way. She'd always think of their first date as the meal they'd shared after being rescued from the gondola.

Always. Here she was using the "a" word in regard to

Josh Tarkington. *Getting a little ahead of yourself there, aren't you, Timberlake?*

After all, she wouldn't put it past her father to be lying in wait, ready to pounce, just outside the ballroom. So she gestured toward the back exit. "I'd like to go for a walk in the garden. Come with me?"

What followed was the very definition of a pregnant pause. Caitlin held her breath. Her mouth went dry.

She tried very, very hard to ignore the thorn of her parents being somewhere in the hotel.

"I would like that, Caitlin. I would like that very much."

"Wait a moment while I grab my bag and shoes."

It took more than a moment, since she was waylaid by college friends saying their goodbyes. Finally, with her shoes on her feet and the darling little Kate Spade evening bag that had been a gift from the bride dangling from her left hand, she and Josh exited the hotel.

He took her hand and held it, and they walked without speaking for a time. Above them, an almost full moon rose over shadowed, craggy mountain peaks. Soft music drifted from the hotel's nightclub on the second floor. Caitlin all but swooned from the romance of the moment.

They walked beside a stretch of grass when the torchy tune of "Crazy" drifted from the hotel's nightclub above them. Josh pulled her into his arms, onto the lawn, and asked, "Can your feet handle one last dance, Ms. Timberlake?"

"Yes," she replied, answering that question and the one he had yet to ask.

He held her close and they mostly swayed. He made her feel petite and protected, and when he nuzzled her, pressing little kisses against her head, he made her feel hot. She shivered with anticipation and literally did purr.

The song ended, the dance ended, and he kissed her sweetly before stepping away.

"I've spent a good chunk of my life wishing things were different. However, it's been a while since I traveled down that particular road. I could easily go there with you."

Wait a minute.

"I've had a great time with you these past two days, Caitlin. Not only are you drop-dead gorgeous, but you're fun and witty and . . . well . . . nice."

Caitlin wasn't sure where exactly he was going, but she sensed she wouldn't like it.

"You can't know how much I like that about you. I haven't known all that many nice women in my life."

Now Caitlin feared she did indeed know where this was headed. And she didn't like this road. She wanted to turn around. "Josh——"

He rested his finger against her mouth. "Hush. Let me say what I need to say."

No!

"I'd like nothing more than to take you back to my room and spend the rest of the night making love to you."

Yes!

"But it would be a mistake."

No!

"It would complicate both our lives."

Her heart pounded. "But life is supposed to be a little messy. That's what makes it interesting."

"Oh, sweetheart." Josh gave a humorless laugh. "Believe me. Interesting is highly overrated."

Temper burned through the last of her sensual haze.

"If this is because we ran into my parents . . ."

"It's because Eternity Springs might as well be Regency England."

"Excuse me?"

"I haven't ruined the duke's daughter yet. I can look Lord Timberlake in the eyes as things stand now. But if I did what I want to do right now—he'd be well within his rights to challenge me to a duel. Your brother would be his second and half the men in town would be there egging him on."

"That's ridiculous."

"You're probably right. It's the women who would be out to tan my hide—or have me drawn and quartered or dragged to the altar. Not sure which would be worse. I've never seen such a matchmaking group of mother hens in my life."

"Wait just one minute. Now you're making me mad."

"That's the idea," he murmured. Then he raked his fingers through his hair. "Caitlin, thank you for a fantastic weekend, but like the saying goes, All good things must come to an end. This is it for me. I'd walk you to your room, but it'd be just my luck to run into the Duke. Or even worse, Celeste. If the women of Eternity Springs are matchmaking hens, then she is the high holy queen and ruler of the roost. I find it awfully fishy that she turned up here tonight. Don't you?"

Without waiting for her response, he put his hand at the small of her back and guided her toward the nearest doorway into the hotel.

Caitlin was still trying to process everything he'd just said, so she allowed him to move her along. It wasn't until he opened the door, all but shoved her inside, then took a step back that she realized he didn't plan to walk her even as far as the elevators.

Here? Now? Like this?

"Thanks again. Good night, Caitlin. Goodbye."

Josh turned and took two steps away before Caitlin found her voice. "You should work on your metaphors,

Mr. Tarkington, and get to know your neighbors better. My father isn't a duke, he's a barrister. Mom absolutely isn't chicken about anything. She fricassees chickens. And I don't know what you could possibly have against Celeste Blessing because she's an angel. Ask anybody in town."

"Have a safe trip back to New York, Ms. Timberlake," he called just before disappearing into the darkness.

Caitlin folded her arms and stared at the spot where he'd disappeared. Back to New York, huh?

"Maybe for now, Mr. Tarkington. But not for long."

Journal Entry

The first time I ran away from home I was six years old. I stuffed a backpack full of peanut butter crackers, clean underwear, Ninja Turtles, and three two-liter bottles of soda. As a result, my pack was too heavy for me to carry, so I dragged it behind me all the way to my hiding place beneath the next-door neighbor's shrubs. It was early autumn and the leaves had begun to drop. My trail couldn't have been any clearer.

Only, Mom never came looking for me.

The neighbor's landscaper chased me from the bushes with a leaf rake. Later I went back for my Turtles, but the backpack was gone.

The next time, I put my Turtles in my pocket.

Chapter Four

Josh retrieved Penny from the boarder first thing the following morning, then packed up and high-tailed it for the backcountry, determined to get on with the serious business of vacationing. He hiked. He fished. He threw a tennis ball for Penny to chase. He lazed in a hammock and read a book.

He dreamt about Caitlin Timberlake. Dammit. He dreamt about her constantly. Every blasted night.

By the following Friday when he awoke with yet another raging erection following one more restless fantasy-filled night, he decided he needed a change of scenery. He drove to the airport in Montrose, parked his camper, kenneled his dog, and dug out his checkbook. He chartered a jet and headed off to Vegas for the remainder of his vacation. Sometimes a visit to the old neighborhood, so to speak, was exactly what he needed to keep him grounded.

He returned home to Eternity Springs eighty thousand dollars richer after having hit on a high-stakes bet at the roulette wheel at the Wynn. Most people would have considered that lucky. Because Josh's luck was Josh's luck, when he went to cash out, he'd run into one of his mother's current lovers. That had led to an ugly exchange and a subsequent phone call from his mom that had him eyeing the hotel room bar with longing.

Four days in Vegas had proved to be the perfect medicine to shake off the restlessness that Caitlin Timberlake had roused within him. He'd been more than ready to come home to the real and wholesome atmosphere of Eternity Springs.

One afternoon during Josh's second week back in town, Chase Timberlake came strolling into Tarkington Automotive. Josh wasn't surprised to see Caitlin's brother. He'd expected someone in the Timberlake family to show up to grill him. He'd hoped that Chase's wife Lori might be the designated interrogator, but when had his luck ever been that good? Nevertheless, he was ready to have this conversation and get it behind him, so he could put a final period on the events in Telluride and move on with his blessed, boring life.

"Hey, Tarkington," Chase said. "Got a minute? I've been instructed to—whoa—is that a Lamborghini you're working on?"

"Yep. A Miura P400. 1967."

"I don't think I've ever seen one of these before. They only produced a handful of them, right?"

"A hundred ten."

"Wow." Chase made a slow circle around the coupe.

"Now that's a car! What a beauty. Does she run?"

"She's more at the walking stage right now, but when I'm finished she'll run like an Olympic sprinter."

"Man, I'd love to get behind the wheel of that. Who does she belong to?"

"She's a project car," Josh replied, dodging the question. He gave the nut another twist with his wrench, then wiped his greasy hands on a red shop towel. "So did you bring thumbscrews with you or what?"

"Huh?" Distracted by the 350 horsepower engine on

display beneath the Lamborghini's royal blue hood, Chase took a moment to remember the purpose of his visit. "Oh, yeah. I'm either supposed to beat you up or throw you a parade. You sure stirred up a hornet's nest when you decided to hook up with my little sister."

"It wasn't a hook-up. We went on a date. We didn't sleep together. Parades aren't my thing, and if you hit me, I'll hit back."

Chase rubbed the back of his neck and twisted his lips as he considered it. "All right, then. I'd rather talk about cars, anyway. My dad drives a Porsche. It was his midlife-crisis car. When I was doing *Thrillseekers*, we spent a lot of time on the French Riviera. Friends loaned me their Maserati to drive. Man it was fun. Used to think if I ever settled somewhere, I'd get me one of my own."

"You're pretty settled now."

"Yep. Driving a Jeep. And, a pickup. And more often than not, an eight-passenger van. And I'm happy as a clam doing it. I found my thrill right here at home." He gave the car another long once-over and added, "Wouldn't mind taking a turn behind the wheel of that one once you get her running, though."

"Mmmm . . ," was Josh's only response. He never let anyone drive his cars.

For a couple of years, Josh and his mother had lived in the same neighborhood as a TV personality known for collecting classic cars. After Josh stood in the street and waved down the star to ask about the McLaren F1 he was driving, the star had invited Josh to tour his garage. That visit began a love affair with automobiles that thrived to this day.

"So, if you didn't sleep with Caitlin, what did you say to her to cause such a fecal tempest? What did you promise her?"

"What are you talking about? I didn't promise her

anything. I thanked her for a nice weekend and wished her a safe trip back to New York."

"That's all?"

"Yes, that's all. What is she saying I promised her?"

"Nothing. She hasn't said a damn thing. That's what has Mom and Dad so beside themselves." He paused a moment, stared at Josh through hooded eyes, and said, "Dad thinks she's pregnant."

Josh blinked once, absorbed the charge, then fired, "Well if she is, it's not by me. I didn't touch her, Chase."

"Okay! Okay! I believe you. I think the 'rents are over-reacting. They've been wound tight for weeks now. I don't know what's the matter. Caitlin isn't the secretive type. She's honest and forthright. She says what she means and means what she says. They just don't like what she's saying."

Which is? The words formed on Josh's tongue, but he swallowed them back. He'd thought about Caitlin Tim-berlake way too much as it was. He didn't need to know what she'd said or done to make her parents think she was pregnant. *Not my monkey. Not my circus.*

Nevertheless, the question fought its way past his lips. "What *is* she saying?"

He thought he'd managed to keep the question casual, but he wondered how well he'd succeeded when Chase narrowed his eyes and studied him.

After a moment, Chase shrugged. "Not a whole lot. Just that she has a big announcement to make, but she wants to do it in person. Mom is afraid that she quit her job, and I swear, she's more worried about that than an accidental pregnancy."

Josh returned his wrench to its spot on his workbench. "Caitlin told me she'd been thinking of making a career change for quite a while. Why would your mother want her to stay in a job she's not happy in?"

"It's not that. Mom—and Dad too—just have a hard time seeing her as an adult who knows her own mind. She's the baby of the family, the only girl. And in their defense, she has bounced around a lot job-wise. I think that's the nature of the industry she's in, but to my parents it labels her as flighty. I also think they're afraid she'll find her wanderlust like I did. My previous lifestyle pretty much drove my parents crazy."

Josh had heard the story of Chase's "previous lifestyle." A jet-setting action photographer engaged to marry his coworker, the beautiful star of the TV series *Thrillseekers*, Chase Timberlake all but owned real estate in the tabloid newspapers. All that changed when he'd gone missing in the terrorist-infested mountains of Chizickstan and been feared dead. Eternity Springs had rejoiced when he'd returned home safely. They'd celebrated when he'd married the town's favored daughter—Lori Murphy.

"Now that I've settled down," Chase continued, "the family waters are calm. Mom and Dad like that. I don't think they're anxious to see it change. But look. I'm sorry I dumped you into the family dirty-laundry basket—as long as you didn't knock Caitlin up, that is. So, all is well—except I have a toothache and my dental appointment isn't for another hour. I need a distraction. So where's this wonder dog my bride has been telling me about?"

Josh allowed the change of subject. "Penny is in the office. I expect she's sleeping. Otherwise, she'd have wandered out here at the sound of your voice."

"Mind if I look?"

"Be my guest." Josh hooked a thumb over his shoulder, pointing toward his office. As Chase disappeared into it, Josh took a seat at his workbench and focused his attention on the carburetor he was rebuilding for one of the mowers Brick had dropped off for service.

He intended to studiously avoid the thumb drive his brother had delivered along with it. Just because Brick didn't like bookkeeping didn't mean he couldn't do it. Just because Josh liked to mess around with engines didn't mean he should continue to have his fingers in his brother's financial world. He no longer drew a paycheck from Stardance Ranch RV Resort. They needed a clean separation.

When he'd decided to take Brick up on his job offer, he'd agreed to work as a handyman and general assistant around the park. The bookkeeping aspect of the job had come about in self-defense after listening to Brick moan and groan as he fought with his accounting software. But Josh had never felt good about it because it seemed wrong to know so much about Brick's financial business when he wasn't being honest about his own.

Chase strolled back into the garage with Penny in his arms—wheelchair and all. "Now this is quite a contraption. Lori told me you'd modified the wheelchair design. I get the reason for the fenders on the tires, but what's the purpose of the spoiler?"

Josh surmised that Chase referred to the U-shaped metal support bracket he'd added to Penny's cart. "It's a stabilizer. Although the Callahan twins have convinced me to add a clamp for a flag."

"For safety?"

"That's my reason for agreeing, but they're girls. Girls who have grown up around Sage Rafferty's Snowdrop."

Chase nodded. "Oh. Of course. The best dressed dog in Eternity Springs." He set Penny on the ground, scratched her behind the ears, then added, "You're not going to put this dog in costumes, are you?"

"Are you kidding me? Penny has standards. Now, I

might start putting her in diapers if we don't manage to get that issue on a better schedule, but she's not wearing any tutus."

"That's good to hear." Chase watched Josh scowl down at the dirt in the carburetor and added, "Could I talk you into submitting a bid to service the equipment we have up at the Rocking L?"

The Rocking L was a summer camp established by Eternity Springs philanthropists Jack and Cat Davenport. Chase had just finished his first summer as camp director and by all reports, had done a fabulous job. Josh asked, "What sort of equipment?"

"Lawn equipment, primarily. But we also have utility vehicles and four-wheelers. A couple of vans and an ancient school bus that hasn't run since a donor drove it up the mountain. I can e-mail you a complete list, or if you have the time, you could come up to camp and see first-hand what we have."

"I'll come up and take a look." Josh liked the thought of working on a school bus engine. He'd never tinkered with one of those before.

"Great."

They set a date and time the following week for Josh's visit, and as Chase strode toward the open garage-bay door, Josh called, "Hey, Timberlake?"

"Yeah?"

"When is your sister planning to make her big announcement?"

"Sometime tomorrow." Chase glanced over his shoulder. "They expect her to arrive by mid-afternoon."

Tomorrow. Caitlin was coming to town tomorrow.

It's too soon.

"When you see her, tell her I . . ." Josh's voice trailed off. He hadn't a clue as to what he'd intended to say.

"Yes? You what?"

Idiot. You'd be a fool to so much as crack that door open. "Nothing. Never mind."

A glimmer of amusement sparked in Chase's eyes. "For the life of me, I don't know why I ever thought Eternity Springs was boring. See you next week, Tarkington. If not sooner."

The sound of Chase's laughter floated on the September breeze and caused a flutter of unease to work its way up Josh's spine. The sensation only grew stronger when he heard Chase add, "This is gonna be fun."

Journal Entry

I did—do, I guess—have family. Blood family, to use my mother's term. I always thought she sounded venomous when she said it. Like she'd wanted to spill some blood where they were concerned. Understandable, to a point. My half sister, Amelia, is nine months older than me. My other half sister, Arabella, is six months younger than I am.

Yeah, do the math.

I've never met them. My mother and my father's mistress were bitter enemies.

My half brother is—was—six years older than me. His mother was my father's first wife, a star on Broadway. Her son inherited her voice. He was the lead singer for a rock band that never quite made it. He used to show up on our doorstep from time to time and turn the charm on, thawing my mother's frost. She always let him stay. She couldn't turn him away. He took after our father, tall with black hair and the famous eyes. Movie-star handsome, of course.

His name was Andrew Barrison Trammel, though everyone called him Drew-Bear. I had a big case of hero worship toward Drew-Bear. He liked me. He played with me. He paid attention to me. A healthy kind of attention.

He hung a basketball hoop on our garage without even asking my mother, and we'd play Horse and Pig. One time he brought his baseball card collection and let me look through it. We spent hours and hours and hours talking baseball. Drew-Bear's dream wasn't to be a rock star. He wanted to play shortstop for the Dodgers. He had a big case of hero worship for Pee Wee Reese.

When we weren't shooting hoops or playing catch or studying stats, Drew-Bear played board games with me. Candy Land, Chutes and Ladders. Some marble game you played on a tin star. I remember trying to get him to play video games, but he wasn't interested. He liked the old-fashioned stuff, he always said.

He committed suicide when I was ten. I saw on the news that he'd overdosed with aspirin, of all things.

He left me his baseball card collection.
Maybe one of these days I'll look at it.

Chapter Five

In the bedroom she used when she visited her parents at their home above Heartache Falls, Caitlin tried to will her brother's Jeep into his customary parking spot on the driveway. She'd arrived twenty minutes ago, and she knew her time was running out. Her parents had a hot seat warmed up and waiting for her downstairs.

It was a miracle she'd put them off this long. They'd tried their best to give her the third degree when she called to say she wanted to visit them. She'd managed to dodge their questions on the phone, and they hadn't hit her with their queries the minute she arrived today, but she knew her parents. They wouldn't let her hide upstairs for long.

But Caitlin really, really wanted Chase here when she broke her news to her parents, so she'd called this morning and given him a heads-up about her intentions.

He'd promised to do his best to be here when she arrived, but had warned her he had a dentist appointment that might delay him.

"Nervy of you to have a toothache when I need you," she'd teased him with only a little whine in her voice.

"I'm definitely a nervy kind of guy today," he'd responded.

She'd caught a note in his voice that suggested he referred to something more than a toothache, but he'd ended the call before she could pursue the question.

Caitlin turned away from the window when a knock sounded on her bedroom door. Her mother said, "Honey? Is everything all right?"

"Yes, I'm fine. Just changing clothes. I'll be down in a minute."

"Okay. I'll put the kettle on. I have the turmeric-ginger tea you like."

"Thanks, Mom."

Caitlin opened her suitcase and pulled out yoga pants, a T-shirt, and sneakers and quickly changed her clothes. She stared at her reflection in the mirror, took a deep breath, then said, "You can do this. You're an adult. It's your life to live. Your decisions to make."

True, but this was the first time in her life she was going to purposefully disappoint her parents, which was why she felt like a nine-year-old going before the bad-report-card tribunal.

They waited for her in the kitchen. Her mother had one of her favorite tea sets out, a fine, hand-painted porcelain set with yellow pansies on the teapot, teacups, and saucers. Her father sat at the kitchen table sipping what she guessed was scotch from a crystal highball glass. *Seriously, Dad? In the middle of the afternoon?* Why did they think she'd come home? To tell them she had cancer?

She found out what her father thought the minute she took her seat.

"You're pregnant, aren't you?" Mac set his glass down hard on the farmhouse kitchen table. "Was it that Oklahoma mechanic?"

That's what they think? That I'm pregnant? Caitlin was appalled not only by the accusation, but also by the scathing tone in her father's voice when he referred to Josh. What did her dad have against Josh Tarkington?

At the same moment, her mother snapped, "Oh, Mac."

"Well?" He flung up his hand. "Why not cut through all the BS? Why else would she make a middle-of-the-week trip home less than a month after her weekend with that . . . that . . . grease monkey. She's in trouble."

"Dad!" Caitlin was flabbergasted. Who was this man and what had he done with her father? Mac Timberlake didn't jump to conclusions. He was steady and deliberate and fair. He'd been a federal judge, for heaven's sake. He never called people names.

The only time she could remember his acting so out of character was when his own marriage was on the rocks.

On the rocks. In trouble.

Caitlin's chin dropped. She darted a glance toward her mother, then back to her dad, then again to her mother. Oh no. Maybe Mac's reaction had nothing to do with her . . .

In trouble.

Oh no oh no oh no.

In that moment the years rolled away and she was a freshman in college once again, reliving the phone call from Mom dropping the bomb that she'd left Denver and Mac. As she recalled that pain, tears immediately welled in Caitlin's eyes.

"She's crying." Mac shoved to his feet, almost knocking his chair over in the process. "I'm right. Dammit. I knew it. I swear I'm going to kill that low-down long-haired, land-thieving carburetor-screwing scumbag pretty boy."

"What?" Caitlin pushed to her feet too. "What are you talking about? I'm not pregnant. Are you?

Is that what's going on here? Are you two splitting up again?"

Now her mother rose to her feet. "Caitlin! You're moving?"

"You're not pregnant?" her father asked.

"Are you and Mom getting divorced?"

"Divorced!" her parents exclaimed simultaneously.

A new voice rose over the chaos. "What in the wide, weird world of Timberlake is going on here?"

Chase strode into the kitchen, his expression curious, but calm. He chose a red apple from the fruit basket on the counter beside the subzero fridge and took a bite as Caitlin and her mother both exclaimed, "Chase!"

Except for the day of his return from Chizickstan, Caitlin had never in her life been so happy to see her brother.

Her father asked, "What are you doing here?"

"Well now, there's a welcome." Chase met Caitlin's gaze and winked. "Bet he didn't greet *you* like that. You've always been the favorite."

Caitlin offered her brother a weak smile and blinked back tears as her mother asked, "Is Lori with you?"

"No, Mom. I'm afraid you're limited to seeing only my ugly mug."

Mac twisted his head and met his wife's gaze. "He's in on this. He knows what's going on."

Ali covered her hand with her mouth. "She needed backup. Oh, Mac. It's worse than we thought."

"What is worse?" Chase asked. "I don't know anything. What's going on?"

"Is their marriage in trouble again?" Caitlin demanded of her brother.

"What?" Chase frowned in confusion. "No. Not from anything I've seen. Recently, I might add. Just yesterday, I can't tell you how embarrassing it is to open the Yellow

Kitchen's supply closet and find your parents mugging down like teenagers."

"You had no business opening that door," Allie snapped.

"Hey, I heard noises! I thought you had a critter in the restaurant. I was trying to do a good thing." Chase shifted his attention to his sister. "Why do you think they're having problems?"

Caitlin hesitated. How could she explain the conclusion to which she'd jumped? It was almost as stupid as what her father had decided. "People around here were jumping to conclusions so I thought I'd join in."

"He dropped the baby bomb, didn't he?" Chase shot his father a disapproving look. "C'mon, Dad. I told you not to go there."

Caitlin's eyes widened. "He rolled his theory by you? Gee, Dad. Did you take out an ad in the *Eternity Times* too?"

Ali held up her hand. "Excuse me. Can we talk about this move? Have you been transferred, Caitlin? Is that what you've dreaded telling us? Where are they sending you? Paris? London? Rome? Or maybe Dublin! Irish textiles are fabulous. Is it a promotion? Surely it's a promotion?"

Caitlin shut her eyes and sighed. "I wasn't transferred, Mom. I wasn't promoted." Shooting a glare at her dad, she added, "And for the last time, I'm not pregnant. I quit my job."

Ali's eyes went as round as the saucer beneath her untouched teacup. "You quit? Why? A better job? You must have gotten a better job."

"Not exactly. I'm not going to look for another job."

A crunch sounded as Chase took a bite of his crisp red apple. Ali ignored the drink in front of her and reached for her husband's scotch.

"I'm lost," Mac said. "Why did you quit your job and why did you ask your brother to show up within minutes of your arrival? What . . . oh, damn." Blindly, Mac reached for Ali's hand. "Are you sick, Pumpkin?"

"I'm not sick. I'm not pregnant. I'm happy as a pup with two tails. I quit my job and I'm going to open a daycare center. In Eternity Springs."

For a long moment, nobody spoke. Nobody moved. Then abruptly, Ali tossed back the entire contents of Mac's glass, then reached for the bottle to refill it. "A daycare center? You want to open a daycare center?"

"Yes."

"A daycare." Ali took a drink.

"Yes, a daycare!" Caitlin snapped, frustration humming through her veins.

Ali drummed her fingers on the tabletop and finally asked the questions Caitlin had expected and prepared to answer. "Why in the world would you do that?"

"Because I want to live in Eternity Springs."

"I repeat, why? You're a city girl, you've always been a city girl. Have I imagined all those times in the past ten years when you griped and complained about being bored here? I do believe you're the one who coined the term 'Boonieville' when referring to Eternity Springs."

"That was a long time ago, Mother. I was angry at you for leaving Dad and Denver, and I didn't see the appeal of small-town life. Especially not this small town. But things have changed since then. *I've* changed since then."

"She met a mechanic," Mac grumbled.

Both women ignored him. Ali said, "Yes, you have an education and an established career."

"And I can take what I've learned and apply it to my new occupation."

"Babysitting."

"Entrepreneurship."

"What do you know about running a business?"

Caitlin's foot started tapping. "As much as you knew when you started the Yellow Kitchen, I imagine."

Chase frowned. "C'mon, Caitlin. Don't—"

"Zip it, bro." She folded her arms and glared at her mother. "I'm not an idiot, Mother. I've given this a lot of thought and analysis and preparation. Eternity Springs needs a daycare center. I can run a fabulous daycare center."

"How do you know? What qualifications do you have? You've never worked with children."

"Sure I have. Think, Mom. You know that my volunteer work has always been child centered, and I've won my company's Community Outreach Volunteer of the Year award for three out of the past five years. On top of that, I've been teaching the preschool Sunday school class at my church for the past three years."

"I didn't know about the awards," Ali murmured.

"There's a lot you don't know about me, Mother."

Mac scowled at Caitlin and warned, "Don't sass your mother, young lady."

"I apologize." Caitlin closed her eyes, summoned her patience, and tried to bury her hurt. Keeping her tone modulated, she said, "I've done my research on this. I know what I need to do to get licensed. I know the personnel and services requirements. I know what facilities I'll need."

Mac rose from his seat and retrieved a second glass from the cabinet. "It'll take money."

"I have my inheritance from Granddad."

Mac winced. Chase whistled silently. Ali gasped and said, "You can't—"

"Yes, I can. He told each of his grandchildren to use the money to finance our dreams. You don't get to tell me what my dream is, Mom. Not anymore."

Ali looked away from Caitlin, but not before she spied the tears pooling in her mother's eyes. The sight brought tears to her own eyes. She loved her mother. She didn't like hurting her. But then, she didn't like being hurt by her either.

"I knew it," Mac muttered as he poured another drink. "I knew the minute I set eyes on the way you were hanging off that free-handed mechanic that there'd be trouble."

Glad to have a different target for her ire, Caitlin whirled on him. "What do you have against Josh Tarkington? He's a nice guy. He takes care of a crippled dog, for heaven's sake!"

"He's from Oklahoma! He came out of the system!"

"What system? What are you talking about, Dad?"

"I asked around about him. He's Brick Callahan's foster brother. He grew up in the foster system."

"So?"

"In Oklahoma!"

"I repeat, so? You did too, Dad. You came out of the foster system in Oklahoma too."

He lifted his drink in a toast. "The defense rests."

Caitlin shot a frustrated look toward her brother. "I'm going to lose it. I knew they'd do this. I knew they wouldn't understand."

"You're doing a sorry job of explaining yourself," Chase pointed out, punctuating his point with a shake of his apple.

"I've tried. They won't listen."

Mac snorted. "I don't need to listen. I heard. You're throwing away your life for a grease monkey."

It was the proverbial final straw. Caitlin fisted her hands, gritted her teeth, and released a screech. "I can't do this. You two are making me feel like I'm a nine-year-old who failed a spelling test, but I'm twenty-nine and I've made a decision, and I'm sorry that you're disappointed, but it's my life and I'm going to live it the way I see fit! Now I'm going for a walk before I say or do something that I'll regret."

Fighting back tears, she rushed out of the kitchen and out of the house, slamming the door behind her like the time she'd left home in a snit because Dad had made her change her too-short shorts. That door slam had earned her a two-week grounding.

"The way he's acting, he's liable to try that again," she muttered to herself.

The way *she* was acting—like a rebellious teenager rather than a mature adult—she'd probably allow him to do it.

Without conscious thought, Caitlin took the path that led toward Heartache Falls. She'd gone maybe four hundred yards when she heard the roar of a motorcycle. Was it coming or going?

Her dad had a bike. Was he leaving? Or was someone arriving? She slowed her footsteps and listened harder. Arriving. Well, good. She'd left just in time. She didn't have it in her to make nice to neighbors.

Another hundred yards or so later, she became aware of footsteps following her. Glancing over her shoulder, she spied her brother. Caitlin didn't slow her pace. Her long-legged brother would catch up with her soon enough.

He did, walking beside her when the width of the path allowed, falling behind when it didn't. They didn't speak, but Caitlin drew comfort from his presence.

The fifteen-minute walk took Caitlin twelve today. She heard the roar of the falls first and her pace increased. When she broke from the trees, she spied the frothing white water and breathed in the scent of mist-saturated air, a lump formed in her throat. She should have come here first for a little Zen moment before going to her parents' house. Something about this spot brought her peace when nothing else did.

She made her way down the slope toward the broad, flat rock that was the Timberlake family's traditional water-watching spot, approximately ten feet from the bank and halfway between the top of the falls and its base. There, she sat cross-legged and stared at the water. Her brother sat beside her and, as was his habit, he scooped up a handful of pebbles and began throwing them one by one toward the falls.

They sat without speaking for a while. Caitlin did her best not to think. Nevertheless, her mind spun. What had just happened in her mother's kitchen?

After throwing at least three handfuls of pebbles off the cliff, Chase broke the silence. "When are you moving, Caitlin?"

"As soon as possible. I have to be out of my apartment in the city by the first of November, so I don't have a lot of time. I hope to find a rental in town tomorrow."

"It doesn't take long to look at rentals in Eternity Springs. You'll find something tomorrow." Chase glanced at his sister. "You don't want to buy a place?"

"No. Not a place to live. Not right away. I'll buy property for the daycare and I want to concentrate on one project at a time. I have my eyes on that empty lot on Aspen between Second and Third."

Chase pursed his lips and considered it. "Not a bad spot."

"The bank owns it and I think I could get it at a decent price. I have a supper meeting with a builder tomorrow night to discuss plans."

"Whoa. No dust on you, is there?"

"I've been thinking about this for quite a while."

"But it didn't occur to you to say anything to the folks about it?"

On the defensive, she stiffened her spine. "It occurred to me. It's my decision, though, and I wanted to make it on my own. Besides, Mom was going to have a cow about it whenever I told her, so I figured it was best for everyone if I waited until it was a done deal."

"And it *is* a done deal?"

"I gave notice at work."

"Okay then. Well . . ." Chase rubbed the back of his neck. "You know, Goober, Mom just wants what's best for you. That's all she's ever wanted."

Caitlin swallowed a lump her throat and shrugged. She pretended that her bottom lip didn't tremble. Her emotions where her mother was concerned were so conflicted. Ali was both her biggest cheerleader and her harshest critic. Caitlin wanted to please her mother, but she didn't want to live her life for her.

Chase shook his head, then took pity on his sister and changed the subject. "Well, here's what I think. I think you'll find a place to live tomorrow before ten a.m. That gives you extra time, so you should come up to the Rocking L and help paint the mural we're doing on the cafeteria wall."

She shot him a look that questioned his sanity. "What?"

He repeated his suggestion.

She couldn't help but laugh. Leave it to Chase to interject the mundane into an insane situation. "No, thank you. I appreciate the offer, but I don't want to spend my day painting a mural on your cafeteria wall."

"But think of the children!" Chase exclaimed, his brown eyes flashing with amusement. "I love Lori dearly, but it's not that she simply colors outside the lines, she doesn't see the lines. She's obliterating Sage's design. If she's left in charge of the mural, rather than it brightening the children's mealtime, it will turn their stomachs."

"You're ridiculous." Caitlin dismissed her brother, gazing back toward the waterfall where the reflection of the afternoon's fading sunlight created a rainbow in the mist. Seeing it, she smiled. Some of the tension in her bones melted.

She loved Heartache Falls—the sounds, the scents, the sight of such majestic beauty. She loved so much about Eternity Springs and its environs. It inspired her. How quickly it had become home to her.

She willed back tears. *Why can't Mom and Dad see that?*

Chase threw an arm around her shoulder and gently tugged a lock of her hair. "C'mon, Goober. Don't tell me you're going to go back on your promise."

"What promise?" As always when he pulled her hair, she elbowed him in the side.

"I seem to remember that when I got home from my Middle East adventure, you promised if I ever needed anything, all I had to do was ask."

Caitlin shrugged off his arm and whipped around to shoot him an incredulous look. The incident Chase referred to was their family's biggest nightmare, the time when he'd gone missing in the terrorist-infested mountains of Chizickstan and their family had feared him dead.

"Seriously?" She shoved him. "You're playing the I-thought-you-were-dead card for an afternoon of mural painting?"

The laughter glittering in his eyes intensified. "Yep. Sure am."

How could she have forgotten how infuriating her brother could be? "That's taking advantage."

Chase shrugged. "How old are you? Thirty?"

Her eyes narrowed. Forget shoving. Now she wanted

to use her self-defense skills and take him to the ground.

"I'm only twenty-nine."

"And for how many of those twenty-nine years have I, as your beloved older brother, taken advantage of you?"

"Twenty-nine."

"Exactly. That's what brothers do."

She sniffed loudly with disdain, even as her lips fluttered with a begrudging grin. "I'm not sure 'beloved' is the proper adjective in this instance."

"Sure it is. You love me big as the moon."

The reminder of the declaration of their childhood warmed her heart. So did the wink he gave while playing his winning card. "And you'll love it when I return the favor by helping you after you change your mind about where you want furniture in your new digs."

Caitlin always had trouble deciding where she wanted things to go. She didn't hesitate. "What time do you want me at the cafeteria?"

Chase laughed. "Let's make it two. That way you'll arrive before Lori, and you might be able to clean up some of her mess before she gets there."

"I can't believe she puts up with you."

"Honestly, I can't either, but the woman is head over heels for me."

"I know," Caitlin responded with an exaggerated sigh. "She always has been. Too bad you wasted so many years being stupid."

"Can't argue with that."

They both fell silent as a hawk lifted from his perch atop a fir tree, his powerful wings pumping the air as he rose high above the waterfall. Caitlin tried to recall the last time she'd watched a hawk take flight. It had been way too long.

Finally, she'd found enough calm within herself to be

able to say, "I knew Mom and Dad wouldn't be happy with my decision, but honestly, I wasn't expecting this."

Chase slung an arm around her shoulder and gave her a squeeze. "Me either, Goober."

"It hurts my feelings. They didn't even give me a chance to explain. Dad's making up stuff out of thin air, and Mom is tossing back booze. Talk about Bizarro World."

"Dad's had a thorn in his paw ever since they saw you in Telluride."

"Obviously, since he's decided Josh knocked me up." Chase started to say something, then apparently changed his mind. He shut his mouth and rolled his tongue around his cheeks.

"What?"

"Nothing. I like Josh. He's a good guy."

"Are you friends?"

"I wouldn't go so far to say that we're friends. More like acquaintances. I know him through Brick—Josh worked for him at the Stardance Ranch RV Resort—but we haven't socialized together much. He's quiet. Seems content to be by himself. I like what he's done with the renovation of his garage. Built a new house, too."

"But you said he's a good guy. How do you know?"

"Brick says he is and Brick knows him. They're foster brothers."

"Yes, Dad mentioned that. So, what happened to Josh's parents?"

"I don't know. Like I said, he's a quiet guy, but my veterinarian bride thinks he's fabulous. He adopted a special-needs dog. That says quite a lot about a man."

"That he's crazy?" Caitlin asked with a laugh, recalling the three-times-a-day bladder expression Josh was required to do for Penny.

"'Dedicated' is the word I'd choose."

Caitlin thought back to the care Josh had taken of Penny during the gondola stoppage. "He is sweet with her. That is appealing in a man."

Chase gave her a sly look. "So was he sweet with you, too? What did happen between the two of you? Care to give me the lowdown?"

Caitlin sighed. "I'm sure you heard all about it."

"Yes, but from the 'rents. Not from you. I'd like to hear your version."

She told him with more detail than she would have anticipated and finished with the decision she'd made in the moonlight following a barefoot dance. "I'm going to marry him, Chase."

"What?"

"I'm going to marry him."

"Holy crap." In the midst of gathering up another handful of pebbles to throw, Chase froze. He looked at his sister with shock in his gaze. "At the risk of sounding like Dad, you're being straight with us about the pregnancy thing?"

She gave him another elbow to the side, a little harder this time. "I'm being straight. I haven't slept with him yet."

"Yet."

"I hope to rectify that soon."

"So Dad is right about one thing. You *are* chasing him."

Caitlin unfolded her legs and leaned back on her elbows. Watching rainbows of light float in the waterfall mist, she said, "Technically, that might be correct, but it's not an attractive charge. I'd prefer to say I intend to make a run at him. Look, I know it sounds crazy, but I just know he's the one. I can't explain it."

Chase's tone was incredulous as he asked, "On the basis of one broken-down gondola ride? That blows me away, Goober."

Sunshine warmed her skin, and she lifted her face toward the sky. "I know. I can hardly believe it myself. I've never been one to believe in love at first sight, and honestly, I still don't. I'm not in love with him. I don't know him well enough for that. Yet. But I believe I will be in love with him. It will come in time."

"Would you be moving to Eternity Springs if he didn't live here?"

"I think so. Maybe not quite this soon, but I've been headed here for quite some time. Everything changed when you went missing."

"So this is my fault now?" He asked, a bit of a bite to his voice.

"Only if you agree with Mom and Dad and think I'm throwing away my life. I've been looking for an excuse to come home ever since you did, Chase. I miss my family. I want to play summer baseball with you and Lori. I want to go to yoga class with Mom and Dad. And after you get around to knocking Lori up, I want to babysit your little girl."

"Boys. I told my wife we're going to have five boys. I want a basketball team."

"And I see marbles rolling out of your head even now."

They shared a grin, then Chase rolled to his feet and went in search of something bigger than pebbles to throw into the water. He gathered a half dozen fist-sized stones and pitched them one by one toward the waterfall. When his hands were empty, he turned and faced Caitlin.

"I get the family part of this decision. That aside, mind if I play Devil's advocate regarding Tarkington?" Without waiting for her answer, he pressed on. "I know you're not like most girls——"

"Women."

"Excuse me. I know you're not like most women, but this whole marriage idea . . . don't you think this is probably the common new-relationship high? You know what I'm talking about. That gaga dippy dreamy-eyed emotion that lasts six weeks or so before fizzling out?"

"I know what you're talking about and this isn't that." She wrapped her arms around her knees. "He's the one, Chase. The *one*. I know it in my bones."

Chase shook his head. "That's just weird. You spent . . . what . . . two days with him?"

"Not even that much. Look, I know it's weird. I also know I'm meant to be with him. Be *here*, with him. In Eternity Springs."

"That's woo-woo, Caitlin. You've never been a woo-woo kind of person." He paused a moment, then added, "I hate to see you risk your heart this way. I'm afraid you'll get hurt."

Caitlin rose, walked over to her brother, stood up on her tiptoes, and kissed his cheek. "I love you, Michael Chase. Honestly, I'm a little afraid that I'll get hurt, too. But I'm convinced I must follow my instincts in this instance. I just need to convince everyone else in my life that I'm right."

Chase's smirk signaled his surrender. "Probably need to let Tarkington in on it, too."

"Oh, I will." Now it was Caitlin's turn for a sly smile.

Seeing it, Chase laughed out loud. "I almost feel sorry for the guy. He doesn't stand a chance."

"I can be a little determined." Caitlin made a dusting motion with her hands.

Chase snorted. "And the summit of Murphy Mountain can get a little cold in January."

"Yeah, well, so can Mom's smile." Caitlin closed her eyes and groaned. "I slammed the door when I left the house. I can't believe I did that."

"Yep. She'll make you pay for that one. So, are you

going to go back to the house and face the music or throw yourself into Heartache Falls?"

Caitlin massaged her brow with both hands. "Sometimes it's hard to be a grown-up."

"Don't you know it." Chase's smile softened to tender. "One reason to take heart, Goober. Celeste rode up shortly after you left the house. Nobody calms choppy waters like Celeste."

"True." Caitlin sighed and turned toward the path that led home. "Unfortunately, I feel like I left a hurricane behind."

Journal Entry

They sent me to a therapist for the first time one week before I turned twelve. The doctor asked me what I wanted for my birthday.

I didn't explain that every year, my mother threw a huge party for my birthday. Hundreds of people came, but they were always all adults. No kids. And the party always had a theme. "A night in the jungle" when I turned nine. I got life-sized stuffed animals—a giraffe and a gorilla and a zebra. Somebody gave me a live monkey. Guests wore Tarzan and Jane costumes and before I finished opening all my gifts, someone had rigged a rope swing from the second floor into the pool.

I liked the sweet, fruity drink the waitstaff served. Jungle juice, they called it. I drank a lot. I fell asleep on a lounge chair beside the pool.

I woke up surrounded by naked people having sex. The sound of a Tarzan yell still scares me.

I told the therapist I wanted a tent for my birthday.

I wanted to run away for real that time, to go up into the hills and camp out. I wanted escape.

Chapter Six

Mac Timberlake stood in front of the big picture window at the front of his house and watched Celeste Blessing give his wife one final hug before pulling on her helmet and mounting her Gold Wing. Thank God for Celeste. She had a way of saying exactly what a person needed to hear, when he needed to hear it.

In today's brief ten-minute visit, she'd managed to remind him that the Timberlake family support system was dedicated and deep, that he'd married a woman of uncommon strength and fathered three children who would never turn their backs on family. "It'll be okay," he murmured, shoving his hands in the back pockets of his jeans. "No matter what, it'll be okay."

Ali waited, waving, as Celeste topped a hill and disappeared down the other side. Not for the first time, Mac half expected that the woman dressed in gold-trimmed white leathers would sprout real wings and she and her motorcycle would rise up into the sky. If anyone could manage that little trick, it would be Celeste.

Ali turned and met Mac's gaze. The smile she offered was bittersweet, and she didn't try to hide the tears rolling down her cheeks. He turned away from the window and started toward the door, intending to walk outside and join her, but a shooting pain in his leg had him reaching for the support of a chair back and gritting his teeth instead.

By the time the pain eased, Ali was reentering the house. Mac did his level best to hide his pain, but his wife of almost forty years knew him too well. The brittle worry in her smile showed him he hadn't fooled her, so he attempted to distract her instead.

"Any sign of the kids on the trail?"

"No. Not yet."

"Could I have handled it any worse, do you think?"

"Of course you could have handled it worse." Ali waited a beat and added, "Though you'd have had to put some real effort into it."

Releasing a half laugh, half groan, Mac crossed the room to his wife and took her into his arms. He buried his face in her hair and sank into the comfort of her embrace. "Should I go after Caitlin?"

"No. Chase will herd her back after she's calmed down." Ali sighed heavily. "We forget because we're not around her all the time, but our girl can have a hair-trigger temper upon occasion. No sense risking making matters worse."

"True."

"Not that I handled the situation any better than you, Mac. Caitlin living in Eternity Springs? Now? I'm not sure I have the energy for this."

Mac took a long look at his wife. These past few weeks had been hard on her. She did more tossing and turning than actually sleeping at night. The lines on her brow etched a little deeper, the creases at her eyes stretched a little longer. He honestly thought this whole thing was harder on her than it was on him.

Oh, Ali. I'm sorry to be doing this to you.

He cleared the sudden lump from his throat. "No matter what happens, you need to take care of yourself, Alison. I'm going to insist on it."

She went up on her toes and kissed him. "Right back at you."

"With that in mind, since our daughter is apparently home for more than a quick visit, maybe we should go down to yoga class tonight after all."

"That's not a bad idea." Ali's mouth flickered in a grin as she added, "We could catch dinner at the restaurant afterwards. Tell Caitlin to fend for herself."

"Yeah. Right. Ali Timberlake opts out of feeding one of her chicks on said chick's first night home? And I'm going to wear hot pink yoga pants to class, too."

This time Ali actually laughed. "If you had hot pink yoga pants to wear, I'd definitely do it. I'd want a camera set up in the room first."

"No can do. Remember, cameras are off-limits in yoga class. However, why don't I join you in the kitchen and you can boss me around while I help you get dinner started? Cooking relaxes you, and there's no reason you can't serve our chick her feed a little early so that we can make the couples class."

"You're truly up to going?"

"I am. I'm glad Celeste reminded us about it. I think we both can use a little Eternity Springs Zen tonight."

They walked hand in hand back into the kitchen. Armed with a knife and a cutting board, Mac sat at the table and sliced zucchinis, tomatoes, and garlic under his wife's watchful eye.

"A little thicker on the tomatoes, please. It's for Caprese salad."

Mac shifted his knife. "Like this?"

"Perfect."

They worked in comfortable silence for a time while

Mac's thoughts bounced from subject to subject, finally settling on his daughter. "So you really thought she had come home to tell us she was moving to Europe?"

"I did. It's the next logical step in her career."

"You had no inkling that she wanted to move home?"

"Not at all. There's nothing logical about her moving to Eternity Springs."

"Sure there is," Mac grumbled. "He's opened a garage on Sixth and Spruce."

"Mac, you need to zip your lips about Josh Tarkington when she comes home."

"I know. I will." He sliced the tomato with a little too much zest.

"Celeste had nothing but nice things to say about the man."

"Yeah well, Celeste never has anything bad to say about anyone."

"Now, that's not true. She's an excellent judge of character, and she'll speak up if she believes it necessary."

Yeah well. Harrumph. "Is this enough tomatoes?"

Ali eyed the cutting board. "One more. Lori loves Caprese."

Mac did too. But then, he loved almost everything his wife created in the kitchen. The only way he'd managed to avoid packing on the pounds after she'd begun cooking professionally was by embracing the active lifestyle made easy to achieve when semi-retired and living in the mountains.

I miss that already.

"Here come the kids," Ali said.

Mac rose from his seat and joined his wife at the kitchen's big window that offered a breathtaking view of the San Juans. Love swelled within him as his gaze landed on his younger son and daughter who were making their way toward the house. His heart gave a little twist. *Dear God, I'm not ready for this.*

"Mac . . . ?" Ali spoke quietly and with a note of hesitance. "Maybe we should tell—"

"No!" He fired out before she'd finished her sentence. "—them."

He repeated, "No. Not yet. Not until we hear what they have to say in Boston."

"But—"

"Honey, I don't need the drama and neither do you. Please. Let it go."

She sighed. "All right. It's just . . . fair warning. Chase is your typical clueless guy when it comes to noticing undercurrents. Caitlin is more perceptive. If she's living in Eternity Springs and around us all the time and we act out of character like we did earlier, she's liable to figure out something's up. And we don't want a situation like Lili had with her parents. They kissed and made up, but the hurt was real and it did some damage."

"You have a point. I'll be careful. I'm calm now."

Ali studied him closely, then nodded. "It's the Celeste effect."

"True." Mac gave her waist a little squeeze. "The bourbon didn't hurt anything either."

When Caitlin and Chase entered the room a few minutes later, Ali stood in front of the stove. Mac was setting the table. The mother and father met their daughter's gaze and all three spoke simultaneously. "I'm sorry."

The tension deflated somewhat. Mac motioned to the table. "Sweetheart, Mom and I want to start this over. Please, sit down and share the news you need to share. We won't interrupt." After a moment's pause, he added, "If we can help it."

Caitlin's eyes watered up. She blinked rapidly and swallowed hard. "Thank you."

Taking a deep breath, she added, "I know I could have handled this better. I've been afraid to be honest with you. But the truth is"—she shot her brother a quick, teasing grin—"it's all Chase's fault."

He snorted. "Some things never change."

"The truth is the truth," their father observed.

At her father's quip, Caitlin's tension visibly eased. "Seriously, though. This did all begin when Chase went missing. Those horrible weeks brought home to me just how short life is. It made me want to make every single day count. You understand that, don't you?"

Mac's gaze flicked toward his wife. *Oh hell.* Caitlin couldn't have made a comment more certain to bring on the waterworks if she'd tried.

Two big fat tears overflowed Ali's eyes and rolled down her cheeks. "Yes. We understand."

"Oh, don't cry, Mom." Caitlin impulsively stood and reached for her mother and hugged her. "Please, don't cry. I know I've disappointed you and that rips me in two."

"That's not . . . oh . . . don't mind me, honey. I'm just hormonal these days. Continue with your explanation, please. Dinner will be ready in twenty minutes. Chase, I texted Lori to let her know we'll be eating a little early tonight."

"Will she be able to get away from the clinic?"

"She said she'd be here. Caitlin, please go on."

Caitlin exhaled a heavy breath, then said, "I'm glad I went to New York and lived that experience. It was fabulous and exciting and I'm proud of what I accomplished. But I've been there, done that, and I dream of something else now. I'm ready for the next step."

She faced her father, and met and held his gaze. "Dad, I'll tell you one more time that I'm not pregnant. However, I want to be. I'm ready to be. That's my new dream. I want children, a house full of kids—the mess and the mayhem and the pandemonium. I want to drive a carpool and bring homemade snacks to Little League games. I want to read bedtime stories and quiz spelling words."

Mac raised his hand. "I'm sorry. I just . . . I know I'm not supposed to interrupt, but I have this one question . . ."

"Yes, Dad. I want to have a husband too. A husband first."

"Okay. Good. That's good. I'll shut up now." He shoved his hands in his pockets and added, "Except . . . don't you think the odds are better for that somewhere other than Eternity Springs?"

Caitlin smiled and shrugged. "Actually, I don't. From what I've seen, Eternity Springs is the happy marriage capital of Colorado. Besides, that's the other part of my dream. I want to share the mess and mayhem and pandemonium with my family. I want you to be part of it. I want my babies to have grandparents and uncles and aunts and cousins who are an intimate part of their lives, not just people they see on holidays and vacations. That's a lot more important to me than designing pretty sheets and visiting Rockefeller Center at Christmas."

His daughter's heartfelt declaration brought Mac to the verge of tears. He was thankful when Chase lightened the moment by saying, "You do make awfully pretty sheets, though, Goober."

"Thank you."

Ali glanced up from the pan of risotto she stirred and cut to the heart of the matter. "Are you serious about Josh Tarkington?"

Caitlin obviously chose her words carefully when she responded. "I haven't known Josh long enough to be serious, Mom. But I am seriously going to see if I can be serious about him."

Mac opened his mouth, Ali shot him a warning look, and he caught his words just in time. "Want me to fill the water glasses, Alison?"

"Please."

He'd give himself an extra big glass. Maybe he could swallow the wrong way and drown himself. Just solve all his problems here and now.

Ali said, "You've told me you work from home quite a bit. Is it possible that you could arrange a long-distance position? Do your designing here then travel to New York when it's necessary?"

"I couldn't do that with my current job, but I could freelance. But Mom, that's not what I want to do. I want to work with children."

"But—"

"Please, Mom. Listen to me. Believe me, this wasn't a spur-of-the-moment decision. I spent a lot of time trying to figure out what I wanted to be now that I've finally grown up. I made a lot of lists. I want to work with children and I want to operate a daycare. Eternity Springs desperately needs a daycare and I'm going to establish a fabulous one. I'm already at work on the licensing and I'm counting on you to help me with other legal stuff, Dad. Will you do that?"

"Of course."

Caitlin shared her plans about renting a place in town and her thoughts about the empty lot on Aspen. Under other circumstances, Mac would have suggested she move back home, but that wasn't doable with their current situation. He exchanged a long look with Ali, silently communicating in that way of long-time partners, and she nodded her agreement.

Caitlin glanced curiously between them, but continued, "If the lot doesn't work out, I plan to ask Celeste if she has any properties that might suit. I'd try to coax Jax Lancaster into doing renovations for me."

"Jax does great work," Chase said. "You'll need good luck to get him away from that baby of his and Claire's. In a town of doting fathers, he's one of the dotingest."

"Is that a word?" Caitlin asked.

Chase shrugged. "I dunno. It suits."

Just then Mac's old dog, Gus, lifted his head from his bed in the mudroom, perked his ears, and thumped his tail. "Lori must be here," observed Mac. "The only time Gus gets that enthused anymore is when Captain comes up to play."

Chase pushed away from the pantry door where he'd been leaning. "So, are we done here? Goober, do you have any more grenades you plan to launch?"

"I've pretty much said what I wanted to say. Mom? Dad?"

Mac arched a brow toward Ali, silently giving her the floor. She said, "It's your life, Caitlin. You have to live it. If this is what you want . . . I won't say I totally understand it . . . but your Dad and I will support you."

"She wants what you had, Alison," Mac said gently. "What you created."

Ali instinctively pulled back. The shock in her expression both amused Mac and frustrated him. Even after all this time, after the undeniable success of their family as a unit, Ali didn't appreciate what she meant to the Timberlake clan. For some inexplicable reason, she had never valued her value to the family.

"Dad is right. You are my hero, Mom. If I can do half as good a job at being a mother and a wife and a businesswoman and a friend and a community supporter as you are, I'll be thrilled."

Ali shut her eyes, but that didn't prevent the tears from

trailing down her cheeks again. Mac's heart twisted. As a rule, Ali wasn't a crier, but these days, tears hovered constantly at the ready.

Chase opened the back door and Captain galloped in, making a stop at everyone's feet to be scratched, petted, and loved on for a moment. Then he escaped with Gus to create their usual havoc with the dog toy box just as Lori entered the house, a wide smile on her face as she called, "Caitlin! Welcome home!"

Once again, Mac and Ali shared a long look, silently communicating their hopes and fears, their worries and concerns, and their regrets. Ali nodded and Mac spoke the words he should have said earlier that day, but had withheld. "Yes, Caitlin our love. Welcome home."

Journal Entry

I ended up at the Christophers' house by dumb luck. Good luck, I guess. One of the few times in my life that I'd say luck fell that way for me.

It was the last movie I made. I played the part of ten-year-old burn victim turned psychopath in a thriller filming three months on location in Oklahoma City. We worked mostly at night so I'd get to bed really late, sleep to mid-afternoon, then do a few hours of school. Listen to my mom's crazy emotional phone calls with the drummer—it was an ugly breakup. Go to work again. Makeup took forever. Mainly I remember feeling exhausted.

The night of the wrap party, Mom attempted suicide.

Someone found her in time to revive her, but she went into the hospital and I got shuffled into the system. I went a little bit crazy myself then. I was still just a kid and I'd had a lot of suicide in my life. My dad, my brother, now my mom—gave me a bit of a complex. What was wrong with me that people in my life kept offing themselves?

Then a social worker introduced me to Paul and Cindy Christopher. We used my mother's surname instead of my own, and my whole first name instead of my initials. Out with J.B. Trammel and in with Joshua Tarkington.

Mr. and Mrs. Christopher took me home with them to suburbia.

I thought I'd landed in outer space. They had a half dozen bicycles in the garage, a trampoline in the backyard, and kids everywhere I looked. At six o'clock sharp when the cuckoo clock in the family room started chirping, you'd damn well better be sitting in your seat for family dinner. They said grace before eating.

Like I said . . . outer space.

Paul and Cindy knew about my California life, but they didn't share it with the other kids. I was just one of them, a regular kid. I had the same rules to follow. The same chores to do. Paul and Cindy didn't treat me one bit different.

Outer space. Oklahoma.

The closest place to heaven that existed on earth.

Chapter Seven

Exiting his garage on a crisp October morning, Josh took a moment to drink in the beauty of the day. The soft breeze was crisp, the sky a brilliant blue. The mountains were on fire with the colors of autumn. He planned to take a hike this weekend up above Brick's river camp. His brother had told him of a remote spot where the forest was a symphony of quaking aspen, burbling creeks, and warbling songbirds. He wanted to experience it himself.

He wanted to go someplace where he knew without a doubt that he wouldn't run into Caitlin Timberlake.

Her brief visit home had turned his world upside down. Nobody knew for sure what big announcement she'd made that weekend, but the rumors were driving him nuts. Some people said she'd come home to tell her parents she'd quit her job. Others said she'd eloped with a professional athlete. The possibility that caused Josh the most grief was the tidbit he'd heard while standing in line to buy milk at the Trading Post. There was some speculation that she just might be planning to move home to Eternity Springs.

Knowing his luck, that's exactly what would happen.

But nobody knew for sure what big announcement she'd made. Mac and Ali Timberlake had left town right after their daughter's brief visit, and Chase hadn't confirmed any of the rumors before departing on a second honeymoon trip with Lori.

So Josh walked on eggshells every time he left the garage.

Maybe he shouldn't have worked so hard to avoid her during her September visit. Shoot, no maybe about it. Hadn't he learned by now that the only way to beat your demons is to face them?

He should have sought her out and said hello and put the first post-Telluride visit behind him. Maybe then he wouldn't be seeing her in line at the post office or playing pool at Murphy's or walking a dog down Spruce. The woman haunted him. The what-ifs haunted him. The might-have-beens left him sad and lonely and alone.

Luckily for his cranky mood this morning, he wouldn't be alone for long. He had a house call to make.

Mechanics didn't ordinarily make house calls, but his across-the-street neighbor's pitiful excuse of a Buick sat stranded in her garage. It took less effort to haul the tools he'd need across the street than hook the Buick up and tow it over to his place.

Besides, Harriet loved to love on Penny, and if he did his work in her garage, she'd bring him cookies hot from the oven. Harriet Rosenbaum could be counted on for that.

The 1981 Buick Skylark needed a Viking funeral. Instead, at Harriet's insistence, he'd do his best to get the old junker running again. The starter was shot. He wouldn't bet on the alternator. For Harriet's safety and that of the people of Eternity Springs, a brake job was a priority. That was just the beginning of the list. When he'd first lifted the hood to give it a quick once-over last night, Harriet mentioned that she hadn't had her car serviced since her husband passed a year and a half ago.

He'd swallowed a groan. Josh understood the love of a great piece of machinery and the desire to keep it running at all costs. However, a 1981 mud brown Skylark didn't qualify as great machinery.

Josh lay on his wheeled creeper scowling up a hole in the Buick's muffler when he heard the squeak of a screen door. Because he'd been smelling the aroma of baking cookies for the past ten minutes, like Pavlov's dog, Josh began to salivate. He had a serious sweet tooth, and Harriet made one fine cookie.

With a shove against the Buick's underbelly, he rolled out from beneath the car. "Do I smell chocolate chips?"

She carried a serving tray containing a plate piled high with steaming cookies, a second plate filled with dog treats, and two glasses of milk. "Oatmeal chocolate chip. Oatmeal is good for you, so I don't feel quite so guilty when I indulge."

Harriet Rosenbaum was a tiny, spry woman in her early seventies. A former math teacher from Texas, she and her husband had retired to Eternity Springs seven years ago. As was her habit, she wore yoga pants and one of a dozen oversized T-shirts that advertised the national parks. She and her husband had been avid campers, and after making the acquaintance of members of the Tornado Alleycats, an all-female camping club who had camped at Stardance Ranch RV Resort the previous summer, she was toying with the notion of joining the organization.

Josh hoped she'd do it. Based on her reminiscences about camping with her husband and his own knowledge of the welcoming nature of the Alleycats, Josh thought that glamping with the girls would be a great way for the active widow to occupy her time. She obviously wanted more to fill up her days than cookie baking—as wonderful as that was.

"I thought we'd sit on the front porch and enjoy our morning snack," she said. "I don't know if you've noticed, but there's been some action across the street at the place next to yours. I'd like to sit and eat my cookies and be nosy. Does that sound all right with you?"

"Harriet, I'd follow you to the top of Sinner's Prayer Pass for those cookies."

He rose to his feet and tugged his red shop rag from the back pocket of his jeans to wipe his hands.

Smiling with pleasure, she led the way out of her garage and up the side steps to her front porch. "So, what's the verdict on Mabel?"

Mabel being her name for her car. "I'll get her running for you, and then you should drive her into Gunnison and trade her in on a truck to pull your new camper."

"I don't have a new camper." She set the serving tray onto the small table that sat between two white porch rockers adorned with parrot green cushions.

"Brick has a connection." Josh took a seat, snagged a cookie, fed Penny a biscuit, and added, "He could hook you up with a sweet little eighteen-footer for ten percent above cost."

A wistful look entered the older woman's eyes. "I'd be afraid to try. Peter always pulled the trailer. I never learned to do it."

Josh took a bite of warm, oatmeal chocolate chip cookie and gave it the reverent moment of silence it deserved. "It's up to you, of course, but I'd think a former teacher would be one to agree with the idea that one is never too old to learn."

She laughed. "Overcoming objections one-oh-one. You should be in sales and marketing, Josh. Or maybe politics, but I wouldn't wish that on anyone I like. And

I do like you. You remind me of someone, you know. I just can't put my finger on who."

Good.

"It will come to me eventually. It always does."

Bad.

He went for the distraction. "These are spectacular cookies. Any time you feel like baking, I'm happy to take some off your hands. So, what's the scoop on the Munster Mansion next door to me?"

She laughed at his reference to the sixties sitcom about a quirky family filled with cliché monsters and fed Penny another treat. "I think we're getting new neighbors."

"Your kind or mine?"

By "kind," Josh referred to residential or commercial neighbors. Eternity Springs was in the midst of a renaissance that gave city planners nightmares. Basically, zoning didn't exist, but it worked for the little town. For the most part, residential properties peacefully coexisted with business concerns in what served as the downtown commercial district. Long-empty buildings and unoccupied homes had mostly disappeared, with the vacancy rate at the lowest level since the silver mines closed a hundred years ago.

Josh's garage sat on a corner lot at Spruce and Fifth. It had been a Sinclair filling station before it closed in the 1960s. He'd bought the station, the lot next to it, and the lot behind it, vacant but for a storage shed packed with prizes—original Sinclair Dino signs, old gas pumps and gumball machines, and a cash register that dated back to the 1920s. He'd been like a kid in a candy store going through the shed.

He'd instructed the architect he'd hired to design the remodel and expansion to stay true to the historic look of the structure. The result was a simple expansion that allowed for entrance on Spruce with drive-through bays and an exit on Fifth. Because a man could never have too much storage space, he'd even kept the shed when he'd had the one-story, two-bedroom Victorian replica cottage built on the adjacent lot. There was a lot to be said for being able to walk to work on a snowy day in January.

After taking her time in an inner debate over which cookie to choose, Harriet responded to his question.

"Honestly, I'm not sure. Celeste owns the property so there's no hint there. I saw her arrive, but I missed the arrival of whoever is driving that maroon SUV. It's a large vehicle, a large house, so I suspect we could have a family moving in."

"Jax Lancaster's truck pulled away from there a few minutes ago," Josh observed. "It looks like they'll be doing some remodeling."

"Yes, but that doesn't tell us much about the visitor, however. That house has been vacant for so long, it surely needs major work. I do hope they don't tear it down. She's a grand old place. I went through it the last time it went up for sale. Not long after Peter and I moved to town. Why, it's made for a big family. Wouldn't it be lovely if a large family moved in?"

"I don't need curious kids underfoot at the garage."

"Oh, don't try that. I've seen you with some of our curious youngsters here in town. Why just last week you all but taught a class to the Wilson boys when you let them help work on your motorcycle engine."

"Their father is deployed. I'm just doing my civic duty."

Penny begged one more treat, then rolled over to a sunny spot on the porch and plopped down to sleep. Josh eyed the dilapidated house under discussion. It had been a showcase in its day. Queen Anne–style with steeply pitched, irregular rooflines that included a tower and turrets. Elaborate brackets of gingerbread adorned the exterior, and turned posts and spindles dressed its three porches. A lot of possibility there. He'd briefly considered buying it himself rather than building something new, but the place was way too big for a bachelor. Since he had no intention of ever changing that status, he'd gone with his new cottage that looked old from the outside, but was equipped with a media room and a steam shower.

"You could wander over and ask," Josh suggested as he lifted his glass of milk to his lips for a sip before reaching for cookie number three.

"Maybe I will. I could take some cookies. I have two more sheets ready to come out of the oven any minute. Why don't we fix a plate and walk over and introduce ourselves? Be neighborly. And if we don't like the people or plans for the house, we can roll out the haunted story.".

"What haunted story?"

"Well, I don't know, but I'm sure we can come up with one if we need it. The place has the look of a haunted house, doesn't it?"

Josh was tempted. He'd wanted to explore the house ever since Celeste refused to show it to him during that short time he'd considered it. *"No, it's not the right place for you,"* she'd replied when he asked about it. *"I've something else in mind for that property."*

That refusal still rankled, even if she'd been right that it didn't suit him. Josh didn't like anyone to tell him no.

"I shouldn't, Ms. H. I've taken a long enough break as it is. My boss will fire me."

"You're your own boss."

"Right. And the guy is a slave driver. I can't be changing starters when I'm getting nosy with the neighbors, and if I don't do it this morning, I won't get to it until next week. I'm booked this afternoon on."

"Mabel can wait. She hasn't run for a month and a few more days won't make a difference. Come with me, Josh.

Having someone with me makes me look less like the nosy stalker neighbor that I am. Besides, if I get a little exercise this morning I'll probably feel like baking a cake this afternoon."

He chastised her with a look, then acquiesced saying, "You drive a hard bargain."

"No, I drive a Buick. Or, I will be again soon. Isn't it lucky that a mechanic moved in across the street from me and is willing to barter for baked goods?"

He laughed just as the timer on Harriet's phone buzzed. "All right, Ms. H. Plate up the cookies and I'll accompany you to meet our new neighbors."

"Potential neighbors," she cautioned.

Josh shrugged, but he didn't believe it. If Celeste Blessing was showing the old house to someone and they'd already called Jax Lancaster in, the deal was done. "I hope if the family has children that they are older and well-behaved and will leave Penny be. She got a little snappish with Racer Rafferty the other night at Murphy's."

"That boy is a tornado on ten toes. Sage and Colt do their best with him, but he is going to keep them hopping. Speaking of Penny, she's welcome to stay in my backyard while we're across the street. The squirrels have been running amok between my trees today. Penny will have a fine time chasing them."

"Sounds like a plan."

A few minutes later Harriet left the house carrying a plate piled high with warm cookies and a stack of napkins. Josh toted a gallon of milk and a package of red Solo cups. The pair crossed the street and stepped up the walk toward the vacant house's front door.

Harriet knocked on the doorframe. "Hello? Hello. It's the neighborhood welcome wagon bearing cookies fresh from the oven."

"Harriet?" Celeste's voice called from a room off the

house's broad entryway and toward the back. "I'm in the kitchen."

Harriet's and Josh's footsteps echoed through the empty house as they followed the sound of Celeste's voice. She sat at a folding card table in the spot where a kitchen table belonged and she had two piles of paperwork in front of her. Contracts, Josh thought as Celeste looked up and smiled delightedly. "Harriet, how did you know I was craving something sweet? And Josh, what perfect timing. Jax was going to tote a small, but heavy trunk down from the attic for me, but we both forgot when he received a call from Claire and hightailed it home. You just missed him, in fact."

"Is everything okay with Nicholas and the baby?" Harriet asked as she set the plate of cookies on the table.

"Yes, all is well at the Lancaster home. This call was about Nicholas's dog. She's having her puppies."

"Finally!" Josh said. He poured milk into a red plastic cup for Celeste. "Nicholas has been on tenterhooks for the better part of a week."

Harriet clicked her tongue. "Yes, the poor boy. Jax said he wasn't half this excited when his baby sister was born. But enough about puppies." Harriet took a seat in the card table's other chair. "What about neighbors? Have you sold the place?"

"Yes, I have—to a wonderful owner, I'll have you know. This property is perfect for her and she for it." Celeste chose a cookie, gave a reverent sniff, then asked, "Would you please see to that trunk, now, Josh? The new owner is up exploring in the attic. She'll show you which one."

He was honestly more interested in the house than in the neighbor, so he nodded and asked, "Where do you want it when I get it downstairs?"

"If you'll set it in the back of the maroon SUV out

front that'll be wonderful. It's unlocked." Celeste took a bite of her cookie and said, "Oh, Harriet, your cookies are sinful. I dare say you could give Fresh Bakery a run for its money with these."

Josh exited the kitchen as Harriet replied with self-deprecating words in a voice brimming with delight. Celeste did have a way of finding the perfect words to please everyone.

Josh peeked into the first-floor rooms before heading up the staircase. The long and skinny floor plan meant that the house had a good portion of its square footage on the ground level. While he'd always preferred tinkering with machines to running power tools, he could see the promise in this place. Wonder what the floors looked like beneath that vinyl? And why in the world would anyone have laid that monstrosity to begin with?

The word reminded him of the Munster reference earlier, so he was grinning as he climbed the stairs. He was halfway up when Harriet poked her head out of the kitchen.

She smiled upon seeing him and said, "Oh, good. I'm glad I caught you before I had to climb the stairs. The beauty shop just called, and Elizabeth is able to work me in for a perm so I'm scooting on home. Also, my call reminded Celeste that she has a mani-pedi appointment, so she's headed back to Angel's Rest. She's asked for you to pass along a message to the new owner. She's to bring the attic trunk and the papers Celeste left on the table with her to Angel's Rest any time after three o'clock today."

"Will do."

"Don't forget the cookie tin I filled for you. You left it on my front porch."

"Oh, I won't forget."

He waited until he heard her leave before continuing

up the stairs. On the second floor, he took a thorough tour of all the bedrooms. Again, the place had promise, though it needed a lot of work. If Jax Lancaster was the contractor, Josh hoped he liked stripping wallpaper.

At one end of the hallway an open door revealed stairs to the attic. Josh's boots scuffed the steps as he started up, and in an effort not to startle the new owner, he called, "Hello? Celeste sent me up to get a trunk."

A muffled feminine voice responded, but he couldn't make out the words. He stepped into the attic, glanced around, and murmured, "Cool."

It was a dusty, mostly empty rabbit warren that called out to the child inside him. One of few good memories he had of visiting his father was the visit they'd made to the Trammel family summer house in Maine. It had rained for the majority of the visit, and he'd spent hours exploring the contents of the attic. Trunks of old costumes had been a treasure trove for a nine-year-old who'd learned at a young age how to lose himself in make-believe.

This particular attic wasn't stuffed to the rafters with trunks and crates and old furnishings. He spied one rocker, a wardrobe, three trunks, and a harp with all of three strings intact. What he didn't see was any sign of his new neighbor.

Take that back. He did see footprints in the dust. They led to the wardrobe and disappeared.

"Huh," he murmured. Then speaking louder he added, "Hello?"

"I'm here," came a muffled voice. "The door is jammed on this side and I can't find another way out."

Josh felt a little silly as he opened the wardrobe door looking for a lady. The wardrobe was empty, but a crooked sliver of light made the false back obvious. "Well look at that. A secret passage."

Delighted, Josh slipped his fingers into the opening and jiggled the back. The piece was heavy and it took some work, but he finally managed to slip it into its track. He then slid the false back open to reveal a square tunnel about ten feet long. Of course, Josh had to see where it led.

He bent over and crawled a couple of feet inside.

"Hello?"

"You fixed it!"

The voice sounded familiar. *No.* A shiver of apprehension skittered down his spine. *No. No.* This was the new owner? His new next-door neighbor? *It can't be. Not right next door.* He must be imagining things. That voice wasn't hers. This was his paranoia at work. His imagination was running away with him.

Nevertheless, Josh's instincts screamed at him to play the Cowardly Lion and back right out of the tunnel.

"I'm so glad," she said. "I admit I was starting to worry a bit."

Oh, hell. It *was* her. His new next-door neighbor. *I am so screwed.* Josh filled his lungs with air, then blew it out slowly. He'd never been clairvoyant, but he was certain that this wouldn't be the last time that Caitlin Timberlake brought him to his knees.

OMG. OMG. OMG.

Caitlin's pulse raced. Her mouth went as dry as a good martini. She'd expected Jax Lancaster. That wasn't Jax. That was Josh.

OMG. OMG. OMG.

This wasn't how she'd planned the meeting. She'd imagined it happening a dozen different ways, but never had it involved a surprise encounter when she was dusty and disheveled and trapped in a secret attic bedroom.

Although . . . wasn't a bedroom exactly where she wanted to get him?

OMG. OMG. OMG.

Okay, girl. Planned or not, this is the hand you've been dealt. Like Dad always says, start like you mean to go on. So, that meant casual and friendly and real.

She resumed the search she'd been making of the walls of the room when Josh's face moved into view. Those eyes. Those cheekbones. She hadn't remembered how he really was good-looking. Movie-star handsome. "Well, hello, Josh. I wasn't expecting you to be the one who came to my rescue."

He froze and closed his eyes. In a resigned voice, he said, "Hello, Caitlin. So it *is* you."

"Live and in person and stuck in this room. But isn't it cool? I've been searching for another exit, but if one exists, it's not obvious. Now that you've rescued me, I don't need to look for it so hard. Thanks, Josh. You're my knight in shining armor."

He exited the tunnel and climbed slowly to his feet. Was that a faint light of hope in his eyes? "You're visiting?" he asked. "You're a friend of the person who bought this house from Celeste?"

Caitlin worked hard to keep her nervousness hidden and show only excitement in her smile. "I *am* the person who bought this house from Celeste."

"Why?"

Here you go. Roll your dice, woman. "I'm moving home, Josh."

His only reaction was a wince.

She continued. "I'm going to open a daycare center." Now he gawked at her. "In Eternity Springs?"

"In this house. I was going to buy a lot and build, but Celeste suggested this place. It has so much potential and she made me a heckuva deal. Honestly, she all but gave it to me."

"No."

"No?"

"This house will make a terrible daycare." This house was built for children. The Haberstroh family, in fact. They had twelve."

"Twelve what?"

"Children!"

"Children?"

"Children? Twelve children? In one family?"

"Yes. There is a whole stack of family history paraphernalia in one of the trunks in the main attic, including a stack of letters exchanged between Mrs. Haberstroh and her sister. In one of them, Mrs. Haberstroh writes a paragraph on each child. It's fascinating. The Haberstrohs weren't one of Eternity Springs' founding families, but by its twenty-fifth anniversary they were definitely one of the most prominent. Mr. Haberstroh founded our first bank."

"Great for him, but what does that have to do with little children tumbling down the staircase?"

"Baby gates prevent that. Jax is going to create a custom design for me."

Caitlin tried not to be discouraged by his obvious lack of enthusiasm for her news. Yes, it would have been nice if he'd lit it up like a Fourth of July sparkler when she told him she'd moved home, but Caitlin never expected this to be easy. Experience had taught her that more often than not when it came to dealing with men, patience won the race. Lori's relationship with Chase was the textbook example of that.

Josh dragged his hand down his face and stared at her for a long, silent minute. Then he glanced slowly around the room, his gaze landing on the thick featherbed that was covered with a beautifully stitched quilt in shades of crimson and gold—in the double wedding ring pattern. "A daycare."

"Yes. One is sorely needed in town."

"Did it really need to be next door to me?"

"Celeste assured me that you like children."

"I do. One or two at a time. Not by the dozens."

"You really don't need to worry, Josh. It's not like they'll be running in and out of your house or business. The whole idea of a daycare is to take *care* of children. They won't be running wild up and down the street, and they'll be gone by six o'clock."

"But you're a textile designer with a dream job in New York. Why would you come to Eternity Springs?"

"Now you sound like my mother," Caitlin grumbled. She was beginning to get peeved. The man acted like she'd just killed his cat. "I told you this in Telluride. My job might be a dream job, but it's not *my* dream job."

He dragged his gaze away from the bed. "And corralling little snot goblins is?"

"Yes." She waited a beat, then asked, "Do you make a habit of raining on parades, Josh?"

He closed his eyes. "No. Not usually."

"So why are you raining on mine?"

Now his eyes flew open, hot and accusing. "Because you've backed me into a corner. Or more specifically, lured me into a secret room."

"I didn't lure you anywhere," Caitlin fired back. "You crawled in here all by yourself."

"Yes, I crawled," Josh said, a bitter note in his tone. He took a step toward her. "I crawled and I'm not proud of it. I knew better, but I did it anyway."

The look on his face turned brooding as he stared at her. "I've been kicking myself the last few weeks for the choice I made in Telluride. I should have taken you upstairs that night. Maybe if I had, you wouldn't have haunted me ever since."

Caitlin's heart went *thud-a-thump*. "I haunted you?"

"Yep. You sing a siren song, Caitlin Timberlake. You threaten me."

Threaten him? Caitlin's mouth went a little dry. That look in his eyes—he was a predator about to pounce. "What do you mean?"

His gaze narrowed and began to smolder. "You know what I mean."

"No, I don't." She took a step backward and asked, "Where's Celeste?"

"Gone. You and I are here by ourselves. We're all alone." Josh took another step forward. "We're all alone and you know exactly what I mean when I say you threaten me. I'm beginning to think you're as witchy a woman as Celeste is."

"I beg your pardon?"

He snorted. "Am I supposed to believe that it's simply coincidence that in all the neighborhoods in all the towns in America, you found the perfect location for your business right next door to me?"

"Yes," she snapped, retreating until her shoulder blades touched the wall. "That's the truth."

"Not hardly. Like my nanny used to say, I was born at night, but not last night. I'll tell you what it is, beautiful. Not coincidence, but my usual rotten luck showing its head again. Bad luck. It follows me everywhere. It's my birthright, goes back generations. It's my destiny. My own personal curse."

Caitlin believed there was an insult toward her buried in there—even if he had called her beautiful.

"Now I seem to have my own personal ghost." His arms shot out, his hands rested against the wall, trapping her between him. "Harriet was right. This place is a ghost story come alive, so of course you'd buy it. It's perfect for you. Because you have haunted me ever since we met. In my sleep. In my daydreams."

Trembling and trying to hide it, Caitlin lifted her chin. "Are you trying to flatter me or insult me?"

"Neither. I'm just telling you how it is. There was a time in my life when I denied myself nothing. You remind of those years. The need. The craving. You make me wonder why I denied myself in Telluride."

His gaze dropped to her mouth. Heat rolled off his body as electricity surged between them. "You know what, Caitlin? I'm tired of the question. I do believe I'm done with it. You don't mind a little dust, do you? It's not as thick in here as it is in the other room. Let's do this. Let's scratch this itch and be done with it."

Scratch this itch and be done? She tried to put some venom in her tone, but he was so close. So hot. "Just so you know, you've definitely managed insulting."

"So tell me no. Shove me away." Deliberately, he leaned forward and fitted his body against hers. "Tell me I don't turn you on and you don't want to have sex with me and we'll go on about our business being nothing but neighbors. Chances are that would work too, because I don't go where I'm not wanted. But this haunting can't go on, not with you living next door."

Caitlin caught her breath. His erection pressed against her, hard and thick and obvious, even through the layers of their clothing. "Tell me no, Caitlin."

She should. She should absolutely tell him to take his itch elsewhere. Instead, when he slowly lowered his head, she lifted her face toward him.

At the first feather light touch of his lips against hers, Caitlin knew. She'd come home. He was her home.

This was right. She'd made the right decision. Josh Tarkington was the man she'd dreamt of finding.

Her heart soared. He groaned low in his throat as he deepened the kiss, licking into her mouth, and their tongues danced. He tasted of cinnamon and chocolate, and Caitlin's knees went weak. If she hadn't been clutching his shirt with both hands for support, she'd have melted to the floor. His left hand slid down the wall to grip her hip. The right thrust deep into her hair as he kissed her and kissed her and kissed her with slow, savoring deliberation.

Her body throbbed with arousal. Her heartbeat slammed against her chest wall. Her blood turned to steam.

Yet, even as they exchanged what had to be the hottest kiss of her life, Caitlin sensed the resistance within him. Despite the way he'd advanced on her, he wasn't all in.

So she wasn't surprised when he broke the kiss and lifted his head to gaze down at her, his enthralling gray eyes gleaming with heat and challenge. His voice low and gruff, he said, "Just so we're crystal clear, this doesn't change anything. Moving next door to me doesn't change anything. I swore off relationships years ago. Sleeping with me won't change that, Caitlin."

And here comes the cold water to douse my fire.

Pride made her lift her chin. "Wait a minute. I haven't said yes yet."

He smirked. "Sure you have. You've been saying yes since the moment we met."

Caitlin opened her mouth to protest, but he stopped her by swooping in and nipping at her lower lip.

"You want me. You broadcast it with the gleam in your eyes, the knowledge in your smile, the sensual stroke of your touch." As he spoke, the hand on her hip skimmed up and down her back. The rough, husky note in his voice reverberated through her, strumming her nerves, rekindling the heat that his words had banked. Everything within her seemed to swell in response to him. She wanted nothing more than to abandon herself to the sensual spell he wove.

And he dares to call me witchy.

"I'm not the only one who's been sending out signals," she defended, not yet ready to surrender.

She spoke the truth. Nothing about the sexual chemistry that flowed between them from the very beginning had been one-sided. The air fairly crackled with it whenever they were together, and there was no mistaking the signal pressed up against her right now.

And she wanted to feel the hard, thick heat of him inside her with a desperation that frankly shocked her.

"I won't argue that," he murmured, something dangerous glittering in his eyes. "It's definitely mutual."

His hands on her hardened. His hips pressed her, pinned her against the wall, his intent unmistakable. "I want you more than I want to breathe and I'm through fighting it. We're alone in a private hideaway that comes complete with a bed. Like the saying goes, There's your sign. I'm through fighting fate, Caitlin. It's wasted effort. I will never win. So, I've offered terms of surrender. Do you accept them? Yes or no?"

This was all happening way too fast. He'd caught her off guard, caught her unprepared. Caitlin was accustomed to being in control of the pace of her relationships. She wasn't in control here. Not at all.

The man had waltzed in here, taken one look at her, and was ready to throw her on the bed and have his way with her.

Yes, please. Total fantasy-come-to-life.

Except . . . he didn't *want* her. Also, he appeared more ready to conquer than surrender.

So why was he rolling out surrender? Surrender meant

defeat. There was *nothing* defeated about the Josh Tarkington who'd just demanded sex. Sex with terms!

"I'm confused," she breathed.

"About what?"

"Terms." Terms of surrender that felt more like a declaration of war than capitulation. In that moment, Caitlin felt like her back was against the wall in more ways than one. "Your terms. You're offering me sex and nothing more?"

He studied her face with unnerving intensity. "I'm offering *great* sex—here. Now."

She waited. He'd definitely put a period at the end of the sentence.

So, sex . . . great sex . . . and nothing else.

"How do you know it will be great?"

"Honey, trust me. We will be great together."

Yes, she wouldn't argue that. Okay, then. She couldn't fault the man for being upfront and forthright, could she? Just because she didn't like what he was saying didn't mean she didn't appreciate his honesty.

At any other time in her life, with any other man, Caitlin would have said thanks, but no thanks, and gone about her business. This time was different. Josh was different. *She* was different.

She wanted him. She intended to have him. Not just for sex. Not just for today. She wanted Josh Tarkington for great sex—and everything else.

The war metaphor didn't work for her. Chess made much more sense. She needed to be thinking two or three moves beyond the moment.

Unfortunately, she could barely think at all because he'd slid his hand upward and cupped her breast. His thumb scraped across her nipple and she felt it clear to her toes.

"What say you, Ms. Timberlake?"

"I'm thinking."

"Think fast."

Think. Yes. She needed to think. She needed to think strategically. She needed to concoct a strategy of her own. It was a mistake to let him define the narrative here, which was exactly what he'd done by declaring both war and surrender from the outset.

Think, Caitlin. Think. But, oh, that was difficult to do with his hard body pressed up against her.

She forced herself to concentrate. She had grown up with two older brothers. She'd learned the science of battle tactics long ago. But the restless glitter in his eyes told her she was running out of time. This was not a moment for negotiation, but for action.

Caitlin wanted to act. With every fiber of her being, she wanted to act right now. But natural caution caused her to hesitate. "We don't have protection."

"In that respect, I'm a Boy Scout. Always prepared."

Okay, then. Well, good. Sleeping with him now, like this, would be a big enough risk as it was. Josh Tarkington wasn't one of the pliable men of her past who fell for her quickly and allowed her to call all of the relationship shots. He might be in lust with her, but he wasn't in love with her.

I could lose this war. He could break my heart.

"Tick tock," he murmured. He shifted his head and nipped at her ear. "Time to make your choice."

Her choice. Yes, that summed it up nicely, didn't it? *He* was her choice.

Caitlin licked her lips and decided to trust her instincts. She loosened the hold she had on his shirt and skimmed her hand upward until she cradled his stubbled jaw in her hand. "You, Josh. I want you. Here. Now."

The gray eyes blazed. He turned his mouth into her hand and deliberately nipped the inside of her palm.

She went woozy with need. He made a low growling sound and swept her up into his arms as if she weighed nothing at all. He carried her the few short steps to the bed and deposited her in the middle of the quilt. He put a knee on the featherbed, paused to give her a slow once-over, and the carnal gleam in his eyes almost caused her to let the rest of her words die on her tongue.

But the man had been honest with her. She could do no less than return the favor.

As he lowered himself atop her, she stalled him with a hand against his chest. "Just one thing. I heard what you said. I accept that you consider this surrender, but it's only fair to tell you that I see the situation a little differently."

He narrowed those steaming gray eyes. "I don't think I want to hear this."

No, he probably didn't. "I'm giving you fair warning, Josh. I want you here and now, but I also want forever. You can throw down surrender all you want, but I'm declaring that you are under siege."

Journal Entry

Women.
Enough said.

Chapter Eight

Josh froze. *"Under siege?" "I also want forever?" Of course she does. Isn't that just my luck?*

Every ounce of self-preservation he possessed clamored at him to stop this immediately, to drag himself up and away and save the life in Eternity Springs that he'd been building for almost two years now.

Because no way would he come out of this unscathed. Caitlin was an Eternity Springs princess with ties on her mother's side going all the way back to the founding of the town. Sleeping with Caitlin Timberlake beneath her father's and brother's noses was bound to earn him a beating or twelve, even Brick might line up against him.

And the women in town . . .

I might as well put a For Sale sign in the windows of both the garage and the house right now.

But no matter how loudly his better sense talked to him, other parts unfortunately screamed a whole lot louder. Sometimes, a man's base nature drove the bus and good sense simply had to hang on for the wild ride.

This apparently was one of those times.

He *was* going to do this, and he *was* going to regret it. The outcome had been all but inevitable since the moment that gondola ground to a halt. At least he'd been honest with her about his lack of intentions. He could hold his head high and give her father and brother—maybe a few others too—a good angle for the shot to the jaw they'd surely want to give him. Once word got out—and it would—they'd line up to do the deed.

As far as they knew, he was nothing but a grease monkey from Oklahoma. If they found out the truth . . . no. That wasn't going to happen.

Under siege, my ass.

"You'll change your mind," he told her right before his lips met hers in a deep, slow, hungry kiss.

His hands went to work, and her blouse and front-snap lacy peach bra fell away to reveal full, coral-tipped breasts. He paused for a reverent moment in order to fully appreciate the sight. "You are so beautiful, Caitlin. You take my breath away."

Her eyes softened with pleasure at his words and she smiled.

Josh realized he'd made a tactical mistake. Perhaps he could salvage the situation yet. "You'll change your mind about me. I'm really not very good at sex."

The stubborn woman dared to laugh. "I'll just bet."

"It's true." He stroked her silken skin. So soft. He bent his head and traced the path of his touch with worshipful kisses. "I'm a selfish lover. I worry only about pleasing myself."

Then he set about doing exactly that.

Unfortunately, what pleased Josh was to drive her insane with pleasure. He loved slowly stripping off her clothing piece by piece, revealing her glorious form to his hungry gaze. He adored touching her, using his fingers to stroke and caress, to play and explore and find and fondle that exact spot that roused her to a fevered pitch. He enjoyed using his mouth to lick and nibble and suck a scream right out of her.

The flush of passion on her face pleased him. The arch of her back and press of her soft flesh against the hardness of his own pleased him. The way she clung to him and squirmed against him and kissed him like she simply couldn't get enough of him pleased him. He found the way she gripped his shoulders and whimpered with need until he joined his body with hers to be more pleasurable than anything he'd experienced in a very long time.

So pleasurable, in fact, that he drew the moment out and made it last. He delighted in the tremors of completion he coaxed from her and decided it suited him to make it happen again.

The next time she literally wept, and Josh finally gave into his own needs. He savored every second of his release before collapsing on top of her, needing to catch his breath, too spent to be careful that he didn't squash her.

The scratch had been well and truly itched.

They lay without speaking for a full minute, Josh's head buried in the curve of her neck and shoulder, his face planted in the center of one of the rings on the quilt. Eventually, Caitlin wriggled out from beneath him saying, "You weigh a ton."

"See? I'm selfish."

Her snort wasn't at all ladylike.

He sensed that she'd rolled onto her side and lay with her elbow propped up, her head resting in her hand. He didn't have the energy to lift his head to confirm that, however.

Another minute ticked by and then two. He was drifting toward sleep when she lifted her hand and trailed a finger from his shoulder, down his side. "Josh?"

Oh crap. She wanted to talk. She was a talker. He wasn't. He didn't talk after sex. He slept. A little five-minute nap did wonders for a man. "Mmmm . . ."

"I have to tell you, that was definitely the Worst Sex Ever."

His eyes sprang open. He turned his head just enough to look at her. She wore a cat-in-the-cream smile that sent shivers running up and down his spine.

Under siege. Oh crap.

She leaned forward and repeated. "Worst. Sex. Ever." Following a moment's pause, she added, "When can we do it again?"

Josh ran. Not literally, but that pretty much described what happened next. He mumbled. He made excuses. He beat feet as fast as humanly possible. It was the closest thing to a wham-bam-thank-you-ma'am sexual encounter he'd ever participated in. When he was sober, anyway.

He wasn't proud of himself. He tried hard not to be a jerk when it came to women. That was part of being the man he'd fought hard to become. The thing with Caitlin . . . he felt like he'd given into a craving and fallen off the wagon.

Wonder if there is a twelve-step program for jerks?

Still, he'd warned her, hadn't he? He'd given her the opportunity to say no. It wasn't all guilt rumbling around inside him. Josh was angry. Seriously pissed off. At himself. At her. At the circumstances.

At Fate, the bitch.

For all the good that did him. He could stand in his front yard and wave his fist at the clouds like Homer Simpson, but it wouldn't change a thing. He could dig up the roots he'd sunk in Eternity Springs and go somewhere else, but that wouldn't keep trouble from following him. He couldn't change his past or the path of tornadoes or the identity of the new girl next door. Once Fate decided to play with him, he might as well lie back and enjoy it.

In the meantime, he had three cars waiting for him that needed oil changes.

Josh halfway expected Caitlin to come knocking on his door that afternoon, but it didn't happen. Neither did she seek him out the following day. When a third day passed without his hearing so much as a peep from her and he'd developed what he feared was a permanent crick in his neck from looking over his shoulder all the time, he decided something needed to be done.

What sort of siege was this, anyway?

Deciding reconnaissance was in order, he went to Murphy's for a burger and a double scoop of gossip.

Shortly after dawn the following morning and after tossing and turning much of the night, he got up, put on his running shoes, and jogged to the rental house on Third Street which he'd learned she'd leased for a year. When she answered his knock looking mussed and sleepy and delicious, he said, "You want to go running?"

She gave him round owl eyes. "What?"

"You told me you like to run. Come with me."

"It's not even seven o'clock yet!"

"Early bird catches the worm. Besides, I open the shop at eight thirty."

She scowled at him. "Why do you call it a shop? It's a garage."

He shrugged and checked his watch.

"If you say 'tick tock' I'll slam the door in your face."

"Are you coming?"

"Give me five to get dressed." She opened the screen door and said, "C'mon in."

He was too curious to wait outside.

The house was small, a two-bedroom Craftsman that appeared to have been updated within the past few years. A tower of moving boxes sat stacked against one wall, yet to be unpacked. The only furnishings in the front room were a sofa and a reading lamp.

He picked up the paperback lying on the sofa and checked the title. A romance. "Figures."

He opened the book and started scanning the pages. Cindy Christopher had read historical romance novels when he lived with them. Josh would never admit it, but he'd read a few of them. Okay, a lot of them. Back then, he'd liked escaping to a world of rules.

"Don't make fun of me for my reading choices," Caitlin said when she entered the room zipping up a running jacket.

"I wouldn't dream of it." He meant it. "You ready?"

"As I'll ever be. It's cold out this morning."

"Great running weather." Then, because Fate was running the show, after all, he bent down and gave her a quick friendly kiss. "Let's go."

Caitlin was right about the chill in the air. When Flynn Brogan brought his Explorer in for an oil change yesterday, he'd mentioned the possibility of snow by the end of the week. While some of his neighbors claimed to dread the arrival of winter, Josh enjoyed the changing seasons for the same reason he liked the mountains. Nothing Malibu about Eternity Springs.

They didn't speak as they took his usual route through town, running side by side. He turned up the winding road to Cemetery Hill and at the cemetery gate, Caitlin called, "I need to sit for a few, Josh. Altitude."

He let her take the lead. She wove in and out of the rows of headstones until she reached an iron bench. There she bent over, rested her hands on her knees, and caught her breath. Josh removed his water bottle from his waist pack and silently offered it to her. After quenching her thirst, she sank onto the bench.

"This is killing me. I haven't run since I left New York."

"You should have told me to skip the hill."

"No. No. It's good. It's all good."

Josh took a seat beside her. He gestured toward a marker off to their left. "You have family here. Roots. Your people were an Eternity Springs founding family. I've toured the historical society's museum."

"Yes. The Silver Miracle mine provided the basis of my mom's family's money. I inherited a share of it when my grandfather died. That's the money I'm using to open Gingerbread House."

He pictured the Munster Mansion and imagined it restored to its former glory. "Nice name."

"I like it."

"Are you going to live there?"

"No. I've worked from home enough to know that I'm happier keeping my work place separate from the place where I live." She glanced at him then and asked, "So what are we doing here, Josh?"

"You're catching your breath." He sucked in a breath, then added, "It's what I've been doing since I made a beeline out of your attic."

She nodded. "You did escape awfully fast."

"Yeah. I'm sorry about that. It wasn't well done of me." After a moment's hesitation, he added, "At least I remembered to haul that trunk to your car. What was in it? Lead bricks?"

"Silver bars."

"Seriously?"

Caitlin nodded. "It's quite the find. In addition to the silver, the chest held a pair of photographs and some legal documents. Celeste is going to attempt to track down the rightful owner."

"Cool."

After that, they both fell silent. Josh watched the sun rising above the mountain peaks and searched for the words she deserved. Eloquence seemed to be beyond his capabilities at the moment, so he decided to keep it simple.

"I owe you an apology and an explanation. I wasn't thinking clearly the other day. Lust has a way of hazing a man's mind."

"A woman's too," she said lightly. "Apology accepted. You needn't worry that I've been sitting around stewing about it."

"Good." He darted her a look. "So . . . you haven't been around. Have you changed your mind about . . . well . . . laying siege?"

"After the Worst Sex Ever?" Caitlin stretched out her legs, crossed them at the ankles. "Not hardly. But I've been busy. We started demo yesterday. Jax gave me a long list of decisions to make."

Josh really wished she hadn't brought up the sex. He didn't need to be distracted. "Ah . . . okay. Well, in that case, you should know why I'm dead serious about my intentions—or, I guess I should say my lack of intentions. I'm not just being a guy who isn't ready to settle down or someone who shuns commitment. I'll never change my mind and after what happened between us the other morning, I think you should know why."

"You are making it sound ominous."

"'Ominous' is a fitting word. So is the graveyard location for the telling of it."

Caitlin gave him a searching look. "Someone broke your heart, didn't they?"

"Not in the way you're thinking. Let me start from the beginning."

He pushed to his feet and began to pace. Caitlin watched him, distracted by the way his sweaty running shirt clung to his torso. He was a fine-looking man. Very fine.

He dragged his hand down his face, then began. "Growing up, my life was anything but normal. I will not talk about it, so don't bother asking questions. The pertinent information is that a few years back, I was feeling pretty good about life. I decided to make a run at normal."

Now she was intrigued. Nothing like someone telling you not to ask about something to make you want to ask about it.

"There was a little girl living upstairs in my apartment building, Kelsey. I met her when she was four years old."

A child? Caitlin sat up straight upon hearing the obvious pain in his voice.

He turned away from her, his hands braced on his hips. "I haven't talked about this in a very long time. It's not easy to do."

"Why don't we walk?" she suggested. "I always find that difficult things are easier to talk about when I'm moving."

He nodded his agreement and Caitlin led the way. They walked almost to the end of the line of grave markers before he continued. "She was a little redhead with big green eyes. Eyes like yours. She was cute as a button, a little shy, but once she got to know you, she opened up. She and her mother had a hard time of it. Janie—her mom's name was Janie—worked retail and her ex was always late on his child support. She struggled to keep a job." He darted a look toward Caitlin and with a rueful smile added, "Daycare was a problem."

"It certainly can be," she replied, keeping her tone even. Now was not the time to say I told you so.

"I helped her. Took care of the kid a time or two. Janie and I got to be friends and then more than friends.

Kelsey's dad was never around. She took to calling me Daddy."

The naked pain in his voice caused her heart to catch, and Caitlin knew in that moment that this story was not one she wanted to hear.

"I loved her. I fell head over heels for that little girl. Janie and I decided to get married. I was happy. We were happy. We were in the process of creating a family. We picked June tenth as our wedding date because she wanted to be a June bride." He stopped abruptly and his jaw went as hard as the gravestones that surrounded them. "But April tenth came first."

Caitlin had an idea of where this story was headed. She wanted to hug him, but his manner held her off. Instead, she reached out and gave his arm a comforting touch.

He glanced down at her. "Have you heard the story already?"

"Not details, no. I know there was a storm." She had not heard about a fiancée, however.

He leaned back against a Davenport family gravestone and folded his arms. "Springtime in Tornado Alley. When a storm is brewing, the air has a certain feel to it. It's heavy and still. There's a sense of anticipation to it. We call it tornado weather, and if you live there, you know what it is. When the weather feels that way, you learn to keep an eye on the sky, an ear out for phone alerts.

"The afternoon of April tenth felt like tornado weather. Janie managed a health food store in a strip mall, and she was due to get off at five. I didn't like the way things were shaping up—I had a weird feeling in my gut—so I asked her to close a little early and come on home. I picked up Kelsey from daycare and brought her home. Janie drove up just as I pulled into the garage. I'd bought a house by then. The girls had been living there four months.

"A little after four p.m. the storm sirens went off."

Though he gazed off toward Murphy Mountain, his thoughts were obviously somewhere else. He cleared his throat. "I will never forget stepping out onto my back porch and seeing that thing coming toward us. It was huge and black, horrible and compelling at the same time. You wanted to watch it. I couldn't take my eyes off of it. Kelsey started crying. She was scared." He dragged a hand across his mouth and repeated, "So scared."

Tears welled up inside Caitlin. She wanted to tell him to stop. She didn't want to hear it. She didn't want to know, didn't need to know. Instead, she bit her lower lip and listened.

"We huddled up in the bathroom at the center of the house. I even had a little helmet for Kelsey to wear. But as my luck would have it, this turned out to be an F4. Wind speeds well over two hundred miles an hour. You know how they always say that a tornado sounds like a train? It's true. A train bearing down upon you. This happened almost a decade ago, but I hear that sound in my dreams. A big black monster of a train."

He swallowed hard, then said matter-of-factly. "We took a direct hit. Things started flying and falling down. Then the wind roared over us. Picked us up. It sucked Kelsey right out of my arms. I couldn't hold her." He blew out a heavy breath and repeated, "I couldn't hold on to her."

Caitlin covered her mouth with both hands. She couldn't hold back the tears. Such raw pain filled his expression. Her heart literally broke for him. "Oh, Josh. No. I'm so sorry."

He closed his eyes against the sorrow in hers and allowed the memories to wash over him. The brutal, unstoppable force. Bone-chilling fear. "Something whacked my head and knocked me out. The last thing I remember

was losing my grip on Kelsey. The next thing I recall is
Janie screaming."

*"Help me. Help me. Josh, get up. You have
to help us."*

"The storm didn't carry us far. Dropped all three of
us into what had been the front yard. The only injury I
had was a bump on the head. Janie . . ." He blew out another heavy breath. "The wind blew a shard of wood
through her leg. Sliced an artery. She was bleeding out."

And she was crawling . . . crawling . . . trying to get to
her daughter. Screaming. *"Kelsey! Kelsey! Oh, God.
Kelsey! Get up. Get up, baby!"*

Kelsey, a little rag doll lying still and broken in the
debris of what had been their lives.

*"You didn't hold on to her. Why didn't you hold on to
her? For God's sake, Joshua. Get up! Get up! Help me.
Help me. Help us!"*

He gave his head a shake, flinging away the memories. Then he cleared his throat and said, "Janie bled to
death. Kelsey's neck was broken. The great irony I
learned later was that neither Janie's store nor the daycare
were hit."

Tears had spilled from Caitlin's eyes and trailed down
her cheek. "Josh, that's the most horrible thing I ever
heard. My heart breaks for you."

"It . . . messed me up. And, it fundamentally changed
me."

"I'm sure it did. How do you deal with something like
that?"

Mainly drugs and booze.

"How do you get over it?"

You don't. He shrugged.

"Did you talk to someone afterward?"

"A shrink, you mean?" Josh laughed and pushed away
from the headstone. He continued the walk, his gaze

snagging briefly on a stone angel set among the markers. *If she only knew.*

"A mental health professional of some sort. Anyone would need help dealing with the aftermath of an event like the one you went through."

"Yes. I talked to a shrink." *Every day for three months, twice a week for months after that.* "I thought I had a handle on it until the next storm got me a couple years later. Well, not me exactly. It took out my car. I'd loaned it to a friend. A girl I was dating."

Caitlin looked at him with dawning horror. "Josh . . ."

"She wasn't hurt. Storm blew through the parking lot where she worked. After that, I . . . backslid . . . a bit." That was a nice way to put it. "The girl and I didn't make it."

"You stayed in Oklahoma?"

"Yep. Three more years." Though of course, he'd been in California a good chunk of that time. Clawing his way back seemed to take longer the older he got. "I mean . . . I'd been hit twice. I figured the odds of it happening again were slim to none."

"But it did?"

"Yep. An F3 blew through my home and business, a marina that the bank and I owned on a lake about an hour from Oklahoma City. Only a hundred and eighty mile-an-hour wind this time and no one was hurt. We rode it out inside a tornado shelter. However, it flattened everything I owned. I had seven employees at the time. The previous owner had lost the business during the drought, but the year I bought it, the lake filled up and boats came back and were doing great."

"I can't believe that. Three times? You've been hit by a tornado three times? What are the odds?"

"Four times, if you count the house and business separately. As far as odds go . . ." He shrugged. "I'm snakebit."

"I understand why you would feel that way. What I don't understand is why these horrible events have caused you to swear off relationships."

He took her hand and laced their fingers. "I'm tired of fighting my way back. Bone-tired of it. I honestly don't have the fight left in me to do it again. I decided to make some changes so that I will never again be put in that position. First, I moved away from Tornado Alley. Second, I decided that I'll never again be responsible for another person's livelihood. I'll either work for someone else, or for myself in a one-man operation. Finally . . ." He tugged her to a stop, released her hand, and placed his hands on her shoulders. Looking her square in the eyes, he stated, ". . . I decided that I'm done with relationships. I will not love again. Not a woman. Not a child."

He saw her subtly stiffen, but he pressed on. "Caitlin, before you and I go any further, I need you to hear what I'm saying. I refuse to be responsible for anyone else, ever again. I'll be your friend. I'd like very much to be your friend. I'll be your lover. I'd like that even more. But I will not fall in love with you. Ever. You need to believe me when it say it."

Some emotion he couldn't name flickered in her eyes, but he didn't let it stop him.

He released his grip on her shoulders and slid his hands down to hers. Squeezing them gently, he insisted, "You deserve more. You deserve to be loved. You are a 'forever' kind of girl and you deserve a 'forever' guy. I can't be that for you, Caitlin. I have nothing to offer you beyond the casual. You can't let the notion that you might find 'forever' with me get in the way of finding 'forever' with somebody else. Call me a superstitious fool. Call me a coward. Both are probably true. But I'm not going to marry anyone, ever. I'm not going to fall in love with anyone, ever. You can lay siege all you want, but it's not going to change those basic facts. It's not going to change me."

Caitlin pulled away from him and took a step back. "That's quite a speech, Tarkington. The end of it bordered on insulting, but I do understand why you said what you said. The question I have is where do we go from here? You're suggesting more than friends, but less than a couple? Do you really think that will work here in Eternity Springs?"

"If we're careful about it, yes. But only if that's what you want. If simple friendship is off the table, I'll accept that too. As long as you agree to my terms, you can call the shots."

"I think you must have been a battlefield general in a past life, Josh. Or a corporate-takeover specialist. We're doing a lot of negotiating." Caitlin stared at him for a long minute. "It could be sort of exciting. The secrecy of carrying on beneath the noses of our friends and neighbors."

"And family," he pointed out.

"Definitely, and family," she agreed with a little laugh. "I've never acted illicitly in my life. I'm usually up for a new experience. I think it might be fun, this . . . what shall we call it?"

"'Friends with benefits' is the popular term."

Caitlin wrinkled her nose. "No. I don't like that. Too pop culture. You and I, Tarkington, are going to have a friend affair."

With that, she went up on her toes and kissed him hard, but fast. Then she took off down the hill to finish their run.

Josh had no choice but to follow her.

Journal Entry

Anniversaries. Why do people mark anniversaries? What the hell good does it do to look backward? Can't turn on the radio or the damn TV without hearing newscasters with their panties in a wad. "Today is the third anniversary of the F5 tornado that cut a fourteen-mile swath across our state, killing sixty-three and injuring hundreds."

Well, whoop-dee-do. Happy anniversary.

Birthdays aren't much better. So you were born. Big damn deal. You're not special. Everybody was born. Everybody dies. Why do those everyday events require flowers on a grave?

Screw that. I'm over it. I'm not looking backward any more. No more rearview mirrors for me, no sir. Someone else will have to put birthday flowers on Kelsey's grave next week. I'm over it.

I hate anniversaries.

I just placed an order for daffodils.

Chapter Nine

By mutual agreement, Caitlin and Josh went different directions at the bottom of Cemetery Hill. Caitlin's mind spun as she made her way home. The more she thought about Josh's experience, the more sober she grew. What a seriously awful thing to have happened to him.

In the past few days, she'd done some snooping around about Josh. Small-town gossip was an extraordinarily powerful resource. With only a few casual questions, she'd managed to learn quite a lot. Eternity Springs labeled him as a nice, quiet, friendly guy who didn't cause trouble. He was a good neighbor who kept his lawn mowed, and he paid his bills on time. People knew he'd been Brick Callahan's foster brother, but the circumstances that led to his being in that system remained a mystery. Colt Rafferty had said Josh could make an engine hum, but of course, Caitlin had already discovered that for herself.

He wasn't a consummate flirt like Brick had been before falling for Liliana Howe, but he could turn on the charm when he wished. Townspeople had general knowledge of his storm-filled past, but she doubted anyone had heard the tragic details that he'd shared with her this morning.

All in all, Eternity Springs had a positive opinion of Josh Tarkington. Caitlin had learned nothing to cause her to change her strategy until he'd opened up to her this morning.

She pondered his revelations as she showered and dressed and watered her houseplants. He'd been sincere. She couldn't doubt that. Had her impulsive, emotion-based decision to continue seeing him been a mistake? If she went forward, she needed to do so with her eyes wide open. He had meant everything he'd said. That had been obvious. He was more than a guy who's just gun shy from being hurt in the past. This kind of hurt was more than most people could even imagine. He may never get over it. There was a real chance that she could lose this war. How would she deal with that?

Maybe she should reassess.

Her goals were different from Josh's. She wanted marriage and children. He absolutely, positively did not. Now that she knew that his position was pretty much chiseled in stone, should she cut her losses? Abandon the whole friend affair idea?

Josh Tarkington could break her heart.

"Wonderful," she said aloud as she opened her refrigerator and stared at the scant contents. Well, she had gone for a run, hadn't she? She could justify a trip to Fresh for her breakfast. She'd been craving Sarah Murphy's croissants for months. Besides, she needed company.

What she needed was a girlfriend to talk to. Unfortunately, her best friend was now also her sister-in-law. She couldn't confide in Lori, because she wouldn't ask her to keep secrets from Chase. If Chase found out that she and Josh were having a secret affair, it wouldn't remain a secret for long. She grumbled, "Brothers."

She pondered her predicament.

Part of her reason for moving to Eternity Springs had

been a desire to expand her circle of good friends. She'd made friends in the city, but not dear, friends-until-you-die friends. Her mother had a circle like that—Nic Callahan, Sarah Murphy, Sage Rafferty, and Celeste being particularly close to Ali—and Caitlin wanted the same thing.

Dad had been right about one thing the day she told them about her move. She did want a lot of the things her mother had.

She glanced at the clock. It was early yet. She didn't need to be at the house this morning. Jax had the demo well in hand. She might as well use the opportunity to reach out to a potential bosom bud. She grabbed her purse, drove to Fresh and bought four breakfast croissants, then made the short drive to Stardance Ranch.

As Caitlin had hoped, she found Liliana Howe in the camp's office and general store, restocking the shelves. She'd first met Lili at the Callahan family Fourth of July picnic the summer before last. They'd hit it off immediately, and Caitlin had hopes that Lili could become a dear friend. "Hello, Lili. How is the bride-to-be this morning?"

"I'm doing fabulous, thank you."

"Are you nervous?"

"A little. I'm worried about the weather, mostly, what with all the family coming in from Texas and Oklahoma. It'd be just my luck to have the first snowfall of the season be a blizzard that closes roads and mountain passes on my wedding day. If we have to delay the wedding again, I don't think my mother and the Callahan women will survive. They are the planning-est women I've ever seen."

Lili and Brick's original spring wedding had been postponed due to the decline and subsequent death of Lili's dear friend, Patsy Schaefer, last spring. Patsy had been the founder and soul of the Tornado Alleycats, the camping club that had brought Liliana and Brick together.

"I don't think you need to worry about a blizzard," Caitlin reassured her. "I've been keeping an eye on the forecast, myself, because we're scheduled to put a new roof on Gingerbread House later this week. Saturday is supposed to be lovely."

"From your mouth to God's ears."

"Hey, I'm not going to step on Celeste's toes." The two women shared a smile and Caitlin held up her bakery bag. "I come bearing gifts. Do you have a few minutes to visit?"

"I do. Though I shouldn't go near anything Sarah baked if I'm going to fit into my gown on Saturday."

"It's her bacon-and-egg-stuffed croissant. You probably can use the protein."

"You're the devil, Caitlin Timberlake. Let's go sit on the deck, shall we? Want some coffee or orange juice to go with the roll?"

"I'd love a glass of juice."

A few minutes later, they were seated in deck chairs placed around a fire pit savoring the contents of the bakery sack. "This is nice," Lili said. "I needed to sit and relax a bit. I've been going a mile a minute the past few weeks."

"I thought you might need a break, and since I need a friend to talk to, I thought it might work out nicely."

"Is something wrong, Caitlin?"

"No. I don't think so. Honestly, I don't know. Lili, when did you realize you'd fallen in love with Brick?"

"Well . . . hmm . . . I was probably nine. Maybe twelve." Caitlin knew that Lili and Brick had known each other when they were young. It was one of the reasons why she'd come to Stardance Ranch this morning. "You went to school together?"

"He wasn't in my class—he's older than me—but we

attended the same school. He and my brother were best friends."

"Maybe I asked the wrong question. Maybe I should have asked when Brick fell in love with you. He resisted it, didn't he?"

Lili gave a little laugh. "To use his grandfather's term, he ran like a scalded dog."

"So what did you do? How did you handle it? Did you simply have faith he'd come around? Were you afraid he wouldn't?"

"Are you having romantic troubles, Caitlin?"

"Always," she replied, a glum note in her voice. "It should be easier than this. Why is it never easy?"

"Because we're human? Tell me what's going on with you."

Caitlin tore a bite from her roll and popped it into her mouth. "Well, there's this guy . . ." She let her voice trail off as she searched for the right words.

"Isn't there always?" Lili said wryly. "Do I know him?"

"He's not from around here." The dodge was technically the truth, but since he was in the wedding party, it probably should count as a lie. She quickly forged ahead. "I really like this one. *Really* like him. I've dated a lot of guys, and this one has been different from the very beginning."

"So what's the problem?"

"He flat out said he isn't interested in marriage, and I believe he means what he says. But I want marriage and children. I'm not getting any younger. I don't know how much time I have to invest in him."

"That is a legitimate concern," Lili agreed.

"It is. Maybe I'd be better off stopping things now before I get in any deeper. My head is telling me that's probably the right thing to do, but my heart . . . my heart wants to take a chance on him. What do I do?"

Lili considered the question a few moments. "First, you're far from old, Caitlin. You have plenty of time to marry and make babies. And a lot of guys resist falling until they hit the ground. Maybe your guy is one of those."

"Maybe, but it's a risk."

"There you go. Love is a risk. Risk and reward. But the reward . . . it's spectacular."

Just then, Brick Callahan rounded the corner of the office building, a spring in his step and a shovel over his shoulder. Lili looked at her fiancé and her face beamed with so much love that Caitlin thought she needed sunglasses to shade her eyes.

Having eyes only for his bride-to-be, Brick called. "Hey there, Lili-fair. What are you doing slacking off in the middle of the workday? Think you've started your vacation already?"

"I'm not going on vacation. I'm going on my honeymoon."

"Oh, yeah. Where you going?"

"I don't know. My hardheaded groom won't tell me."

He grinned, winked at Caitlin, then said, "Hello, Ms. Timberlake. Welcome to Stardance Ranch RV Resort. I take it you're the reason my soon-to-be wife is lollygagging around on this bright, shining morning three days before our wedding?"

"Lollygagging, Callahan?" Lili interjected. "In that case I guess I was too busy lollygagging to figure out the discrepancy in your inventory figures."

"You found the problem?"

"I did."

Brick tossed the shovel to the ground, grabbed Lili up and planted a kiss on her lips. "Woman, you are a goddess."

"I know."

He set her back on her feet. "Don't let me interrupt your lollygagging. I need to get back to my chores."

"What are you doing with the shovel?"

"Off to maintain the dog park. Getting a little hard to walk in there. You girls enjoy your hen party." He slung his shovel back over his shoulder and sauntered away.

"Hen party," Lili grumbled. "I hate it when he uses that term. It's so sexiest."

"But he sure is sexy when he says it," Caitlin observed.

"That teasing twinkle in his eyes makes your toes curl, doesn't it?"

Lili heaved a heavy sigh. "It's a cross I bear. But back to your question. Brick was slow to come around, and I honestly believed he never would. I loved him, but I left him and Eternity Springs."

"I remember that."

"So, I did experience the loss, even though it turned out differently in the end."

"That's what I want to know about. The time between your departure and his grand romantic gesture . . . how did you bear it? Did you wish you'd never met him? Never loved him? If he'd never come after you, would you have been glad to have had the experience of loving him? Or was the pain so much that you'd have preferred never to have known him?"

Lili gave the questions serious consideration. "It wasn't easy, I'll admit. What made it easier for me is that I stayed focused on Patsy, helping her live the good days she had left the way she wished. But if I'd been all alone during those weeks . . . well . . . I don't recall who said 'Tis better to have loved and lost than never to have loved at all,' but he had it right. I never regretted loving Brick. Love is such a gift. Not just the receiving of it, but the giving of it too."

"True," Caitlin agreed. "Celeste once told me that loving is aerobic exercise for the heart. It makes the heart stronger."

"I think she's right. A stronger heart survives pain better than a weak one. I know that when we lost Patsy, I took comfort in the fact that I'd loved her fiercely the last ten months of her life. Saying goodbye was hard, don't get me wrong, but the love I had for her added a layer of protection around my heart."

"That's nice, Lili. I'm glad for you that you had that experience." Caitlin popped the final bite of croissant into her mouth, then licked her fingers. "Thank you. This is what I needed to hear."

"Are you going to tell me who the mystery man is?" Caitlin's smile went a little sly and shy. "No. Not now. For now, he's going to remain my scandalous little secret."

"*My Scandalous Little Secret*. Sounds like a good title for a romance novel?"

"No," Caitlin corrected. "It would need to be simply *My Scandalous Secret*. There's nothing little about my guy whatsoever."

Lili snorted a laugh and said, "You go girl."

The conversation returned to the upcoming wedding. Caitlin asked if she could be of any help with preparations, and Lili assured her she, her mother, and the Callahan women had everything in hand.

"I'm looking forward to Saturday," Caitlin said as she took her leave. "In my experience, any party that involves the Callahans is not one to be missed. I'm sure your wedding will be just the same."

Josh gazed around the acres of the North Forty, the Callahan family compound on the shores of Hummingbird Lake, and gave a soundless whistle. He'd been to his fair share of weddings, but he'd never seen anything like this. Not because the event was overly extravagant, but because it had such a festival air to it.

At noon in a mass at Sacred Heart church, Mark Christopher Callahan II had married Liliana Howe in front of family and a few close friends. That was all the church could hold. An hour later, they repeated their vows in an outdoor ceremony at the North Forty attended by almost every citizen of Eternity Springs, and what seemed like half the states of Oklahoma and Texas.

"I'll bet there's well over five hundred people here," Josh observed to Harriet as he lifted two glasses of champagne from a tray offered by a waiter as the reception got underway. He handed one to Harriet and scanned the crowd for the face he most wanted to see.

"It's a crush. I thought their Fourth of July parties were large. I'll bet there's not an empty hotel room—or campsite—in a two-hundred-mile radius."

"Nic Callahan said it's the biggest family event since the brothers reunited. They're serving beef from their own ranches. And the Tornado Alleycats have come out in force to see Liliana wed. She won the camping club member's hearts with her devotion to their founder. Look at Liliana. Doesn't she look fabulous? So radiant and happy?"

His gaze had snagged on Caitlin Timberlake. "Gorgeous. Simply spectacular."

And he had plans for her during this wedding reception.

Since they'd defined this "friend affair" on their morning run earlier this week, they'd indulged in a few stolen steamy kisses, but nothing more. He had to admit he was enjoying what he considered to be extended foreplay. Caitlin was playful and lighthearted and imaginative about it. The things she could say silently with just her eyes and her lips when they were in the company of others made him want to howl at the moon.

Josh managed to pull his attention away from Caitlin when the groom's aunt Torie approached to tell him that the Callahan family patriarch requested his presence. She looped her arm through Josh's, then escorted him through the crowd to a spot where Branch Callahan sat in his wheelchair holding court.

"I found Josh, Branch," Torie Callahan said.

"Good. Good. Boy, step over here. Don't you look all dapper dressed up in a monkey suit."

"You're looking fine yourself, Branch. I like the bow tie."

"Thank you. It's my marryin' and buryin' suit. Getting more use with the latter than the former of late. I don't like it."

"No sir."

"Now, enough chitchat. Did you escort a young lady to this shindig of ours?"

"No sir."

"Good. I want you to meet a couple of pretty girls, relatives of ours on my late wife's side. If you have a lick of sense you'll cut one from the herd and show her a good time. Torie, take Josh over and introduce him to the McBride twins."

Josh knew better than to waste his time arguing with Branch, so he didn't try. Torie introduced him to the twins and they spent a few minutes telling Branch Callahan stories. The conversation had moved on to Colorado ski resorts when the circle opened up and Caitlin, Devin Murphy, and Lori and Chase Timberlake joined the discussion. A few minutes later when Brick announced over the sound system that the buffet was open,

Chase suggested they get in line. They moved forward as a group.

Caitlin looped her arm through Devin's. When she reached up and twirled a lock of her hair around her finger, Josh's lips twitched with a grin. She was teasing him.

She'd done the same thing this morning when he was standing outside at the shop talking to a customer about an engine overhaul. She'd sat on the side porch at her Gingerbread House and twirled her hair around her finger while she slowly and lasciviously ate a banana.

He plotted to fire back with a salvo of his own. After they made their way through the buffet line, he positioned himself so that he secured a seat catercorner to Caitlin at one of the rows of rectangular tables draped in white floor-length tablecloths and yellow runners. He glanced at her over a centerpiece made from white hydrangeas, yellow Gerbera daisies, greens, and little glass camping trailers. Caitlin had turned her attention to her meal and Devin Murphy's tale about sharks off the coast of Australia. Josh made small talk with the McBride sisters as he enjoyed his dinner. The steaks were fabulous and the sides worthy of five stars. He'd waited until Caitlin had finished about half of her steak to kick off one of his dress shoes.

Watching Caitlin from the corner of his eyes and praying that his aim was true, he stretched out his leg and trailed his foot up the bare calf of her leg. She startled and fumbled her fork. Josh smothered a smile and got a little bit friendlier with his foot.

Caitlin's voice was pitched a little high when she spoke to Devin Murphy. "So, Dev. Are you home to stay this time?"

With the sound of his native Australia strong in his voice, Devin chewed his meat thoughtfully, then said,

"Hadn't planned on it. However, you could make both our families happy and marry me and tie my feet to Eternity Springs."

Through the years, Caitlin and Devin had been paired at many family events. The spark had never been there for either of them, though, but they liked each other, so they didn't protest the subtle pushes made by the match-making moms. They'd agreed to be each other's backup plan, should they reach the age of forty with no prospects and a desire to marry. Josh knew this because Devin him-self had told him when he brought a four-wheeler in for work. With nothing else to do, the Aussie had hung around to watch.

Caitlin blew Devin a kiss. "I'd consider it, but I haven't found any tie-downs strong enough to work on your feet."

Beneath the table, Caitlin's bare foot began tangling with Josh's.

Devin chewed his steak thoughtfully and nodded in agreement at the observation. His sister Lori smiled at the McBrides and added in a teasing tone, "You'd think he was from Kansas rather than Australia. Devin is Dorothy on steroids. It doesn't take a tornado to blow him away. A little breeze will do it."

Caitlin's gaze flew up to meet Josh's, and he read the question in her eyes. *Does talk about tornados bother you?*

Josh answered her with an almost imperceptible reas-suring wink, then asked, "Do the women in your life al-ways give you this kind of lip, Murphy?"

"These two sure do," he said.

"If it were me, I'd give 'em some of that lip right back," Josh lifted a forkful of lobster mac-and-cheese to his mouth and licked it like an ice cream cone. "Mmmm . . . mac-and-cheese is my favorite."

Caitlin's gaze locked onto his fork. She didn't notice the figure sauntering up the aisle behind her until Mac

Timberlake's hand landed on her shoulder. "Hello, everybody."

Josh's foot fell back to the floor.

"Dad, you're back!" Caitlin said. "When did y'all get back?"

At the same time, her brother asked, "How was the leaf peeping? Was it really any better in New England than it is here?"

"What?" Mac said, apparently perplexed by the question.

Now it was Chase's turn to look perplexed. "Isn't that where you've been? Or did I get your trips mixed up? You and Mom are gone so much it's hard to keep up sometimes."

"Oh, yes. We got back late last night. We didn't want to miss the wedding."

"So how was the color?" Caitlin asked.

"Fine. Nice. It's a beautiful part of the country." His smile looked somewhat strained as he met his family members' gazes in turn. "It looks like you three are through eating. If your friends will excuse you, I'd like you to join Ali and me. We want to introduce you to someone."

Caitlin glanced down at her plate where she'd crossed her knife and fork, then briefly met Josh's gaze before she stood. "Sure."

Josh watched her trail after her brother and his wife with both amusement and consternation. Mac Timberlake didn't like him any more now than he had the last time their paths had crossed—in the grocery store the day after Caitlin returned to New York. Mac had nodded, said a stiff hello, and continued to the produce section. Wonder how the return of her parents to Eternity Springs would affect their little affair.

He still expected to look up one day to see Caitlin's father's fist headed toward his jaw.

And I can't say I'd really blame him.

Josh returned his attention to the McBride twins and tuned into their conversation with Devin. When he next glanced up to scan the crowd, he'd lost sight of Caitlin, but the look in her father's eyes stayed with him. Josh had never been one to back down from a challenge.

Surreptitiously, he pulled his cell phone from his pocket, double-thumbed a text, then entertained himself by imagining her reaction when she read it.

This whole friend affair thing was kinda fun.

Journal Entry

My mother called me today to tell me she got married. I think this is the fourth time, although it could be the fifth.

I phoned the Christophers after my mother called me. I wanted to tell them that I love them. They will celebrate their fortieth wedding anniversary this year.

I guess some anniversaries are worth noting, after all.

Chapter Ten

Mac took Caitlin's hand and led the way through the crowd of wedding guests toward the rose-covered arbor where her mother stood with Devin's parents, Nic and Gabe Callahan, and a guy about Caitlin's age wearing khaki slacks and a blue sports jacket. The young man's face was animated as he gestured with his arms and told a story that had the other members of the group laughing.

Mac placed his hand at the small of Caitlin's back and steered her toward the gathering.

Seeing her children, Ali's expression lit up. "Hello, you three. I wondered where Mac had disappeared to."

"I caught a glimpse of them and knew you'd want to say hello."

"You look pretty, girls," Ali said. "I love your dresses."

"Thanks, Ali," Lori said.

Caitlin kissed her mother's cheek. "I like yours too, Mom."

Mac looked at the stranger in the sports coat and said, "Boone McBride, I'd like to introduce you to our son Chase and his wife Lori, and our daughter Caitlin. Boone is an attorney—a prosecutor—from Fort Worth."

"Your kind of peeps," Chase said, shaking the other

man's hand. "Nice to meet you. I suspect we might have had dinner with relatives of yours. They're twins?"

"My sisters," Boone replied as he greeted first Lori and then Caitlin with handshakes.

Lori said, "They said you and Brick are cousins."

"Distant cousins." He shared an entertaining story of his first encounter with Branch Callahan, and Caitlin found herself laughing. While her brother replied with a Branch tale of his own, a faint ding sounded from the small handbag she carried.

Caitlin wasn't one to jump to attention at every sound her phone made, but she thought it strange that she would receive a text message right now. Everyone who usually texted her was at the wedding.

She stepped a little behind Chase so her actions wouldn't be obvious, slipped her hand into her purse, and found her phone. A quick glance caused her eyes to widen. She quickly shoved the cell back into her bag.

Wow. Oh wow. She stifled a little embarrassed giggle.

Phone foreplay.

When she dragged her attention back to the conversation, Ali was explaining how she and Mac had met Boone and his father at one of Branch's birthday parties in Texas. To Boone she said, "Your sisters weren't there that day. You'll have to introduce us before the wedding is over."

"I'll do that," Boone replied.

Lori asked if this was his first visit to Eternity Springs, and conversation turned to a comparison of Fort Worth and Colorado Springs. Mac guided the conversation like the skilled attorney he was, and soon it sounded like an Eternity Springs sales pitch. When Mac brought up the fact that he intended to retire soon and needed a lawyer to take over his practice—news to both Caitlin and Chase—it was clear he dangled the possibility of an Eternity Springs–based job in front of Boone Mc-Bride.

Caitlin wasn't really surprised that her dad would want to officially retire. The practice had grown bigger and faster than he'd anticipated, and professional obligations had thrown a wrench into her parents' travel plans more than once.

But why was he chatting up Boone McBride about it? He'd met this guy once, five years ago, and he was ready to hand over his practice? And why was he talking about it here and now?

Caitlin frowned as her father continued his pitch. "I was amazed at the amount of business a little town like Eternity Springs produced. The great thing is that for the most part, the matters are all low key. Leaves you plenty of time for outside interests. You said you like to ski?"

"I do. You make it sound attractive, Mac. I love the outdoors, and I need a change from what I've been doing. The last few cases I prosecuted have wiped me out. When kids are involved . . . I see things I don't want to be seeing."

At that point, Mac's questions turned probing and more personal, and his comments subtly drew Caitlin into the conversation. Before she quite knew how it had happened, she'd shared how she'd recently decided to make a big career change and her reasons—beyond family—for choosing Eternity Springs for her new home.

Other friends of the Timberlakes joined the group. Chase and Lori drifted away. Slowly, as Mac continued to guide the conversation with his queries and opinions, Caitlin began to get a clue.

He's trying to set me up.

She stared at her father in amazement. It was the sin-gle biggest moment of Dad-weird in her entire life. Mac had always been protective of her. When she'd started dating in high school, he'd been a gruff old bear every time she brought a new boy around. During her college years, he'd only gotten worse, subtly campaigning against the two semi-serious boyfriends she'd introduced to him. More recently, he'd tolerated Doug. Caitlin had actually believed that Mac might eventually welcome Doug to the family gracefully. Of course, then Doug had dumped her, so she'd never tested the theory.

But her dad had never, ever thrown a guy at her like he was throwing Boone McBride today. *What the heck?*

Her phone dinged again, but she knew better than to check it. Her parents had been fierce disciplinarians where phone etiquette was concerned. She'd remember to her dying day her mortification when, after she'd checked her phone during an inappropriate time, her father had grabbed it from her hand and read the text stream aloud. All she needed was for her dad to get a glimpse of another X-rated text from Josh.

She decided she had to fight fire with fire. She did her own bit of conversation-steering by asking if Boone was familiar with his cousin's Eternity Springs business concerns.

"The story of how his bride pushed that movie star into a creek at his high-dollar glamping resort is established family lore at this point. The Callahan brothers love to crow about that one."

"Have you had a chance to pay a visit to Stardance River Camp?" she asked.

"No, I haven't. I do want to see it."

"The tents are awesome, but the tree houses are spectacular. Have you seen the one they built here at the North Forty?"

"No."

"It's not nearly as big or extravagant as those at River Camp, but it is seriously cool. Brick says it's one of his favorite places in Eternity Springs. I'd be happy to show you."

"I'd like that."

Caitlin turned to her father. "Dad? Will you excuse us?"

Mac Timberlake beamed. "Of course. You two go on. I've been neglecting Alison as it is. Boone, you and I will talk some more about my practice another time."

"I'd like that, Mac."

They made small talk as they crossed the yard headed for the passage between Luke and Maddie Callahan's home and that of Brick's father, Mark, and his wife, Annabelle. The tree where the tree house had been built stood just beyond. Along the way, they were stopped numerous times. She introduced Boone to people from Eternity Springs. He introduced her to Texans.

They reached the tree house only to discover that the ladder had been removed. Caitlin said, "That's disappointing."

"Probably a liability issue to leave access to it with such a crowd around."

Spoken like a lawyer, Caitlin thought.

"It does look pretty cool, though. I don't know that I've seen a two-story tree house before. Bet the Callahan kids have a great time in it."

"Callahan kids of all ages, from what I hear."

One side of Boone's mouth lifted in a crooked smile, and Caitlin silently observed that the good-looking gene bred true on the McBride side of the family. Abruptly, she said, "I'm sorry my dad acted so obvious back there. He's not ordinarily like that. I don't know what got into him. You don't need to worry that I'll start chasing you. It's not my style."

She wasn't chasing Josh, she was laying siege to his walls.

Boone's crooked smile turned into a full-fledged flirtatious grin. "Hey, I think it's a good practice to keep fathers happy. Happy dads are less likely to come after me with a shotgun. And I've never minded being chased by a beautiful woman, so be my guest."

"Thank you." She smiled at the compliment, but added, "I actually already have a man I'm . . . um . . . pursuing. My dad doesn't like him."

"Aha! The plot thickens."

"Or something. I'm beginning to think this whole retirement thing is messing with his mind. Has he spoken to you prior to this about joining his practice?"

"He floated the idea in general terms when we were on a hunting trip that Brick's uncle Luke organized last year. To be honest, I didn't think he was serious."

"The trip to Montana? Elk hunting? You were on that trip?"

"Yes." Boone pinned her with a look. "Is there a reason why I shouldn't consider it?"

"No, not at all. Dad just hasn't mentioned to me that he was thinking about retirement. I'm glad he's considering it. I think it's long overdue. And no matter how crazy he's acting toward me, I know he wouldn't have broached the subject of retirement with you if he wasn't serious about it."

At that point, a trumpet fanfare rang out from speakers that were part of the sound system covering the compound. "That sounds like a summons to me." Boone gestured for Caitlin to precede him. "Shall we?"

They emerged from the pathway between the two Callahan homes as Mark Callahan took the microphone on a raised stage where the music-loving family brought in bands for live music a few times a year.

"Ladies and gentlemen, the Howe and Callahan families wish to welcome you to the North Forty as we celebrate the marriage of Liliana and Brick. We hope everyone enjoyed their meals. While the band sets up and the caterer clears away tables up here at the front to make room for dancing, we're going to get the speech-saying part of the evening over with so I can enjoy the rest of the party. I hate speaking before a crowd, and boy, do we have a crowd! Thank you all for coming."

"Thanks for the steak!" someone called out.

After a pause for the cheers and laughter to die down, Mark continued, "The waitstaff is coming through the crowd with champagne, so everybody grab one. Brick and Liliana, come sit in these two chairs we have on the stage so everyone can see you. Wedding party, y'all come on up here too."

Caitlin forgot all about Boone McBride as Josh Tarkington took the stage. On a stage filled with sexy men, he stood out from the crowd. *It's those eyes*, she decided. *And those high cheekbones*. The man was movie-star handsome.

Lili's father made a speech and a toast, and then it was the best man's turn. Paul Christopher made a brief but moving statement about his pride in the man that Brick had become. After he toasted the bride and groom, the maid of honor made her toast and brought many in the crowd near to tears with her mention of Patsy Schaefer keeping an eye on things from heaven.

Caitlin sighed at the romance of the moment when Brick and Lili danced the first dance to "At Last." Her heart gave a little twist watching the father-daughter dance, and the mother-son dance was one of the sweetest things she'd ever seen—Brick danced with Cindy Christopher, then Annabelle Callahan, followed by Torie, Maddie, and Nic Callahan. The man didn't lack for mothers.

When Brick invited everyone to join in the dancing,

Boone looked at Caitlin and asked, "Would you like to dance?"

She saw that Josh was dancing with one of the bridesmaids, so she gave Boone a bright smile. "Might as well make Daddy happy."

They danced two dances before her brother cut in. Caitlin thanked Boone, then arched a brow at Chase. "If it isn't my fifth-favorite groomsman."

"Out of five. Gee, thanks."

"Abandoning your wife already?"

"I figured I'd be a good egg and rescue you from Dad's set-up."

"You noticed too?"

"The birds in the trees noticed. The trout in the lake noticed. The worms in the dirt noticed. Josh Tarkington sure put a burr in Dad's saddle, didn't he? And speaking of Tarkington, what's happening there? I haven't heard a word of gossip about the two of you."

"Have I mentioned how handsome you look in a tux, Chase?"

"You're not talking, hmm?"

"Does it remind you of the bad old days when you were gambling in Monte Carlo and being fodder for the tabloids?"

"Okay, now bringing that up is just mean."

"I love you too, Goober. Don't let Dad get you down. I think he's just going through a phase."

She lifted her shoulders in a shrug. "Or something. His retirement talk sure caught me by surprise tonight. Guess I thought he'd scale back at some point, but to stop practicing law completely? What's he going to do?"

"Drive Mom nuts, I imagine."

Caitlin sighed, then shook her head. "Oh well. Enough about that. I want to relax and have a little fun."

Chase took the hint and gave her a twirl. And then another one. And another. Soon, Caitlin was laughing like the children playing hide-and-go-seek among the Callahan cabins. At the end of the dance, she hugged her brother then stepped toward the back of the crowd. Finally alone, she had a chance to check her phone.

Holy cow. And here she'd thought the dancing had made her hot.

She'd better never, ever lose her phone.

Slipping her cell back into her purse, she began to casually look around, hoping to spot Josh. The crowd was too thick and she was too short, but when she spied her father, she made an educated guess and turned in the opposite direction.

Josh was nowhere to be found.

He wouldn't have left. He was a groomsman. Maybe he was overseeing the decorating of the jeep Brick would drive up to the river camp where the newlyweds intended to spend their wedding night before departing for a two-week honeymoon, the destination of which Brick had kept to himself.

So intent was she on searching the crowd that she failed to notice the waitress trying to get her attention until the college-aged girl tapped her on the shoulder. "Excuse me. Miss?"

The girl's impatient tone told Caitlin that the waitress had spoken to her before. "Oh, I'm sorry. Yes?"

"A guy asked me to give this to you." She handed over a business card for Tarkington Automotive.

A smile flickered on Caitlin's mouth. On the back, strong male handwriting had written 4:27—THE TREE HOUSE.

"Four twenty-seven?" she murmured. "Not four thirty? Or four twenty-five?"

However, the odd number was intriguing.

The tree house, however, was not. It was way too public a spot for them to steal even so much as a kiss. They certainly wouldn't be disappearing up into it. Caitlin could climb a tree with the best of them, but not in a silk dress.

She had to admit that she was a little disappointed. For a man that inventive with text messages, she'd expected something a little more imaginative.

She checked her watch. 4:19. Eight minutes to kill. Knowing her luck, her dad would show up two minutes from now with some other guy in tow. She'd better make herself scarce until it was time to wander back to the tree house.

Caitlin decided that the best place to stay hidden was on the crowded dance floor, so she mingled with the dancers and killed another five minutes before slipping off toward the tree house, keeping her head down and moving fast. She arrived there to find . . . nothing. She was alone. She checked her watch. 4:27. She folded her arms and said a snippy, "Well."

But then the sound of an engine caught her attention. It was one of the utility vehicles used by the caterers. The driver wore a white cook's shirt and chef's hat, and the dishtowel draped around his neck obscured his features.

The driver braked to a stop beside her. Gray eyes gleamed at her, and in an anxious tone, Josh said, "Quick, get in the back. Lie down and cover up. Move, darlin'. Go go go."

The urgency in his voice had her moving instinctively. Tablecloths were piled high on the back seat. "Down. Get down."

She got down and covered up and, as the vehicle sped off, she wondered what in the world he was doing. Where was he taking her? The vehicle bounced and jostled over uneven ground. Lying across the back of the seat unable to see anything, Caitlin felt like he drove eighty miles an hour, though he probably topped out at ten.

In less than five minutes, gravel crunched beneath the tires as he applied the brakes and the vehicle slid to a stop. The motion almost threw Caitlin off the seat and onto the floor. "We're here."

Josh reached for her arm and helped her from the utility vehicle. He placed his hand at her back—okay, on her butt—and propelled her up three steps into a . . . seriously?

"A food truck?" Caitlin exclaimed as he shut the door behind them, then locked it. "You brought me to a food truck?"

"Yeah. I did." He turned to face her and waggled his brows. "I'm hungry."

He stepped toward her and his big hands cupped her cheeks. Holding her like she was precious to him, he lifted her face toward his and gave her the longest, steamiest, sexiest kiss she'd ever received. By the time he lifted his head, her mind was as fuzzy as cotton candy.

"You look drop-dead gorgeous today, Ms. Timberlake."

"You do too, Mr. Tarkington. Well, you did until you covered up your tux with a cook's uniform."

"I'd rather be naked. With you." He skimmed his hand from her butt where it rested up along her spine.

Caitlin heard the rasp of her zipper and said, "Whoa. Wait a minute."

"I'm not waiting a whole minute." His practiced fingers made quick work of the catch on her bra. "We only have seventeen of them. We have to use them wisely."

Then his hand was full of her breast and his mouth was back on hers. They kissed and kissed and kissed. At some point, her dress slid off her shoulders and fell to her waist. He kept one hand wrapped around her waist as the other played with her breasts, but he didn't try to take things further.

When she managed to formulate a thought, she told herself she was glad. She didn't think she was ready to have sex in a food truck. That was just wrong.

The notion made her giggle. Her giggle stilled first with his hand, and then his mouth. He lifted his face and stared down at her with an eyebrow arched above a twinkling eye.

She asked, "A food truck?"

"The catering vans were all locked."

"The odd time?"

"Added an element of mystery, don't you think?"

Her giggle intensified to a chuckle. "Why the car at the tree house? Why didn't you just ask me to meet you here?"

"I thought the getaway cart added a measure of excitement to the process. Besides, I saw that Texan chatting you up while you stood beneath the tree house. I don't want you thinking about him when you see that tree house. I want you to think of me."

They kissed for a few more long, luscious minutes. Josh Tarkington was *good* at it. He seemed to honestly enjoy kissing for kissing's sake. She hadn't made out like this since high school.

The thought of high school had her giggling again. "I can't believe we're doing this. It's silly. It's ridiculous."

He kissed her again, slid his hand sensuously over her breasts, then said, "Absolutely."

"It's fun. You're fun, Josh."

He grinned down at her, then kissed the tip of her nose. "Thank you. That's a compliment I treasure."

He stepped away from her, reached behind her, and fastened her bra before helping Caitlin back into her dress. "Turn around. I'll zip you."

After he did so, Caitlin picked her bag up from the floor where she'd dropped it and pulled out a compact. Her hair was a bit of a mess, but that could just as easily have happened from dancing as hiding beneath table-cloths and making out among the . . . she glanced around. "What sort of food truck is this, anyway?"

He rolled his tongue around his mouth and dodged the question. "It's owned by the same bunch out of Vail who catered the wedding. I don't know why they brought it with them unless they needed backup ovens or some-thing."

He checked his watch, then began unbuttoning the chef's shirt he wore over his tux. "I have three minutes before I must leave. I still have a few groomsman duties I need to do. Do you want to walk back with me or make our way separately?"

"Oh, let's not blow this now. Separate is good. It'll ex-tend the afterglow. I'll give you a five-minute . . . no, make that a seven-minute head start."

Josh laughed softly, then turned and unlocked the door. He opened it cautiously, glanced around, then paused long enough to look at her and say, "Thanks for the canoodle, Caitlin."

She laughed again. Now there's a word she hadn't thought of in a very long time. "Thank *you*. I enjoyed every minute of it."

Josh exited the truck and pulled the door shut behind him. Caitlin leaned back against the work counter, her arms folded and a grin on her face as she relived the past seventeen minutes. To think that the words she most of-ten heard when friends and acquaintances described Josh were "quiet" and "serious." Did anyone know he had this kind of playfulness inside him? He'd certainly never shown this side of his nature to her before now.

She liked it.

She liked him.

She wondered what had gotten into him. She didn't have a clue. *I'm not going to figure it out tonight in a food truck.*

She'd better get back to the reception before her father sent out the rescue dogs. Caitlin gave her reflection one more check in the mirror, decided not to refresh her lipstick so as not to draw more attention to her swollen lips, and after checking to make certain she wouldn't be observed, stepped down out of the food truck.

As she made her way around to the front, one of her questions was answered. The truck's name was painted across the side: THE WIENER WAGON.

She laughed all the way back to the reception.

Journal Entry

Genetics.

They tell me I look exactly like one of my great-something-grandfathers. They tell me my talent came to me through my grandmother's line. I inherited one person's eyes and another person's mannerisms and someone else's money. Can't leave the money out of the equation.

Which of my ancestors was the first to beat his kids?

Was one of them a regular at an eighteenth-century opium den?

How many of the nuts on my family tree offed themselves?

Is it possible to ever overcome genetics?

Chapter Eleven

On a snowy morning the week before Thanksgiving Josh turned on his shop radio to the classic rock station, tossed a treat to Penny, then went to work. He had a tune-up to do on Maggie Romano's SUV and an oil change for Colt Rafferty waiting for him. After that, he wanted to put in a few hours on the Lamborghini. He'd worked hard the past few weeks. He figured he'd earned the time for playing with that classic engine.

Speaking of play, he'd done plenty of that of late too. He and Caitlin spent at least two nights a week together, alternating between her rental home and his house. A third night usually found them in the same group at a social event of some sort. Because Eternity Springs had a shortage of citizens in the twenty-five to thirty-five age group, it was usually all hands on deck when any one of them threw a party or held a game night. Keeping to the secret spirit of their affair, Caitlin and Josh avoided being seen as a couple, treating one another no differently than they did their other friends.

Once or twice Caitlin had mentioned experiencing a twitch of guilt about it, especially where Lori and Chase were concerned. Just last week as Josh cuddled with Caitlin after a stolen hour in his bed, she'd twirled her finger in the hair on his chest and confessed, "Before I moved back, I told my brother I had a crush on you. I know he wonders why I appear to have changed my mind."

Josh had asked, "Do you want to go public?"

"No. I'm enjoying this. As long as I don't have to outright lie. I can't abide liars, so I'm walking a fine line, personally."

"Well, if you ever decide you need to spill the beans, it's all right with me."

And it was. In fact, a part of Josh wanted to go public with their affair just to get under Mac Timberlake's skin. The man had a serious hard-on against Josh, and it was beginning to seriously annoy him.

When Springsteen's "Born to Run" came on the radio, he turned his attention away from the Timberlakes and toward tuning up the engine of Maggie's 2014 Ford. Once that was done, he tackled Rafferty's oil change and was finishing up when he heard the sound of a motorcycle engine. A skipping engine.

Celeste drove into his shop on her Gold Wing, switched off the engine, kicked down the stand, then removed her sparkling gold helmet. "Hello, Joshua."

"Good afternoon, Celeste. Something tells me you need me to look at your carburetor."

"And my spark plugs," she observed, beaming at him. "She's been hard to start the last few times I've ridden her, and I'd hate to get stuck somewhere on a winter's day."

"We're not exactly heading into motorcycle weather."

"True. Tomorrow certainly won't be a good day for riding. Our forecast for tonight calls for a mix of sleet and snow. But I want to be ready for the next clear, cold winter's day because I find a ride under those circumstances to be especially invigorating. Don't you agree?"

Josh considered the question as he grabbed the tools

he anticipated needing from his toolbox. "It can be. It can also be a miserable experience."

"How soon do you think you can get to her, Josh?"

"I've just finished what I needed to do today. I can look at it right now."

"Excellent. Do you mind if I wait? I have a little time to kill before I meet Savannah Turner to plan our Thanksgiving feast."

"You're welcome to wait. This shouldn't take long. I put some new magazines in the waiting room this morning." He put a wrench to a nut and got to work.

"Oh, I'll just stay here and chat with you. It seems like forever since we've had a chance to visit. Plus, I want to ask your impressions of our Fall Festival. It was your first time attending, was it not?"

"Yes." He set about removing the carburetor from the motorcycle.

"Did you enjoy it?"

"Yes, very much. It's not often a guy gets to compete in a game where a former pro basketball player."

"I heard you gave our Lucca Romano a run for his money."

"It was fun. And the Cakewalk . . . I don't have words to describe that. I never guessed a game like that could be a full-contact sport."

"It's become quite the tradition. I'm curious to know if you have any new ideas for us to try next year. The festival is our biggest school fundraiser, and I'm afraid our activities are growing stale. I'd be so pleased if you'd join our organizing committee for next year, Josh. May I count on you?"

Her carburetor definitely needed to be cleaned. "I'm not much of a committee person."

"That's why you'll be so perfect. Our first meeting is December fourth at seven p.m. I'll count on seeing you there. Which reminds me, do you have Thanksgiving plans, Josh?"

A quick image of what the Timberlake family Thanksgiving table might look like flashed into his mind and was banished just as quickly. It would be a cold day in hell before he'd get that invitation. Josh dropped the carburetor into the pail of cleaner, then took the wrench he needed from his toolbox to tackle the spark plugs.

"No, I don't."

"So you're not going home to California to see your mother?"

The wrench clattered to the garage's cement floor. Josh shot Celeste a look that was half panic, half outrage.

"In that case, consider yourself invited to Angel's Rest." Then with kindness in her tone, her eyes filled with compassion, she added, "You need not worry, dear. I recognized you the first time we met. I haven't told a soul who you are, nor do I intend to ever do so."

Josh bent and retrieved his tool. He briefly considered trying to bluff his way through this, but when Celeste Blessing gazed at him with those clear blue eyes, he couldn't lie. "I don't understand. How did you recognize me? Nobody ever does. I haven't made a movie in over twenty years. I don't look anything like I did when I was J. B. Trammel."

"True. But you are the spitting image of your namesake, your great-grandfather Benjamin."

That took Josh aback. No one had said that to him since puberty. In fact, to this day on the rare occasions that he did see his mother, she always waxed on about how much he looked like the men in *her* family tree.

"I'm honestly surprised that no one else has noticed," Celeste continued. "Cary Grant. Rock Hudson. Benjamin Trammel. Oh my. Heartthrobs of women across the world, back in the day. And I know that I'm not the only woman in town who watches the classic movie channel. You should prepare yourself to be outed, Joshua. Someday it will happen and it might not occur at the most opportune time."

Oh hell. He'd never even thought of that. "I'll grow a beard."

"Then, you'll look like your father."

"I'll die my hair blond."

"Your uncle Franklin."

"Okay, I'll give myself pink tips!"

"You don't read the gossip magazines, do you? Your sister Arabella has pink and purple tips. While the resemblance with your sisters isn't as strong, it does exist."

"Well, I'm going to try to think positively about this." What else could he do? "Not everyone has your intuition, Celeste. I've gone this long without anyone noticing. And even if someone else here in town does see the resemblance, they have no reason to think it's anything more than a coincidence. People do have doppelgängers. That's what they'll think about me." Then he closed his eyes and added, "Except I have the most god-awful luck."

Celeste clucked her tongue. "About that, Joshua. It's true that you've had a terrible time with tornados, and losing your fiancée and her daughter was truly a tragedy. But I do believe you are wrong in the way you think about your luck. You've certainly brought a positive energy with you to Eternity Springs. Why Brick might have lost everything if you hadn't been sharp enough to realize that Courtney was stealing from him."

Josh turned his focus to the motorcycle's spark plugs. "That's different, Celeste."

"Is it? I have something I want you to think about."

He braced himself, instinctively knowing he wouldn't like hearing what she had to say.

"Open your mind to the idea that much of what you've

perceived as bad luck is actually good luck that simply hasn't manifested itself as of yet."

Oh. Well. That wasn't hard. Because it was nonsense.

"It takes a little faith, Joshua. But I want you to consider the idea that the most recent tornado that destroyed your business and home might have been the luckiest event of your life."

He couldn't hold back his bitter laugh. "I'm sorry, Celeste. That's a little too far into woo-woo land."

"Open your mind," she repeated. "You wouldn't have come to Eternity Springs if not for that storm. That's already proven to be a lucky happenstance for Brick. Who knows whose life you'll affect next? Why, it could easily have been me. If you hadn't opened your shop, then I'd have ridden my motorcycle to South Fork to have it worked on. I might have been caught in a sudden, freak snowstorm at the top of Sinner's Prayer Pass. So there you go. You've probably saved my life today."

He couldn't help but laugh. "Your mind is an amazing thing, Celeste."

She crossed to his workbench where her carburetor and spark plugs now sat and placed her hand on his arm. "You are a good man, Joshua. You have a good heart. You're building a new life in Eternity Springs that has the potential to be something wonderful if only you will allow it."

Josh didn't know why a lump suddenly formed in his throat.

"Now, I should have just enough time to walk over to Heavenscents to be on time for my meeting with Savannah. I'll tell her you're joining us for Thanksgiving. And don't forget to mark the Fall Festival planning meeting on your calendar. I'll pick up my Gold Wing before you close this afternoon. See you later, dear."

He could do nothing more than reply, "See you later, Celeste."

She'd been gone no more than a minute when he saw she'd left behind a notebook with a pattern of angel's wings on the cover. "Bet she'll need that," he murmured.

He picked the notebook up and walked out of the work bay. Celeste was just beyond Caitlin's Gingerbread House and striding rapidly away. He called out to her and broke into a jog. She turned around and he held the notebook up. "You forgot this."

"Oh, heavens. I'd forget my head if it wasn't attached. Thank you."

"No problem." He caught up with her and handed over the notebook. Then he took two steps back toward his shop and paused. "Celeste?"

"Yes?"

"Thank you. For keeping quiet about . . . well . . . you know. And for the Thanksgiving invitation. And for . . . well . . ." He waved his hand around. "Everything."

Her eyes sparkled. "You are quite welcome. Promise me you'll think about what I said."

"Yes, ma'am."

He started back toward the shop, slipping his hands into the front pocket of his sweatshirt to keep them warm. Walking past Gingerbread House, he could hear the sound of a skill saw and the pounding of hammers. Caitlin's renovations were coming right along. She'd told him last night that Jax had told her they were running ahead of schedule. He hoped to be finished by the first of February. She'd tentatively set her grand opening for the first of March.

Josh thought it would be nice to have kids playing in the yard next spring and summer. He glanced toward Harriet's house. Bet she'd sit on her front porch watching them all the time—if she wasn't off camping by then. He'd noticed the Tornado Alleycats membership application lying on her counter the last time he was in her kitchen.

Back inside the garage, Josh went into his stockroom to check his supply of spark plugs, making sure he had what Celeste needed. He was distracted as he did so, but he didn't know by what. Something bothered him. Niggled at his consciousness. He removed a box of plugs from his stock shelves and reentered the work bay. What was wrong?

He set down the box and walked back outside. Had he noticed something odd at Gingerbread House? Or maybe at Harriet's?

He eyed his neighbor's house. Her newspaper wasn't in her yard. The flyers that had arrived in today's mail weren't sticking out of the mailbox on her porch. Nothing wrong there.

Giving into his instincts, he started up the sidewalk toward Gingerbread House. He'd reached the front walk of his own house when it hit him.

Her bird feeder. Harriet's bird feeder was empty. She filled her bird feeder up like clockwork after she brought in the mail each day. Letting it remain empty wasn't like her at all.

Josh changed direction and crossed the street. He climbed her porch steps and knocked on the door. "Harriet?"

She didn't respond. He knocked again. "Harriet? Are you home?"

Was that a sound coming from inside?

Damn. He had a really bad feeling about this. He tried the doorknob. Unlocked. Opening the door, he stepped inside. "Harriet?"

Then he heard her, her voice weak and thready. "Josh! Oh, thank God, Josh."

He rushed toward the sound and found Harriet Rosenbaum lying on her kitchen floor. Streaks of tears stained her cheeks.

"I can't get up. It's my hip. I'm afraid it's my hip. Help me, Josh."

"I will. I'm here. Hold on, Harriet. I'm going to call the paramedics." Except he didn't have his phone with him. "Do you have a landline or just your cell?"

"Just a cell. It's in the living room. Beside my chair."

"Okay. I'll get it. Hold on, Harriet. We'll have help for you in just a few minutes."

"Thank you. Oh, thank you, Josh. God bless you. The day you moved across the street from me was my lucky day."

Autumn faded to winter and in the valley that nestled Eternity Springs, two inches of snow fell on Thanksgiving Day. Caitlin spent a lovely day with her family, though she wished circumstances had been such that Josh could have shared the day with them. Next year, she told herself.

Renovations on Gingerbread House continued to progress well. She settled into a routine where she worked from home in the mornings then wandered over there in the afternoon and spent a few hours tackling whatever jobs Jax Lancaster deemed appropriate for her. Her sense of accomplishment and pride of ownership built every time she swung a hammer.

Her attachment to the mechanic next door continued to grow too.

Mid-afternoon of the first Saturday in December, she sat on a workbench in his garage with Penny in her lap. Idly, Caitlin scratched the doxie behind her ears and watched Josh's shirt pull tight across his shoulders as he reached above him to do something to the muffler of the car on the lift. She clucked her tongue and observed, "I do like a man in flannel."

"True, that."

With temperatures hovering in the twenties, Josh had his bay doors closed, even though he was open for business until three. Caitlin had tried to talk him into closing a little early, but the man was infuriatingly responsible. He closed at three, so he'd stay open until three on the dot. Working until three on the dot.

Penny started squirming, so Caitlin scooted off the workbench, carried the dog over to her wheelchair, and fitted her into it. Penny rolled over to her bed, burrowed her long red nose into her pillow, and closed her eyes.

Caitlin wandered back toward the workbench. She picked up a ratchet and twirled it around, liking the clicking noise it made. It reminded her of working with her grandfather in his shop.

Without looking away from the muffler, Josh slipped his wrench into his tool chest and withdrew another smaller one.

"You should wear a leather tool belt like Jax does."

"Mechanics don't wear tool belts."

"Why not?"

"We just don't."

"Well, you should. Tool belts are sexy."

That distracted him long enough to arch a brow in her direction. "You shouldn't be ogling Jax Lancaster's ass. He's married."

"Don't be sexist, Tarkington. I've noticed you looking at Claire's butt. I can't help it that tool belts make me hot. If I give you one will you wear it for me?"

A smile flirted at the corners of his mouth. "Maybe."

"Without pants?"

"If you promise to hold my hammer."

Caitlin laughed. She was so gone over this man. "How is Harriet doing?"

"Good. I stopped by to see her yesterday. She thinks she'll be sent home from rehab next week."

"That's good. I know she's ready to come home. Is her son going to stay with her?"

"No. He's got to get back to work. He's hired a live-in nurse for her."

"She's going to hate that."

"Yep. But she knows she's lucky. The break could have been so much worse."

Caitlin set down the ratchet and picked up his socket set. She lifted the three-eighth-inch deep socket from its slot and peered through it like a telescope toward the clock on the wall. "Five minutes to three, Tarkington. Time to start putting away your tools, don't you think?"

"If you'll stop playing with them, maybe I'll do just that." He gave the wrench one last twist, then stepped out from beneath the car. He wiped his hands on a shop rag and flipped the lift switch to lower the car.

Caitlin replaced the socket and jumped down to the ground. "I had to keep my hands busy. What I wanted to play with wasn't available."

Josh grinned and pulled her into his arms saying, "C'mere."

He kissed her hello for a long, lovely minute. *Yep, over the moon gone for him.*

"So, what's on our agenda?" he asked, then immediately clarified. "As in, where are we watching football? Your place? Mine? Murphy's?"

"Football!"

"It's conference championship Saturday. If we go to your house, maybe you can bake us some cookies?"

"Aren't you afraid my Mom will drop by?" Caitlin asked dryly.

"Good point. I can make a quick run by the Trading Post and pick up some eggs. I think I have plenty of everything else you'll need."

She gave an exaggerated aggrieved sigh. "Oh, all right. Only because you said my sugar cookies are better than Harriet's."

"Hey, I know which side of my cookie is iced." Josh gave her one more quick kiss, then released her to begin tidying up his already tidy shop.

"Tell you what. I have eggs at home. I'll run by there and grab the eggs and pick up the dress I'm wearing to-night. I can get ready at your place."

In the process of stowing items into his toolbox, Josh paused a moment. "Oh, yeah. I forgot about the date to-night."

The very absence of an expression told Caitlin just how unhappy he was about tonight's event at the Yellow Kitchen. She couldn't blame him. She wasn't happy about having to attend the dinner party either, but honestly it was his own fault. She'd been ready to bring him as her date.

They'd argued about it, but he'd been resolute in his refusal. He didn't think that the celebration dinner wel-coming Boone McBride to Eternity Springs and her father's law practice was the right time and place to take their relationship-that-wasn't-one public.

"It'd be waving a red flag at a bull, Cait," he'd told her. "If we decide to go public, then let's do it at a time and place when escape is possible."

So, tonight she was going solo to her father's big event, which made Mac happy as a clam. He hadn't tried to hide his hope that she and Boone would hit it off.

Josh, on the other hand, seemed more aggravated by her father than normal. *Serves you right, Josh Tark-ington.*

This friend affair of theirs wasn't going to last forever. Either he'd have to finally admit that their relationship was a relationship or . . . well . . . she didn't want to think about "or." Not yet. Not until after Christmas.

"I'll meet you back your place then?"

"Sure." He still wore a scowl.

Caitlin decided to leave him in a better mood. "Do you have butter?"

Sure enough, the reminder of the promise of fresh baked cookies cheered him up. "I have some. Maybe one stick. How much do you need?"

"Don't worry. I'll bring it." She gave him a quick kiss, then said, "See you in half an hour."

"I'll preheat the oven."

She paused at the door and gave him a saucy look. "Darlin', my oven *always* stays heated around you."

Journal Entry

Put a toe tag on me and leave me the hell alone.

My therapist pretended he didn't hear me say it, so I said it again. Louder. I meant it, too. I'd rather have a coroner do a Y-cut on me than have that asshat poking around in my head any longer.

Therapist. The rapist. Kinda apropos, don't you think?

Hour after hour. "How does that make you feel?" "What are you feeling?" "Do you feel like you're making progress?" "Tell the group about your feelings." "And that will be two hundred dollars an hour, thank you very much."

It's all bull. If they're so smart, they should tell a person what to do. Instead, they ask questions and we're supposed to do all the work figuring the stuff out.

What a crock.

And this is supposed to help me how?

Chapter Twelve

Josh couldn't keep his mind on football. For one thing, the game was boring. Alabama was pounding their opponent. *So what else is new?* He had a sugar rush going on because he had way overindulged on Caitlin's cookies. His body was still humming from shower sex, and she was in his bathroom blow-drying her hair so she could go out to dinner with another man.

Josh couldn't put his finger on why, exactly, but it really chapped his butt. He wasn't worried that she'd actually fall for the lawyer, was he? No. Absolutely not. Caitlin wasn't the type to dangle two men on her string at the same time.

So, she'll dump me.

She'll dump me and in a month she'll be wearing a rock on her hand and in June her happy daddy will march her down the aisle and this time next year she'll be pregnant with twins.

"No," he muttered aloud. "She's not going to do that." *Well, it's not like you didn't tell her that you aren't into marriage and kids. If she does move on to someone who can give her that, then what right do you have to say anything? Fool.*

He grabbed the remote and started channel-surfing.

When a familiar black-and-white movie flashed on the screen, Celeste's words reverberated through his mind. *You are the spitting image of your great-grandfather.*

Was he?

And of course, it was just his luck that Caitlin walked past the media room door right at that moment wearing nothing but her makeup and one of his fluffy white towels. "Ooh," she said. "I love this movie. There's a scene coming up where Benjamin Trammel and Grace Kelly stare at each other and you think the film is going to burst into flames."

Damn. Josh's thumb pressed the remote buttons and returned to football. "I'm not a fan of old movies, myself. Didn't you say your dad wanted you at the restaurant at seven? You'd better get moving or you'll be late."

She sighed. "You're right."

She disappeared into his bedroom and returned ten minutes later wearing a little black dress, three-inch heels, and a strand of pearls. Josh's stomach sank. "You look fantastic."

She made a little curtsey. "Thank you."

"Nice pearls." *From an old boyfriend?*

She fingered them, smiled, and gave him the information he wanted. "They were my grandmother's. My grandmother gave them to me."

Mollified and a little embarrassed by his reaction, Josh stood and walked over to where she stood. "They suit you and what you're wearing tonight. Understated and classy. Though I think colored jewels would suit you better. Emeralds to match your eyes."

She grinned. "Yes, emeralds are the perfect accessory for changing diapers and wiping three-year-olds' snotty noses."

Words formed on the tip of Josh's tongue asking her

to stay, to stand up her parents up. To tell Solicitor Mc-Bride that she was taken. In a relationship.

A cheer erupted from the television and halted the dangerous direction of his thoughts.

"Alabama wins," Caitlin said. "Imagine that."

She opened his front closet and removed her dress coat. Shaken by what he'd almost done, he rose and said, "I'll drive you."

"I can walk, Josh. It's two blocks."

"It's cold. Your toes will have frostbite by the time you get there. I'll take you." He made his way to the back door in the mudroom and lifted the keys to his truck from their customary hanger.

Abandoning her argument, Caitlin followed him to his truck and climbed into the passenger seat. He turned the ignition switch and sat in his drive for a few minutes as the engine warmed up. Caitlin said something about a cookie sheet and the dishwasher and a soap pod, but he barely heard her. Josh was in a stew.

He didn't speak as he drove her to her mother's restaurant. He badly wanted to walk her up to the front door and claim her with a public kiss, but better sense prevailed. He pulled up to the curb in a shadowed spot around the corner from the Yellow Kitchen. "Will you come back to my place afterward?"

"Probably not. I don't know what time we'll be done, and I'm sure either Chase or my dad will offer to drop me off at home." She leaned over and kissed his cheek. "I'll see you tomorrow. Maybe you could take me up to Stardance River Camp and we could do some cross-country skiing? I haven't been yet this season, and I know after eating my mother's lasagna, I'll be ready for exercise."

"Sure. Whatever."

He pulled away from the curb and turned the corner before she did. He drove past the Yellow Kitchen, and upon seeing Caitlin's parents and Boone McBride approaching from the opposite direction, he turned into the church parking lot down the street and positioned his truck so he could watch the front door.

Parents and daughter greeted each other with a hug. McBride shook Caitlin's hand. But as they started toward the restaurant's entrance, he saw one of Caitlin's shoes slip and for a moment, she teetered on those high heels. McBride reached out to steady her, setting both hands on her waist.

Josh gripped the steering wheel so hard that his knuckles went white.

McBride kept one hand at the small of Caitlin's back as he escorted her into the restaurant. Josh sat in his truck, not moving, for at least ten minutes.

He wasn't so clueless that he didn't recognize the emotion burning in his gut like a bad burrito. He was jealous. Pea-green, hard-breathing, jaw-clenching, ready-to-hit-something jealous.

He took his foot off the brake, pulled out of the parking lot, and onto the street. He drove the parameter of the eighteen-block rectangle of Eternity Springs proper. Twice. Then two more times. After making the fifth full circuit, he stopped in front of a house on Aspen between Third and Fourth. He walked up to the front door and knocked. Loudly.

Moments later, he heard footsteps approaching the door. It swung open. "Tarkington?"

"Hello, Mr. Whitfield. I'm sorry to bother you this time of night, but I need a favor."

"A favor? Well, all right. I'm happy to help any way I can. I told you that when you discovered the brake fluid leak in my wife's car last summer."

"Yes sir. You did. That's why I'm here. I need you to let me into the bank, into my safety deposit box."

"All right," the bank manager said. "I can do that. When . . . ?"

"Tonight, sir. I'd like to go right now."

Caitlin eyed the tiramisu on the dessert plate before her and wondered if she dared take one more bite. While her mother had turned over much of the everyday operation of the Yellow Kitchen to trusted management, she'd been hands-on preparing tonight's celebration meal. The food had been divine, and Caitlin's seams were feeling a little too tight at the moment.

She'd enjoyed the evening. She would have enjoyed it more if Josh had been sitting beside her, but the company had been good, the conversation lively and interesting, and her parents had seemed happier and more relaxed than she'd seen them in some time. Dad was almost giddy to have Boone McBride joining his firm.

She glanced across the table to see him joking with Lori's dad, Cam, and her mother, Sarah. Perhaps he sensed her gaze, because he glanced her way and upon meeting her gaze, smiled. It was an easy smile. An honest one. Seeing it made Caitlin's heart do a little squiggly dance. Things had been tense between her and her father since she moved home. He invariably seemed to be pushing her—shoving her—toward settling down and getting married and having 2.3 children. It drove her crazy.

Maybe he had a bigger issue with his youngest child turning thirty than she did. Whatever. Though she liked seeing him without a frown line marring his face for a change. Maybe he *had* been working too hard. He was trying to balance the travel and his work really was too much for him. Maybe he really did need to retire, but he felt like he needed all his chicks settled first. He was old-fashioned that way. Sadly.

It was something she'd file away and think about. Later. Boone McBride was speaking to her.

"I think this meal ranks in the top five I've had in my entire life," he said.

"Just the top five?"

"Okay, maybe top three. I can't rank your mom above my own mother's Thanksgiving dinner. That would be just wrong."

"So whose is the third out of the three?"

He named a famous restaurant in Napa that was the holy grail for foodies.

"Name-dropper," Caitlin accused.

"You asked." He shrugged, a grin fluttering on his lips.

Caitlin asked him a question about the food and wine pairings at the renowned restaurant. That led to a discussion about California wineries that Caitlin enjoyed until she caught sight of her father's satisfied expression. She wanted to roll her eyes. *Really, Dad? Could you be a little more obvious?*

She did like her father's new partner. He was intelligent and witty and genuinely interesting. Under other circumstances, she might have been attracted to him. But these weren't other circumstances. Josh was in her life. In the past couple of months, he'd *become* her life. She was head over heels in love with him.

And to him, I'm just the friend he's sleeping with.

On that depressing note, Caitlin gave into temptation and speared the last bite of tiramisu.

The mood stayed with her as the party broke up. Beneath her father's encouraging stare, Boone asked if he could see her home. Caitlin accepted the ride, deciding this was as good a time as any to apologize for her father's obvious attempt at matchmaking and let Boone know she was otherwise involved so he need not feel pressured.

The Texan drove a small, sleek BMW sports car—not exactly the ride one needed in a Colorado mountain town—and he mentioned his intention to get something more appropriate. "Lots to do with a move like this. I didn't realize just how much going into it."

"Having second thoughts?"

"No. I needed to get away from Fort Worth."

His tone didn't invite questions, which of course, made her want to ask them. Instead, due to the brevity of the ride home, after she gave him directions to her place, she got to the point. "Boone, this is a little embarrassing—actually, it's a lot embarrassing—but a person would have to be blind to miss the fact that my dad is trying to set the two of us up. I don't know why he's decided to play match-maker, but I hope you'll ignore him. I certainly plan to do so. First at the wedding and again tonight."

"Don't be embarrassed, Caitlin. You're a beautiful woman and under other circumstances, I'd definitely be interested. But I'm not in the market for a relationship right now."

Relief washed through her. "Oh. Oh, good. That's ex-actly what I was going to say—well, except for the woman part. Nothing womanly about you. You're a hot guy. But I'm already with a hot guy. Please, don't tell anyone I said so. Especially not Dad. And I'm babbling."

He laughed. "I'm glad we're on the same page. I don't need a girlfriend in Eternity Springs, but I can use a friend." After a second's pause, he repeated, "I need a friend."

He sounds like he really means it. Adding a bit of perk to her voice, Caitlin said, "Hey, I can do that. I'm a good friend." *Ask Josh.*

On second thought, don't ask Josh.

As Boone pulled to a stop in front of her house, Caitlin added, "I'm glad we're simpatico too. So let me say with total sincerity, welcome to Eternity Springs. I'm happy you're here."

The dome light came on as she opened the passenger side door to exit the car. Boone leaned over and kissed her cheek. "Thank you, friend. I'm glad to be here."

The December night was bitter and Caitlin hurried toward her front door. She'd neglected to leave a light on when she'd gone to Josh's house earlier, so the room was pitch-black when she stepped inside. She was hanging up her coat when his voice came out of the shadows.

"You let him kiss you."

Journal Entry

Rage.

As long as I can remember, it's been a beast living inside me. It mostly sleeps, though sometimes it slithers around, restless, stirred. That last visit with my dad before he died . . . after that last backhanded slap . . . I named him Sherman. Sherman has red eyes that glow in the dark. He has big pointed yellow teeth.

He's hairy and he stinks and when I was a kid, he frightened me. As I grew older, he made me feel strong.

Feel. "How do you feel?" "How does that make you feel?"

The rapist.

But when Sherman escapes . . . when he is free . . . he looks just like my father.

Sherman scares me.

My new friend makes me forget about him. I call my new friend Charlie.

How do I feel? How does Charlie make you feel? Good. Great. Invincible.

Chapter Thirteen

Josh switched on a lamp and a part of him relished the startled look on her face. From his position beside the window where he'd watched for her to come home, he said, "Good thing it was only a kiss on the cheek. I'd hate to have to track him down and whip his ass."

"Excuse me?" Caitlin folded her arms. "Did I invite you here?"

"No. I don't get invited to Timberlake family events."

"I invited you tonight," she muttered.

He ignored that. "Even better you didn't ask him in for a nightcap. The mood I'm in, I might have killed him."

"Josh—"

He crossed the room to her in a few long strides and cut off her words with a kiss filled with fire. He backed her against the wall, knocking down a small framed picture of her family. It clattered to the floor with a satisfying crash.

He was rough with her and she was rough with him right back. He yanked up her dress. She tugged his jeans open. Their tongues battled like swords.

He took her there against the wall, jealousy and lust and some other emotion he was afraid to name pulsing through his blood. When it was over, when he could breathe again, he picked her up and carried her to her bed. He stripped her naked but for her pearls, and for a long moment, he stared down at her.

She gazed up at him, her heart in her eyes. A lump of emotion choked his throat, but he couldn't say the words. He just couldn't.

Slowly, Josh removed his own clothes, pulling the necklace from his pocket as he did so. He knelt over her, slipped her pearls from around her neck and replaced them with *his* grandmother's necklace. It nestled between her full breasts. The Sokolov emerald pendant, a gift to a great-something-grandmother from a Grand Duke of Russia a century ago.

"There," he murmured. "I've pictured this. Pictured you like this." Lovely and lush, wantonly mussed, the scent of him clinging to her glistening skin and his gift nestled between her breasts. "You are my dream."

Then Josh lowered his head and kissed her, gently this time, sweetly. Reverently. He made love to her in a depth and manner he'd never shared with any other woman. Afterward, when they lay silent and spent and satisfied, Caitlin lifted the pendant and studied it.

The rectangular emerald was as big as his thumb, set into an intricate and uniquely styled pendant of white gold, surrounded by diamonds, and hanging from a heavy chain.

"This is beautiful, Josh."

"It suits you." A fierce rush of possessive pleasure washed through him.

"I'm surprised you have something like this lying around." She arched her brow and spoke with a hint of starch in her tone. "An old girlfriend's?"

He grinned. He liked that she wasn't immune to jealousy, either. "No. Not an old girlfriend's." He picked up the pendant and thumbed the jewel named Heart of Spring. His voice husky with renewed desire, he said, "I do believe it was made just for you."

She smiled sweetly at him, then sat up and switched on the bedside lamp. She studied the pendant closely. "I love antique jewelry. You've probably noticed. A lot of what I have came to me from my grandmother's sister. She had a ton of costume jewelry. My mom isn't into it, so she gave it all to me. She didn't have anything as spectacular as this, though. Where did you find it?"

He paused a moment, then spoke the truth. "I inherited it from my grandmother. She left it to me so my father wouldn't get his hands on it."

And sell it for pennies on the dollar on one of his lows or give it away during one of his highs.

"This is the first time you've mentioned your birth family to me."

He regretted it already. "It will be the last. They have nothing to do with who I am."

She looked like she might pursue it, but at his sharp glance she took the hint. She tugged the necklace over her head and attempted to hand it back. "Thanks for showing it to me. It's—"

"A gift. My gift to you."

"Oh. Well. Thank you, Josh, but I can't accept this. It's a family heirloom."

He took it from her and returned it to where it belonged. "I don't have a lot to give you, but this I can do. Accept it graciously, Caitlin. Wear it for me when you're naked. It will give me immeasurable pleasure."

To demonstrate the truth of his claim, he made love to her again, drawing it out, indulging himself in the picture she made lying against her crisp white sheets with her long blonde hair fanned around her, in the scent of her arousal, in the sounds she made when he brought her to climax again and again and again.

Long after she'd drifted off to sleep cuddled against him, Josh stared up at the ceiling. He'd done it. He'd thrown sense out of the window. He'd gone and done the one thing he'd sworn he wouldn't do.

He was in love with her. He'd fallen in love with her. Stupidly, ridiculously, idiotically in love with her. Passionately in love with her.

He loved her. So what now? Could Celeste be right? Dare he take a chance? Could it possibly work between them?

The idea hovered at the edge of his dreams like the whisper of an angel's wings.

Maybe . . . maybe . . . maybe.

Caitlin awoke the following morning toasty warm from lying beneath her down comforter and spooned up against her own personal furnace. The man put off heat like the hot springs at Angel's Rest.

She liked waking up with Josh Tarkington lying beside her. He slept soundly, his soft, rhythmic breaths blowing softly against her neck. Not wishing to disturb him and enjoying the moment, she remained right where she was. Her thoughts began to whirl.

She adored the necklace, but why had he given it to her last night? Christmas was only weeks away. Why didn't he wait until then?

Which brought up another concern. Now what in the world was she going to give *him* for Christmas? Was he one of those people whose love language involved gift giving? She couldn't tell. This was the first gift he'd given her and it was pretty wonderful.

Would he expect something just as wonderful from

her in return? She'd always been one who demonstrated her love through actions. Her gifts were that of time and effort. Baking him cookies yesterday had been a gift to him. Would he recognize that—at least without her having to whack him over the head with it?

What can I get him for Christmas?

The necklace was breathtaking. She loved it, she truly did, though she wasn't sure where in the world she would wear it. To the Trading Post to buy paper towels and toilet paper?

Why had he given it to her? What was he trying to say to her? What was he trying to say? Part of a fantasy of his? Was it simply just a sexual prop? Or was he trying to express an emotion he wasn't quite ready to say?

The answer was something for which she'd dared not hope.

Had her patience paid off? Was it love? Had Josh fallen in love with her?

She shouldn't get ahead of herself. It was a piece of costume jewelry, not a diamond ring for her left hand.

Nevertheless, the possibilities sent energy pulsing through her. She needed to move. As she scooted out from beneath his embrace and slipped from bed, she figured what she should do was face the morning's cold and the overindulgence of last night's dinner by pulling on her gear and going for a run. Instead, she decided to get up and make waffles for Josh. She'd break out the good maple syrup instead of the cheap stuff she ordinarily used.

Love language. Maybe neither one was to the point where they'd put it into words, but Caitlin was ready to think that maybe, just maybe, they had a future together.

He ate four waffles, three slices of bacon, and used half the bottle of syrup. Caitlin considered the meal a rousing success.

Upon draining his third cup of coffee, he said, "So, you mentioned cross-country skiing. Want to go this afternoon? I can use the exercise."

"Me too. I'd love to go skiing with you this afternoon." Adopting a casual tone, although she didn't feel casual about it at all, she added, "How about you come with me to church, and we go after that?"

In the process of licking syrup off his thumb, Josh gave her a sharp look. "Come again?"

"Come to church with me this morning. Sit with me. Afterward, we can go skiing. I'll pack a lunch before we go."

"Caitlin, that's not a good idea. That's about as public a place as you get in Eternity Springs. News that we were together will be all over town before the end of the Altar Society's bake sale."

"I know. That's fine by me. I'm over the whole secrecy thing. It's been fun, but I'm tired of sneaking around. I'm tired of my dad trying to set me up with Boone McBride."

Josh's brow furrowed with a scowl. It had not missed Caitlin's notice that her father's efforts on the Boone front stuck in Josh's craw.

"Will your parents be there?" he asked.

"Yes. They don't miss church when they are in town."

Josh drummed his fingers on the table. "I don't know. Maybe we should think about this some before we jump off and do it."

"I have thought about it. All we will be saying is that we are dating. It's okay for me to date. I got that privilege on my sixteenth birthday."

"They made you wait until you were sixteen?"

"Oh yeah."

Josh rose from his seat and carried his plate to the sink. She could all but see the wheels turning in his head as he began to rinse the dishes and load the dishwasher.

She topped off her coffee mug and leaned against the counter, waiting.

After almost a full five minutes of thought, he said, "Your dad wouldn't cause a scene in church."

"No, he wouldn't."

"Okay, then. Well." He shot a look at her over his shoulder. "I'll go to church with you this morning, Caitlin. You'd better hurry and get dressed. We should arrive early in plenty of time to say our prayers. I'm afraid we're going to need them."

He was right. This turned out to be her father's day to usher. A smile blossomed on his face when she stepped into the church. It quickly died when he saw just who had come with her.

"Good morning, Dad," she chimed, pretending she didn't see the tension.

"Good morning, honey." Mac bent and kissed her chin, then nodded stiffly toward Josh. "Tarkington."

"Good morning, sir."

Josh's amused smirk didn't help the situation any, but Caitlin knew when to pick her battles. The door opened again behind him, and elderly Mrs. Wilson shuffled inside. Caitlin seized the opportunity. "We'll find our own seats, Dad. You help Mrs. Wilson."

Caitlin dashed up the aisle to take a seat a few rows behind her mother. No way would she sit in the path of her father's laser eyes.

Reverend Montgomery gave a thought-provoking sermon about modern influences on the season of Advent that struck a chord with Caitlin. She gave Josh a sidelong look and decided that they'd have the gift-giving talk soon.

After the sermon, the congregation sung a hymn, and her father and another usher walked up the aisle carrying the offering baskets. When Mac was two rows away,

Josh reached into his pocket for his wallet. Caitlin saw the two men's gazes meet, and then the strangest thing happened.

In the process of handing the offering basket from one row to the next, Mac dropped it. He didn't fumble it. He simply dropped it. Bills and change and church envelopes went flying everywhere.

But the act of dropping the offering wasn't what Caitlin considered strange. It wasn't the first time a basket had been spilled and it wouldn't be the last. The strange part was the expression that flashed through her father's eyes as his gaze flew to meet her mother's.

Her father looked stricken. He looked scared.

In that moment, fear rumbled through Caitlin too.

Shortly before noon the following Tuesday at the end of a hectic morning, Josh took Penny outside to tend to her physical needs, then saw her settled on a dog bed in his theater room. Caitlin had smiled tenderly at him when he told her that Penny enjoyed the colors and sounds of TV, then she suggested the Disney Channel. Now *Paw Patrol* was a definite favorite. And if Josh sat and watched with his dog for an episode every so often, well, what was wrong with that?

Today, Penny would be watching by herself. He hung the OUT TO LUNCH sign on his front door, grabbed his wallet, and headed for the Mocha Moose to pick up the order he'd placed an hour ago. He'd learned an important lesson about life in Eternity Springs over the course of the past two days. Any time business started lagging, all he needed to do in order to goose his sales was to show up to church with a girl.

There'd been a near steady stream of people in and out of the shop since he opened Monday morning. Both regulars and new customers. An amazing number of folks just happened to stop by to purchase a soft drink from the machine he kept in the front office. He had a rush on oil changes and brake fluid checks and tire rotations—all by people who lingered to visit either before or after the service.

Every one of his visitors attempted to pump Josh for information about Caitlin—How long had he'd been seeing her? Was it exclusive? Was it serious? He managed to deflect most of the questions, though Sarah Murphy surely won the persistence prize because she hadn't quit until she wormed out of him the fact that no, he wasn't dating anyone else. He and Caitlin had definitely gone public—with a capital P. It surprised him that he didn't really mind.

He arrived at the Mocha Moose to find his order ready and waiting for him. "I switched out one of the turkey sandwiches for pimento cheese," the proprietor, Wendy Davis, told him. "Caitlin Timberlake is wild about my pimento cheese."

"I don't recall mentioning Caitlin when I ordered."

Wendy rolled her eyes. "You ordered one turkey with horseradish. There's only one person in town who eats turkey with horseradish—Jax Lancaster. If you're buying this many sandwiches and one of them is for Jax, then you're buying lunch for his whole crew. And Caitlin is at Gingerbread House today because she's meeting the designer. It just makes sense that one of these sandwiches is for her. You and Caitlin have a lunch date."

Small towns. Living in one was a love/hate relationship.

But Josh couldn't argue with her logic. She'd gotten it exactly right. He picked up the crate stacked high with bags of sandwiches and sides and headed for the door saying, "Thanks, Wendy. I'll be sure to tell Caitlin she has you to thank for the pimento cheese."

"'Preciate you. Now you be careful with your hands so full, and watch your step on the sidewalk—there's still some icy patches in the shade."

"I will."

"See you Thursday."

"Am I that predictable?"

"Nah . . . you having a thing for Caitlin was a total surprise. I had you paired with that friend of Chase's from college who visits from time to time."

Josh didn't have a clue as to whom she was talking about, but as he walked the few short blocks to Ginger-bread House, he marveled at the power of the Eternity Springs telegraph. It was a minor miracle that he and Caitlin had been so successful in keeping their secret.

The topic of secrets brought the incident in church on Sunday back to mind. Caitlin had brooded about it throughout the afternoon they'd spent cross-country ski-ing up at Stardance River Camp. He hoped she'd learned something from her mother on their shopping spree yes-terday that settled her worries.

At Gingerbread House, he found Caitlin with a paint-brush in her hand in what would be the two-year-olds' room downstairs. "Hello, beautiful."

Her face lit up like the town Christmas tree in Daven-port Park. She set down her paintbrush and rushed toward him. "Josh!"

She gave him a one-armed hug, keeping the hand wet with green paint safely away, and kissed him. "I missed you yesterday."

"I missed you too. How did the shopping extravaganza go?"

She rolled her eyes. "I'll tell you when we are alone. Maybe after I have a glass of wine."

"That bad?"

"Not bad. Frustrating. Now, let's get sandwiches

passed out before the crew gets restless. You're their favorite person now, you know. People don't ordinarily spring for lunch."

"I'm trying to butter them up to do some fixes at my place."

"Fixes? Already? Your place is brand new!"

"Nothing major. Just a few minor changes I've realized I want after living there a while."

She folded her arms. "Don't even begin to think of stealing the crew away from me before I'm finished with them."

"Yes ma'am." He winked at her, and then together they passed out sandwiches and chips, potato salad and slaw. Caitlin gave him a quick tour of the latest renovations, then they settled into the front porch swing to enjoy their own meal. Josh set it swaying with a push of his foot and sighed with satisfaction. "Beautiful weather. Beautiful woman. A roast beef sandwich that's a work of art." He gave her a quick, hard kiss, then added, "It doesn't get any better than this."

He unwrapped his roast beef and took a bite, a contented man.

"We're lucky to be able to sit outside this time of year," Jax Lancaster said from the porch step where he sat plowing through his turkey sandwich with extra horseradish. His gaze kept drifting toward the house across the street. His wife had called a few minutes ago to say she and their daughter were visiting Harriet and they would stop by on their way home.

"We'd better enjoy it while we can," Caitlin licked pimento cheese off her fingers. "I'm happy to see the sun again. It's been so dreary the past few days, and I'd have sworn I heard sleet hitting the roof last night."

"I heard it too," Jax said. "I was up with the baby around three and it was pinging against the windows. It was nice to wake up to sunshine this morning. The forecast says . . . oh. There's Claire and Julianna. Excuse me." He rose and strode away toward the pretty redhead who was trying to maneuver a stroller through the front doorway of Harriet's house.

"He is so over the moon about that baby," Caitlin said, smiling. "It's fun to watch. I keep wondering when Chase and Lori are going to take the leap into parenthood. I suspect Chase will be even more giddy about fatherhood than Jax."

The topic sent unease slithering up Josh's spine. He quickly pivoted to another subject. "So tell me about the shopping trip. Did your mom give you the third degree?"

"Yes. And the fourth and fifth. Of course, I was doing the same thing to her, so we had a bit of a grilling standoff."

"You asked her about your dad's reaction to dropping the collection basket?"

"I did. I actually talked to them both about it. I spoke to Dad when I picked Mom up at their house yesterday morning. I flat out asked him why he looked so disturbed about it. He blew me off. Told me I was imagining things, that it was nothing more than a flash of embarrassed regret. When I brought it up to Mom, she did exactly the same thing."

Josh took a thoughtful bite of his sandwich and considered swallowing the question hovering on his tongue. The little line of worry between her brow settled it for him, so he said, "I'm aware that I'm probably stepping way out onto a limb here, but isn't it possible they're telling you the truth? The lighting inside the church isn't great on a sunny day, and it rained Sunday morning. It was dark inside St. Stephen's."

"I know," Caitlin sighed and slapped his hand when he stole a potato chip off her plate.

He shared one of his corn chips. "I suspect if you saw anything, it was embarrassment. You dad caused a minor scene. He doesn't strike me as the type to be happy about that."

"He's not. You could be right, Josh. Maybe I was seeing things. Nevertheless, it was a weird moment. Another in a long list of weird parent moments of late. Maybe it's the whole retirement thing. Chase and I are both a bit baffled by that. He's never suggested that he wanted to hang up his shingle for good."

"I think you should take them at their word and let it go." He gave the swing another push and added, "If you need to fret, do it over the poor choice of paint color you made for the two-year-olds' room."

She went stiff. "What? What's wrong with it?"

"It's green." Josh smothered a smile.

"Yes, a lovely shade of green."

"It's pee green. Not with an 'a,' but with an 'e.' With a room full of two-year-olds, don't you think you're going to have all that color you can manage as it is? Why plant suggestions in their heads?"

"It's not pee green," she chided. "It's parakeet green and it's part of the color palette Sage helped me choose."

He shrugged. "Whatever you say."

When she frowned and began digging around in her bag for the notebook that had become her Gingerbread House bible, he knew he'd managed to distract her from her worries about her parents, which had been his goal. He'd made a mistake by bringing the subject up in the first place.

Although he didn't regret shifting the conversation away from babies one bit.

"Parakeet green is a fine color," she muttered as Jax started up the steps carrying his daughter, Julianna. At eleven months old, she was a beautiful little butterball who'd taken her first steps last Wednesday. If Jax was over the moon about her, Claire was giddy. Their son Nicholas was the Lancaster who amused Josh. He loved his little sister, he was quick to tell anyone who asked, but she wasn't anywhere near as awesome as his dog.

"Hi, Claire," Caitlin said. "I love Julianna's hat. Where did you get it? Do you know if they come in adult sizes? A stocking cap with hound dog ears would be a perfect stocking stuffer for Lori."

"Actually, they do come in adult sizes. I stock these hats at Forever Christmas in the Dog House. Nicholas insisted. I think I have a boxer and a dachshund left."

"Perfect. Hold the dachshund for me, would you please? I'll stop by this afternoon to get it. Speaking of holding . . . are you going to hog your daughter, Jax, or share?"

"I'll share. For a few minutes, anyway."

As Jax handed the baby over to Caitlin, Josh asked, "Claire, would you like a sandwich? We have a few left over. Turkey and ham, I think."

"No thanks, I ate with Harriet."

They discussed their friend's recovery for a few minutes, then at Caitlin's insistence, they all went inside to view and discuss parakeet green. To Caitlin's smug satisfaction, Josh was outvoted. The conversation had turned to plans for Christmas when the baby started fussing and Jax got a call from one of his suppliers.

Josh met Caitlin's gaze. "Lunch break is over. I need to get back to work. Are we still on for supper?"

"Absolutely. I pulled pork chops out of the freezer before I left home this morning."

"Awesome."

"I'm leaving too," Claire said. "I need to get back to the store and put Jules down for her nap." She finger-waved to her husband and walked outside with Josh and

Caitlin where she settled Julianna into her stroller and said her goodbyes.

"Thanks for lunch," Caitlin said to Josh, going up on her toes to give him a quick kiss.

"You're very welcome. I'll see you tonight."

"See you tonight. You're going to love my pork chops."

"I already do, babe." He gave her a teasing wink, stole a quick kiss of his own, and headed toward the shop.

He was a few yards behind Claire when a loud crash boomed from inside the house along with the sound of Jax's pain-filled shout. At that point, time slowed to a crawl.

Oh God.

Josh saw Claire whirl around, take a step . . . and land on a patch of ice. Her feet flew out from beneath her and she fell, losing her grip on the stroller. The stroller began to roll down the sloping driveway toward the street— and the approaching car.

Josh ran. Seconds ticked by like hours. He ran as hard and as fast as he'd ever run before. Dread filled him. In that place where his nightmares lived, he'd have sworn he heard the freight-train roar of a tornado.

The stroller rolled downhill and out into the street. In front of the car that showed no signs of stopping.

No, God. No. Not again. Not another child.

He lunged toward the stroller handle with his hands outstretched, touched it, and gave it a mighty shove.

My damn bad luck strikes again.

Pain exploded and the world went black.

Journal Entry

Sherman, meet your new neighbor, the new monster on the block. He's Italian. Call him Tormento.

Chapter Fourteen

Caitlin stood trembling in shock outside the Eternity Springs Medical Clinic as the air ambulance lifted off the ground. The *whop, whop, whop* of the helicopter's blades beat like her heart, reverberating through her bones, stirring up a bile of fear and disbelief and helplessness in her stomach.

"Here honey," her mother said. "Let me see your hands."

The child in her accustomed to obeying lifted her arms. Ali clucked her tongue and murmured soothing words as she used a damp washrag to wipe the blood from Caitlin's hands and arms.

Josh's blood. Red. Sticky. Everywhere. It had been everywhere.

A band of tension wrapped Caitlin's chest, and she could barely breathe. Her gaze remained locked on the blue and yellow helicopter as it rose high and headed north. When it faded to a speck in the sky, she said, "I need to go. I need to go now."

"Dad is bringing the car. He's on his way."

"He needs to hurry, Mom."

"He'll be right here."

The sound of a fussing child finally snagged Caitlin's

attention away from the sky. She turned to see Jax rolling Claire out of the building in a wheelchair, Julianna tucked safely in her mother's arms.

Ali asked, "How are you? How's the baby?"

"The baby is fine," Jax said. "Just a little scrape on her face from when the stroller tipped over. Claire sprained her knee and she has a knot on the back of her head where she hit the driveway, but she's not concussed. I'm fine. Six stitches on my shoulder where I didn't move fast enough."

"What happened?"

"Entry hall light fixture fell. My bad luck to be standing beneath it. But what about Josh?"

"Yes," Claire said, "How is he?"

Caitlin tried to speak, but a knot of emotion closed her throat.

Her mother said, "Dr. Cicero and her team placed a chest tube for a pneumothorax and got him stabilized. He's on his way to the trauma center in Gunnison."

Dragging his hand down his face, Jax nodded. "Good. That's good. They have excellent doctors there."

"He saved her life," Claire said, her voice shaking with emotion. Fresh tears pooled in her eyes and ran down her cheeks. "Josh saved our baby's life."

"So I understand," Ali said. "How is Reverend Thomas doing?"

Reverend Bobby Thomas was the driver of the car that had hit Josh. The sixty-three-year-old was the pastor at the local Methodist church.

Jax said, "So far, so good. It's definitely a heart attack, but Dr. Cicero is cautiously optimistic."

"That's good."

"I think the best news they could give Reverend Thomas and all of us is the news that Josh will be okay." A thready little moan escaped the noose around Caitlin's throat. "Where's Daddy? I need to go. I'll just drive myself."

"No you won't," her mother said firmly. "You're in no shape to drive, sweetheart. Mac will be here . . . now. Here he comes."

Ali waved toward the black SUV turning into the clinic's drive and Mac slowed to a stop in front of them. Caitlin opened the back passenger door and climbed inside. Her mom took the front passenger seat. "Go fast, Daddy. Please?"

"I'll get you there as fast as is safely possible, sweetheart. I promise."

"Thank you."

Ali fastened her seatbelt saying, "Celeste texted me a few minutes ago. Caitlin, she thought that you would probably want your phone with you, so she retrieved you purse from Gingerbread House. She's waiting for us at the Angel Creek footbridge, so Mac, if you'll pull over to the curb, she'll bring it to us."

"Will do," he said. "I have some news too. Liliana called to tell us that Brick made a run into Gunnison this morning. He'd just started home when she called him with news of the accident, so he turned right around. He'll be at the trauma center shortly, and he's promised to phone us with updates on Tarkington's condition until we arrive."

"Josh!" Caitlin snapped, suddenly done with her father's attitude. She rubbed her eyes. "His name is Josh, Dad. Please hurry."

Her father pulled onto Cottonwood Street and headed north, and a few moments later, the car slowed. Her father hit the window buttons and both Caitlin's and her mother's rolled down. Celeste approached the SUV, took Ali's outstretched hand, and squeezed it.

"Thank you," Ali said.

"Happy to help," Celeste replied.

She handed Caitlin her purse, then reached into the back and took Caitlin's face in her hands. "My sweet angel," Celeste said, capturing Caitlin's gaze with somber blue eyes. "In the giving of your heart, you open it to fear. The trick is to remember that fear is the springboard for courage. Acknowledge your fear, and courage will become the wind beneath your wings."

Caitlin's eyes filled with fresh tears, her throat with a fresh lump of emotion, and she could do no more than nod at Celeste.

As her father pulled away from the curb and headed north, she turned her head and gazed out of the window, lost in thought. She was only vaguely aware of her parents' softly spoken conversation in the front seat as she silently prayed. *Please, God. Let him be all right. Please, God. Please God. Please God.*

Mac managed to shave ten minutes off the two-hour drive to Gunnison. Brick had called twice to report that he had nothing to report, that Josh was still in surgery.

"That's good news, don't you think?" Caitlin asked her mother. "He's alive. If he's still in surgery, he's still alive."

"Yes, I think it is good news," her mother replied.

By the time they finally approached the trauma center, tension coiled within Caitlin like a snake. One part of her wanted to dash from the car before it came to a stop. Another part wanted to pull her jacket over her head and hide until her daddy proved the monster waiting for her didn't really exist.

As they arrived at the trauma center, Celeste's words echoed through her mind. *Fear is the springboard for courage.*

She took three deep bracing breaths, and when her father pulled to a stop in front of the entrance, she sprang from the car and hurried inside.

A volunteer directed her to the surgical waiting room. She spied Brick sitting with his legs spread, his elbows resting on his knees. He stared down at a paper coffee cup, his expression strained and heartsick.

Her stomach sank. Her steps faltered. Her heart in her throat, she croaked. "Brick?"

His head snapped up. He rose to his feet and walked toward her. "As far as I know, he's still in surgery."

"Still? Why is it taking so long? And why did you say 'as far as I know'?"

"Things have gone crazy around here. They started flying in victims of a four-car pileup not long after Josh arrived, and it's all hands on deck. They're too busy trying to save lives to provide updates."

"So . . . what are you . . . you don't mean . . . he's dead. He's dead and they're just not telling us! That's not what you're saying!"

For an instant, she saw the doubt and uncertainty roll across Brick's eyes, and she knew he had the same concern she did. She swayed and her knees turned to jello. He reached out and caught her as she started to fall. He guided her into a chair saying, "No. No. Don't do that. Don't go there. We have absolutely no reason to think that. We have to think positive. They're busy, Caitlin."

Fear is the springboard for courage.

"Okay. You're right. Of course. Lives come first."

"Waiting sucks, but Josh couldn't be in better hands. The trauma center is new, with state-of-the-art facilities. The doctors and nurses are excellent. I know this because my grandfather is a major donor here. One thing about Branch Callahan, he looks after his own best interests. Once he realized how much time various members of the Callahan clan would be spending in the area, he made sure we'd have top-notch medical facilities available when we need them."

Caitlin had known the Callahan family had joined other prominent Eternity Springs residents to update and expand the medical clinic in town, but she hadn't known they'd taken their philanthropy this far. "That's reassuring."

"Yep. We need to keep the faith." If the intensity of his declaration seemed to be a reminder for himself, well, there was nothing wrong with that.

Movement in the doorway of the waiting room got their attention, and both stood as Brick's wife Lili enter the room with Caitlin's parents. Brick opened his arms as Lili crossed to embrace him. She asked, "Any news?"

"Not yet."

"No news is better than bad news," she added.

"Amen to that."

Lili turned to Caitlin and gave her a hug too, saying, "I'm glad you're here."

"I wanted to go with him on the ambulance. They wouldn't let me."

"Well, you're here now. You'll be here when he wakes up."

When he wakes up. Whether it was the confidence in Lili's voice or the compassion in her eyes, Caitlin couldn't say, but Lili touched off the storm of tears that had been building inside Caitlin since she saw the car strike Josh. She broke. "Oh Lili, I'm so scared. I can't lose him. I love him. I love him so much."

"I know. I know you do, honey." Lili wiped the tears from Caitlin's cheek, then took her hands and squeezed them. "You won't lose him. I haven't known Josh for very long, but one thing I learned right from the start is that you can count on him. He won't let you down. He won't quit. He is a fighter. He will fight his way back to us."

"She's right," Brick agreed. "You should have seen

him the time that—" He broke off abruptly when a nurse entered the waiting room.

"Tarkington family?"

"Yes," Brick and Caitlin said simultaneously.

"Doctor Draper is on his way. He'll speak with you in the conference room. This way, please."

As Caitlin stepped forward to follow the nurse through a pair of swinging doors, Brick grasped Lili's hand and motioned to her parents to join them, 'family' or not. The nurse gestured to a smaller room just on the other side of the doors.

Tension rolled through Caitlin's stomach and she felt lightheaded. *Please God. Please God. Please God.* The five of them had no sooner entered the conference room than a man wearing blue scrubs joined them.

His gaze swept the small room and he got straight to the point. "He's alive, and barring the unforeseen, I expect him to stay that way. I'm his surgeon, Alex Draper, and I have another patient being prepped for surgery, so I'll be brief.

"In addition to multiple rib fractures, Mr. Tarkington suffered lacerations to his spleen and a kidney, which caused extensive internal bleeding and required surgery. The good news is that as of now, he still has all his parts. We'll keep a close eye on the spleen especially, over the next few hours and days, but I'm optimistic. He's in recovery, but he's heavily sedated for pain control. Immediate family should be able to see him within the hour. I apologize for the brevity of this meeting. I'll be back to address your questions just as soon as I possibly can. It'll be at least an hour—probably more—but if you'll leave a phone number with the volunteer outside the waiting room, someone will call when we can give you a better idea of when I can tackle your questions."

The doctor exited the waiting room, and for a moment,

they all stood in stunned silence. Then Brick released a heavy breath and bent over, resting his hands on his knees.

Lili said, "Whoa."

Relief swept over Caitlin and she began to shake. She sank into the nearest chair, closed her eyes, and focused on breathing as she offered up silent prayers of thanksgiving.

A few moments later, Brick said, "I'd better make some calls. Let people know the good news."

"I know we weren't the only people making the drive from home," Lili added. "The waiting room is already getting crowded with families of the traffic-accident victims. I wonder if we shouldn't pick a spot for everyone to meet and wait together?"

Caitlin shook her head. "The doctor said we could see him within the hour."

"He said immediate family," her father pointed out.

Caitlin folded her arms, lifted her chin, and stated defiantly, "Who here is going to tell them I'm not immediate family?"

"Not us," her mother was quick to say. "Lili, I think choosing a meeting spot is a wonderful idea. Why don't Mac and I scout something out?"

"That would be good," Brick said. "Thanks."

Mac asked, "Is anyone hungry? We could make a cafeteria run too. Cait? How about an ice cream bar?"

Caitlin recognized the question as the peace offering it was. She gave a little smile and shook her head. "No thanks. Nothing for me, Dad."

"I'm fine," Lili said.

"I could use a sandwich," Brick told him. "Ham if they have it, but anything is fine."

Mac nodded and opened the conference room door. Before Ali stepped outside, she crossed over to the chair where Caitlin sat, bent over, and kissed her daughter's head. "I'm glad he's doing well, baby."

"Thanks, Mom."

Once her parents had gone, Brick excused himself to make his phone calls. Lili indicated her need for the ladies' room and stepped outside.

Alone, Caitlin bowed her head. Exhaustion rolled over her like morning fog in the valley. She wasn't sure she could have stood if she'd wanted to. The only other time she'd been this afraid had been those awful, terrifying weeks when Chase had been missing in Chizickstan. Fear was a powerful emotion, and it occurred to her now that the depth of its experience went hand in hand with love.

She'd known she'd fallen in love with Josh, but today had proved to her just how deeply her heart was involved.

I'm in this. All the way in this.

And he doesn't want a relationship.

He's afraid of relationships.

He's going to hurt me.

"Fear is the springboard for courage," she murmured. Josh had certainly put his fear and courage on full display today. He'd feared for Jax's daughter and sprang courageously to save her. So what did that tell Caitlin? She believed he loved her. Maybe he never said it, but he showed it with his actions. So what had the events of today proven to her? That he was courageous with his body but cowardly with his heart?

Or maybe he hadn't been tested yet. If she'd been the one closest to Julianna Lancaster, she liked to think she would have acted courageously too. If their situations were reversed right now, what would Josh be thinking? Would he still be standing on that springboard testing the bounce? Or would fear have provided the nerve he needed to jump into the deep end of the love pool?

The love pool? Seriously? Caitlin, you've cracked. She'd embarrassed herself with the cheesiness of that analogy.

And why was she worrying about this now, anyway? Josh was lying in a hospital bed fighting for his life. She should be thinking about that.

Except, she didn't want to think about it. It was scary. Still way too scary. She didn't want to lose him—physically or emotionally. She loved him. Madly, truly, deeply loved him, and she'd be lost without him.

"Fear is the springboard for courage" didn't cut it in this situation. She needed Celeste to show up and give her some words of wisdom that fit the current situation.

Knowing Celeste, she might well be out in the waiting room right now. She had a way of being there when she was needed.

The thought propelled Caitlin to her feet, and she exited the conference room and returned to the waiting room. What she found there reminded her of one of the reasons she'd moved to Eternity Springs, and it brought forth a fresh flow of tears.

The waiting room was packed. Yes, Celeste was here. So were Chase and Lori, Nic and Gabe Callahan, the Murphys, the Garretts, the Turners, the Davenports, Brogans, Ciceros, Raffertys, and Romanos.

Eternity Springs had come to support its newest hero.

Mac and Ali Timberlake spoke with a volunteer at the information desk who suggested a waiting room not far from ICU where those waiting for word about Josh could gather. Then they went to the cafeteria, ordered soup and salad for themselves and a sandwich for Brick, and spoke with the manager about putting together an afternoon tea type of menu for their group. Ali gave the manager her phone number and said, "If you'll call when the trays are ready, we'll send some people down to pick them up."

Mac was hungry and he polished off half his salad before broaching the subject that had been plaguing him for hours now. "She's serious about this guy, isn't she?"

Ali looked at her husband over the top of her soup-spoon. "Yes, she is."

"I don't know why she doesn't see how perfect Boone is for her."

Ali set down her spoon hard. "And I don't know why you won't accept that she's chosen Josh Tarkington."

Mac speared a cherry tomato with his fork. "I don't like him."

"Yes, that's obvious to everyone. You've done everything but rent a billboard. We've been down this road before and I still don't understand, Mac. By all appearances, Josh is a good guy. Look at what he did today. He saved that baby. He's a hero."

Mac shrugged. "Well, we'll see what he is. I've hired an investigator."

"You what?" Ali said, her voice a near screech.

"I hired an investigator." He squared his shoulders. "I need to know who and what he is, Alison. I need to know where he came from."

"What you need to do is trust your daughter!"

"I do . . . well . . . except when it comes to men. Face it, Alison, she's made some terrible choices in the past. If Tarkington is another one of those, I want to know while I still have the faculties to do something about it. Sure, she usually figures it out in time, but I don't have time. I want . . . I need . . . to see her settled with a good man before I die."

Ali reared back as if from a physical blow. Seeing her stricken look made him feel guilty, and the sensation intensified when tears pooled in her eyes.

"Dammit, Ali," he muttered.

She scooted back her chair and rose. "Excuse me. I need another napkin. I'll be right back."

Mac closed his eyes and dropped his chin to his chest. He was physically weary and emotionally exhausted. And underlying all of it was a bubbling, seething slough of anger that didn't go away.

He should apologize for making her cry and say something comforting. But he was tired. He was heartsick. And dammit, he was more than a little afraid.

Then he dropped his soupspoon and the anger erupted.

Mac shoved to his feet and stalked from the cafeteria and through the nearest door that led outside. Cold air enveloped him. He wanted to run, to pick up his heels and run as hard and as fast as he could. He wanted to outrun the monster nipping at his feet.

Instead he shoved his hands into the back pockets of his jeans and paced the half-empty parking lot. Up and back. Up and back. Up and back. His blood churning. His thoughts spinning. He had so much to do. So much to get settled. For Ali. For Caitlin. The boys were both okay. They would manage.

He'd wanted to be a granddad to children of Chase and of Caitlin. Stephen's little ones were the light of his life, but they lived in Texas now. He'd had dreams of being more involved in his grandkids' lives. He'd wanted to take a grandson hiking and fishing and camping. He'd wanted to buy a pony for his granddaughter. Every little girl wanted a horse at some point in her childhood. He'd wanted to ride bikes with them to Fresh for donuts on Saturday morning. He'd wanted a grandchild on his lap Sunday morning in church.

"Mac?"

At the sound of Ali's voice, he halted. He took a moment to blink away the moisture in his eyes before turning around to face his wife.

"Are you okay?"

He couldn't keep the bitterness from his voice as he laughed and repeated, "Okay? For a guy who's dying, I guess I'm okay."

At that, Alison's temper flared. Her eyes fired and the hands at her side fisted. One part of Mac observed and admired her. Ordinarily calm, cool, and collected, Ali's classic, sophisticated beauty had always attracted him. But when she got angry, when color flooded her cheeks and her eyes glittered and attitude blasted from every pore, she'd always turned him on.

"Mackenzie Timberlake!" she snapped.

"That's me," he fired back.

She wanted to fight. He did too. This wasn't the best place, the most opportune time, but this had been a long time coming. He looked around, spied the evergreen hedge that he knew from previous visits enclosed the trauma center's prayer garden. Considering the increasingly bitter bite to the afternoon air, he thought chances were good that they'd have the place to themselves.

"C'mere." He took her arm and propelled her toward the garden. "We're not doing this in public."

She shook off his grasp and increased her speed, walking ahead of him. Once inside the enclosure, Ali whirled on him, braced her hands on her hips, and declared, "You have to quit saying you're dying."

"Why? Because you don't want to face the truth? Well guess what, Alison? I have to face it. I have to face it and prepare for it and make sure that you and Caitlin especially will be okay once I'm gone."

"Stop it! Just stop it! You don't know that you're dying."

"I wonder if Lou Gehrig's wife tried to bury her head this deep in the sand too."

Ali screeched, balled up her fist, and socked him in the stomach. "I might well kill you before ALS gets the chance!"

Suddenly, Mac's anger died. With complete sincerity, he said, "I wish you would, Ali-cat. I really wish you would."

His words and tone were a cloudburst that doused the fire of her anger. Ali buried her face in her hands and began to cry. Mac wrapped her in his arms, and just for a few moments, allowed himself to cry with her.

But his need to comfort his wife rose above everything else. "Hush, honey. It's okay. I'm sorry I was so blunt."

She lifted red, tear-swollen eyes that pleaded with him. "I can't give up hope. You can't ask that of me. We don't know for sure that you have ALS. Every doctor we visited said it takes nine to twelve months to get a definitive diagnosis. The soonest we'll know for sure is when we return to the specialist in March. We still have over two months to hope. Don't steal that from us."

"Oh honey." He leaned down and kissed the tracks of her tears. "I'm not trying to steal anything. I haven't given up all hope that time will prove the diagnosis wrong, but neither can I deny the truth that is staring me in the face. My symptoms grow worse every day. Look at what happened in church last Sunday. Today, I couldn't hold my spoon. I broke down and used a cane this morning. My body is beginning to fail me. It would be negligent of me not to get my affairs in order."

"That sounds so . . . funereal."

"Okay. I won't use that term again." Mac tenderly pushed Ali's hair away from her face. "Alison, I need you to do something for me."

"Anything."

"You know that I am a very controlling person."

"Uh, duh!" She snorted. "Why do you think Chase hid your judge's gavel?"

He shared a smile with her. "Well, that particular quality of mine just makes this whole situation more difficult to swallow. I can deal with dying, Alison. We're all going to die sometime. But the idea of losing control of my body bit by bit while my mind remains the same— that scares the living daylights out of me."

"I know, Mac."

"Because of my nature and what I'm facing with this disease, I have this fierce need inside of me to take care of my loved ones while I can. I need you to let me do it."

"Oh Mac. I understand. Honestly, I do. But if our greatest fears come true, if you truly do have ALS, then don't you see how important it will be for Caitlin to have someone she can lean on?"

"I know. That's why I want to see her settled."

"If that's your motivation, then you need to take off your blinders where Josh Tarkington is concerned. Caitlin loves him. You saw that today. She's made her choice. You need to trust in her judgment and accept it—accept him. Otherwise, you will both be miserable and it will spoil the time you have left with her, whether that's one year or fifty years."

Mac touched his forehead to hers. "You have a point. I accept that. Watching Caitlin worry for the man broke my heart today. I don't want conflict with my daughter these last months, so I will promise to try where Tarkington is concerned."

"Good."

"However, that doesn't mean I'm calling off my private investigator."

"You should rethink that decision. You're risking your daughter's wrath and possibly her respect."

"It's a risk I must take, Alison. Josh Tarkington might be Eternity Springs' newest hero, but he has his eyes on one of my prizes. I intend to make sure that he is worthy of her."

Journal Entry

Detox.

The word itself is enough to give me the shakes.
Withdrawal is a bitch with teeth and claws who leaps at me in sneak attacks, one after the other. That's what I remember about the first time in rehab. Fix one misery, another pounces. The sweats? I can deal with that. Hot. Cold. Shudders.

Craving.
Shoot me up with something else.
Then, my eyes. I'm crying . . . only I'm not. Tears pour from my eyes and my nose runs and runs and I start to ache. My back. My legs. The worst flu of my life.
Craving.
Shoot me up with something else.
The bugs . . . the bugs are crawling all over me. I vomit.
I crave it.
Hell. I am in hell.
I am fourteen years old.

Chapter Fifteen

"Mr. Tarkington? Mr. Tarkington? I'm Jenny. I'll be taking care of you until we get you into a room."

Jenny. Penny. Copper Penny. *Did I feed her today?*

"You're not Penny."

"Jenny Hill. I'm going to take care of you while you're with us in recovery. I'm going to raise the bed a little now."

A motor hummed, and Josh felt himself rising.

"Here's your water." She handed him a plastic cup with a bent straw.

"This is your PCA pump, Mr. Tarkington. It allows you to control your pain medication. The anesthetic will be wearing off, Mr. Tarkington. We want you to stay on top of your pain. When you begin to hurt, press the button and it will give you a dose of medicine. You don't need to worry that you will accidentally overdose, because it's set to prevent that."

Overdose. Shoot me up. Just shoot me.

"You're in control."

Control. Awe . . . no. No. No. No. No.
Push the button. Push it. Push it. I'm lost.

* * *

Josh opened his eyes. Above him loomed a smiling woman wearing green scrubs. Her blue-gloved hand stretched out toward him holding a small cup with two capsules inside. His head swam. Disjointed thoughts fluttered through his mind like tattered ribbons floating on a breeze. There was something . . . something important. Just beyond reach.

He tried to sit up. Pain sawed through him like the blade of a serrated knife. He gasped.

"No. No." She placed a gentle hand on his shoulder. "Don't get ahead of yourself. Here. "I want you to swallow these. We want you to stay ahead of the pain."

She tipped the cup and the capsules spilled into his hand. He simply stared at them. "Swallow the capsules, Mr. Tarkington."

She bumped his hand a little and he instinctively raised it to his mouth. She lifted an insulated cup from a bedside tray and guided a straw to his mouth. She waited until he sipped and swallowed. "Good. That's good."

Josh stared up at her, straining to catch the thought that hung like a black cloud just beyond his consciousness.

Jenny. Penny. Copper Penny. Money Penny. Crap. What the hell is wrong with me?

He didn't care. He closed his eyes, drifted away. *I'll care later.*

Pain. Fire. God help me. Make it stop. Make it stop. Pain. Fire. God help me. I can't do this. I shouldn't do this. Not again. Not again. I can't do this. I can't go through this again. Please, God, make it stop.

"Stand up, Mr. Tarkington. There you go. We have you. Want you to take a few steps."

Mother lovin' son of a ball bustin' bitch. It hurts.

"Great job. You did great. Here is your next dose of Percocet." *God help me, I'm down the rabbit hole again. I'll never climb out.*

Josh's eyes flickered open and he gazed up at an unfamiliar ceiling. He blinked. *What the . . . ? Where am I?* "Josh?"

He turned his head toward the voice. "Caitlin."

She smiled like an angel. "Hey there, handsome. Are you back with us?"

He took stock. His chest hurt. His gut was on fire. He had an IV tube stuck in his arm and . . . aw hell . . . a catheter up his dick. *Hospital. I'm in a hospital.* He closed his eyes and gave his head a little shake. "What happened?"

She spoke in a soothing tone. "There was an accident. You were hit by a car, but you are going to be fine, Josh. Don't worry. You're going to be just fine."

He studied her face and read the truth in her expression. Something gave him the impression that this wasn't the first time she'd said those words to him.

An accident. He frowned. He felt weak as a sick kitten and his mind was mush. "I was hit by a car."

"Yes." Caitlin stepped closer to the bed, took his hand, and explained what had happened. Josh struggled to make sense of it. The baby. Oh hell. He remembered the stroller. "Is she all right? Jax's little girl?"

"She's fine. She's wonderful. You saved her, Josh. You're a hero."

Him? A hero? He'd snort except he thought doing so would hurt.

Caitlin continued her explanation of events since the accident, but Josh had a difficult time concentrating on what she was saying. He hurt all over. Breathing was a bitch. And his belly . . . he reached inside him and ripped out his guts, He lifted his hand to his chest. Big bandage there. "What . . . um . . . ?"

"The doctor was in this morning and he said you're healing well," she continued, then gave him a summation of his injuries.

Bruised lung. Spleen. Huh. Josh tried to recall the purpose of the spleen. He couldn't. No wonder he felt so sore inside. His guts *had* been ripped apart. "You said how many broken ribs?"

"Three. I have to tell you, Josh, when I saw you dive in front of that car, saw you bounce off the grill and hit the windshield, those were the longest seconds of my life. The worst."

He couldn't remember anything after seeing the stroller roll. "How long have I been here?"

"This is the morning of the third day."

Three days. He'd lost three days? The last time he'd lost three days he'd been strung out on junk. At the thought, Josh's heart began to thud. "Did I hit my head?"

Caitlin's smile turned sympathetic. "Yes. You have a knot on your left side, a little above and behind your ear. But it's just a bump, not a brain injury. You don't need to worry about that."

Josh didn't know if that made him feel better or worse.

"I can't remember any of this."

"I imagine it's because of the pain meds you're on."

He went totally still. Pain meds. Of course they'd given him pain meds. *Oh, holy hell.*

His voice emerged with a croak. "What were they, do you know?" Aspirin? Ibuprofen?

He knew long before she flashed a grin and said,

"You've been on the good stuff. Dilaudid first. Percocet the last couple of days. We had a couple of interesting conversations. The first time I didn't realize that you weren't aware."

Sickness spread through Josh. Bile rose in his throat and he reached for the plastic kidney-shaped bowl on the bedside cabinet because he feared he would vomit.

Josh closed his eyes, willing his stomach to settle. He needed to think. He needed to assess. He needed to plan.

"I need to be alone."

"Excuse me?"

The hurt in her voice was unmistakable, but he didn't have the patience or energy to pick and choose his words. He needed action. He searched the bedclothes for a call button for a nurse and pushed it. "I need a nurse. I want to use the john."

"Oh. Of course." She gave his leg a pat before moving toward the door. "I'll tell her you're awake and with us this time."

Josh stopped her at the doorway. "Caitlin? Thanks for being here."

"I wouldn't be anywhere else."

Yeah. That's what Josh was afraid of. One of many things he feared. He looked at the IV bag hanging beside his bed as fear like he'd seldom known before overwhelmed him.

He ripped the line from his arm. He shoved the IV pole and sent it crashing to the floor.

A nurse rushed into the room, Caitlin on her heels.

"What happened here? Oh, Mr. Tarkington, you shouldn't try to get up by yourself. You must wait until someone is here to help you."

She righted the IV pole, then reached for Josh's arm

to inspect it. Using his opposite hand, he grabbed her arm and stopped her. "Nothing else. Nothing else until I speak to the doctor."

"No!" he snapped. "Not another fluid or drug or line goes into my body until I've spoken to a doctor or I'll sue this hospital and everyone in it!"

The nurse was taken aback. Josh released her arm and she stepped away from the bed. Caitlin stepped forward. "Josh—"

He cut her off. "Cait, I've got this. I'm sure things at home need your attention."

"But—"

"I've asked for privacy. Nurse, please. Surely I have some rights as a patient."

He might as well have hit her. Caitlin's face drained of color. Her eyes shone with pain. Without another word, she turned and fled.

Josh knew he was being an ass, but he had bigger problems than that right now. He hurt like a sonofabitch from head to toe, but that was nothing compared to the dread—the fear—that had settled in the marrow of his bones.

He shut his eyes and dropped his head back onto his pillow. *Oh God. I can't. I can't do this again. All I've built. This great new life. And Caitlin. Caitlin. I'll lose it all. Poof. Gone. Better the damn car had squashed me like a bug.*

Josh would rather be dead than fight this fight again.

He heard the sound of his door opening and footsteps clicking against the tile floor. The nurse said, "Doctor Davis. Mr. Tarkington is awake and . . . well . . . we seem to have a problem."

Josh opened his eyes to see a fifty-something brunette

wearing a white coat and a frown approach the computer that he assumed registered his medical records. Records that had one vital piece of information missing.

He should tell the doctor about his past. He knew he should. It was stupid to keep that part of his medical history from his caretakers.

But . . . hell . . . he couldn't. He was so afraid. Hurting like hell. And dammit, ashamed. So ashamed. Shamed to the marrow of his bones.

The shame and the pain churned in his gut, creating a sour bile that bordered on panic. Screw this. Screw this. Doctors might be great in emergencies, but when had they ever helped him with this particular problem? How many doctors had he seen? Dozens? How many had helped him? Zero!

He'd had to fight this fight, battle this monster, alone.

The doctors hadn't helped. His mother damn sure hadn't helped. Hell, even the Christophers hadn't helped, though they'd tried.

He had to do this alone. Again.

He cleared his throat. "I'm not a prisoner. You can't keep me here. I'm checking myself out. I'm going home today."

"He can't stay by himself," Caitlin told Brick and Lili Callahan later that afternoon in the hallway outside Josh's room. "It wouldn't be safe."

"He can stay with us," Brick and Lili said simultaneously.

Caitlin shook her head. "You're still newlyweds. He wouldn't want to invade your privacy. Believe me, he's big on privacy today."

"Paul and Cindy are seriously upset that they can't be here to help," Brick said.

Caitlin asked. "How are they feeling today?"

"Not much better, I'm afraid. It's apparently a wicked strain of flu. Paul is worried that Cindy might end up in the hospital herself. If that happens, I'm heading to Oklahoma no matter how hard they argue against it."

"Please send them my get-well-soon wishes," Caitlin said. "As far a Josh goes, I could take him to my place, but I think instead I'll stay with him at his house. He'll be more comfortable there."

"Are you sure you want to do that, Caitlin?" Lili asked. "I've been around bad patients in the past, but after our visit today, I have to say that he takes the prize."

"He says it's the hospital, that hospitals give him the heebie-jeebies. I think he'll be better when we get him home." She paused a moment before adding, "I hope."

Brick showed her a crooked grin. "Well, if you need any help, don't hesitate to call. I know the Lancasters would like to help in any and every way possible."

"I predict you'll get so much food delivered that you won't need to cook until Valentine's Day," Lili said.

"Easter, I imagine," Caitlin agreed. "There is something you could do to help, Brick. If you'll drive him home, I could go on ahead and get things ready for him. Change the sheets and turn up the heat. Pick Penny up from Lori's so that she'll be there to welcome him when he gets home."

"That would be good. It's always nice to come home to a dog ecstatic to see you."

Moments later, Caitlin slipped back into Josh's room in order to explain the arrangements, but he was sleeping. Later on the drive back to Eternity Springs, she reflected on the day and silently admitted that playing nurse to a healing Josh might take every bit of patience she possessed.

He'd been a jerk to her that morning. After his shower,

he'd asked her to return to his room, and he'd offered a perfectly acceptable apology and explanation for his rudeness.

A hospital phobia might be part of it, she thought, but she'd bet pain also contributed to his aggressive mood. He roared like the lion with a thorn in his paw. Caitlin had never been much of a mouse, but she guessed there was a first time for everything. In the wake of this trauma, he needed time for everything. She'd seen the same thing with Chase. He'd been a five-star grouch. He'd needed time and space and a dog and Lori to heal. He'd needed Eternity Springs.

Caitlin sang along to songs on the Christmas music station during the two-hour drive home. Upon arriving in Eternity Springs, she stopped by the Trading Post for groceries and picked up Josh's dog from the vet where she'd been boarded. At his house, she changed the sheets, made a pot of potato soup for their supper, and in deference to his sweet tooth, mixed a batch of chocolate chip cookies.

She felt disturbingly like a housewife.

Brick and Lili arrived with Josh at half past four. It quickly became apparent that his mood hadn't improved with the drive. Brick helped him to his room and into his bed for a two-hour nap. When they sat down to supper, Caitlin was encouraged to see that his appetite was strong. He ate two bowls of soup—a half dozen cookies.

The meal mellowed his mood, and she talked him into watching a Christmas movie with her. As the closing credits rolled, she glanced over to see that the furrows in his brow had deepened. She rose and walked into the kitchen where Lili had left a collection of amber pill bottles. She read the labels and returned to the media room with a glass of water and two tablets in the palm of her hand. "You'd better take your pain meds, Josh. Remember they told us it's important to stay in front of it."

He stared at her outstretched hand for the longest of moments before taking the pills, popping them into his mouth, and swallowing them. Afterward, he rose and said, "I'm going to bed. I need to sleep. Caitlin . . . ?"

"Yes?"

He raked his fingers through his hair. "I'm sorry I was such an ass to you today. You don't deserve it. I'll try to do better."

"Don't worry about it, Josh." She went up on her tiptoes and gave his cheek a sweet kiss. "Remember what the doctor said. You'll feel better every day. By Christmas you will almost be back to new."

"Christmas. I'd forgotten. I've lost track of time."

"We're less than two weeks away." She tilted her head and studied him. "Since I'll be staying here, do you mind if I do a little more decorating? The wreath on your door is lonely."

He shrugged. "I got shamed into Deck the Halls Friday decorating."

"Yes, I've been meaning to talk to you about that. It was a pitiful effort, Tarkington."

"You're welcome to have at it. I'm done for today." He started toward his room, then abruptly halted. "Are you sleeping in my room?"

"And risk elbowing you in the ribs? Not hardly. I'm in the guest room."

"Okay. That's probably for the better. You'll see to Penny for me?"

"Of course."

"Thank you. Good night, Cait."

"Good night, Josh."

He didn't kiss her. She told herself not to be silly. The

man hurt every time he moved. Kissing would be the furthest thing from his mind.

Caitlin didn't know how right she was. As Josh brushed his teeth and undressed and settled carefully into bed, he was thinking about one thing. Only one thing.

He needed another Percocet.

Journal Entry

Every time I go to rehab, they make me journal. It's supposed to boost my mood and lower my blood pressure. They tell me I'll spend fewer days in the hospital if I write my feelings down. I don't know if I buy that. I never did in the past.

But I've changed. A lot of things have changed. Are changing.

Dying does to that guy. Dying has given me a new perspective.

I admit, I kinda liked it. It was surprisingly easy to do, and it would be even easier to do it again. The thought of floating away into that nice, warm blanket has a real appeal. Only, next time I'd do it right—somewhere far away from anybody who is ready with a snort of naloxone to pull me back.

I could do it. The idea is tempting. It's a craving. One giant craving that trumps all the others. I think about it. I think about dying a lot.

Dying makes me think about living, too. It's a choice. Die or live. Surrender or fight. Easy or hard.

Coming back is a bitch of a trip. That I never ever want to do again.

So I have to choose. I think about dying a lot. But when have I ever done things the easy way? This is my journal. This is my journey.

Chapter Sixteen

The first casserole arrived at nine the following morning. By noon, they had a dozen. By dinnertime, they could have fed every cadet at the Air Force Academy.

Visitors began stopping by on Josh's third day home. Brick and Lily put up a Christmas tree in the front window, and Claire brought so many decorations that Josh grumpily questioned if she'd emptied the shelves at her Christmas shop. Celeste dropped off a stack of vintage motorcycle magazines. Gabi and Flynn Brogan stopped by with a prototype model of a remote-controlled car Flynn had designed, and shortly before school was dismissed for the day, Hope Romano's kindergarten class congregated on the front lawn and sang Christmas carols.

Sarah Murphy dropped off a dozen Snickerdoodles with the promise of regular deliveries.

Josh bore it all with a stoic smile and seemingly genuine appreciation. And when everyone left, he went straight to bed.

Each day he grew more taciturn. Each day he became more withdrawn.

"I don't know what to do," Caitlin said to Dr. Rose

Cicero two days before Christmas when their paths crossed at the Trading Post grocery store. "He's never been gregarious, but now, he barely talks. When he does talk to me, he's as likely to snap at me as speak civilly. Sometimes I feel like the silverware are about to burst into song."

"You've lost me."

Beauty and the Beast. He's not playing Gaston."

"Ah, I see."

"Do you think he could be depressed?"

"First, I'm a doctor, but I'm not his doctor, so any opinion I express is purely conjecture. That said, post-operative depression is not uncommon. Feeling bad emotionally and physically often go hand in hand. How is his appetite?"

"Good. His sweet tooth definitely hasn't been affected. The guy can plow through more cookies than a Little League team."

"Is he eating more than normal?"

"Not really. He's always been a cookie monster."

"Is he sleeping significantly more or less than before the accident?"

Caitlin pursed her lips and considered it. "More, I guess. I mean, we weren't living together before, so maybe he often took an afternoon nap." And slept late. And went to bed early. "Is it his pain meds, do you think? Could they be making him drowsy?"

"Possibly. I expect his doctor told him to walk. Is he doing that?"

"Yes. He does take at least one walk a day, even when it's snowing." Alone. He didn't want her coming with him. "But he watches a lot of movies. He has a media room and he sits in the dark and watches movies." Again, alone. He didn't want her sitting with him.

That was one reason why she was loitering in the grocery store this afternoon. When he'd started the Lord of the Rings trilogy earlier, she'd popped a bag of popcorn, put it into a bowl for them to share, and sat down beside him to watch. He'd just about bitten her head off when her phone rang.

She was seriously thinking about going home. Maybe she wasn't cut out for nursing. Or dealing with cranky men. Grouchy heroes.

Rose asked, "Is he going back to his physician in Gunnison or did he transfer here? When is his next follow-up appointment? Who is he seeing?"

"Here. The appointment is tomorrow with Dr. Alvarado. Josh thinks the doctor is going to let him go back to work."

"He could probably do desk work. Counter work. That might be the best thing for him. Will he allow you to speak to the doctor?"

"I honestly don't know."

"Try. Be honest with him, Caitlin. Tell him he needs to be screened for depression."

"If he says no?"

"Do you think he's a danger to himself or others?"

"No. Not at all. Well, except for his cholesterol count. Those cookies can't be good for him."

Rose laughed and gave Caitlin's arm a comforting pat. "It's still early yet. He probably simply needs a little more time to heal. Perhaps an increase in the amount of his pain meds. Alvarado is a good doctor. He will ask the right questions."

Reassured, Caitlin finished her grocery shopping—all she really needed was more aluminum foil and fresh fruit for breakfast because the casseroles were never-ending— then she headed back to Josh's house, detouring long enough to check on changes at Gingerbread House. She found Jax in the three-year-olds' room, checking the foot pedal on the sink. She asked, "Is it weird of me to think that those short little commodes are just the cutest things?"

"Pretty much. Yep." He slipped his wrench into his tool belt and grinned at her. "What are you doing January fifteenth at ten a.m.?"

"I don't know. What's happening January fifteenth at ten a.m.?"

"Final walk-through."

"Really?" Delight flowed through her. "You'll be done?"

"Barring a disaster"—he knocked on the wooden doorframe—"yes, we'll be done."

Caitlin's thoughts began spinning. She hadn't spent much time thinking about her business since the accident. She'd been too busy worrying about Josh and, frankly, playing housewife. Not exactly the recipe for professional success. *Idiot.*

"That's fabulous, Jax. I'd better get my butt in gear if I'm going to be ready to open for business on March first."

On the advice of almost everyone who'd dealt with construction delays, she'd waited to order furniture. Undiscovered plumbing or electrical issues could easily set things back for weeks. As far as staffing went, she'd targeted the people she wanted as teachers and discussed the possibility with most of them, but she had no official employment agreements in place. She would need to take care of that—right after the holidays.

"So, when can Claire and I sign up for a slot for Julianna? Nicholas also wants to attend your after-school program. We don't want you to fill up before we can put down our deposit."

Caitlin waved away his concern. "I don't need a deposit from you guys."

"Caitlin. Caitlin. Caitlin." He chastised her with a frown. "A piece of advice from one business owner to another. Start as you mean to go on. Create policy and stick to it—friendship or not."

She gave him a two-finger salute. "Yes, sir." After a moment's pause, she added, "I'm still saving Julianna a spot, no matter what."

His chuckle followed her out the door and buoyed her steps as she crossed the yard to Josh's house. He was asleep again when she arrived and her worries returned. She decided she'd definitely bring up the subject of depression at some point before his doctor's appointment the next day. In the meantime, she had gifts to wrap. The area beneath the Christmas tree was looking sadly bare here a few short days until Christmas.

In the guest room where she was sleeping, she went down onto her knees and pulled the gifts she'd purchased for Josh from under her bed. What to get him had been a major problem. How did one follow up a fabulous gift like the necklace he'd given her? It had been a darned near impossible task—until she'd discovered the stack of writing journals in his closet while putting away his laundry.

Though tempted, she hadn't snooped beyond opening one just long enough to confirm that they were written in Josh's handwriting. She'd been both surprised and delighted with the discovery. Surprised because Josh didn't strike her as the journaling type. Delighted because she finally knew what gift to give him for Christmas.

She'd dug out the card of an artist she'd discovered at an arts festival the previous year and called to check his inventory. Yesterday the handcrafted leather journal with handmade paper and a vintage door-hinge closure had arrived via priority mail. It was even lovelier than Caitlin had hoped. She couldn't wait to give it to him.

She wrapped it, along with gifts for her family and friends, and placed them beneath the tree.

Christmas Eve arrived along with six inches of new snow, transforming Eternity Springs into a picture postcard. Josh had awakened that morning feeling mean as a hungry bear. He'd dreamt he was high—that euphoria of pleasure and well-being had ended in the crash of awakening to pain from head to toe. The need for relief was a rampaging force inside him, and it took all his energy to beat it back.

The phone call from his mother shortly before noon didn't help his mood any. She was drunk. It was an hour earlier on the west coast, and she was already high as a kite. *Merry Christmas, Mom.* Some things never changed.

Josh hated the Christmas holidays. For as long as he could remember, his holiday season was one crisis after another, one disappointment after another, one lost stretch of time that he survived rather than lived. The only enjoyable Christmas he could remember was the lone holiday he spent with the Christopher family when he was sixteen.

He sat in his office at the garage with a stack of paperwork in front of him. His right hand held his phone. His left massaged the bridge of his nose. "I'm sorry, Mom," he said into the phone. "You deserve better than that from the men in your life."

"You're one of the men in my life," she accused in a quavering voice. "I deserve better from you! It's Christmas and I'm all alone."

It was a waste of breath to attempt to defend himself. Never mind that up until yesterday when her latest lover dumped her, she'd planned to be in Hawaii for the holiday. Then there were the little details of three broken ribs and internal sutures and the fact that he wasn't supposed to drive—not that he had any intention of sharing that little detail. She'd only twist things around to make it about her. Mainly, though, he wasn't going visit his mother or invite her to visit because she was a pill-popping alcoholic and he couldn't be around her.

"I'm going to hang up now, Mom. This conversation isn't helping either one of us."

"But . . . but . . . wait. There's something else. I need . . . would you . . . Joshua, I need you to send me some money."

Of course. The real reason for this call. "I made your regular deposit last week."

"Yes, but I need more. You have it, Joshua. You can give it to me. Today, before everything closes."

"All right. Fine. I'll make a deposit this afternoon." *And I'll go to hell for being an enabler.*

Josh ended the call, telephoned his personal banker, and authorized a transfer. He knew he shouldn't do it, but a man could only fight so many battles at one time, and he was hanging on by a thread as it was. The craving was a constant temptation pulling on his sleeve.

He needed a distraction, so he called home to Oklahoma. Cindy sounded a little better, he thought. Her lingering cough didn't interrupt their conversation every few sentences on this call like it had on the last. That was a definite improvement, and he felt that little knot of tension reserved for his foster parents' health dissolve.

"We'll do our best to get up to see you in January," Paul Christopher said.

"No. I don't think the winter mountain air could possibly be good for your lungs. I'll come to you as soon as I'm able."

"Speaking of which," Cindy said, "how are you managing your pain, Josh?"

He hesitated. The Christophers knew his history, of course. Under other circumstances, he might have confided in them. But they were fighting their own fight right now. His mother, especially, had been seriously ill. He wouldn't add another burden of worry on them. "Good. I'm doing really good. With all the wonder drugs around we forget how powerful a pain reliever plain old aspirin can be."

They wished each other Merry Christmas and ended the call. Josh decided he'd been sitting too long, so he rose from his chair and headed for the kitchen to raid Caitlin's cookie jar. As he walked by the Christmas tree, his gaze snagged on the package that had arrived by messenger the previous afternoon. It had come gift-wrapped at his instruction, but he found he was curious to see what he'd bought. Careful not to tear anything, he peeled back the red foil paper, revealing a small jewelry box. He opened the box and silently whistled.

The Sokolov emerald earrings matched the necklace he'd given Caitlin before the accident. He'd purchased them through an intermediary from his half sister, Arabella. He'd put the ring that completed the set, Amelia's inheritance, and now his possession, in his safety deposit box. His half sisters both had been quick to accept the offer he'd made for the pieces. An ex-pat living in London, Arabella had expressed a desire to meet him the next time she visited the States. It was a vague enough request that he'd agreed to it. She'd said she'd bring Amelia along too. If it ever happened, his mother would blow a gasket.

Josh studied the earrings. The emeralds in the triple teardrops glowed an appropriate Christmas green, the diamonds surrounding them twinkling like tree lights.

They'd be pretty as a Christmas ribbon dangling from her ears, wrapping the perfect package.

Caitlin had certainly been a gift to him. He'd needed help doing just about everything those first few days out of the hospital. She'd refused to let him hire a nurse and she'd moved right in.

She was both his salvation and his damnation. He knew that for both their sakes he should send her away, but that was another thing he didn't have the strength to do. Because even though he didn't want to admit it, he liked having her around. He liked the way she fussed over him, and he didn't want to be alone, even when the pain and craving turned him in on himself. He kept telling himself that after Christmas, he'd send her home, knowing if he had any honor whatsoever, he'd do it today.

Because he had no future with Caitlin Timberlake. He wouldn't drag her down into the quagmire of misfortune and bad luck that sucked at his shoes wherever he went. He wouldn't saddle her with a man who might sink into the slop again at any time. Disaster was his destiny and he cared too much to suck her into it with him. But in the meantime, it was Christmas and she'd decorated his home and his sugar cookies. He looked forward to giving her this gift.

He rewrapped the earrings and slipped the box into the pocket of his jacket. Maybe he'd give it to her tonight. He didn't know if she was a Christmas Eve opener or the type who waited for Christmas Day. He knew she planned to go up to her mom and dad's house at Heartache Falls tomorrow morning after church. Supposedly, he'd been invited to tag along, but to his relief, the Callahan clan was in town for the holiday and he would spend Christmas Day with them.

Maybe.

Or maybe he'd lie to everybody and stay home.

He felt like crap. Maybe he'd go for a soak in the hot tub. The doc had yanked the staples at his last appointment, so he'd been given the all-clear for a soak.

Maybe he'd ask Caitlin to join him. He needed a distraction right about now. Doing some hot-tub skinny-dipping was bound to help that. It might cause a different sort of pain, but that sort he would welcome.

He found her seated at the kitchen table with a pencil in her hand making notes on a square of green paper. A steaming cup of tea sat off to one side. Penny lay snuggled in her lap and Christmas carols played softly in the background. In that moment, he craved her, craved what she represented, almost as much as he craved the Percs.

"Are you making a list?"

"Yep. Checking it twice."

"Since you brought up naughty, I'm headed for the hot tub. Want to join me?"

Her brows arched. "The hot tub? Surely you're not . . . I mean, you can't . . . not so soon. You'd rip your stitches!"

Josh gave his first honest smile in days. "A soak, Caitlin. A simple, restful soak."

Skepticism filled her frown. "You're the one who brought up naughty."

"Hey, fantasies won't strain a stitch. Meet you there in five?"

"Sure."

The hot tub was recessed into his back deck and was surrounded by a privacy screen that included an outdoor fireplace. It offered one of the pleasures of mountain living during winter, the contrast of the steaming water below and freezing air above.

He stepped carefully into the tub and sank into the heat, which then seeped into his sore muscles and bones. When Caitlin joined him a short time later and they sat in comfortable silence, his pain eased, his craving diminished. It was as if he'd popped two pills.

He'd written about it in one of his journals.

It's . . . peace. It's like being inside a cabin in the woods when there's a foot of snow on the ground and it's still falling. It's sitting on a comfy sofa next to a crackling fire, wrapped up in a blanket with a dream girl, watching a good movie. You're relaxed and content and you don't have a care in the world. That's the euphoria of percs.

He needed Caitlin here in his house with him. Just for a little longer. Just until he got a little stronger.

"Josh?" Caitlin asked.

He didn't open his eyes. "Hmm?"

"Do you think you might feel up to attending Celeste's open house tonight at Angel's Rest?"

He considered it. The Christmas Eve gathering was becoming quite the tradition here in Eternity Springs. He wouldn't mind a little company tonight, a little more distraction. If he could hang on a few more days, he might just dodge the bullet.

He opened one eye and looked at her. "I think I'd like that."

Her expression lit up like the flashing star atop their Christmas tree. "That's fabulous. I'm excited. It's always one of the best parties of the year. Did you go last year?"

"No, I spent Christmas with the Christophers."

"Well, wait until you see Angel's Rest all angeled up. Celeste is almost always happy, but on Christmas Eve, she's joyful. It's fun to watch."

Caitlin was fun to watch as she bubbled on about the party. "I have a new red dress to wear. I bought it because it has the perfect neckline to show off the necklace you gave me. I'll have to go home to get it. Maybe I'll shower and dress there. That way I can make an entrance when I come back here to pick you up."

"You always make an entrance, Cait. You do that naturally. And you know what . . . I think I'm all right to drive. I can pick you up. We're only going a half a mile."

"No. Absolutely not. The doctors said six full weeks."

He scowled at her. "Makes me feel like a wuss letting you drive me around everywhere."

"Get over it. You know what else would be nice if you're up to it? Going to the midnight service at church."

"I thought you were going in the morning with your parents."

"I'd rather go this evening with you."

He started to shrug, but remembered his broken ribs. "I can give it a try, I guess. I can sleep in church as easy as I can here."

"You do that and the reverend will call you out," she warned with a twinkle in her eyes. "He did that to Chase one year."

She launched into a tale about Christmas Eves of the past and soon had him laughing, a first since the accident. Later after he showered and stood in front of the mirror shaving, he told himself he'd turned a corner. Physically, he felt halfway decent; and mentally, he wasn't nearly on edge.

He finished shaving then opened his medicine cabinet where he kept his aftershave. His gaze snagged on a row of amber bottles that didn't belong there. He froze. Well, hell. Caitlin must have picked up the prescriptions the doctor had sent in at his last visit. Temptation coiled like a rattlesnake.

Josh slammed the cabinet door shut and backed away. He was still standing staring at his reflection in the mirror when he heard his front door open. Caitlin called, "I'm back."

"Sorry. I'm running late." Slowly, he opened the medicine cabinet and found his aftershave. Ten minutes later, he walked into his living room to see Caitlin standing before the Christmas tree.

She turned and smiled at him and took his breath away.

Her dress was Christmas red, a simple fit-and-flare style with three-quarter sleeves and a modest neckline appropriate for church. It showed off the Sokolov necklace to perfection. Green and red. She'd give Claire Lancaster a run for her money for the title of "Miss Christmas."

She folded her arms, tapped her lips with a finger, and said, "I spy with my little eye something new beneath your Christmas tree, Mr. Tarkington."

"I can't see anything but you. You are a vision." And he should give her his gift right now to complete tonight's outfit.

"Well, the gift tag reads 'to Josh from Penny'. I wonder what she got for you?"

"Penny?" Surprised, he laughed. "Shall I open it and see?"

"Oh. No. What blasphemy. It's not Christmas yet. You get to open one gift—after church."

"So I guess that means you won't open my gift to you now?"

"Nope."

"That's a mistake. Just saying."

"Why is it a mistake?"

"Guess you'll have to wait and see."

"Does it have something to do with that other new box beneath the tree?"

"Your little eye did quite a bit of spying, didn't it?"

"It's tradition. I'm all about tradition."

Apparently, pestering him with guesses was part of

her tradition too, because she did exactly that during the drive to Angel's Rest. They arrived shortly before Celeste asked her guests to gather in the central hallway for a special announcement. She climbed the stairs to the second-floor landing and stood at the banister, waiting for stragglers to make their way into the hallway. The space quickly grew crowded, and when another guest accidentally elbowed Josh in the ribs, he decided he'd find an out-of-the-way place to listen to Celeste's big announcement.

Later, the guests all said it was a miracle that someone had been standing in just the perfect spot to catch Celeste when the banister broke and she lost her balance and tumbled toward the ground. The fact that the "someone" was Josh and the impact damaged his mending ribs was a terrible bit of bad luck.

Journal Entry

*I looked back in a previous journal and found
something I wrote shortly after I arrived in Eternity Springs. I wrote:*

*I have found a place. They claim it's a little
piece of heaven, a place where broken hearts
come to heal.*

*I'm not here to mend a broken heart. I'm not
exactly sure why I'm here except I needed somewhere to go and I landed here and liked it.*

*There's this woman here. I don't know how to
describe her. It's like she's everybody's grandmother, everybody's best friend, everybody's port
in a storm. Everybody's angel. She'll give you hell
if you need it and a pat on the back when it's deserved.*

I like her. She's . . . soothing.

Boy, was I wrong. She damn near killed me.

Who says angels can fly?

Chapter Seventeen

At the local medical clinic, tests and X-rays revealed new damage to Josh's ribs, but thankfully, no troublesome issues with internal organs. He remained at the clinic overnight on doctor's orders and went home to his own bed on the afternoon of Christmas Day. There, Caitlin handed him a glass of water and a pain pill.

Josh swallowed both.

He told Caitlin to enjoy Christmas dinner with her family and not to rush home because he intended to sleep. He did exactly that until he awoke to debilitating pain. Josh took another Percocet.

A week passed. On New Year's Eve, Josh stood in his bathroom staring at the lone pill in the bottle of painkillers for almost five minutes before he dumped it into the toilet.

On New Year's Day, the Beast was back.

The bitter wind of the mid-January morning brought tears to Caitlin's eyes as she hurried up the street toward the vet clinic where she needed to pick up Penny's heartworm-prevention medicine. At least she tried to tell herself that the wind and not the exchange she'd just had with Josh was the source of her tears.

After the last two weeks, a part of her wanted to elbow him in the ribs just out of spite. He'd been impossible to live with. More than once she'd considered moving back to her house and leaving him to fend for himself. She wasn't quite there yet, but . . .

A door chime jangled as she opened the door and stepped into the clinic to the sound of loud barking. "I'll be right with you," her sister-in-law called from an exam room.

"No rush," Caitlin called back. She sat in one of the waiting room chairs, picked up a *National Geographic*, and began flipping through it. She found an article about the Great Wall of China and began reading. Her mind wandered by the time she turned the page. What was wrong with Josh? She couldn't figure him out. She could understand his grumpiness right after Christmas because, in many respects, the act of catching Celeste had sent him back to recovery Day One. But he'd been much nicer to her that week after Christmas than he was now. Aloud, she muttered, "I swear, if he snaps at me one more time, I'm going bite back."

"You having trouble with a dog, Caitlin?" Lori asked as she exited the exam room carrying her dad's sedated Boston terrier, Mortimer, in her arms. Gently, she placed the dog into a kennel, shut the door, then turned a curious look toward Caitlin.

"More like a horse's ass."

"Ahh . . ." Lori nodded sagely. "Dare I surmise that Josh is being a difficult patient?"

"Difficult? Hah! That doesn't begin to describe him." Caitlin shot to her feet. "He's impossible. Do you know what he snapped at me about this morning? He was toasting a bagel and he burned it and it was somehow my fault because I'd turned the dial when I cleaned the toaster. Never mind that all he had to do was check the setting. Then he grumbled because I put the jam in the door of the refrigerator when everyone knows it belongs on the shelf. He even growled at Penny this morning!"

At that, the amused smile on Lori's face faded. "He was mean to his dog?"

"Yes!" Caitlin exclaimed before almost immediately qualifying. "Well, not really. Josh was emptying the kitchen trash can and he set the bag on the floor behind him while he dealt with the liner. Penny bit into it and made a mess. He scolded her."

"As well he should."

"Loudly!"

Caitlin had a long list of other complaints she could make, but whining was so unattractive. "I need to pick up Penny's heartworm medicine."

"All righty." Lori walked to the cabinet where she kept her retail goods and removed a package of pills. "How is Josh set on pet shampoo? Savannah Turner just dropped off a new batch of pet products that smell heavenly. Here." Lori opened a bottle of shampoo and held it out for Caitlin to sniff. "Isn't that fabulous?"

Caitlin smelled coconut and orange and something else she couldn't place. "It makes me think of summer. On a day like today, that's a good thing."

"Tell me about it. We're supposed to get another foot of snow overnight."

Lori held up the shampoo, a question on her face, and Caitlin nodded. Through no fault of her own and as a result of her back injury, Penny was a very stinky dog. Caitlin nodded. "Definitely add the shampoo."

While Lori wrote up a sales receipt and bagged the purchases, Caitlin retrieved Josh's credit card from her wallet. Seeing his name on the card turned her thoughts in his direction once again. "He's shutting himself off from me, Lori. He's been a different man since the accident, but especially since Christmas. I don't know why, and I don't know what to do about it."

Lori accepted the card Caitlin extended toward her saying, "Could he be depressed? A lot of people suffer from holiday depression."

"I talked to Rose about that, but when I brought the subject up with him, he waved it off and claimed nothing was wrong. He made a stupid joke about being depressed about the Broncos' loss in the playoffs."

"Chase is still a bit depressed about that loss too."

"Yeah. Well, Josh isn't. He didn't even watch the game."

Lori's eyes rounded in alarm. "Seriously? Chase and I have watched Bronco football with Josh in the past. He was into it. We even talked about it because he's a recent Bronco convert. He grew up a Raiders fan. I can't imagine him not being interested in the game. Maybe he turned it off after one of the team's numerous miscues."

"He didn't watch at all. I was there. He went for a walk. A long one." Josh had been taking lots of long walks of late. By himself. In all kinds of weather. More than once she'd asked to tag along and he always refused the request. He always had an excuse, though generally, a poor one.

Caitlin sighed and continued, "I don't know what to do. Some days I think it would be best for me to pack up my things and move home. He doesn't need me there any longer. He's well enough to live by himself again."

"So move home. He'll miss you."

"Possibly. Probably. Except I'm afraid if I leave, he'll never invite me back. Any hopes I have of building a life with him will wither away to nothing."

"So this mood of his hasn't changed your mind? You still want to be with him?"

"Yes." Caitlin recognized that she said it with less certainty than she had even two weeks ago. "He's trying to drive me away and I'm afraid he just might succeed. But I sense that something else is going on here, Lori. Something I don't understand. It's as if there's a puzzle piece missing and he knows where it is, but I don't."

"That's tough. Have you said that to him? Just like that?"

Caitlin thought about it a moment. "No. Not just like that."

"Maybe that's a place to start."

"You could be right, though I expect he'll just blow me off. Or snap and growl at me."

"You're not happy with the way things are now. What do you have to lose?"

The bell on the door jangled again as the local banker's wife walked in with her cat. The three women exchanged small talk for a few minutes, then Caitlin took her leave. Outside, she turned her face into the wind. This time when tears leaked from the corner of her eyes and she blamed it on the bitter wind, she told herself the truth.

With a renewed sense of purpose, Caitlin began the walk home to Josh's house. She was halfway there when a car pulled up beside her and her mother rolled down the window. "Hello, sweet pea. This is kismet. I had just decided to call you to see if you could steal an hour away. I'm on my way to the spa at Angel's Rest for a pedicure. Want to tag along? My treat."

Caitlin looked up the street toward Tarkington Automotive where Mr. Grumpypants had probably gone to do paperwork or hide from her or both. A spa date with her mom sounded like just the pick-me-up she needed.

Twenty minutes later, she and Ali sat side by side in pedicure chairs, their feet soaking in scented, toasty warm water. Caitlin talked to her mom a couple times a week on the phone, but they hadn't seen each other since

Christmas because Mac and Ali had taken one of their getaways. "So how was Cabo? Did Dad catch any fish?"

"Cabo was beautiful as always and yes, Dad is a happy fisherman. So, tell me what we missed while we were gone. Is Jax wrapping things up at Gingerbread House?"

"Yes. Work slowed down a bit last week. Claire had a stomach bug so he stayed home with the kids and that delayed our walk-through. It's now scheduled for next Monday."

"That's exciting. Though I hate to hear that Claire has been ill. She's better now?"

"Yes."

"And how about your hero? I trust his ribs are healing all right?"

Caitlin hesitated. She'd like to pour out her heart to her mom, but she feared if she started, she wouldn't stop. "Yes, I think so. He's pretty grouchy, though."

"That's understandable. Broken ribs are painful to begin with and to have them injured twice . . ." Ali shuddered. "That poor guy."

Had Caitlin not been watching close, she wouldn't have noticed the sheen of tears in her mother's eyes.

"Mom? What's wrong?"

Ali closed her eyes and gave her head a little shake. "I'm sorry. It's nothing. I'm just tired. Traveling gets harder all the time."

Unease rippled through Caitlin. "When was the last time you went to the doctor?"

Ali rolled her eyes. "I went in December, Moth-er. I'm fine. You have my word. Like I said, traveling is harder than it used to be. It doesn't help that Dad and I stayed out late last night. I planned to sleep on the plane, but the ladies across the aisle from me never stopped talking."

At that point their nail techs arrived, and Caitlin knew

better than to pursue any serious line of questioning in front of them. Her mother was a private person. To Ali Timberlake, there was a time and place for intimate conversations, and the salon wasn't it. Instead, she entertained Caitlin and the nail techs with tales of shopping at a Mexican market and her ideas for a Taste of Mexico menu at the Yellow Kitchen.

Of course, Ali's penchant for privacy didn't exactly extend to questions she wished to ask of others. While the technician slathered a salt scrub on her calves, she glanced at Caitlin and asked, "So after all the drama of Christmas Eve, did you and Josh ever exchange Christmas presents?"

"We did." Caitlin smiled as she recalled how the gift exchange had gone down.

After Christmas Eve party goers helped both Celeste and Josh back onto their feet following Josh's miraculous catch, Dr. Rose Cicero insisted he be taken to the clinic for new X-rays. She'd kept him for observation overnight, and rather than spending the first minutes of Christmas Day seated beside Josh at the midnight church service, Caitlin had sat between her parents and her brother and his wife. No sense spending the night at Josh's bedside. The man was dosed up on painkillers and out like Santa on December 26.

The week slowly passed with Josh spending much of the time in bed. Traditionally, Caitlin's family kept their holiday trimmings up until Epiphany, but on New Year's Eve, a little depressed and with nothing to do but watch a movie by herself, Caitlin began taking down decorations and stripping the tree of its ornaments and lights. She had everything boxed up but the Twelve Dogs of Christmas ornament set when Josh came out of his bathroom, still damp from a shower. He wore loose-fitting drawstring pants and a button-up flannel shirt. It was the first time all week he'd dressed in something more than pajama bottoms and rib wrap.

Maybe the worst of it is over, Caitlin thought, even as she observed the furrow of pain on his brow and the tightness around his lips.

"Wow. It looks barren in here now."

Caitlin nodded. "It does, but at the same time, I always like getting the clutter put away and creating a sense of a new start for a new year. I have a pan of hot chocolate on the stove. Would you like a cup?"

"I'd love one, thanks."

Caitlin went into the kitchen and filled a mug with the steaming drink, then returned to the family room. Josh stood in front of the fireplace, his gaze focused on the pair of wrapped packages sitting on the mantel in place of the Santas she'd already boxed up to put away. He accepted the mug, then nodded toward the mantel. "What are you planning to do with those?"

"I was waiting for you to tell me."

"I think we'd better open them now. If we wait until after midnight, then they'll be next year's gifts."

"I'm not quite sure I follow that, but okay. Let's exchange our gifts. I'll admit it's been difficult for me to wait."

"Think I got you something good, hmm?"

"Actually, I'm more excited to see what you think of my gift."

"Well, let's see, shall we?" He retrieved the package tagged to her and offered it, saying, "Merry Christmas and Happy New Year, Caitlin. Here's hoping we get through New Year's Eve without something—or someone—falling from the sky."

"I'll drink to that." They clicked their mugs in toast, then Caitlin handed over her gift to him. They both set down their mugs and began opening their gifts.

Josh was a ripper, Caitlin discovered. She liked to carefully untie bows and peel back tape, so he had his box opened first. She paused in her efforts to watch his reaction.

Alarm. His gaze shot up to meet hers, and she immediately recognized his fear. Hastily, she assured, "I didn't read your journals, Josh. I would never invade your privacy that way. But I noticed the one beside your bed and the stack of them in your closet."

He held her stare for another moment, then visibly relaxed. He turned his attention to the handcrafted journal. "This is beautiful. I've never seen anything like it. The clasp looks old. Is it a door hinge?"

"Yes. It dates to the 1890s, as does the lock and key."

"Handmade paper, too," he mused, flipping through the pages.

"Yes."

"It's great. Seriously awesome. Thank you." He started to lean toward her and lower his head. She lifted her face in anticipation of a kiss—that never happened. Instead, he grimaced, straightened, and grumbled, "Damn ribs. Open your gift, Caitlin."

She decided she'd claim that kiss the next time he was horizontal, and then she returned her attention to his gift to her. She uncovered a small white box. Inside sat a black velvet jewelry box. Not a ring box. It was bigger than that. She silently scolded herself not to be disappointed.

She'd never anticipated getting a ring for Christmas. Dreamed about it, maybe, but never anticipated.

She flipped open the lid and caught her breath.

At the spa at Angel's Rest, the nail tech lifted her right foot from the bowl and began to rub the bottom of her foot with a pumice stone. As always, it tickled and jerked Caitlin's thoughts back to the present.

Presents. Her mother had asked about Christmas presents, "I gave him a journal and he gave me a gorgeous pair of earrings that match the necklace he gave me a few weeks before Christmas."

"The one you wore Christmas Eve?" At Caitlin's nod, Ali continued. "I've been meaning to ask you about that. I want a closer look at it. It's fabulous. A true statement piece."

"The earrings are just as gorgeous. The setting is unique and truly, the loveliest vintage jewelry I've ever seen. A bit fancy for Eternity Springs, but I don't care. I love them."

"You'll have to find out the designer's name and—" Ali broke off the thought when her phone rang. She glanced down at the number and thumbed the green button. "Hello, Mac. I'm with Caitlin at Angel's—"

Ali broke off abruptly and listened for a moment. "Oh no. Mac." She pulled one foot from the tech's hands and the other from the bowl and motioned toward a towel. Into the phone, she said, "I'm going to hang up and call nine-one-one."

Caitlin sat up. "What's wrong? Mom, what happened?"

Ali ignored her daughter and swiped the towel over her legs. "Are you sure?"

"Mom!"

Ali shook her head at Caitlin and spoke into the phone. "All right. Yes. All right. Stay where you are, Mac. Don't try to get up. I'll be right there. I'm going to leave Angel's Rest now. Here, reassure your daughter while I put my shoes and socks on."

Ali shoved the phone toward Caitlin, who took it and said, "Dad?"

Mac spoke in a determined and cheery voice. "I'm

okay, snookums. I just tripped on something and twisted my ankle. No big deal."

Relief washed over her. "Oh, Dad. Are you sure it's not broken?"

"Positive. It's not even that bad of a strain. I wouldn't have bothered your mother about it except I'm at the bottom of the basement stairs and—"

"Dad! Tell me you didn't fall down the stairs."

"I didn't fall down the stairs. What I did manage to do is lock myself in the basement."

"How in the world did you do that?"

"Long story, baby girl. One that makes me look really foolish, I'm afraid."

Caitlin lifted her feet away from the pedicure chair's bowl saying, "I'll ride up with Mom."

"No!" The harsh snap in his tone took her aback. He said it again, more gently this time. "No, honey. Thanks, but don't bother. I promise you, I'm just fine. A little embarrassed, but just fine."

By now Ali had donned her shoes and crossed the salon to the coatrack. She slipped into her jacket, then returned for her phone, wiggling her fingers to signal Caitlin to hand it over.

"Mom wants her phone."

"Give it to her. Come see me tomorrow, okay?"

"Okay," Caitlin said reluctantly, then she handed the phone back to her mother.

"Sorry for the interruption. Finish your pedicure. Tell Josh I said hello. Maybe we'll come down and visit with you two tomorrow. Dad and Josh can compare injuries."

"Mom, are you sure that—?"

"Gotta run. Bye." Ali leaned down and kissed Caitlin's cheek, then blew out the front door just as Celeste stepped inside carrying a box and a stack of magazines.

"Well," Caitlin muttered. "That was . . . strange."

Dad locks himself in the basement? Mom goes from brittle to boisterous to bizarre in the time it takes to soften the callouses on her feet?

Her parents were getting stranger by the day.

And Caitlin continued to worry about her father. Mac Timberlake had never been a clumsy man. *First he drops the collection plate and now he trips and manages to lock himself in the basement? What the heck?*

"Hello, Caitlin," Celeste said. "What a lovely color you've chosen for your toes. Nothing like sunshine yellow to brighten up a winter day."

Yellow? Caitlin hadn't picked yellow. She glanced down at the tray between her chair and her mother's and saw her choice of Valentine red and . . . sunshine yellow. Her mom had chosen sunshine yellow! Ali Timberlake seldom wore any nail polish bolder than a pastel pink. She *never wore yellow. Yep. Stranger not by the day, but by the minute.*

"I suppose you're right." Caitlin smiled up at Celeste as the nail tech picked up the bottle of bright yellow polish and shook it. "A little sunshine never hurts."

"Speaking of sunshine, how is our resident hero doing today?"

What Mr. Grouch-and-gloom had to do with sunshine, Caitlin couldn't hazard a guess. "He's doing well," she replied. She wasn't at all certain she spoke the truth, but Celeste had felt so guilty about the Christmas Eve fall that Caitlin wouldn't dream of saying otherwise. "Harriet brought him cookies again this morning, and that always perks him up."

"Harriet looks good, doesn't she? I visited with her yesterday, and she's getting around on that new hip of hers quite well."

"Yes. She's back to her old self. Plus, she told us she's

put a down payment on a new camper. She's joining the Alleycats for their first camping weekend in May."

"Harriet has joined the Tornado Alleycats?" Celeste's blue eyes gleamed with delight. "Exceptional news. I think that's just what she needs. Now, I'd best toddle along. I still have a long to-do list for today. Will life ever slow down, I wonder? Before I go, I have a stack of new magazines. May I interest you in *Architectural Digest, National Geographic,* or *People?*"

Caitlin had stopped even scanning the front cover of *People* at the grocery store checkout line when they started publishing pictures of Chase during his globetrotter phase. Since she'd paged through that issue of the *National Geographic* today at the vet clinic, she smiled at Celeste and said, "*Architectural Digest,* please."

Celeste handed over the magazine. "Enjoy, my dear. And remember, even the longest, darkest winter days eventually end. Hold onto your faith in spring. Keep your eyes on your sunshine nail polish."

Smiling, Caitlin wiggled her sunshine toes, opened the magazine, and began idly turning the pages as she waited for her polish to dry. A men's cologne ad caught her attention—steel gray eyes and bristled jaw—if the model's hair was a little longer, he could be Josh. She sighed, skimmed a two-page story about an eighteenth-century Italian villa, then turned the page to see a photo of a distinguished man with salt-and-pepper hair leaning against an American luxury car. He could have been her dad.

Josh. Her dad. What was the deal with the tight-lipped men in her life? Both of them had something going on that she didn't understand. In her dad's case, she feared it might be health related.

There. She'd admitted it. She'd been circling the idea for a while now, afraid to put it into words. Based on the way her parents were acting, it was the only thing that made sense. Caitlin's stomach took a sick tumble.

But if that was the reason for his unusual behavior, why keep it secret? That wasn't the way her family rolled.

That more she thought about it, the more annoyed she grew. Honesty was part of their bedrock. Obfuscations, denials, and lies had no place in Timberlake family relationships. *Dad should know better.*

Maybe it was time that she called them on it.

She flipped back to the men's cologne ad and glared at the gray-eyed man. *You too, Josh. I've been patient. More than patient. I've been patient. I've kind and caring and understanding—I don't understand why you run hot and cold more often than a kitchen faucet.*

It was more than sore and aching ribs, more than the frustration of physical limitations. Something had built the castle walls of his emotions. Someone, most likely, had handed him the shovel to dig the moat.

She drummed her fingers against the magazine. She'd bet her bottom dollar that family was the crux of the what, who, and why. He spoke of his foster family easily, but he'd never told her anything about his birth family or what calamity had placed him in foster care. She'd asked, but he'd always dodged the questions.

I'm tired of dodges. I'm tired of dodges and secrets and sidesteps. Problems can't be solved if they're never acknowledged. Even heroes can be challenged—except it's hard to have a good battle with a warrior who's wounded.

Frustrated, she turned a half dozen more pages of the magazine, not paying real attention to either the articles or the ads until she reached the magazine's center spread and her gaze fell on a familiar face. She did a double take. Whoa. It was a vintage black-and-white photograph of a 1927 stage production of *Hamlet*. The actor was the spitting image of Josh. The caption beneath the photo identified him as Thomas J. Trammel. The article was about the Trammel family "summer house" estate in Maine.

She knew of the Trammel family, of course. They were an American acting dynasty whose beginnings traced back generations. A smile played across her face as she studied the picture. She'd have to get a copy of this magazine and show it to Josh. *Wonder if he'll also see the resemblance.*

She started reading the article, learned about the 1835 marriage of an Irish comedian to an actress who'd made her first stage appearance at the age of five. The next generation gave the family their first major star, and the tradition continued through the transition to silent films and then talkies. By now the Trammels were considered Hollywood royalty. Benjamin Joshua Trammel made a name for himself on stage as one of the finest Shakespearean actors the world has ever seen. His daughter Eleanor was an established movie star in the Golden Age of Hollywood. The Hollywood queen had married an Arabian sheik who loved to shower her with gems, and a competition ensued. Every time Richard Burton made news by giving Elizabeth Taylor a fabulous new jewel, Eleanor's husband made a point to outdo him.

A photo near the bottom of the page showed a sparkling ruby-and-diamond broach.

Caitlin turned the page and read the next paragraph in the article. *Eleanor's favorite gems—the Sokolov emeralds—were said to be those gifted to her upon the birth of her son.*

Caitlin glanced at the corresponding photograph and froze. Holy cow. Those were her necklace, her earrings!

No wonder they were so beautiful. The design was a

copy of a famous set. And with today's technology, manmade jewels often outshine the real ones.

But as she continued reading the article, unease rippled through her. There was that portrait . . . .

No, surely not.

Caitlin dragged her attention back to the article and read about Eleanor and her siblings' descendants. Toward the end of the piece, a name jumped out at her.

Ben's son J. B. by actress Jana Tarkington began his career at just fifteen months of age when he landed his first job in a cat food commercial. The release of Martin Holberg's blockbuster hit, Starseeker, *made him a star at the age of eight. Audiences and critics alike praised young J. B.'s performance with his extraterrestrial friend. When asked about the boy's early success and his future plans, his grandfather said, "Acting is part of J. B.'s DNA. The profession is his destiny. He will return to the set and/or the stage someday. He has many more roles to play, many more performances to give."*

The photograph was a still from *Starseeker.* Caitlin studied it, searching for a sign of the man in the boy. The eyes. His eyes had always been unique. He looked sweet and innocent. Angelic. Time had taken care of that.

Caitlin's fingers trembled as she deliberately shut the magazine. She felt lightheaded and dazed. The article had been a two-by-four to her head.

She set the magazine aside, then leaned over and tested the polish with the pad of her index finger. Dry. *J. B. Trammel.* She pulled on her socks over sunshine yellow toes. *Jana Tarkington.* She shoved her feet into her boots and tied the laces. *The Sokolov emeralds.*

She stood and stared down at the *Architectural Digest* cover and read the article headlines. *"American Royalty's Summer Escape."*

Benjamin Joshua Trammel. Jana Tarkington. The Sokolov emeralds. J. B. Trammel.

The doppelgänger portrait.

Josh Tarkington.

Josh Tarkington, auto mechanic.

No. No. No. There must be an explanation. This was coincidence, that's all. A wacky series of coincidences. So he looked like the guy in a vintage photograph, and the costume jewelry he'd given her was a copy of real stuff. So his last name was the same as some movie star's mother's maiden name, and he never breathed a word about his birth family. Coincidences do happen. That's all. Otherwise, what was she to think? That a movie star was hiding in Eternity Springs pretending to be an auto mechanic?

Maybe he's researching a part. It fit. All of it. It fit!

But no. That's crazy. He wouldn't have ended up in Oklahoma City if he was a Trammel. *It's a coincidence. It has to be. He'll probably laugh when I tell him about this. If he's in a good mood, that is.*

But what if it isn't a coincidence? What if I'm right? I can't be right. "I have to ask him," she murmured. "I have to ask."

After paying their bill—her mother had neglected to do so in her hurry to leave—Caitlin stuck her head into Celeste's office and asked to borrow the magazine. "There's an article I'd like to show Josh. I'll return it by the time you close today."

"Of course you may borrow it," Celeste said. "No need to make a special trip to return it, either. Next time you're headed this way will be fine."

"Thanks."

"And Caitlin?"

"Yes, ma'am?"

"On the way into the spa, I noticed something that

made me think of you. It's about halfway between the sidewalk and the big blue spruce to the north, halfway between the front door and the parking lot. In the snow. Take a look as you leave, will you, please? It's a sign, one should hold close to your heart in coming days."

She didn't have the patience to translate Celeste's cryptic advice right now. Distracted, she said, "Sure. Thanks, Celeste. I'll see you soon, I'm sure."

"Goodbye, dear. And please tell Josh that I pray every day for his speedy recovery."

"I will." Caitlin retrieved her coat from the hall tree and exited the building. Halfway to the parking lot, she remembered Celeste's request and looked northward. Since she didn't have a clue about what she was looking for, she didn't know whether to look high or low or . . . there. Snowdrops. White teardrop flowers on green stems pushing skyward through the blanket of snow. A promise that spring will come.

A sign. One I should hold close in the coming days.

Apprehension blew through Caitlin like a blizzard.

Journal Entry

Tormento has become a problem. He is a bad influence on Sherman, feeding him, suggesting evil things.

It is not good to have monsters running around inside one's mind and body. They destroy one's soul.

Chapter Eighteen

Josh sat on the side of his bed trying to work up the desire to move. His chest hurt worse than it had yesterday. He needed to cough, but coughing damn near killed him so he tried to stifle the urge.

He probably should call the doctor. He'd been warned that pneumonia was often a complication of broken ribs, and pneumonia could kill you. Dying didn't worry him all that much, but the thought of having to cough his way to the grave did give him pause.

The need to cough won out over will and by the time the fit was done, he'd felt as if he'd hacked up both lungs—and broken at least two more ribs. He looked toward Penny standing in his doorway with head cocked to one side, watching him.

"Wipe that look of pity off your face," he grumbled. "It's demeaning to be pitied by a crippled dog."

At the sound of his voice, she padded over to his bedside. Under other circumstances, Josh would have scratched her belly and behind her ears, but bending over wasn't an option. Instead, he rubbed her with his foot. "You're looking pretty today. Caitlin takes good care of you, doesn't she? She takes good care of us both. The woman is a saint."

She deserved better from him, too. The worse he felt, the bigger an ass he became. He couldn't explain how she sometimes wandered into the line of fire between his demons and himself. He'd been hungry for the first time in ages and decided to toast a blueberry bagel. He couldn't say why, but the scent triggered his cravings. She'd walked into the kitchen while he was riding the high of the memory—his heart racing, his nerve endings tingling in anticipation. She'd said something—he hadn't a clue what—and he'd damn near bitten her head off.

Afterward, he'd crawled back into bed and slept the sleep of the shamed.

"I should send her home," he muttered to Penny. "If I had an ounce of integrity, I'd send her home today."

Good thing he had no integrity, because he didn't want to do that. He desperately didn't want to do that. He loved having her company, loved being the recipient of her care and concern and first-class pampering. He loved . . . her. Still.

He met Penny's solemn brown-eyed gaze and observed, "I am so screwed."

Speaking triggered another cough that was longer and harder than the last and left him seriously wondering if he might have broken something else. Maybe a hot drink would help. Soothe the cough tickle away. He walked into the kitchen, filled the kettle with water, and set it onto the stove.

While he waited for the water to boil, he brooded over the truth he'd avoided thinking about since the accident. What the hell was he going to do?

Face reality, that's what.

This was bad. Hell. Love was hell. Hell was exactly what he deserved.

He'd lied to himself. Right from the very beginning,

he'd lied to himself. He'd known he was playing with fire. Friends and sex never mix. He loved her, and although she'd never said it, he knew she loved him, too. She showed it every hour of every day.

So what the hell are you going to do about it?

Nothing, that's what. Even if he wanted to throw caution to the wind and take a run at happy-ever-after again, he couldn't . . . wouldn't . . . do that to her. Because he loved her, he had to give her up.

Not because he actually believed that he was cursed with bad luck—he knew that was an easy way to kid himself and deflect others. Yes, he'd had a run of bad luck. No doubt about it. But did he honestly believe that daring to commit to something permanent with Caitlin would doom her to being swept up in a freak tornado or hit by a car or fallen upon by an angel-sans-wings? No.

The bottom line was that Caitlin deserved someone better than him. She needed someone she could trust. Someone she could count on being there when she needed him. Someone who wasn't a ticking time bomb.

He was close to exploding now. Closer than he'd been since he'd crawled his way out the last time. If he hadn't had that one moment of strength that allowed him to dump the Percs again, he'd be swirling down the toilet bowl himself right now.

It was going to happen. Someday. Sometime. He'd fight the good fight for as long as he could manage, but eventually, he would tire and weaken. He would surrender, and when that happened, there would be no coming back. Not again. He knew it in his soul. His sobriety, his life, was one weak trigger moment away.

He loved Caitlin too much to tie her to the disaster in waiting that was his future. She deserved so much better, so much more. She deserved a happy-ever-after that actually lasted ever-after.

The kettle began to whistle, and as Josh poured boiling water into a Tarkington Automotive mug, Penny's whining caught his notice. She stood at the back door, her attention locked on something outside. Had she been able to shake her tail, he knew it would be whipping up a wind.

He opened the door and she dashed off, surprisingly fast in her two-wheel chair. He figured she was after a squirrel or maybe a bird. Dachshunds had been bred as hunters, and Penny's disability did not affect those instincts. Just last week, she'd managed to take out a bird, which spoke to the truth of "bird brain." How dumb must a bird be to allow a dog in a squeaky wheelchair to sneak up on him.

When Penny disappeared around his outdoor kitchen, he turned away from the door opened his walk-in pantry in search of teabags. As he reached for a box of Earl Grey, the need to cough overwhelmed his ability to stifle it. In order to minimize the pain, he tried to hold himself completely erect during the event. Coughing with broken ribs competed with withdrawal in the pain department. Pain awoke the cravings.

He very much feared that having Caitlin Timberlake around was the only thing keeping him sober.

Furious and hurting, he swept a row of canned goods off the shelf. They clattered to the floor. He panted like Penny after a run up the hill.

He needed to let Caitlin go. He needed to break this off, to send her away. He needed to save her from himself. But dammit, he wanted just a little more time. He wanted to make love with her one more time. He couldn't do that now. The pain wouldn't allow it.

The devil whispered in his ear. *There are ways. There are positions you could manage. You could do it if you refilled the prescription. That's all you'd have to do. Re-*

fill the prescription, grovel a bit, and lure her into bed. You could do it.

Barking from outside yanked him from his reverie and he exited the pantry to look through the window to see . . . trouble. Penny had slung her tires going over his stepping-stone walk and now she'd managed to get herself caught in his woodpile. Josh muttered a curse, lifted his coat from its hook in the mudroom, and then tossed it aside because he couldn't put it on by himself. He stepped into his backyard coughing, hurting, filled with despair, and trying to pound his demons back into submission.

Penny's path through the backyard was obvious. From the spot where her wheelchair lay tipped over beside a stone, she'd carved a path through the snow to his out-door kitchen. There, she'd dragged herself up to and over rough bricks and mortar barely softened by a scant two inches of snow. The streaks of blood began just beyond the patio furniture where she'd dragged herself over the cast iron chair's L-shaped legs. "Oh, Penny."

It was a problem with her. She couldn't feel her belly and legs, so when she escaped her wheelchair and dragged herself, she scraped her skin raw. But dang it, she'd managed to climb the woodpile! What was she after? Not a skunk, he hoped. *Please, not a skunk.*

She continued to bark, continued to claw her way across snow-dusted logs. "Stop that, Penny," Josh called. "Stop before you hurt your—"

Logs rolled. Crashed. Penny yelped. Josh spat a curse. A fox scurried out of the woodpile.

"At least it's not a skunk." A cold breeze battered Josh as he hurried toward the woodpile taking care to secure his footing. The last thing either he or Penny needed was for him to slip and fall. She was trapped in the center of the woodpile with at least six heavy logs on top of her. Her pained whimpers shot arrows into his heart.

Josh looked around for help. Nobody in sight—not exactly a surprise since the garage was closed and the temperature hovered in the twenties. He was on his own. His surgeon had told him not to lift anything as heavy as a gallon of milk or risk tearing his stitches, but what was he to do? Let his dog be crushed or freeze to death?

He studied the woodpile that stood shoulder high. He couldn't lift the log that had shifted and blocked Penny's exit for fear of bringing the whole thing down. He'd have to start from the top and work his way down to her. And of course it was the part of the stack that had the heaviest logs. He'd need to be careful about the order of their removal too, so as not to risk a collapse.

This is going to hurt like a sonofabitch. Praying he wouldn't hear or feel the pop of stitches or staples, Josh gritted his teeth, tugged the top log, and dropped it to the ground. It took him ten long minutes to free his dog, and by the time he lifted Penny into his arms, he was breathing hard and sweat ran in rivulets down his temples. He hoped he could get back to the house without passing out.

Although, he'd heard that freezing to death was a good way to go. You just go to sleep and go away.

Penny whimpered. Her warm, sticky blood slid across his forearms. She had some bad abrasions on her belly. He'd need to tend to them before he crawled back in bed or into a snowdrift to die. Upon reaching the stepping-stone walk, he stared at Penny's wheelchair and wondered if he had the intestinal fortitude to bend over one more time to pick it up.

If I do it and fall down and can't get back up, that's not suicide, right? I'm caring for my dog.

He figured he must be delirious from the pain when he heard Celeste speak to him. *Now, don't be silly, Joshua.*

He let out a cry like a warrior on a battlefield as he bent and scooped up the wheelchair by the frame. He carried it and the eight-pound dog into the house, then sat Penny into the kitchen's farmhouse sink. He was vaguely aware that his hands were shaking as he washed the scrapes and applied the ointment Lori had prescribed for situations like these. He was acutely aware of the pain in his gut as he carried the dog to her bed, and of the coughing fits that wracked him as he rinsed the blood from his sink. As his whole body began to shake when he changed out of his bloodstained shirt and the thought of lying in the snow took hold, he accepted that he could take no more.

The war was over. The battle lost. He picked up the phone, dialed the local pharmacy, and surrendered. *Maybe it's better this way*, he told himself as he warmed up his tea and sat at the kitchen table to drink it. The choice had been made. The die cast. The Rubicon crossed. It was too late to second-guess himself. Too late to indulge in maybes or what-ifs.

It was time for Caitlin to go home.

"I should have stopped by the yoga studio for a class before coming here," Caitlin muttered as she approached Josh's house. If she were in a cartoon, she'd be Wile E. Coyote's round black bomb with its sparkling, steadily shrinking fuse. She was about to explode.

She'd made the twelve-minute walk from Angel's Rest to Josh's house in eight minutes thirty seconds, fueled by adrenaline, her thoughts whirling like falling leaves on an autumn wind. She had questions, lots of questions, and she wanted answers. Immediately. From her father. From her lover. She was tired of being kept in the dark by the men in her life. *When I finish with Josh, I'm going up to Heartache Falls and having it out with my dad.*

But first, Josh owed her an explanation. She intended to be calm, cool, and collected when she showed him the magazine article and asked her questions. After all, she could be way off the mark.

She didn't think she was, though.

She opened the front door and stepped inside, pulling off her gloves and tucking them into her pockets. He wasn't in the family room. She checked his office, then the media room, and finally, the kitchen.

He was sitting at the table staring down into a mug of something hot. He didn't look up when she came in, and his lack of attention fanned her smoldering fuse. She demanded, "Are you J. B. Trammel?"

So much for calm, cool, and collected.

Her heart pounded. Her mouth went dry. A full thirty seconds passed before he answered with a simple, "Yes."

Caitlin released a heavy breath and tried to absorb the news. Josh was J. B. Trammel. She gaped at him, waiting for further explanation—explanation that never came. He didn't give her anything. Didn't say a single word. She wanted to smack him. In the ribs! "'Yes'? That's all you're going to say?"

He shrugged slightly and after a long pause asked, "Want my autograph?"

She couldn't explain why, but that hurt more than anything. It sliced right through the defense of anger and wounded her heart. She stood there speechless, trying not to cry, wondering how life had taken such a fast, terrible turn when he finally spoke again. Rather than providing answers, he casually asked a question of his own. "How did you find out?"

She pulled the magazine folded to the article out of her tote and dropped it onto the table in front of him. His lips twisted in a wry grin. "Ahh. I was cute, wasn't I? They told me I was an angel."

Finally, she found her voice. "Has it all been a lie, Josh? Or, should I call you J. B.? Is it some sort of Hollyweird experiment? Go live like the common folk for a while to add authenticity to a role? How could you do this to us, to me and the people of Eternity Springs who invited you into our lives and hearts? Why the masquerade? Does Brick know the truth about you? Has he been lying to us, too?"

Again, there was a long pause before Josh responded. "Brick doesn't know. He's never known. The Christophers respected my privacy. Will you? Are you going to out me, Caitlin?"

"Why shouldn't I? I'm not a liar, unlike someone else in this room. Why shouldn't I let everyone in town in on your little secret? Explain it to me, Josh. Make me understand!"

"Technically what I've told the people of Eternity Springs is the truth—just not the whole truth. I am Josh Tarkington just as much as I am J. B. Trammel. *Why* I have two separate and distinct lives is my business. My privacy is important to me, and I told you from the beginning not to have expectations where I'm concerned. You're my friend, not my wife. There are limits to what friends need to know."

Caitlin took the words like a blow and she reached for a chair back to steady herself. It only got worse.

"I've enjoyed your company," he went on. "I really enjoyed the sex. But I'm afraid I haven't been at my best of late, so I didn't notice the signs. I think the events of the past month gave you the wrong impression about where you and I might be headed. It's getting a little too . . . domestic . . . around here. I appreciate having had your help. You've been a great friend and a real help to me, but I'm getting along fine now. I think it's probably time you moved back home."

She sucked in a breath. "You're breaking up with me."

"I'm a selfish bastard. I enjoyed you and I let it go too far for too long. I'm sorry, Caitlin. It was poorly done of me."

He's breaking up with me.

Her knees went weak and it was all she could do not to double over from the blow. Suddenly, she wanted away from Josh J. B. Trammel Tarkington as fast as she could possibly manage. She was going to cry, and pride wouldn't let him see her tears.

Without a word, she fled the kitchen, blinking back tears, her heart breaking, her stomach churning with a combination of fury and hurt unlike anything she'd felt before. In the guest room she opened the closet and yanked her suitcase from a shelf. Luckily, she didn't have all that much to move since she'd only brought everyday items with her. It took her less than five minutes to empty the closet and bureau drawers. In the bathroom, she tossed makeup and toiletries into a backpack.

The last piece of furniture to empty was the bedside nightstand. She picked up the paperback she was currently reading and tossed it into her suitcase along with her computer and electronics cords. Then she drew a deep breath and slid open the nightstand drawer to reveal the two black velvet jewelry boxes.

With a trembling hand, she removed them, opened them, and stared down at the contents. What were they called? S-something-emeralds. Sorbek? Saracen? No, Sokolov. The Sokolov emeralds. Guess she'd been a real idiot not to recognize these as real.

Although she'd pretty sure she'd never seen jewels like these outside of a museum. And why in the world would it have occurred to her that they were anything other than costume? The man portrayed himself as an engine mechanic. Why would she think he had real jewelry to give? Should she have suspected him of burglary?

He'd gifted her with a fortune in jewels—right before he sent her away. *I'm like the duke's mistress in a romance novel, dismissed after he meets his heroine.*

A soft, sour laugh escaped Caitlin's lips. Josh had warned her. He'd been totally honest about his wishes and his walls. She'd been the one to ignore them. She'd been the pursuer in their relationship, not him.

She'd believed she could overcome his objections. A siege? Hah. She'd launched her catapults, shot her arrows, swam the stupid moat . . . and his walls stood strong as ever. She'd failed. She'd been vanquished. The castle walls weren't in ruins—she was.

She'd lost.

Caitlin snapped the boxes shut and tossed them on the bed. She lifted her backpack, picked up her suitcase, and headed for the mudroom and her coat. Josh—or J. B.— had yet to move away from the kitchen table.

In a perfect world, she would have the perfect parting shot sitting on her tongue. In reality, the sight of him saddened her, and she couldn't think of anything clever so she crossed the room in silence. He didn't look up from his drink.

She set down her luggage in order to slip into her coat. Penny rolled up beside her and Caitlin took a moment to pet her before removing her gloves from her pocket and pulling them on. "I left Penny's heartworm tablets on top of the washing machine."

"Thanks."

She slung the strap of her backpack over her shoulder. *Come on, Timberlake. Think of a zinger.* She opened the door, picked up her suitcase, and couldn't think of a single thing to say to him other than goodbye. She wasn't quite ready to say that.

So she remained silent as she stepped outside. As she reached for the doorknob to shut the door behind her, Josh finally spoke. "You deserve better, Caitlin."

"I know that, Josh." At this particular moment in time and under these particular circumstances, she knew there was nothing else to say.

So Caitlin closed the door.

Journal Entry

Today, I looked at baseball cards.

It's an awesome collection. There's a Joe DiMaggio, a Ted Williams, a Hank Aaron—too many prizes to count. It took me a while to figure out that he had them grouped by league, then team, then position—infield, outfield, catchers, and pitchers.

I thought about Drew-Bear. Wondered why he'd called the game early. Did he have a Sherman of his own? A Tormento? Did he spend a lot of time thinking about it? Planning it? Or was it an impulsive, reckless act?

I flipped through the box. Second basemen—Joe Morgan, Pee Wee Reese, Bump Wills. Shortstops—Ozzie Smith, Maury Wills, Derek Jeter. Hmm . . . why are Lou Gehrig, Roberto Clemente, and Lymon Bostock out of order?

I thought a few minutes and figured it out. They died. They were all players who died young.

Guess that answered my question. Not recklessness, then. Genetics.

Chapter Nineteen

Caitlin nursed her wounded heart overnight in the privacy of her little rental house on Third and Pinion. She lay awake tossing and turning and mentally replaying the events of this day and those of the past four months. From that electric moment in Telluride when her and Josh's gazes first met to the wicked games they'd played at Brick and Lili's wedding. To the laughter they'd shared. The early morning runs. The late-night conversations. Had none of that been real? Had it all been as false as his name?

She didn't want to believe it.

She didn't know what to believe.

She felt lost. She wished she were home. She wished she could go beg a hug from her mom or crawl up into her daddy's lap and bury her head against his chest and cry.

Except, that was a whole other problem, wasn't it? Her parents had a problem they hadn't shared with her. She knew it as certain as . . . well . . . as certain as the fact that her lover was a liar. She finally drifted off to sleep thinking that she seriously couldn't deal with another secret for one more day.

When she awoke the following morning, she decided to do something about it. She picked up some cinnamon rolls from the bakery, drove up to Heartache Falls without calling ahead, and walked into her parents' home through the kitchen door without knocking. "Mom? Dad?"

"Caitlin?" Her mother's surprised voice came from the front of the house. "We're in here."

Caitlin set down the bakery box then walked to the great room. There, an open book and reading glasses showed that her mom had obviously risen from her usual spot on the sofa. Her father reclined in a big leather chair that hadn't been there the last time Caitlin had visited. He didn't get up, which was understandable if he'd twisted his ankle. Except, his ankle wasn't wrapped or swollen at all.

Mac Timberlake looked tired. Pale. Definitely not the vigorous father Caitlin was accustomed to seeing.

Although if she was being honest with herself, when was the last time she'd taken a long, hard look at her father?

You've been avoiding it. You know you have. She'd been so wrapped up in Josh and his problems that she'd ignored the troubles up at Heartache Falls.

Well, no more. No more ignorance where either one of these stubborn men were concerned. "Enough of this. I'm not stupid, Daddy. What's wrong with you? Something is wrong with you. Tell me what's wrong."

Mac shot Ali a quick look. "I'm fine, honey. I think Mom told you I twisted my ankle."

"Yes, she did. While her face drained of all color." Caitlin folded her arms. "There's a recliner in Mom's living room. As long as I can remember, Mom swore she'd never have a recliner in the living room. Your office was okay. The den was okay. The living room was not okay. You are sick, aren't you, Dad? I need to know the truth. Please, just tell me the truth!"

Mac closed his eyes, swallowed hard, and took a deep breath. Caitlin's heart dropped to her toes.

Her father said, "I've had some worrisome muscle weakness and tingling in my hands. But I don't want you to fret about it. I had a complete barrage of tests and they didn't find anything."

Relief flowed over Caitlin like snowmelt in the spring. And yet . . . "But you're still having symptoms? They're bad enough that you need a recliner?"

"My symptoms come and go. The recliner is . . . um . . ."

"I'm expanding my boundaries," Ali said. She lifted her chin and a militant light gleamed in her eyes. "Your dad and I agree we don't want to get in a rut."

Caitlin's eyes went round. "A rut? When have the two of you ever been in a rut?"

"I rest my case. But enough about us." Ali offered her daughter a bright smile and asked, "So, is there a special reason for the visit? How is Josh today?"

Caitlin tilted her head and studied her parents. As always, they presented a united front. Her father's gaze never wavered as he watched her, and Mac Timberlake didn't lie to her. "You'll tell me if it's something serious, Dad?"

"I'll tell you as soon as anything is confirmed, sweet-pea. You have my word."

"Okay then." Caitlin drew a deep breath and returned to her mother's questions. She didn't have an answer for the second one, of course, so she answered the first. "I brought cinnamon rolls from Fresh. That's always special."

"I'll make fresh coffee," Ali said. She looked at her husband. "Shall we have a tray here by the fireplace?"

"No." His voice was firm. "We'll sit at the kitchen table."

Ali began, "But——"

"I'll use the cane, Caitlin, what's the latest on Gingerbread House?"

Caitlin was glad to keep the conversation away from Josh and on daycare matters, and she left a half hour later reassured about her father's health. It cleared her mind for further brooding about her own problems. And brood she did. For the rest of the morning and the entire afternoon, it was all Josh, all the time.

She'd been vanquished from the battlefield, true, but what about the war? Was she ready to give up? For months now, she'd said she loved him. If she truly loved him, would she walk away? Let him push her away? Wouldn't she fight for him?

If she truly loved him.

That was the question, wasn't it? How could she love a man whose name she didn't even know?

Who was he? What were his values, his beliefs? Why was he hiding in Eternity Springs? Why had he hidden himself from her?

Without answers to those questions, how could she have real, honest, true feelings for the man?

But could her instincts have been so completely and totally wrong?

Caitlin looked deep within herself. In her heart of hearts, she didn't believe she would be so wrong. But how could she be sure? How could she trust herself?

At that point, she did the only thing she knew to do. She called her best girlfriend.

Lori closed the vet clinic half an hour early, and by five the two women were sitting at Caitlin's kitchen table with a tub of rocky road and every ice cream topping the Trading Post had on the shelves set out in front of them. As they dug in, Caitlin explained the situation and poured out her heart, ending with, "He didn't ask me to keep the movie star thing a secret, but I don't feel right about spreading it around, so . . ."

"I'll keep quiet," Lori assured her. "It's a fascinating bit of news, though, isn't it? I'd sure love to know the backstory there."

"Or maybe not," Caitlin observed. "It could be really awful, for him to have hidden it so deeply."

"True." Lori gave her spoon a thoughtful lick. "So you think that's why he broke up with you? You discovered his big secret?"

"I don't know. I imagine that's part of it, but who knows? He hasn't exactly been the king of communication lately."

"Well, men can be total jerks, but we know that about them."

"Truer words were never spoken."

"So what are you going to do?"

"I don't know. I admit that this has given me some doubts I didn't have before. That's kind of scary."

"That's kind of normal, if you ask me. The man didn't tell the truth about his identity. Big red flag there. Of course you have questions."

"You want to know the really scary part? I'm pretty sure I know the answers. Well, the one answer that seems to matter most, anyway. I love him. I still love him. The way he's acted . . . the secrets . . . they don't seem to matter." She set down her spoon and rubbed her eyes. "I can't explain it, Lori, not even to myself. I just know I love him. I love him. That frightens me. What if I'm totally off base here? What if I'm wrong about him? What if he's been playing a role all along and I'm just too blind to see it? Although, I don't know that it matters one way or the other because he broke up with me yesterday, didn't he!"

"Break up, shmake up." Lori squirted a dab of chocolate sauce onto the last of the ice cream in her bowl. "If you want him, you'll fight for him. If you fight for him, you'll win. That's what you do, Caitlin."

"Why?"

"I don't know about that," Caitlin said, frowning.

"I do. The question is, do you want him? Honey, I'm going to be honest here. I think you need this break as much as Josh does."

"This love affair happened very fast. I know you've been sure of your feelings right from the beginning, but this whole thing has been out of character for you. I think this break is a good opportunity for you to give yourself time to be sure of your surety."

Dryly, Caitlin asked, "Are you sure?"

Lori shook her spoon at her sister-in-law. "I am. Besides, it's not like you don't have anything to do to keep you busy."

"That's true. I've a million things to do before Gingerbread House's opening day."

"Then get to them." Lori scooped the last of her ice cream onto her spoon, swallowed it with sinful relish, then stood. "Now, I do believe my work here is done. I'd better get home to your brother. It's my night to cook and I promised him Tuscan chicken—though I don't know how I'm going to eat a bite after all this ice cream. You're welcome to join us, Caitlin. I have plenty."

"No thanks." She rose and gave her sister of the heart a hug. "All of a sudden I'm anxious to get started on work."

"Good."

"Yes, good. Thank you, Lori."

"My pleasure." Lori gave her wink and added, "It's also going to be my pleasure to watch Mr. Hollywood mend this break-up fence. Winter can be long in Eternity Springs. I'll be glad to have the entertainment."

Caitlin watched through the kitchen window as Lori backed her veterinary practice's van out of her driveway and pulled away. A faint smile played upon her face as she rinsed the dirty dishes and loaded the dishwasher. The two visits with family today had improved her spirits tremendously.

Tonight, she thought she'd do a yoga video on You-Tube and then take a nice long bath. She'd go to bed early and there would be no tossing and turning this time.

She wasn't going to worry about her dad.

She wasn't going to wallow around feeling heart-broken.

She would pour her energy and efforts into Ginger-bread House and give herself time to think about exactly what she wanted from the man who lived next door.

The minute Caitlin shut the door, Josh surrendered to the coughing fit he'd fought to hold back since he'd asked her to leave. When the delivery he requested from the pharmacy arrived, he didn't hesitate to throw back the maximum dose. After that, he went to bed, where he pretty much stayed for the next three days until a pound-ing on his door roused him.

Harriet took one look at him and called his doctor. Josh was too sick to protest when the physician did the small-town solid of making a house call. Ten days of an-tibiotics later, he began to feel human again and by the first week of February, he decided he just might survive. Lonely as hell, hooked on painkillers, but alive.

Dammit.

He remembered something one of his rehab doctors back in the day had said. "Pneumonia is God's gift to old people—it's not a bad way to die." It would have been easier if he'd just died. If Harriet hadn't been over here hounding him to take his antibiotics every damn day, he might have pulled it off.

And now he was out of Percocet and wondering where he could get some more.

Dr. Alvarado wouldn't refill his prescription so soon. Neither would the doctors in Gunnison. Doctor shopping had netted him nothing. He was so effed. Why hadn't they just let him die?

He hadn't heard one word from Caitlin since the day he sent her away, and he was fine with that. He didn't need her hovering over him. Neither did he need Celeste or Harriet or Lili knocking at his door. Unfortunately, they didn't take his hints. On Groundhog Day, Harriet had watched Punxsutawney Phil predict six more weeks of winter on the television in his kitchen while he hid in the bathroom shaking and shivering and puking his guts up as he tried to resist the urge to take a pill. Three days after Valentine's Day when Claire Lancaster dropped by with a plate of iced sugar cookies after the baby's afternoon nap, he could move without his ribs barking at him too bad, but he was completely out of Percs and contemplating driving somewhere—anywhere—to score some.

Or I could pay her a visit and ask to use the john, rifle through her medicine cabinet, and steal whatever she has.

He thanked Claire and walked her to the door. As he started to shut it, movement across the street caught his notice. A thought occurred. Harriet had broken her hip. Harriet had taken pain medication. What were the chances that she had a few left over? Pretty good, he'd bet. He could ask to borrow a couple.

A wave of relief washed over him at the thought, but that was immediately eclipsed by a tsunami of shame.

You'd steal pain medicine from an old lady? You don't deserve to live, asshat.

Shaken by the knowledge that he had sunk so low, Josh backed away from his front door and shut it, stared at it as if it were a snake. The Snake. Temptation. Evil waited on just the other side and if he stepped into it . . .

"I have to do something," he murmured. Dammit, he had to do something now before he did something soul-destroying. He needed something. Needed it now.

Needed.

On the third Monday in February, Caitlin stepped away from the bulletin board and beamed. "Is that cute or what?"

Her mother eyed the construction paper ladybugs, green grass, and bright yellow sun along with letters that spelled WE'RE BUGGY ABOUT SPRING and grinned. "It's cute, and it's so you. You have always been a ladybug girl."

"I don't know why I love them so much. They are kinda creepy. And the nursery rhyme is downright scary."

A wistful smiled played about Ali's face. "I know why you love them. After-dinner tag in the summer. Remember? All the neighborhood kids would come play in our front yard."

"I do remember that. The boys wouldn't let me play."

"*I* wouldn't let you play. You were little and it was a rough and tumble game. But you and I would sit on the front stoop and there were always ladybugs flying around." She let out a long sigh. "I miss those days."

Both Ali and Caitlin turned at the sound in the doorway. Mac stood there pulling on his jacket. "I finished your fence, Cait. Want to come see it?"

"I do!" She walked toward her father and saw his gaze glide over the bulletin board. His smile was bittersweet. "Sometimes it's hard to believe that spring will ever come."

"I know," Caitlin agreed. "They are forecasting six inches of snow before morning and even more during the next few days. The extended forecast looks pretty hairy too."

Ali glanced toward the window. "I know. I'm worried the weather will interfere with Stephen's ski trip."

Caitlin's eldest brother lived in Dallas now with his wife and three children. He and a group of old college friends had a ski trip to Wolf Creek scheduled for the first week of March. He intended to visit Eternity Springs for a few days afterward before heading home. Mom had started planning her menus already, giddy at the thought of having all three of her children under the same roof for a time.

"Don't fret, Alison," Mac called over his shoulder as he led them toward the front hall. "Stephen won't let the weather prevent this trip home. He'd hire a dogsled team to get over Sinner's Prayer Pass for a pan of your lasagna."

"It's true, Mom. Stephen won't—oh!" Caitlin spied the short, white picket fence attached to the hallway walls. She clapped like a child. "Oh my gosh. That's perfect!" Then she shook a finger, saying, "Wait a minute." She dashed into the kitchen and returned a moment later carrying a Spiderman backpack. She hung it over one of the pickets, stepped back, and clapped again. "Totally perfect. Can't you just see all the little backpacks lined up on the fence?"

Ali nodded. "I can. This was a darling idea, Cait."

"Wait until you see the nursery now that the furniture's in. It's my favorite room in the house."

"Show me, show me," Ali said with a smile.

Mac held up a hand, palm out. "I'll wait for another time, if you don't mind, sweetheart. I have a few errands I need to run before the stores close."

"No problem." She went up on her toes and kissed her father on the cheek. "Thanks for all the help, Dad. I truly do appreciate it."

"Glad to be of service." He returned his daughter's kiss. "Anything else for my Daddy-do list?"

"No. I think that does it. I have a few final touches to do myself, but Gingerbread House will be ready to open its doors on schedule next week."

"In that case, I'll see you two later." He strolled out the door.

Caitlin watched her father leave with a combination of tenderness and concern. "He's been in a good mood lately."

"Yes, he has. He's had fun helping you around here."

"His muscles don't seem to be giving him much trouble."

Ali glanced after her husband. "He hasn't complained. I don't bring it up. He's enjoying life. That's what matters."

Caitlin couldn't argue with that. She didn't have time. The past few weeks had flown by as she'd readied Gingerbread House for its opening. The work had been a godsend, especially after she'd learned that Josh had developed pneumonia. It had taken all of her willpower not to rush over to his house with chicken soup. Maternal instinct proved difficult to ignore.

Lori had talked her down from the soup pot, and the pinecone telegraph—as Celeste sometimes called town gossip—kept Caitlin up-to-date on Josh's condition. She understood he was improving, so much so that she'd spent Valentine's Day in reluctant expectation. After all, she'd slept with the man for months. It wouldn't have hurt him to send a friendly card. She hadn't heard a word from him, and she'd taken the card she'd purchased for him and tossed it in the garbage. A real shame, considering the price of greeting cards these days.

"Are you going to show me the nursery?" Ali asked, tugging Caitlin's attention back to the present.

"Yes, I'm sorry," Caitlin led the way upstairs to where two former bedrooms were now one big room. Six white dressers sat next to six white Jenny Lind cribs. Caitlin planned to give parents the option to decorate their baby's individual area if they so desired. If not, the nursery worker would choose between a variety of themes Caitlin had on hand.

"It's lovely, honey," her mother said. She sat in one of three oversized rockers. "These chairs are fabulous. Good choice."

"You're the one who suggested them. Everything is wired, of course, so that parents can check in on their little ones whenever they wish."

"It's homey, peaceful, and pretty—I love the dotted Swiss window curtains."

"I want parents to consider us more as nannies than a daycare facility."

"I expect you'll pull that off." Ali glanced around the room. "Didn't you put an entrance to the secret room in here?"

"No. We changed that. My insurance guy said we'd be better off having only one doorway that I can keep padlocked. Liability issues. I still plan to use it as a storeroom, but I think it's best the kiddos don't know it exists."

"That's probably a good idea." Giving her daughter a sidelong glance, Ali added, "Speaking of good ideas . . . a little birdie told me that Josh—"

"Mom, please," Caitlin interrupted. "I don't want to hear about Josh Tarkington today. I'm in a good mood and I'd like to stay that way. Say, have you seen the glass mobile Cicero made me for the sunroom? It's fabulous."

"All right," Ali said with a sigh. "I guess you'll talk to me when you're ready. No, I haven't seen the mobile."

"Come see it while the sun is still shining. It's almost like having a disco ball hanging from the ceiling."

Moments later, they stood in the sunroom gazing upward where colors danced all over the room. Ali smiled with delight. "You're right. It's wonderful. The children are going to love it."

"I think so too."

"You're building something special here, Caitlin. Eternity Springs will be a better place because of it. Dad and I are proud of you."

Her mother's words warmed Caitlin. She kept her voice light as she asked, "Still think I should have stayed in New York?"

"No, and I should have known better." Ali linked elbows with Caitlin. "You are the most project-oriented person I've ever known. Once you set a goal, you don't give up until you achieve it."

Movement outside the window caught Caitlin's gaze. Josh was leaving his house and walking toward the automotive center. "I don't know, Mom. There is such a thing as lost causes."

"Nonsense. You know what Celeste would say about that, don't you? 'To risk all for a lost cause is the way great victories are achieved.'"

The heater kicked on and stirred the air. The mobile pieces moved and clinked together, sounding just a little like bells.

Josh paced his living room like a caged lion. Finally, he grabbed his wallet and went hunting for his keys. He hadn't used them in so long, he didn't know where to look. He wasn't sure where he'd go once he found them.

He hadn't had a dealer in years. He could fly somewhere. Load up. Shoot up. He'd be free of this all-consuming yearning. But that would take hours and hours. Gunnison? He could probably score something in Gunnison. Might take him a little while to track down a source, but there would be one. Sources were everywhere.

Except for Eternity Springs. Eternity Springs wasn't like any other place in the world. It was truly a place out of time.

Josh found his keys hanging on a key rack in his mudroom. *Where did that come from?* Caitlin, of course. He found her little touches all over the house.

He slipped the keys into his pocket, pulled on his coat, and stepped out into the winter afternoon. Though the sun was shining, clouds rolled in from the west. Looked like it might snow before long. Driving might be a bear.

He just wished it wasn't so damn far to Gunnison. Halfway to his garage and the bay where he left his car, he glanced across the street and his feet slowed. Maybe he could ask Harriet for a pill. Just one. That wouldn't be so bad, would it?

Yeah, it would. It's a slippery slope. Best not go there at all.

He walked on to the garage. There, he climbed into his car and started the engine, giving it some time to warm up. It was the first time he'd been behind the wheel in a long time. It felt good. Never mind that his hands shook like a palsied old man's.

He pulled out onto the street and drove at a snail's pace through town. While approaching the stop sign at First and Spruce, his gaze fell upon Murphy's Bar and Grill. Without making a conscious decision to do so, he pulled over and parked, then went inside.

Shannon Garrett stood behind the carved wooden bar drying pint glasses. She smiled at him in surprise. "Josh, this is a nice surprise. You haven't been in since before the accident. You're feeling better?"

"Yeah."

"Here for a burger?"

He hesitated. A burger wouldn't hurt. "Yes. A cheeseburger, please."

"Something to drink?"

He sucked in a deep breath. "The Macallan. A double."

"Coming up." She offered him a brilliant smile and added, "Take any seat you'd like."

He sat at the end of the bar away from where she was working, which should indicate that he didn't want to make small talk. She poured a glass of water and set it on a coaster in front of him. "Do you want me to put in your order now or would you like your burger to arrive after you've finished your drink?"

"Why don't you wait on it."

A moment later, Shannon set a double scotch in front of him. Josh touched the glass, stared at the amber liquid inside, but didn't immediately lift it. He remembered being twelve years old . . . and drunk.

Hey kid. Aren't you a pretty boy? Whatcha hiding in those pants? Let's see it. C'mon. Don't be shy. Look. I'm not shy. Want to touch it? C'mon. Touch me.

He remembered being seven and watching a drunk.

Hey kid. Damn, you're a good-lookin' kid. You look just like me. Damn sure a Trammel. Camera loves you. Bet the booze will too. It's our curse, you know.

He remembered sitting in a circle surrounded by others with hollow eyes and the slumped shoulders of the hopeless.

I hate it here. I don't want to be here. I don't belong here.

Josh ran his index finger around the lip of his glass. He still didn't pick it up.

Go ahead. You'll love it. It's the best high ever. Tons better than booze or grass. Here. Give me your arm. I'll show you how. Don't worry. It's a clean needle.

"What the hell are you doing, son?"

Mac Timberlake swooped in and grabbed the glass out of Josh's hand. He set it out of Josh's reach and signaled for Shannon to come get it.

"What the hell are *you* doing, old man?" Josh fired back, leaning past Caitlin's father and reaching for his drink.

"Saving your ass, apparently."

"You can't—"

"Shut up," Mac interrupted. "Shannon, don't serve him. He's still on medicine. Drug interactions. Guess the idiot just forgot. Bring us some food, would you, please? I don't care what. Something fast."

With a curious look from one man to the other, Shannon said, "He ordered a cheeseburger."

"That'll work. Make it two." Taking Josh's forearm in a firm grip and with a little more force than necessary to deal with a man with healing ribs, Mac hauled him to his feet. "Let's get a table."

Josh yanked out of the older man's grip and considered marching out the door, but he couldn't make himself do it. He was hungry for news of Caitlin. Sullenly, he followed Mac to an isolated corner table.

Once they were seated, Mac scowled angrily and asked, "What the hell? You trying to kill yourself, J. B.?"

"She knows? Huh. That's a surprise. She never let on. J. B." She told you."

"I didn't think you'd told her."

"I didn't. She figured it out herself."

"Ah . . ." Mac nodded as if a puzzle piece had just fallen into place. "No wonder she left you. You lied to her. That's one of her big taboos."

Josh knew he should keep his mouth shut, but he felt compelled to defend himself. "I didn't lie to her. I am

Paul and Cindy Christopher's son. They are my family. I am Joshua Tarkington—I changed my name legally."

"So I understand."

That took Josh aback. He hadn't shared that particular fact with Caitlin. "How do you know?"

"Before the accident in December, I hired a private investigator to check you out."

Josh's eyes rounded in surprise. Guess he should have anticipated that. "What did you expect to learn? That I was a thief? An ex-con? A father of five who'd deserted my family?"

"I didn't know what to expect." Mac shrugged. "My little girl was starry-eyed over you, and all I knew about you was that you'd come out of the Oklahoma foster care system. I had concerns."

"I'll just bet you did," Josh muttered. "So why haven't you outted me to the entire town?"

"I considered it." Mac paused when he saw Shannon approaching with two glasses of ice and a pitcher of water.

"Burgers will be right out," she informed them as she filled the glasses.

"Thanks, Shannon." Mac smiled up at their hostess, and when she walked away, he sipped his water and said, "Look, I didn't like you because you reminded me of myself. Did Caitlin ever tell you that I came out of the Oklahoma foster system too?"

Josh looked at him in surprise. "She never mentioned that."

"I don't go around bragging about it, believe me. My mother was a bitch on wheels. Drug and alcohol abuser. A grifter. She'd steal the wimple off a nun whether she had use for it or not. More than once, she abandoned me in flea trap of a motel, and it's but by the grace of God that I didn't follow in her footsteps. It could have gone the other way just as easily. So when you caught Caitlin's attention, it worried me. I looked at you and I saw myself. I wasn't very nice to you."

"Really?" Josh drawled. "I hadn't noticed."

Mac grinned. "Smart-ass."

Josh was just grumpy enough to press it. "Weren't you a federal judge once upon a time? I thought judges waited for evidence before they reached a verdict."

"I'm a father first. That means I automatically don't like any hairy-legged boy who comes sniffing after my little girl. That's probably never going to change because no guy will ever be good enough for her."

Shannon delivered two platters piled high with burgers and fries to the table, and Mac waited to say more until they'd both consumed half their meal. The cheeseburger tasted surprisingly good to Josh, and the meal, together with the company, managed to distract him from the clawing need that had sent him from his house in search of relief.

Feeling more mellow than he had all day, he decided to offer Mac Timberlake a gift. "Don't worry. I know I'm not good enough for her. That's why we're not together anymore."

"Excuse me?"

"BS. You're not together anymore because you're trying hard to make the same mistake I almost made. They say girls look for men like their father to marry. I'd hoped Cait would choose better than that, but the girl has always been hard-headed."

"Whoa, whoa, whoa. Marry! I've never said anything about marriage!"

"That's because you're being an idiot. You're letting

your past control your future without any acknowledgment of the person you've become in the present." Mac popped the rest of his fry into his mouth. "I did the same damn thing. I let fear rule my actions and emotions and almost ruined my relationship with the love of my life. Be smarter than me. Life is short, Tarkington. Too damn short. Don't waste it by living in the past."

Mac took his napkin from his lap and wiped his mouth, then removed his wallet from his pocket and pulled out a twenty. "I heard what I wanted to hear from you today. You're Tarkington, not Mr. Movie Star. That's good."

He tossed the bill onto the table. "I understand you gave Caitlin some fancy jewelry. That's a nice start, but you can do better."

Better than the Sokolov emeralds? "Um . . . I'm wealthy, but I'm not stupid rich."

"Just stupid," Mac muttered, making a disgusted roll of his eyes. "Caitlin gave you something infinitely more valuable than diamonds and emeralds, Tarkington. My daughter gave you the most valuable gift in existence. She gave you her heart. Treasure it. Cherish it. Be worthy of it."

Despair rose within Josh. "But that's just it. I'm not. I never will be. I'm . . . I have . . ." He gritted his teeth and at Caitlin's father. "I'm not whole."

"Hell, pup. None of us are whole. You gotta slap on a bandage and keep on going."

"You don't understand."

Mac's voice softened. "You'd be surprised at what I understand. My PI created a thorough file."

He knows. Josh shut his eyes as shame washed over him. "I'm surprised you haven't shot me."

"Why? Seems to me that you had plenty of help getting into that dark world. That wasn't your fault. It shows character that you had the balls to get out."

"You're never out. Not really. You take it day to day, so you're never really out."

"Maybe so. But you have something—someone—to keep you looking forward to the next day." Mac rose to leave, but stopped beside Josh and put a hand on his shoulder. "Don't give up, son. You have friends here. You have family. You have people who love you. A fine, fabulous woman who loves you. You don't have to do this alone. Let us help you." He gave Josh's shoulder a squeeze, then departed.

Minutes ticked by as Josh sat without moving. *It wasn't my fault? Did he really say that? Did he really believe it? Do I?*

To a point, yes. He'd been thrown into the deep end by parents who should have done better by him. He had managed to avoid drowning and he crawled his way back onto solid ground. He could do it again—couldn't he?

If it meant a future with Caitlin . . .

When he finally stood, his hamburger sat like a rock in his gut. The craving that had subsided during the conversation with Mac returned, crawling on spider's legs up his spine.

A light snow fell from the darkening sky and muffled the sound of traffic on the street. Josh shoved his bare hands into his pockets and sucked in a deep breath, filling his lungs with bitter air and in the process, reminding himself of his illness and that his bones had yet to completely heal. Shivering, he started to walk, not toward his car but toward the building two blocks away where a red neon sign read URGENT CARE.

The moisture leaking from the corners of his eyes was a reaction to the cold, not tears. Not tears.

My daughter gave you the most valuable gift in existence. She gave you her heart. Treasure it. Cherish it. Be worthy of it.

"God, help me."

The clinic's automatic doors swung open and Josh stepped inside. The receptionist smiled at him. "May I help you?"

"Which physician is working tonight?"

"Dr. Cicero has this evening's shift."

Not Alvarado. Does it matter? I like Rose. She might be easier to talk to. "I'd like to see her, please."

The receptionist handed him a clipboard. "Please fill out this paperwork and return it to me when you're done. It's been a slow evening so far. You shouldn't have too long a wait."

"Thank you."

Within ten minutes, he was called back to Exam Room Three. A nurse took his vital signs and asked the reason for his visit. "I'd rather wait and explain to the doctor, please."

"All right. Dr. Cicero will be in shortly."

He listened to a baby crying in a room across the hall and stared unseeing at a poster of the digestive system. A few minutes later, the door opened and Rose Cicero stepped inside. "Hello, Josh. I hope you're not here to tell me you've injured your poor ribs again."

"No. No, that's not it." Josh raked his fingers through his hair. "Rose, I'm in trouble. The pain pills have become a problem for me. I should have told Dr. Alvarado. I . . . need help."

He exhaled hard, shut his eyes, and confessed, "I'm an addict."

Journal Entry

I can't remember the last time I was this afraid. Maybe the night my father died? Or the time when I was eight and realized my mother had left me alone in the house when she went off to Paris with a lover? Perhaps it was the first time I woke up from a heroin overdose. Whatever. I don't guess it matters. Suffice to say that I'm pretty damn scared.

Because I have hope again.

Hope. It's a crazy deal. It can be small as a pinprick but more powerful than a hundred-thousand-candle-power flashlight.

I went by her house. Stood outside in the snow, watching the warm light in her window. She saw me. For a long moment, our gazes met and held. She didn't invite me in. I didn't knock on her door. I'm afraid I should have left well enough alone.

Chapter Twenty

It snowed almost every day for the next week, but the storm never intensified to the blizzard conditions meteorologists had predicted. On Gingerbread House's opening day, the sun shone in a brilliant blue sky and made the icicles hanging from the eaves sparkle like diamonds.

For the most part, the children who arrived for their first day of "school" were delighted. As to be expected, a few of the little ones cried and clung, but Caitlin and her team had been ready with distractions. At the end of the day when she'd shared a glass of celebratory champagne with her staff, everyone agreed that the opening had been a smashing success.

If Caitlin regretted that a certain someone had not been there to share the moment with her, well . . .

"His loss," she said as she turned out the lights and locked the door behind her. She made it a point not to glance next door as she made her way home.

That didn't mean she didn't keep an eye on his house and business throughout each day. She couldn't help herself. Her office windows gave her a bird's-eye view and besides, the man was outside all of the time.

The first time she'd seen him shoveling snow, she'd almost marched outside to scold him. That couldn't be good for his ribs, could it? But an Internet search and a count of the weeks since the accidents reassured her. Still, when she saw him tackle Harriet's drive, she couldn't help but fret that he was overdoing it.

He also went on walks. A lot of them. It seemed like every time she happened to glance his direction he was either coming or going from his house or garage. She told herself it was his way of dealing with the loneliness in his life now that she wasn't a daily part of it. She even believed that. A little bit, anyway.

Her brother Stephen made it home for his visit, and she proudly gave him a tour of Gingerbread House. "This is great, sis," he told her. "You've knocked it out of the park. I'll admit I agreed with Mom's viewpoint that you were making a mistake by moving home and opening this business. I was wrong."

She linked her arm with his and gave him a patronizing pat. "Coming from you, those three little words mean so much."

"Brat."

"I love you too."

The entire family gathered that night up at Heartache Falls for Stephen's welcome home dinner. It was a fun, relaxing evening full of laughter and teasing and reminiscing and, of course, fabulous food. She and Lori and Chase had come prepared to stay overnight in case the forecasted heavy snowstorm transpired. When it came time to leave, the sky was clear, but Ali so wanted all her chicks beneath the same roof for just one night that nobody could tell her no. The promise of Belgian waffles for breakfast sealed the deal. When Caitlin climbed into bed, for the first time in weeks she didn't feel lonely.

Family truly was the best medicine.

Lying in bed next to his peacefully sleeping wife in the master bedroom, her father's thoughts followed a similar path as he reflected upon the evening. He'd enjoyed talking about the old neighborhood with the kids. They'd brought up instances and events that he hadn't thought of in years. The night had been a gift. More than once he'd looked around the room and sent up a prayer of thanksgiving for his family and the love they shared.

It would give them strength in the days ahead.

With the snow coming down heavy and the promise of Ali's Belgian waffles in the morning, they'd all agreed to overnight here at the house. Mac decided that tomorrow after breakfast, he was going to tell them about the diagnosis.

It made sense to do it now while Stephen was home. The appointment was a little over two weeks away, so they wouldn't be on pins and needles for long. Plus, he'd been squirming a bit ever since his conversation with Tarkington had touched on lies. Caitlin would not be happy with him. Technically he hadn't lied to her when he said the doctors had found nothing, but that wasn't the whole story. He'd promised to her face that he'd tell her as soon as anything was confirmed, but she would recognize it for the dodge that it had been. Although since he was dying, she'd probably let him off the hook.

Mac drifted off to sleep feeling more content than he had in months and awoke just after dawn the following morning—feeling frisky. He looked at his wife and as he had done so often during their close to forty years of marriage, he marveled at her beauty and the fact that despite his having been a penniless Oklahoma boy with a hard-scrabble past, she'd chosen to spend her life with him.

He dipped his head and kissed her shoulder, then nibbled his way to her neck. He had her naked and panting even before he seduced her from sleep, and he made sweet love to her until they both lay sated and replete.

He held her, gently stroking a finger up and down her arm, reluctant to break the joy of the moment, but knowing he must. "I'm going to tell them, Alison."

She slowly stiffened. Almost half a minute passed before she asked, "When?"

"This morning."

"Oh, Mac."

"Yeah."

She drew in a deep breath, then exhaled in a rush.

"It's good. I'm glad you've made this decision. It needs to happen. You . . . actually both of us . . . can use their support."

They showered and dressed and went downstairs together. Mac fried the bacon while Ali tackled waffles, and as the kids wandered downstairs and to the coffee bar, a bittersweet combination of sadness and pride filled Mac. He glanced at Ali. She was looking back at him. In the way of couples long together, they communicated without words.

We did good.

Yes, we did.

I wish I didn't have to share this burden with them.

I know, but it's time. A shared burden is more easily borne.

When breakfast was finished, the younger generation rose to tend the dishes. Mac took Ali's hand and said, "I'm going to start a fire in the family room. When you're done, join us there, would you please? You mother and I have some news to share."

The boys didn't appear to pick up on the note of tension in Mac's voice, but the way Caitlin's sharp gaze darted toward her mother's told Mac that his daughter had noticed. Ali kept her smile serene and pretended not to see. Mac felt the tremble in her hand as he tugged her from the kitchen.

Mac and Ali's home had three fireplaces, two of which were outfitted with gas logs. The family room fireplace had been designed as Mac's plaything. Like so many men, he enjoyed playing with fire. Ali took her customary seat on the sofa while he stacked the kindling and nursed a flame to life. By the time the kids wandered in, he had a nice fire burning.

Mac held out his hand toward Ali and she rose and stood beside him, their hands clasped. Seated on the sofa, Caitlin shifted nervously.

Mac drew a deep breath and began. "A number of months ago, I began to notice weakness in my right hand, some tingling and twitches. I figured I had a pinched nerve. When the symptoms worsened and my left hand became involved, I saw a doctor. He identified a whole list of possibilities and he ordered a battery of tests." Mac glanced at Caitlin and added, "They didn't find anything, but they ruled out cancer, which had been my biggest fear."

"Dad," Stephen began.

"Let me finish, son, and then I'll answer questions. I was a referred to a specialist and eventually ended up at a hospital in Boston. In October, we were given a tentative diagnosis. However, due to the fact that this condition is one that is diagnosed by eliminating other issues rather than pinpointing something wrong, we were told to wait six months. So I have an appointment next month for reevaluation and at that point, they'll know if their suspicions are correct."

"What suspicions, Dad?" Caitlin burst out. "Bottom-line it, would you please?"

He nodded, squeezed Ali's hand tight, and broke his children's hearts. "It's ALS. Amyotrophic lateral sclerosis."

Stephen dropped his chin to his chest. Chase shoved to his feet and paced the room. Lori covered her mouth with her hands, and Caitlin gazed from one to the other with a panicked lack of understanding. "What is ALS?" Stephen and Chase spoke simultaneously. "Lou Gehrig's disease."

That, Mac's daughter recognized. She curled her feet up under her and slumped back against the sofa cushions in an abbreviated fetal position as the cloud of an incurable, fatal diagnosis settled over the room.

Chase burst out. "Tentative! You said tentative. So you don't know for sure. It's not one hundred percent."

"That's right," Ali responded. "We still have hope and I actually have a good feeling about it. Even if we do get bad news, medicine is making strides in slowing down the effects of the disease. The FDA recently approved a new medicine that does that."

In a quiet tone, Stephen asked, "All this time and you didn't tell us?"

"Yes," Mac rubbed the back of his neck. "I wanted to spare you. The waiting is . . . hard."

"I understand how you might feel that way, but it's dishonest. That's not the way you raised us."

Mac glanced toward his wife. Her gaze clearly said, *I told you so*. But as he surveyed the pain on the faces of his children, he knew he wouldn't change a thing.

Chase asked, "When is your appointment, Dad?"

"March twentieth."

"The first day of spring," Lori said. She rose from her seat and crossed the room to her husband. Wrapping her arms around him in a comforting hug, she said, "I'm going to take that as a good sign."

Wearing a watery smile, Ali leaned into Mac. "That's an excellent point, Lori. It reminds me of something Celeste would say."

For a time during the past five months, Mac had given hope the good old college try. He'd never managed to pull it off. What he'd found during recent weeks was acceptance. The Timberlake family would mourn him, but they would be okay. Stephen and his family were settled in Texas and thriving. Chase had finally found his way home to Lori, and Caitlin, well, it was good that she'd moved home to Colorado. Ali would have her to lean on and vice versa. If Tarkington ever pulled his head out, he'd be there for them too.

One by one, Mac gazed at his family. The loves of his life. A fine life. A life well lived.

Yes, he'd done good.

Sweat poured down Josh's face as he finished the cool-down portion of his workout on the elliptical. He was whipped, sadly out of shape, and weak as a kitten. Nevertheless, he felt better than he had in months.

His ribs still ached and he needed to be careful when he wielded the snow shovel, but due to the medicines Dr. Rose Cicero had prescribed and the support system she'd help him find, the pain and, more importantly, the cravings were under control. He should have gone to Rose with his problem weeks ago.

The cool down complete, he headed for the shower. Having slept in, he was getting a late start today, though it was a different type of sleep from the heavy, lethargic kind he'd suffered of late. Rather than awakening tired, he'd greeted the morning feeling rested—a true blessing. He stripped and climbed into the steaming shower where he indulged in an extended stay. A long hot shower on a cold morning was one of the good things in life and something to be appreciated. When he reached the stage just short of prune, he lathered up and rinsed, then reached for his shampoo.

He accidentally picked up Caitlin's instead. Because she'd been using the guest bathroom since the accident, she'd missed it when she'd packed. This bottle had occupied his shower since they'd become lovers last fall.

He probably should give it back to her. Salon shampoos were stupid expensive. He just couldn't make himself do it. When he flipped open the lid and sniffed it, he could almost pretend that she was again sharing the shower with him.

Later while he dressed, his thoughts turned to that exchange with her father. He wondered if in the fog of his hunger for relief, he'd imagined the conversation. Had Mac Timberlake really given Josh his blessing where Caitlin was concerned?

Nah, Josh must have been delirious.

Wearing a gray Broncos sweatshirt and jeans, he strolled to his kitchen where Penny lay sleeping in her plastic clothes-basket bed. She lifted her head at his entrance. "Good morning, girl. You ready to get up and rolling?"

As he carried her outside, he planned the day ahead. He had three snowmobiles waiting for tune-ups that he planned to tackle first. Depending on how those went, he might jump into the ATV engine overhauls that Cam Murphy had dropped off late last week. The goal was to stay busy keeping his body and mind occupied. Then tonight, he would attend the twelve-step group that met three times a week at St. Stephen's.

It was a very small group. Last night, he'd been one of only four people to show up. It had been hard to walk into the room the first time because the anonymity offered by the city-based groups he'd attended in the past wasn't available in a town the size of Eternity Springs. But he'd been welcomed and supported, and he'd left the meeting encouraged and wondering why in the hell he hadn't looked for a meeting weeks ago.

Of course, he knew the answer. He hadn't wanted to betray his secret to Caitlin.

With a sigh, Josh set Penny down and let her scamper in the snow, which continued to fall in fat flakes, laying a soft, silent blanket of white upon the land. Spring seemed so very far away.

Penny chased a squirrel into a tree, but when she turned her attention to the woodpile, Josh called a halt to the play. He dried her with a towel, then carried her inside and placed her into her wheelchair. "Do you know what today is, sweetheart? It's canned dog food Saturday."

He wasn't positive that she recognized the words for her weekly treat, but she did make an excited lap around the kitchen while he filled her dog bowl. Then with the dog tended to, he saw to his own breakfast, talking to her as had become his habit of late. It made the house seem less lonely. "I think it's an oatmeal kind of day, Penny, don't you?"

He dawdled over breakfast and for the first time in months read the online versions of the three newspapers to which he subscribed—the *Wall Street Journal*, the *Denver Post*, and the weekly *Eternity Times*. Perusing the ad for the Trading Post grocery store, he made a mental note to stock up on the New York strips that were on sale. A man could never have too many steaks in the freezer, especially now that his appetite had returned.

When he finished his breakfast and loaded his dirty dishes into the dishwasher, he realized he almost felt like a normal person again. That's why when someone knocked on his front door, he answered it with a smile on his face. The smile immediately died. "Caitlin? What's wrong?"

She gazed at him with tormented eyes. "Josh, I'm sorry, I shouldn't have come here. But . . . I need you. It's Dad. Before, he said it wasn't a big deal. But at breakfast this morning . . . he told us . . . oh, Josh, he told us that he's dying."

Josh briefly closed his eyes. His heart aching for her and her family, he pulled her into the house and into his arms. Sobbing, she collapsed against him. He held her, letting her cry, stroking her back up and down, and murmuring soothing sounds. She babbled against his chest, but he couldn't make out the words. Slowly, he guided her toward the big chair sitting in front of the fireplace. He sat, pulled her into his lap, and let her fall apart.

She cried until she had no more tears to shed, and when she finally quieted, he asked, "Can you tell me about it, honey?"

In fits and starts interrupted by hiccups, she did. Josh's stomach sank as he pieced together her tale. *ALS. Oh man, that's tough.* "I'm so sorry, Caitlin. That's frightening. Waiting is the worst thing, and to have to wait six months . . . that's gnarly."

"I knew something was wrong. I knew it and I asked them and asked them and they lied to me." She squirmed out of his hold and sat up. With accusation in her voice, she added, "Like you lied to me. Lies of omission are still lies."

Josh considered his response. He needed to have an honest talk with Caitlin, but now was not the time. She'd come to him for comfort and support. This moment was about her.

"Don't be too hard on your parents, Cait. I don't doubt that they wanted to spare you worry. They protected you.

That's what you do for those you love. Plus, I imagine they needed time to come to terms with the situation themselves. This is your father's journey. He gets to decide the route. Don't beat him up over the choices he made. Now is not the time."

"You're right." She sighed and snuggled closer to him. "Now that I know what he and mom were going through, I understand what I was seeing when I sensed something was wrong. They both have been tense and on edge. Stressed. But something has changed, with Dad at least, and it's happened in the past week or so. He's mellowed."

"Acceptance."

She considered it, then nodded. "Yes, I think he has come to terms, at least in part, with what is happening to him."

"I would imagine he's been going through a grieving process. Acceptance is the final stage."

Sounding like a little lost girl, she said, "I'm just beginning the journey. I have to tell you, Josh. It sucks."

"I know, sweetheart."

She cried a little more, her tears softer this time, more sorrowful than devastated. When she finished, she fell into an exhausted sleep.

Josh was content to hold her. He'd be happy to hold her from now until her family's wait ended with Mac's appointment on the first day of spring. He wanted to be her rock. Be her support. To do for her like she'd done for him in the aftermath of the accident.

Because that's what people do when they love one another, and Josh loved Caitlin—whether he wanted to or not.

She didn't stir for almost an hour, and he spent that time watching her, studying her face and features like he would a masterpiece hanging in a museum. She was a masterpiece to him, an exquisite combination of beauty and emotion and heart.

He was about to doze off himself when Caitlin finally stirred. She sat up and gave him a sleepy smile, and Josh couldn't help himself. He kissed her.

It was a stupid thing to do. A selfish thing to do. Certainly not in keeping with the guidelines by which he was trying to live his life.

But then she kissed him back, and his craving for her eclipsed any other hunger he'd ever known. No medicine could treat this need. No amount of therapy. The only twelve steps that would satiate this desire were those it would take to reach his bed.

Josh simply wasn't strong enough to resist Caitlin Timberlake.

Journal Entry

Love is patient, love is kind.
It is not jealous, it is not pompous,
it is not inflated, it is not rude,
it does not seek its own interests,
it is not quick-tempered,
it does not brood over injury,
it does not rejoice over wrongdoing
but rejoices with the truth.
It bears all things, believes all things,
hopes all things, endures all things.

—1 Corinthians 13:4-7

For the first time in my life, I get it.

Chapter Twenty-One

When the fog of lust finally cleared, Caitlin went from limp as a noodle to strung tight as knotted fishing line. What in the world had she done?

She'd gone crawling to Josh like a needy child, that's what. And what had it solved? Nothing. Her father was still sick, and she'd thrown her righteous resistance under the bus.

Caitlin was ashamed of herself. She'd used him. That was poorly done of her.

Not that he likely cared. He was a man, after all. Pity sex was still sex and he'd been in a dry spell. With his ribs healed, he had probably been pretty itchy and glad to have it scratched.

Now what? Was there a way to get out of this with her pride intact? How should she act?

What did it matter? *Daddy is dying. That's all that matters.*

Despair returned with reality. Without looking at Josh, she rolled out of bed, retrieved her clothing, and fled to the bathroom to dress. Tears had welled up inside her again and she desperately wanted to hold them back, but she couldn't stop the flood. She felt cold both inside and out, so she turned on the shower and stepped beneath the steaming spray.

Her gaze immediately fell upon her shampoo and her conditioner and her heart gave another twist. She'd forgotten all about those two bottles. Why hadn't he moved them? Had he always believed she'd come back? She'd given him no reason to think so. She hadn't spoken to him once since he threw her out. Did he think that all he needed to do was snap his fingers and she'd come crawling back?

He didn't even have to snap his fingers.

The truth of it made her feel raw. She wished she could dissolve and disappear down the drain right along with the soap, the shampoo, and her tears.

And to think that she'd awakened this morning happy as a clam and looking forward to the weekend. If the weather held, she had planned to do some cross-country skiing. Gliding through a silent, snow-covered forest offered the perfect opportunity for thinking. After weeks of avoiding the subject, she had planned to do some serious thinking about the state of her relationship with Josh.

How quickly plans change. Angry at herself, her parents, the world, she twisted off the water. She dried herself with one of his fluffy brown towels and dressed. Then, she could delay no longer. *At least I'm not crying any-more.* Hoping against hope that he'd gone for one of his walks, Caitlin left the bathroom.

He was wearing jeans and a red flannel shirt he'd yet to button and sat on the side of his bed facing the bathroom door. Her gaze dipped to his scar. It looked better. A lot better.

He spoke her name, steady and strong, and then asked, "What do you need from me?"

Love. Support. Honesty. Your heart. Your soul. Your everything. Because that's what I've given you. She cleared her throat and cut to the heart of the problem. "Tell me about J. B. Trammel."

Josh didn't know what he'd expected her to say, but that wasn't it. He'd been thinking about Mac and the Timberlake family. Trying to find ways he could help them navigate these troubled waters. He did have one idea, but he needed to do a little research before he brought it up.

Nor was he ready to talk about J. B. Trammel. He wasn't prepared. It was one thing to admit his problem to a physician, but something else entirely to do it to the woman he loved.

The woman he loved.

He loved her.

And he knew her. She wouldn't let him get by with hitting the bullet points like Rose had. He'd have to tell her the whole ugly truth, the parts she wouldn't find by googling.

Could he do it? Even in rehab, he'd never told anyone the entire story. And he wasn't far enough along in his twelve-step journey to manage it today. "I can't do that, Caitlin."

She held his gaze for a long minute. He thought she might push him on it, and maybe a part of him wished she would. But then she shrugged. Silently, she walked past him and a moment later, he heard the kitchen door open—Josh waited, holding his breath—and close. He shut his eyes and fell back onto the bed.

That afternoon, he took a walk. He walked a lot these days. The cold air and physical exertion cleansed his mind and sapped the energy from the demons that continued to plague him. The walks also helped fill up the empty hours and days without Caitlin.

First he walked north and south, up Aspen Street and down Spruce and up Pinion and down Cottonwood. Then

Emily March

he walked east on the odd-numbered streets and west on the evens until he walked the entire grid of Eternity Springs. After that, he crossed the footbridge over icy Angel Creek to the grounds of Angel's Rest. He didn't know he intended to talk to Celeste until he knocked on the door of her office. She looked up from a computer monitor and smiled. "Hello, Joshua. What a nice surprise."

"Do you have a few minutes, Celeste? I need some advice."

"Of course. Please come in and have a seat." She gestured toward an occasional chair upholstered in cabbage roses. "I'm thrilled to have a distraction from this pesky bookwork. It doesn't matter how many people I hire to help me with this business, there are still things no one but I can do. What can I help you with, my dear?"

Josh took the seat she indicated, but almost immediately popped back up onto his feet. "I need you to do your wise-woman thing."

She sat back in her chair and steepled her hands in front of her. "My wise-woman thing?"

"Yes. You know." He made circles with his hand. "I've heard about it ever since I came to town. People say that time and time again whenever someone is in crisis, you have an uncanny way of showing up and saying exactly the right thing that they need to hear. Then they solve their problems and you give them a necklace and everyone lives happily ever after."

Her ice blue eyes twinkled. "People say that, do they?"

"Yes."

"And you're in crisis?"

"Yes."

"Crisis over what?"

"Well, it's complicated."

"Most crises are."

Pacing the room, Josh raked his fingers through his hair. "Caitlin wants something from me that I can't give. Not with the way things are now, anyway. That's where you come in, I hope."

"Where I come in?"

"I need you to give me that perfect sound bite of wisdom that I need to hear to get past this fear of mine."

"You're afraid of something."

"Terrified. I'm a spineless, gutless, sissified coward."

"So says the man who dove in front of a moving car to save a child."

"Yeah, well, that's different. Physical bravery is easy compared to putting yourself on the line emotionally. There's no pill I can pop for this. That's what gets a person started down this path, you know? Somebody lets you down and makes you feel terrible so you take something to feel better and it's a vicious cycle. I don't want to feel terrible. I don't want to be ashamed. I don't want to fake my way through life. Been there, done that, have the star on the Hollywood Walk of Fame."

"What do you want, Joshua?"

"I want real. My life here in Eternity Springs is real. Caitlin is real. What I feel for her is real. What wisdom do you have for me, Celeste? Give me something like you gave Brick or Cam Murphy or Lucca Romano. People around here talk about it all the time. Tell me to leap like a lunatic. Tell me to forget the past and decide who I am today and discover who I will be tomorrow. Remind me that my trials have made me stronger, that I'm not a walking disaster, that I will triumph over my demons. Tell me that nothing defeats a valiant heart. Or how about the one about peace being a process? Or love being a miraculous medicine?"

"I said all those things?"

"Yes! And hearing them changed lives. Instilled

courage. Look at the people in this town. Nobody goes through life without some bruises. Many of our friends have suffered real tragedies. But they healed. If I've heard it once, I've heard it fourteen times. Eternity Springs is where broken hearts come to heal."

"Well, that is true."

"Yes. And broken hearts come in different forms, but most of them at one time or another are afraid of something. We're afraid to leap in case we might fall. Afraid to risk in case we might fail. Afraid to reach in case we might miss. When you let fear be your guide, you don't live a genuine life. You live a fake life. A Hollywood life. If you're not content with fake, then you need to man up and suck it up and leap and risk and reach. Overcoming the fear will bring healing."

"I see."

"Yeah." Josh stopped his pacing, shoved his hands in the back pockets of his jeans, and nodded. "Yeah. Okay. That's good. That makes sense." He drew in a deep breath then exhaled a heavy sigh. "Yeah. Right." He beamed a smile toward her. "Thank you, Celeste. I knew you'd have something for me."

Dryly, she said, "I'm glad I could help, Josh."

"Me too. Really. I owe you big time. If there's ever anything I can do for you, just let me know. A tune-up. Oil change. Autographs. Maybe a movie premier. I'm your man."

"I'll remember that."

"Great. Well, I've taken up enough of your time. I'd better let you get back to your bookkeeping." He walked around the desk, leaned down, and kissed her cheek. "You are an angel, Celeste. I adore you."

As he sauntered from the room, he heard her say, "Oh, my boy. I adore you too."

He was halfway down Angel Rest's front steps when

he snapped his fingers and turned around. A moment later, he ducked his head back into Celeste's office. "Excuse me, Celeste? One more thing. Do you think I could have one of those necklaces?"

Her laughter floated on the air like feathers. She opened her desk drawer, removed one of the official Angel's Rest blazons that she awarded to townspeople who learned to accept love's healing grace, and tossed it toward Josh.

He caught it on the fly, brought it to his mouth for a theatrical kiss, then held it up and said, "I have a sneaky feeling that this is gonna be my good luck charm."

An hour later, he knocked on Mac and Ali Timberlake's front door. Mac answered, "Hello, Tarkington. Caitlin isn't here. She and her brothers have gone snowmobiling."

"I'm not here to see her. I wanted to talk to you. She told me about the family meeting this morning." From the pocket of his coat, he removed a Tarkington Automotive business card and handed it to Mac. "The name and number on the back . . . you should call him. He's a neurologist who has made a name for himself as a diagnostician. He's—"

Mac read the name and interrupted. "I recognize the name. I tried to get an appointment with him. He couldn't see me for eighteen months."

"Um . . . you have an appointment with him next week if you want to take it."

Mac's head snapped up and he pinned Josh with a narrow-eyed look. "How . . . ?"

"His son and I were in rehab together years ago. I helped him one time when he overdosed. Saved his life. We stay in touch. You should go see him. I won't say anything to anybody if you prefer, but you really should go." He turned and started up the walk to his car.

Mac called after him. "Josh? Thank you."
"You're welcome. I wish you the best of luck."

Caitlin was having a very realistic dream because she smelled bacon. She knew it was a dream because she was home and alone in her house. Her mother might be the Cooking Queen, but she drew the line at breaking into her children's houses and cooking breakfast.

But darned if that didn't smell legit.

Without opening her eyes, she felt along the top of her nightstand for her phone and picked it up. Checked the screen. Seven thirty-three on Sunday? "Why am I awake?"

And why do I still smell bacon?

She sat up feeling a little uneasy. This was really weird. She grabbed her robe from the foot of the bed where she'd left it, slipped her feet into the Minnie Mouse slippers Lori had given her for Christmas, and crossed to her bedroom door. Why was it closed? She'd left it open, hadn't she? She always slept with her bedroom door open.

Her heart began to pound. It crossed her mind to call 9-1-1 but really, what would she say? Someone broke in and is cooking bacon? Truly concerned now, she quietly turned the knob, carefully opened the door, and gasped.

A flower bomb had gone off in her hallway.

Vases filled with cut flowers and potted flowering plants in a rainbow of colors lined a path down her hallway. Yellow daffodils and pink crocuses and white begonias and red geraniums. Pink calla lilies and orange tulips and blue hydrangeas. Carnations and chrysanthemums and peonies.

That *was* frying bacon she'd smelled. She could hear it sizzle. She stepped to the kitchen doorway and her mouth gaped. The hallway had been filled with flowers, but the kitchen was stuffed to the rafters with them. Almost every flat surface was occupied, if not by full flowers then by rose petals.

Josh stood at the stove wielding kitchen tongs. Seeing her, he smiled. Perhaps the smile was a bit nervous. Perhaps. "Good morning, beautiful."

Caitlin didn't feel beautiful at the moment. She really, really wished she'd detoured to the bathroom to brush her hair. And maybe pee. "Which of the obvious questions should I ask first?"

"Let me see if I can answer them without you having to bother. I need to talk to you. I wanted someplace private where we wouldn't be interrupted. I figured the chances of getting you to my house hovered between slim and none. You never asked for your key back so talking here was an obvious solution. I thought that since I am here, I might as well cook breakfast. Why don't you have a seat, sweetheart? Breakfast will be ready in just a few minutes."

And the flowers? What was the purpose of the flowers? His failure to mention them made them the elephant in the room and only made her want an explanation about them more. But damned if she'd ask. If he could pretend they weren't there, then so could she.

"I'm . . . um . . . I'll be right back." She fled to the bathroom and returned five minutes later with her hair and teeth brushed and wearing jeans and a sweatshirt and her garden shoes. If he could make subtle statements, then so could she.

Josh noted the shoes with a ghost of a grin, then handed her a mug of steaming black coffee. He set two plates of bacon, scrambled eggs, and toast on the table. "Dig in."

She didn't see a reason to refuse, so she picked up her fork and tasted the eggs. The meal was no different from the dozens they'd shared over the past six months. He told her a story about Penny and a tennis ball and asked her questions about the goings-on at Gingerbread House. When they'd both finished, he topped off her coffee and insisted she remain seated while he tended the dishes. Caitlin shrugged and lifted her cup. *It's your garden party.*

Through it all, anticipation hummed through her like a bumblebee on a nectar high.

When he'd loaded the last dish into the dishwasher and dried the last pan and returned it to the cabinet, she watched him take a deep breath. When he turned to face her, she held her own breath.

"What do you want to know about J. B. Trammel?"

Hope was the tender sprout of a crocus bulb pushing through a blanket of snow. "Everything important."

"A reference point will help. How much do you know already? Did you google me?"

"Yes . . . but only so far as Wikipedia."

He nodded. "Okay then. Well, I guess the first important point to make is that I was no victim. I was born into a long line of gifted actors going back to silent film. They're Hollywood royalty. I never went without food or a roof above my head. I had every toy any boy could want. I truly did live in the lap of luxury."

"But?"

He sighed. "My father was the poster boy for great, tormented actors. He was an alcoholic. He battled depression. I suspect he was bipolar, but that was never diagnosed. He did marry my mother, but he was never faithful—the two half sisters I have who are close to my age were evidence of that. My mother knew about his infidelity. My earliest memories are of arguments—shouting, screaming, and throwing things. They divorced when I was six. He died not long afterward."

"I read about that," Caitlin said. "He had a heart attack."

"That was the official story. The truth is he committed suicide. I was with the nanny when she found him."

Caitlin covered her mouth with her hand. "Oh, Josh. That's terrible. I'm so sorry."

He shrugged. "Beyond the fright of the moment itself, his death wasn't that difficult for me. I didn't have much of a relationship with him, so I didn't grieve."

Caitlin doubted that, but she didn't interrupt.

"My mom was another story. Despite the sorry way he treated her, she loved him. She was devastated after his death. That's when she decided his great acting legacy needed to live on—in me. I'd done a few commercials already, but after my father died, she started pushing. And pushing. I auditioned for every role that came along and I landed a lot of them. I honestly liked the work. Life was pretty good. But then I got the role in *Starseeker* and shortly after it released, Franco Rinaldi came into our lives."

Franco Rinaldi. She knew that name. "The drummer in Waverunners?"

"Yep. My mom fell hard for him. We moved into his house in Beverly Hills, and that's when my life turned upside down. I got up close and personal with sex, drugs, and rock and roll."

"You were how old?"

"Eight. Almost nine. I'll go into detail if you wish, but I don't know that it serves a purpose. The pertinent highlights—or actually, lowlights—are these: I smoked my first cigarette at eight and my first joint at nine. I was popping pills by twelve and shooting up by the time I was fourteen."

Caitlin caught her breath. "Shooting up?"

"Heroin. I'd done three stints in rehab before I turned twenty-one."

Oh, Josh. She closed her eyes. She'd suspected something like this. It was Hollywood, after all. But she never guessed the extent of it. She'd noticed he didn't drink, but she never really thought anything about it. He was a health-conscious guy. He drank carrot juice, for goodness sake. "I'm so sorry. Where was your mother in all of this?"

"In and out of rehab herself. Still, we continued to work. We were on location in Oklahoma when her life really blew up, and I got shuttled into the system. God was watching out for me because I got placed with the Christophers."

"Brick's adoptive parents."

Josh nodded. "They saved me. They helped me get clean and stay clean. In the Oklahoma suburbs, I left J. B. Trammel behind. I built a life and I was happy, and I seldom thought about my California world. I stayed clean and sober for seven years."

She sensed what he was going to say next. Sure enough, she was right.

"Then wham, I'm tornado bait. When I lost my fian-cée and her daughter, the old days started whispering to me and I slipped. Actually, I fell hard and went back to heroin. Again, the Christophers stepped up to help. Getting clean again almost killed me."

"But you did it."

"Yes, but my confidence in my ability to maintain my sobriety took a serious hit. Then a couple years later, springtime rolls around again. A twister wiped me out again. Brick offered me a change of scenery, and I jumped at it."

Caitlin wanted . . . needed . . . to touch him, but his arms were crossed and his walls were up and a No Tres-

PASSING sign flashed neon across his forehead. Instead she fluffed the satin bow on a pot of daffodils and said, "You built a new life here as Josh Tarkington."

"J. B. is a junkie. Josh isn't." He turned away from her and stared at the kitchen window as he added, "But it was touch and go for a time, Caitlin. Touch and go."

Finally, she put the clues together and things began to make sense. "The accident. They gave you opioids in the hospital. Oh, Josh, why didn't you say anything?"

He didn't respond and she could deny herself no more. She touched his arm and was grateful that he didn't shake her off.

His voice was a low, tormented rumble. "Because I was scared senseless and I was stupid. I didn't want to admit my weakness to anyone, much less you. I was ashamed. So very ashamed. It didn't help anything that the pain was such a bitch because that made it difficult to think straight. So, armed with the medical degree I got out of a cereal box along with a secret decoder ring, I played 'Physician, heal thyself.'"

Dread rolled through her stomach. "What did you do, Josh? What did you take?"

He had a white-knuckled grip on the countertop. "Nothing. I was afraid of getting hooked again, so I flushed my pills and went cold turkey and made your life miserable because I was such an ass. Then the day I sent you away, I threw in the towel. Took the pain pills and couldn't stop."

Caitlin took a moment to absorb the revelation. Then she gave his arm a backhanded slap and stepped back. "Of all the stupid, witless, brainless things to do. You idiot! Surely there is someone who could have helped you. No wonder you were such a jerk to everybody in the weeks after Christmas. Why didn't you say anything to me? Why didn't you ask for help?"

"Because like you said, I was an idiot." Josh released his grip and turned away from the window. He met her gaze with a solemn sincerity in his own. "I was slow, but I did get there eventually. I finally did ask for help. Rose Cicero gave me a lecture the likes of which I've never had before, and we made a plan. One of its elements is my return to a twelve-step program, and that brings us here this morning to this confession."

He reached out and took her hands in his. His striking gray eyes pleaded for understanding as he said, "I wasn't prepared for this yesterday, Caitlin. I was afraid to tell you the truth. I had to work through it. I failed you yesterday and for weeks before that. I'm sorry. I am so very sorry. I hope you can find it in your heart to forgive me."

Her first instinct was to tell him that of course she forgave him. Caitlin had never been one to hold grudges. When someone hurt her, an honest expression of regret and a request for forgiveness usually was all it took for her to let bygones be bygones.

But something held her back. She wasn't exactly sure what.

Okay, she did know what it was. In all this talk, he'd never said the words she needed to hear. Those three powerful little words.

Josh said, "I was wrong."

Okay, those three were pretty good, but they weren't the ones she wanted most. Damned if she'd ask for them directly. She studied him intently and saw no hint of doubt or deceit. He'd confessed to fear about being honest with her about his past. Was fear keeping his lips zipped when it came to what she needed most to hear?

Maybe. So far, this morning had been about facts, not emotions. Maybe he needed a little encouragement. Maybe he needed her to say the words first.

Perhaps, but that really didn't work for her. He'd hurt her badly. His words and actions meant more than those of any other. Frankly, she needed a bit of groveling to soothe her wounded heart.

Isn't that what the flowers are about? A bouquet of flowers had long been part and parcel of a male apology. It made sense that in Josh's mind, dozens of bouquets amplified the effort.

Still, she wanted the words and she wanted him to say them first. "Tell me about the flowers."

He glanced around the kitchen. "Do you like them?"

"Of course. I love flowers. But why are they covering my kitchen?"

Again, he sucked in a deep breath and appeared to brace himself. Then he moved to stand before her and took both her hands in his. He stared into her eyes, and the look in his caused her heart to being pounding.

"I spent a long time yesterday trying to compose the words I wanted to say to you today. You should see all the wadded up balls of paper in my trashcan. Nothing was right. Nothing expressed how I feel. The closest I could come was a metaphor, and the flowers are my effort to illustrate it.

"You see, my life has been winter. Cold and lonely and barren. Then one day last summer, you brought spring into my world. You are my springtime, Caitlin. You are color—bold, rich, explosive hues and soft pastels of peace. You are the exotic fragrance that tempts me and the sweet scent that soothes me. Your heart is rose petal soft, though you stand ready to wield your thorns when necessary to protect those you love."

He brought first one hand and then the other to her mouth for a gentle kiss. "You are everything beautiful in my world. You are love. My love, and I hope, my new beginning. I'm asking you to take a chance on me. I know the addiction thing is great big red flag, but I'm standing here this morning giving you my solemn oath that I will do anything and everything necessary to keep that beast out of our lives. Trust me. Take a risk on me. Believe in me. Marry me, Caitlin. Be my wife and the mother to our children. I love you. Say yes. Please, say yes and be my forever spring."

Caitlin took his words into her heart as joy blossomed into watery eyes and a brilliant smile. "That was good, Tarkington. Really, really good. I love the thought of being your spring. I love you. My answer is yes. Yes. Yes, I'll marry you and have our children. Yes, I'll trust you to never again be such an idiot about asking for help when you need it."

He closed his eyes and exhaled a heavy breath. "Thank God."

Then his arms went around her and he picked her up and twirled her around. Their lips met in a perfect kiss.

The first kiss of spring.

Journal Entry

Dear Diary,

Okay, maybe it's silly to channel my inner teenager as I begin this, the very first page of my very first journal on the very first day of my new life, but I don't care. It makes me happy.

I am so very, very happy. Today at two p.m. I officially became Caitlin Tarkington. Mrs. Josh Tarkington. That's an old-fashioned, anti-feminist manner of identification, but I love it. So sue me. I love him.

It's been a perfect day. The wedding day of my dreams. Mom and I have had so much fun planning it for the past year. I never thought I'd be one to have a destination wedding, but getting married in Telluride felt right and isn't all that far from Eternity Springs.

I had a fabulous dress. A-line with a sweetheart neckline with crystals and a glitter net—I felt like a Disney princess. Belle, of course, because I married my Beast.

We did suits instead of tuxedos. Gray to match Josh's eyes. Dad looked so distinguished, and he joked as he walked me down the aisle. He wasn't perfectly steady, but that had nothing to do with his multifocal motor neuropathy—not ALS, thank God. The medicine Josh's doctor friend put him on *after making the correct diagnosis has improved his condition significantly. Dad said he trembled just a little bit because he was nervous about stepping on my dress.*

We made it through the ceremony without any disasters, and the reception was relaxed and so much fun. I'm still not exactly sure how it happened, but a guy caught my bouquet. Boone McBride. Mom said when the women went up for it, someone accidentally slapped it away and it hit the side of Boone's head and he caught it instinctively. The guys ribbed him mercilessly about it, but Celeste gave him speculative looks the rest of the evening.

And now, the honeymoon begins. We are spending our wedding night in Telluride, and tomorrow we fly to Europe. We'll be gone a month. Tuscany and Venice and the French Riviera. Then Paris. April in Paris. Someone should write a song.

Now, dear diary, I will bring this to a close. It's time to take off my clothes and put on the Sokolov suite—necklace, earrings, and as of today, the ring. Josh has asked specifically that I indulge this particular fantasy of his.

He said, "It's only appropriate that you wear green to our marriage bed tonight. This is St. Patrick's Day, after all.

"And I am the luckiest man alive."